Lynne Graham was born in Northern Ireland and has been a keen romance reader since her teens. She is very happily married, to an understanding husband who has learned to cook since she started to write! Her five children keep her on her toes. She has a very large dog, who knocks everything over, a very small terrier, who barks a lot, and two cats. When time allows, Lynne is a keen gardener.

Louise Fuller was once a tomboy who hated pink and always wanted to be the Prince—not the Princess! Now she enjoys creating heroines who aren't pretty push-overs but strong, believable women. Before writing for Mills & Boon she studied literature and philosophy at university, and then worked as a reporter on her local newspaper. She lives in Tunbridge Wells with her impossibly handsome husband Patrick and their six children.

Also by Lynne Graham

Cinderella Brides for Billionaires miniseries

Cinderella's Royal Secret
The Italian in Need of an Heir

Innocent Christmas Brides miniseries

A Baby on the Greek's Doorstep
Christmas Babies for the Italian

Passion in Paradise collection

The Innocent's Forgotten Wedding

Also by Louise Fuller

Proof of Their One-Night Passion
Craving His Forbidden Innocent
The Rules of His Baby Bargain

Passion in Paradise collection

Consequences of a Hot Havana Night

The Sicilian Marriage Pact collection

The Terms of the Sicilian's Marriage

Discover more at millsandboon.co.uk.

THE GREEK'S CONVENIENT CINDERELLA

LYNNE GRAHAM

THE MAN SHE SHOULD HAVE MARRIED

LOUISE FULLER

MILLS & BOON

First Published in Great Britain 2021
by Mills & Boon, an imprint of HarperCollins*Publishers*
1 London Bridge Street, London, SE1 9GF

ISBN: 978-0-263-28229-0

This book is produced from independently certified FSC™ paper
to ensure responsible forest management.
For more information visit www.harpercollins.co.uk/green.

Printed and bound in Spain
by CPI, Barcelona

THE GREEK'S CONVENIENT CINDERELLA

LYNNE GRAHAM

CHAPTER ONE

EVERY EYE AROUND the crowded conference table locked in astonishment on to Althea Lekkas's exquisite face when she gasped. 'I'm sorry… I'm calling off the wedding!'

'You can't!' expostulated her father, Linus, jumping upright with knotted fists of fury. 'If you call it off this late in the day, I'll disown you!'

Jude Alexandris almost laughed at that melodramatic threat from his future father-in-law, who was embarrassingly keen for the marriage to take place. After all, the Alexandris billions were a living legend and Jude was accustomed to being regarded as a literal golden goose. Not that the huge weight and purchasing power of all that money had ever made anyone in *his* family happy, he acknowledged grimly.

His grandfather was a manipulative, bitter old man who had outlived three wives. His father, an only child like Jude, had been a high-flyer in business but utterly useless on the husband and father front. His mother, Clio, discarded by her husband and denied her son, had thrown her broken heart into creating a world-famous garden and only there had she found some measure of contentment. Jude himself? He recalled being truly happy only once, when he was twenty-one and on top of the world because back then he had loved Althea, and had believed that she loved him. He had truly believed that he could ignore all the cynics and rewrite Alexandris family history.

Sadly, that naive hope hadn't lasted long. Althea had slept with another man, destroying everything he had ever felt for her and, seven years on, they were merely friends, who had agreed to marry for purely practical reasons. Thanks to his grandfather's machinations, and the pressure those had put on him, Jude needed a wife in a hurry and Althea, divorced in the wake of a short, disastrous marriage, craved the freedom from family expectations that a second marriage would give her.

As Althea burst into floods of tears, Jude stood up in one fluid motion to ask if there was an office free. He was very tall at six foot five, lean and muscular with the physique of an athlete. He cropped his riot of black curls short. Flaring ebony brows framed shrewd dark eyes set below lashes long and lush enough to make the average woman weep in envy. A beautiful child, he had grown into an even more beautiful man. Lean, sculpted features, sheathed in olive skin and worthy of a Greek god, completed the vision of a male who turned female heads wherever he went.

One of his English legal team rose in haste to accommodate Jude's request for a more private space and he urged Althea out of the room into one across the corridor.

'I didn't mean to just drop it on you like that…not in front of an audience!' Althea sobbed. 'But I *can't* go through with it! It would be wrong for me…maybe not for you, but for me.'

'Are you sure this isn't just wedding nerves?' Jude asked, leaning back against the door with the cool of a man who rarely lost control of his emotions.

This had been the day the prenuptial agreement was to be signed, and the wedding was to take place within the week. Jude would have been content with a quick civil ceremony, but Althea had wanted a big wedding, which had taken weeks of planning. Thanks to her insistence on all the glitzy trappings, he was now perilously close to the finishing line, which was only a couple of months away. If he didn't have a wife by his thirtieth birthday, his mother, Clio, would be forced to leave her home and her precious garden and there would be nothing he could do to forestall that blow and the devastation it would inflict on her. Unfortunately for Clio, she lived in an Alexandris family property, which Jude would only inherit after his grandfather passed away and his grandfather, Isidore, was using that as a threat to force his grandson into taking a wife. His mother might be a rather difficult personality but Jude still wanted to protect her.

'No, it's not nerves.' The slender blonde drew a tissue out of her bag and dabbed carefully at her eyes, struggling not to dislodge her fake lashes. 'I realised that I was marrying you for the wrong reasons, that I'd be looking for more than you were willing to give and that I wouldn't want to let you go at the end of it. That wouldn't be fair to you *or* me, so I'm backing out now because I do value your friendship and I don't want to lose that as well.

'No, don't say anything,' Althea muttered in a wobbly undertone as he studied her with a troubled frown, his wide, sensual mouth compressing at that explanation. 'I'm doing the right thing for both of us and you *know* it. You're never going to feel anything more for me than you do now. I killed all that when I slept with your best friend. And now I'm leaving you in a hell of a mess and Dad's going to go crazy about the wedding costs I've incurred.'

'I'll cover the expenses,' Jude interposed, reaching for her hand.

'You *can't*, not when I'm the one backing out of our agreement,' Althea protested, tugging her hand gently from his. 'I'm always screwing up, Jude.'

'No, you can blame me for this. I should never have told you what my grandfather was threatening to do in the first place.'

'We're friends. I offered, you didn't *ask* for my help,' Althea reminded him ruefully. 'No, this is on me. Blame it on my never quite getting over you and craving the kudos of walking down the aisle with you. That appealed to my vanity and I'm ashamed of it. You're not a trophy to be shown off.'

Registering that her reasons for not marrying him were *not* reasons he could argue with, Jude expelled his breath in a sharp hiss of grudging acceptance. 'Let's go back in and deal with the fallout.'

'But what are you going to do now?' Althea demanded, searching his face with a more calculating light in her gaze.

'Find me a wife…one without the finer sensibilities that persuaded you to back out on me,' he murmured wryly while fiercely resisting the urge to remonstrate with her about the feelings she was insisting she still cherished for him.

'You won't find anyone at this late stage,' Althea countered. 'You'd be wiser rethinking what you're willing to offer me.'

Jude almost groaned out loud because he had already offered Althea everything he was prepared to offer. Unfortunately, she was still on the rebound from a bad marriage, and fanciful. She ignored the reality that seven years earlier she would never have slept with another man in the first place had she genuinely loved him and that in any case these days they were no longer the boy and girl they had once been. She had been his first love, his *only* love, but fidelity was a hard limit for Jude and, although he had forgiven her as a friend, she had annihilated the deeper feelings he had once had for her. She didn't understand that, couldn't accept that bottom line, but then that was Althea, always wanting most what she couldn't have, always believing that a pretty gesture or the right words could work a miracle. Jude had always had a tougher and less idealistic outlook because his dysfunctional background had stolen his innocence when he was still very young.

His earliest memory was of his parents fighting over his father's extramarital affairs. He remembered his father's arrogant defiance and his mother's agonised hurt and hysterical recriminations. He was the unfortunate baby who had been christened Judas in the cradle by his embittered mother because she had first caught his father in another woman's bed shortly before she gave birth. In that moment, Jude had become the symbol of everything his mother had suffered, and he suspected that even now she had yet to manage to forgive him for it. His grandfather had despised his daughter-in-law and had renamed his grandson Jude and when, inevitably, there was a divorce, the older man had moved heaven and earth to ensure that Jude's father was awarded full custody of his son and that his mother saw as little as possible of her child as he grew up.

'You're an Alexandris male,' Clio had told Jude during one of her brief visits. 'It's written in your genes that you'll lie and cheat with women just like your father. You won't be able to help yourself.'

But, Jude was a natural rebel. As soon as he'd been told that, he had sworn that he would not repeat his father's mistakes. After all, he had grown up with the consequences of his father's inability to maintain a stable relationship with any woman. He had had several stepmothers and his absentee father had taken countless lovers as well. Ironically, his father had never loved any woman the way he had loved Jude's mother, but he had been far too proud to admit that even to himself. Dion Alexandris had lived a life full of thrills and spills, ultimately dying in a racing accident in a car he should not have been driving. Jude was equally volatile, but he also had his mother's common sense and his grandfather's cool, cutting intellect, and he was a renowned 'fixer' in the business world, possessing that rare ability to rise above ego and emotion and see right to the heart of a matter to find a solution to complex problems.

Jude was on the way out of the office when one of his legal team members addressed him. 'What will you do now?'

He glanced down with a frown at the smaller man, struggling to recall his name while remaining disconcerted that a junior executive would approach him in such a familiar fashion. *'Cherchez la femme,'* he responded drily.

Calvin Hetherington squared his slight shoulders. Although he was not tall, he had the smooth, blond, boyish good looks of a fashion model. 'What you need is a woman you can pay to marry you and who won't make a fuss when you walk away.'

'Is that so?' Jude said discouragingly.

'I know someone who wouldn't cause you any trouble, who would marry you for a set fee.'

'I'm sure I can find a gold-digger of my own,' Jude murmured flatly.

'But you need someone discreet, someone willing to stick to *your* rules, not a spoiled and privileged woman from your world,' the older man contended. 'Someone who will do it for a price without hassle or consequences.'

It was a compelling truth even if Jude wasn't in the mood to listen to it. 'And where am I likely to find this wonder woman?' he prompted drily.

A card was settled into his empty hand. 'Ring me if you decide you're interested.'

'Who is she?' Jude demanded impatiently.

'My stepdaughter. I want her out of my home because my girlfriend won't move in until *she* moves *out*,' Calvin offered with a wry roll of his eyes. 'But Tansy has no money, no job.'

'Not my problem, not in my interests either,' Jude sliced in with ruthless bite as he strode into the lift, thrusting the card into his pocket while reflecting that occasionally you met some real weirdos, although he had not expected to discover that even a junior member of his British legal team fell into that category. Where had that presumptuous idiot got the idea that he could freely suggest some random young woman as a bride for Jude? Jude, who had grown up knowing that because of his unlimited wealth he could marry virtually *any* woman he set his sights on. He wasn't desperate enough to consider settling on a complete stranger…was he?

No, of course, he wasn't. Yet the seductive suggestion of a woman who would play by his rules and provide him with no unwelcome surprises could only linger with him in the wake of that messy denouement with Althea. Someone he paid to marry him, someone who had no personal stake in the marriage other than enrichment, he mused. Yes, that option *would* suit him best, a woman without her own agenda, a woman without personal feelings involved in the exchange, a woman who would simply marry him because he paid her handsomely to do so.

Even better, such a woman could be dispensed with as soon as he was able…easily, casually and without consequences. Yes, although Jude might not have appreciated his timing, Hetherington, he thought, glancing down at the card to get the name, had actually made a valid point. Simple guidelines and goals often worked the best. After all, he had already screwed up badly when he'd chosen to rely on Althea and their supposed friendship. Althea had made it all personal and emotional while Jude had seen absolutely no reason why emotion should figure in any part of the arrangement. A woman who could see that truth as clearly as he did would be his perfect match.

Jude had already reached a decision when he strode back into his opulent penthouse apartment. He had to consider *every* option before he ran out of time and that meant checking out the gold-digger possibility. He rang Hetherington. 'I'm willing to meet your stepdaughter,' he said flatly. 'Set up a meeting.'

Tansy scooped her dripping, wriggling baby sister out of the bath and wrapped her securely in a towel. Her stepfather was calling her from downstairs and, holding Posy deftly on her hip, she walked out to the landing. 'I'll be down as soon as I've got Posy settled,' she called back.

Posy tried to roll away while her big sister was slotting her into a fresh onesie, but Tansy was practised at dealing with her playfulness. In spite of her difficult start in life, at ten months old and blessed with a mop of blond curls and big blue eyes, Posy was a very pretty baby with a happy disposition. Sadly, Tansy and Posy's mother had died within minutes of bringing her second daughter into the world. At the hospital, reeling in shock from that tragedy, Tansy had taken one look into her sister's eyes and had realised that, although she didn't like her stepfather very much, she would never be able to walk away from her newborn sibling.

And yet her life, she conceded ruefully, would have been so much easier if she *had* had the strength to walk away.

Her aunt, Violet, had given her some surprisingly hard-hearted advice after her mother's funeral. 'Leave now and go back to that university course that your mother made you abandon. That baby is your sister, *not* your daughter. By all means, stay in touch with her and your stepfather, but let them get on with their lives while you return to yours. You don't owe them or your mother's memory anything more than that.'

But, unfortunately, nothing was that simple or straightforward, particularly when feelings got involved, Tansy conceded ruefully. Posy might not be Tansy's daughter, but Tansy had become as deeply attached to her baby sister as any new mother. Calvin had asked Tansy to stay on to look after Posy and enable him to return to work and she had agreed to that, but she had soon begun to feel taken for granted as an unpaid childminder, and then her stepfather had begun dating again. While acknowledging that Calvin was only in his early thirties, having been considerably younger than her mother, Tansy had still thought his interest in other women had returned tastelessly soon, but she had minded her own business when Calvin's lady friends had begun to stay over for the night. Only when Calvin had begun to pressure his regular girlfriend, Susie, into taking over Posy's care and replacing Tansy had Tansy interfered, because it had quickly become painfully obvious that Susie was too irresponsible to take charge of a baby.

One afternoon Susie had actually gone out and left Tansy's little sister alone and unattended in the house when something more entertaining than childcare had been offered to her. There had been other incidents as well, incidents that bordered on child neglect, which had stoked Tansy's growing concern for her sister's welfare.

It was not as though she could trust Posy's father to look out for his child's welfare. In fact, Calvin Hetherington hadn't the smallest interest in being a father to his motherless daughter, nor did he seem to have developed any natural affection for his child. He had married Tansy's mother, Rosie, a successful businesswoman in her mid-forties, and the last thing he had expected out of that union was to become a parent. Rosie might have been overjoyed by her unforeseen pregnancy, but Calvin had been aghast and his wife's death had not made him any keener to take on a paternal role. He might live in the same household but he behaved as though his daughter did not exist. That was why Tansy had stayed on to look after her sister even though her stepfather had recently made it rather obvious that he thought it was time she moved out.

In her will, her mother had left both her home and her beauty salon to her second husband. Had it not been for her infant sibling and her impoverished state Tansy would immediately have moved out because she felt very much surplus to requirements in Calvin's home life now that he was entertaining other women.

'Is the kid in bed?' Calvin checked as Tansy walked into the spacious lounge. 'Look, sit down. We have to talk.'

'What about?' Tansy enquired defensively, standing straight and stiff, instinctively distrustful of the vain, shallow and selfish man her mother had chosen to marry. She had to force herself to sit down and act relaxed and pleasant, which she had learned to do around her stepfather.

'I'm going to be totally honest with you. I'm facing bankruptcy proceedings in the near future,' the slim blond man informed her as he stood at the window.

Tansy froze and paled. 'That's not possible. For goodness's sake, you only sold Mum's business a couple of months ago,' she reminded him.

Calvin Hetherington sighed. 'The beauty parlour was up to its neck in debt—'

'It was a thriving business!' Tansy argued in startled disagreement.

'*Was* being the operative word, Tansy. Your mother was off work for months during her pregnancy and the business went downhill, even though you tried to pick up the slack. Any money your mother made, she spent on extending the property, hiring more staff or buying new equipment,' Calvin enumerated impatiently. 'There were no savings, nothing put by for leaner times. I had to sell, and the price was swallowed by the debts the business had accrued. Then there's the mortgage on this house.'

Tansy frowned in consternation. 'There's a mortgage on this house?'

'The price of all the improvements your mother insisted on making. I could lecture you for an hour on the financial cost of your mother's passing. I'm afraid we always lived above our means, juggling overdrafts and debts,' Calvin admitted grudgingly. 'I'm sure that you realised that your mother really only liked the finer things in life?'

Tansy pinned her parted lips mutinously closed. While it was true that she had often thought her mother had rather extravagant tastes she had also never heard Calvin complain about their comfortable lifestyle or seek to cut back on the expenses of their fancy cars and even flashier holidays. 'Bankruptcy though?' she breathed starkly, avoiding a pointless exchange of bestowing blame for the debts he had mentioned. 'That's a very serious step—'

'Yes and, unfortunately, this house will have to be sold as well. I don't want to see Posy deprived of her only home.' Calvin sighed heavily. 'But there is another option...a rather strange and unexpected option that has literally dropped right into our laps and which could be the answer to all our problems.'

Tansy sat forward, her green eyes locked to him with brimming curiosity. 'What option would that be?'

'My firm's richest client needs a wife for business purposes, and he's prepared to pay a lot of money to the right candidate.'

'What kind of business purposes?' Tansy pressed suspiciously.

'I'm not in possession of that information. Jude Alexandris is a very private man. He doesn't explain his motivations to his solicitors,' her stepfather told her.

'Does he need a British passport or something?'

'I very much doubt it. But I do know that he needs a fake wife. It would be a marriage of convenience. Sign up for it and the sky will be the limit for you,' Calvin told her with a sudden surge of enthusiasm. 'Not only will he pay a large sum of money up front if you agree to marry him, but he will also make a very substantial settlement on you after the divorce and ensure that you never have to work again.'

'That sounds like a winning scheme for a gold-digger,' Tansy pointed out sweetly. 'But I'm not that way inclined. Of course, I can see the appeal from your side of the fence. Presumably if I agree to this nonsense, *you* would get the large sum of money upfront to settle your debts and retain your lifestyle.'

'Think of the benefits for Posy,' her stepfather urged speciously.

'Calvin, you don't give two hoots about Posy or her needs. You're only thinking about saving your own skin,' Tansy countered ruefully.

Calvin frowned. 'You know that's not true. I love that little girl.'

'No, you don't,' Tansy said with regret. 'You live in the same house and you haven't bothered to even see her in over a week. I'm not judging you for that. I accept that not everyone wants to be a parent but what worries me the most is that you don't care about her welfare either.'

'And how do you make that out?' Calvin riposted, angry colour spotting his cheeks at that criticism.

'Well, you keep on pushing Posy off on your girlfriend even though it's perfectly obvious that Susie hasn't an ounce of interest in acting as her substitute mother.'

'Posy is *my* daughter,' her stepfather reminded her with lethal timing. 'Allow me to decide what's best for her. Now what about this proposition? Don't ignore the fact that there would be substantial benefits in the marriage for you as well.'

'But nothing that I value. Yes, money would make it easier for me to move on with my life and possibly return to university,' Tansy conceded reluctantly, 'but it wouldn't sort out the problem of who is to care for Posy. Right now, I think I'm the best person to look after my sister because I love her. Why can't you sign over custody of Posy to me?'

Calvin studied her in indignant disbelief. 'And what would people think of me if I did something like that? Handing my own flesh and blood over to a girl barely into her twenties?'

'Is that all you care about? What other people think?' Tansy viewed him with helpless contempt. 'At the end of the day what should matter to you is what makes *Posy* happy and secure.'

'Well, it certainly won't be you when you're broke and living under my roof at my expense,' her stepfather reminded her crushingly. 'You have no means of supporting a child, no income, no home—'

Tansy jumped to her feet with knotted fists. 'There's

nothing I wouldn't do to keep Posy!' she snapped back at him angrily. 'Given a little time I could find us a home and I could find a job—'

'Marrying Jude Alexandris would give you a home *and* an income,' Calvin pointed out persuasively. 'You just said that there's *nothing* you wouldn't do to keep Posy. Did you mean it? If you agree to marry Alexandris, I'll consider giving you custody of Posy. In those circumstances, nobody would question me handing her over to you because you would be in a position to offer her so much *more* than I ever could. The Alexandris family are one of the richest in the world—'

'Are you serious?' Tansy gasped in complete astonishment at the suggestion that should she be willing to agree to such a marriage he might be willing to surrender his rights to her sister.

'Yes, you agree to marry Alexandris and hand over that initial sum of money to me and I will agree to relinquish my paternal rights in your favour. But, mind you, it won't be that easy,' Calvin told her, switching into cool, curt business mode. 'You would have to impress Alexandris first and you won't do that by mouthing off to him the way you do to me. He will have a low tolerance level for insolence because he's not accustomed to dealing with it. I wouldn't suggest telling him about Posy in advance either as he will only see a young child accompanying you as a problem and a burden. He wants a yes-woman who will do as she's told, nothing more demanding.'

Tansy let his words wash over her while she breathed in deep and slow. A yes-woman, well, she supposed she had been a weak yes-person for much of her life, constantly striving to please and impress her mother and never quite managing to make the grade. From childhood, Tansy had been a disappointment to Rosie Browne. She had cried when her mother had entered her in beauty pageants, come over all shy when she'd got her a booking as a child model and had failed utterly in the drama and ballet classes that had followed.

It was that sad history, that awareness of past failure, that had made Tansy take time out of the radiography degree her mother had denigrated and come to the older woman's aid when she had asked for her help while she was pregnant. Just for once, Tansy had wanted to succeed in winning her mother's approval because she had badly needed the comfort of believing that in spite of everything she could still be a *good* daughter. Regrettably, she had no memory whatsoever of her father, who had died when she was a baby, and by the time her mother had married Calvin, she had been fifteen years old. He had had no desire to take on a stepfather role and she and Calvin had pretty much avoided each other until she went to university. Currently, she struggled to deal with Calvin without her mother around because everything about superficial, smooth-talking, selfish Calvin irritated her.

'You will be seeing Alexandris tomorrow morning at ten for an interview,' Calvin informed her, startling her with that announcement. 'I'll organise Susie to look after the baby.'

'Tomorrow?' Tansy gasped.

'We have no time to lose and neither has he. He's on

a tight timeline. I need to coach you on what Alexandris expects so that you'll impress him as a viable choice,' her stepfather decreed, disconcerting her even more.

Tansy was taken aback by the concept of being 'coached' by Calvin in anything. Was she even willing to go through some marriage ceremony with a stranger for money? Put that baldly, it struck her as a proposition that only a greedy, unscrupulous woman would even consider, and she was neither of those things. On the other hand, if agreeing to that proposition gave Tansy the right to ensure that her little sister was never again left screaming, hungry and unwashed in her cot, she had to think again about what she was ready to sacrifice to achieve a greater good.

'Will you promise me that if this guy agrees to marry me, you will hand over Posy?' she pressed worriedly. 'Because that would be the only reason I am even prepared to consider this idea.'

'So you say,' Calvin jibed with a curled lip. 'But I refuse to accept that the cash and the lifestyle Alexandris could give you doesn't feature in your decision.'

'If this works and you get the money for me doing this, are you willing to sign over custody of Posy to me?' Tansy demanded a second time, needing that reassurance.

'Tansy, if you can pull this off, I'd sign my soul over to the devil, never mind give up Posy,' Calvin admitted with unusual honesty. 'Right now, I'm facing disaster and I'll do anything to avoid it...'

CHAPTER TWO

TANSY AVERTED HER gaze from her reflection in the mirrored lift wafting her up to the penthouse apartment. She was still a little shaken by the elaborate security checks she had had to undergo to prove her identity on the ground floor and gain access to the building. She was now in a special lift that travelled only to the penthouse apartment, a luxury that impressed her to death with its sheer exclusivity. In truth, getting permission to even enter the presence of Jude Alexandris felt like an achievement of no mean order.

Maybe she didn't look quite fancy enough to impress, she conceded ruefully. Maybe she should have tailored her appearance to exactly what Calvin had advised and trowelled on the make-up and used every beautician trick known to her to ensure the ultimate polished finish. Unfortunately, that extremely groomed look wasn't Tansy and never had been. Although her mother had ensured that her vanity-resistant daughter was taught every cosmetic skill available, Tansy had never enjoyed the artificial aspect of presenting herself as someone she felt she was not.

For that reason, Tansy was only wearing light make-up, but she was also, at Calvin's behest, wearing a dress and shoes she felt would have been more suitable for clubbing than a supposed interview. The last time she had worn the short green dress and perilously high heels had been to dance at her friend Laura's wedding and she had been a different girl back then, she thought sadly.

Only eighteen months ago, she had still been at university studying radiography and looking forward to the hospital career she had planned. And then without warning everything had gone pear-shaped. Her mother's pregnancy had been problematic from the outset and when Rosie had found herself struggling to run her beauty salon it had been her daughter she had turned to for help and support. At the time, Tansy had assumed she would only need a couple of months out of her course and that once her sibling was born she would be free to return to her studies. Yet even now, when she accepted that that miscalculation had concluded her education, nothing could make her regret her sister's birth, she conceded fondly. Sometimes life demanded sudden changes of direction and she had simply had to come to terms with the different path that had opened up ahead of her. And if that meant marrying some weird, rich foreigner, she *would* cope if it was for Posy's essential benefit.

With a soft bell tone, the lift doors whirred back and exposed a vast expanse of marble floor flooded by light from the glass roof overhead. A single metal sculpture took pride of place to one side of a glass hall table. It was very stark décor, but it also struck a highly sophisticated note. Tansy stepped out of the lift just as an older woman in a severe black dress appeared from a doorway.

'Miss Browne, please come this way,' she urged, leading the way into a breathtaking reception area flooded with light and surrounded by fabulous panoramic views of London.

Indeed, so spectacular was that space that Tansy didn't even notice that the older woman had abandoned her or that, as she pirouetted round on one high heel to better appreciate what lay beyond the wall of window glass, a tall man had strolled in off the roof terrace behind her.

Jude studied his visitor with appreciative eyes. She was a beauty and a surprisingly unusual one, distinctly different from the common herd. Broadly speaking, she had blond hair, but it was streaked in shades that ran from light brown to gold to pale honey and it looked as natural as her delicately pointed features. Her hair fell halfway down her back in a thick mass of rather messy waves. She wore a raincoat over a dress that revealed legs that in shape and length would not have shamed a Las Vegas showgirl. Slender in build, she was of medium height. Against her creamy skin, her almond-shaped green eyes glowed as clear as emeralds above her full soft pink mouth.

'Jude Alexandris…' Jude murmured, thinking, yes, she would fit his purpose, *more* than match and make possible that extra dimension to the marriage that he had originally planned with Althea.

After all, why go to all the trouble of getting married

to satisfy and silence his grandfather's demands and not take advantage of that legal union? It would make sense to try to have a child with the woman he married and, in so doing, shift his cantankerous grandfather into long-overdue retirement, which would leave Jude free to live his life and run the Alexandris empire exactly as he liked without interference from anyone. When Althea had bowed out, he had given up on the idea of a child but why should he do that? A woman prepared to marry for money would probably have little compunction about providing him with a child in return for an even richer payday.

At the unexpected sound of another voice, Tansy flinched and jumped and spun round, her coat flying out to catch on the small table beside her and toppling it. 'Oh, for heaven's sake,' she began in incredulous embarrassment, wobbling on the high heels that she had not worn in well over a year, one foot semiskidding on the tiled floor, making her lurch clumsily to one side.

Jude caught her upper arm with a powerful hand to steady her before she could fall and picked up the table with the other. 'Sorry, I didn't mean to startle you,' he drawled.

Tansy froze as his hand dropped from her arm again and he backed off several feet. 'I got lost in the view. I was picking out landmarks like a total tourist,' she confessed unevenly, because in reality even contriving to breathe that close to such a perfect vision of masculinity challenged her.

She had looked him up on the Internet, of course, she had, and could hardly have failed to notice his classic good looks. In the flesh, however, he fell into another category entirely, she thought helplessly, ensnared as she was by stunning dark eyes surrounded by a spectacular fringe of black lashes. In real life, he was as visually dazzling as a golden angel springing to sudden life from a printed page. Quite literally, Jude Alexandris took her breath away. His lean, darkly handsome features were as flawless as his bronzed skin tone, his incredible height as striking as his lean, muscular physique. She had felt his strength when he'd grabbed her before she could tumble over in her stupid heels and even that strength of his had made her go weak at the knees, burying every brain cell she possessed…

And that swiftly, Tansy burned with mortification because if there was one thing she never allowed herself to be with a man it was gullible. Being weak and impressionable had got her heart broken and her trust in the opposite sex smashed when she was only nineteen. The experience had hurt like hell and she had never quite recovered from it or regained her youthful confidence. Ever since then, though, she had been careful to avoid the attention of the kind of good-looking man who was a promiscuous sleaze beneath the superficial charm. And she knew Jude Alexandris was a legendary womaniser because not one of the photos she had seen of him online in female company had featured the *same* woman twice. He changed his bed partners as often as other men changed their socks and, naturally, so experienced a guy was fully aware of the pulling power of his extraordinary physical attraction.

'Mr Alexandris,' Tansy pronounced rather stiffly.

'Come and sit down,' he invited lazily. 'Tea or coffee?'

'Coffee, please,' Tansy said, following him round a sectional room divider into a rather more intimate space furnished with sumptuous sofas, and sinking down into the comfortable depths of one, her tense spine rigorously protesting that amount of relaxation.

She was fighting to get a grip on her composure again, but nothing about Jude Alexandris in the flesh matched the formal online images she had viewed. He wasn't wearing a sharply cut business suit, he was wearing faded, ripped and worn jeans that outlined long powerful thighs and narrow hips and accentuated the prowling natural grace of his every movement. An equally casual dark grey cotton top complemented the jeans. One sleeve was partially pushed up to reveal a strong brown forearm and a small tattoo that appeared to be printed letters of some sort. His garb reminded her that, although he might be older than her, he was still only in his late twenties and that, unlike her, he had felt no need to dress to impress.

Her pride stung at the knowledge that she was little more than a commodity on Alexandris's terms. Either he would choose her, or he wouldn't. She had put herself on the market to be bought though, she thought with sudden self-loathing. How could she blame Jude Alexandris for her stepfather's use of virtual blackmail to get her agreement? Everything she was doing was for Posy, she reminded herself squarely, and the end would justify the means...*wouldn't it?*

'So...' Tansy remarked in a stilted tone because she was determined not to sit there acting like the powerless person she knew herself to be in his presence. 'You require a fake wife…'

Jude shifted a broad shoulder in a very slight shrug. 'Only we would know it was fake. It would have to seem real to everyone else from the start to the very end,' he advanced calmly. 'Everything between us would have to remain confidential.'

'I'm not a gossip, Mr Alexandris.' In fact Tansy almost laughed at the idea of even having anyone close enough to confide in, because she had left her friends behind at university and certainly none of them had seemed to understand her decision to make herself responsible for her baby sister rather than return to the freedom of student life.

'I trust no one,' Jude countered without apology. 'You would be legally required to sign a non-disclosure agreement before I married you.'

'Understood. My stepfather explained that to me,' Tansy acknowledged, her attention reluctantly drawn to his careless sprawl on the opposite sofa, the long, muscular line of a masculine thigh straining against well-washed denim. Her head tipped back, her colour rising as she made herself look at his face instead, encountering glittering dark eyes that made the breath hitch in her throat.

'I find you attractive too,' Jude Alexandris murmured as though she had spoken.

'I don't know what you're talking about,' Tansy protested, the faint pink in her cheeks heating exponentially as her tummy flipped while she wondered if she truly could be read that easily by a man.

'For this to work, we would need that physical attraction. Nobody is likely to be fooled by two strangers pretending what they don't feel, least of all my family, some of whom are shrewd judges of character.'

Tansy had paled. 'Why would we need attraction? I assumed this was to be a marriage on paper, nothing more.'

'Then you assumed wrong,' Jude told her without skipping a beat. 'Neither your stepfather nor any of my legal team are aware of the personal terms I require for this to work. There was no need for them to have access to that knowledge because I had already reached agreement in private with the woman I believed I was going to marry.'

'Your friend…who…er…let you down,' Tansy mumbled, playing for time while she struggled to absorb what he was telling her. 'Perhaps you should be sharing those personal terms with me now.'

'That was always my intention…if you met the initial requirements,' Jude responded calmly.

Tansy was shaken by the discovery that Calvin had not, actually, been privy to the finer details of the marriage of convenience he had told her about, although he had talked with his usual aplomb as though he knew everything. Of course, it had all sounded too good to be true, she reflected ruefully, all that money upfront just to pretend to be the wife of a very rich man.

'Sex *would* feature,' Jude informed her without a shade of discomfiture. 'For as long as we would be together it would be a normal marriage.'

'I'm afraid that would be a deal-breaker for me,'

Tansy responded stiffly. 'I wasn't aware that intimacy would be involved in this arrangement, nor do I understand why it should even have to be.'

'This marriage may well need to last a couple of years. I'm not prepared to be celibate for that length of time. But if I satisfy my needs with another woman, my family will be immediately aware that the marriage is a fake because it is widely known that I believe in marital fidelity,' Jude explained with the same cool that somehow made her want to slap him, trip him up, in some way jolt him, because his complete calm and control while she was embarrassed and flustered infuriated her.

He believed in marital fidelity? Tansy wanted to scoff, and only with difficulty did she keep her tongue clamped in her mouth. No man who bedded as many different women as he did could possibly believe in marital fidelity! Who did he think he was kidding? Did she really look that credulous?

'Look, I wasn't aware of your…er…terms,' Tansy framed awkwardly, rising with difficulty in her high heels from the sofa, clutching at the arm to steady herself. 'There's no point in you telling me any more as I couldn't agree to what you've just suggested.'

Jude sprang upright as well. 'Are you serious? You're saying no, over something as trivial as sex?'

Her heart-shaped face reddened. 'It's not trivial to me.'

'Is there someone else in your life? Some reason why you're taking that attitude?' Jude probed because, the more he looked at her, the more interested he became, and he could not credit that she would turn him down.

No woman had ever turned him down and he had already felt the appreciative weight of her eyes on him, had recognised that spark of mutual attraction for what it was. That streak of individuality he had recognised in her at first glimpse further appealed to him.

'I'd sooner not get into that,' Tansy muttered, stepping back as the older woman swept in with a tray and laid it down on the coffee table. 'But it wouldn't work for me…'

As his housekeeper departed again, Jude recognised Tansy's awkwardness and found it as oddly appealing a trait as the long coltish legs she didn't seem to know what to do with. He gazed down at her, watching her worry at her full lower lip with the edge of her teeth in a nervous gesture and glance up at him from below curling lashes. It wasn't staged and he found it incredibly sexy and he didn't know why—didn't know why it should send a current of primal lust to his groin that made him hard as stone within seconds.

'We could make it work,' he heard himself declare. 'Sit down. We'll talk about this.'

'There's really no point when I'd be wasting your time,' Tansy mumbled, casting a longing look in the direction of the lift.

'Tell me why it would be a deal-breaker for you. I'm curious,' Jude admitted. 'These days everyone is so casual about sex.'

'Not everyone,' Tansy argued, sitting down very stiffly, only staying because he had blocked her path of escape and she didn't want to come across as childish and immature.

He spread fluid brown hands. 'Explain,' he pressed with genuine curiosity.

Tansy lifted her chin although she could feel heat gathering below her skin, but she refused to be intimidated by Jude Alexandris. He was gorgeous and he was rich but neither of those things made him any better than she was. 'I'm a virgin. I didn't plan it that way, but the right guy never came along,' she framed curtly. 'I do, however, know he's not going to be you in some mockery of a marriage.'

His black brows drew together and he knew the very minute she spoke that he *was* going to be *that* guy, no matter what it cost him, no matter how hard he had to work to achieve it. He was an Alexandris: it was ingrained in his DNA to want what anyone told him he couldn't have, and he had wanted her the minute he'd laid eyes on her. He didn't understand why, because she was by no means perfect and he could see that she had a slight overbite and a nose that turned up a little at the tip, giving her a faintly impish expression. And he usually went for blondes and she wasn't blonde, not properly blonde, and yet that streaky, unruly mane of hers kept on grabbing his attention as the light glimmered over the differing shades. A virgin, though. That possibility hadn't even occurred to him with a woman of almost twenty-three, particularly one he had already deemed to be a gold-digger. When had he become so cynical that he expected all young women to be cookie-cutter copies of each other?

'The marriage won't be a mockery and no woman with me will ever be treated with less than respect,' Jude countered levelly. 'Obviously, I would give you time to get to know me. After all, once we're married, neither one of us will be straying very far from the other in the first few months.'

Tansy reddened even more, unwarily connecting with those tawny golden eyes locked to her, feeling the butterflies leap and jump in her tummy, her nipples snap tight inside her bra, horrendously aware of that attraction she couldn't deny or stop in its tracks. 'It's not possible, just not possible,' she proclaimed uncomfortably, shifting a hand in denial when he offered her the coffee on the tray, his manners impeccable even in a tense moment. 'I'm sorry for wasting your time.'

Jude was astonished by her determined departure. Firstly, people never walked out on him before *he* had finished with them. Secondly, people generally bent over backwards to please him. Thirdly, the female sex in particular were his biggest fans.

His long powerful stride caught him up with her before she could step into the waiting lift. He reached for her hand. 'We could make this work,' he told her levelly. 'Give me your phone.'

'Why?'

'So that you can contact me when you change your mind,' Jude responded.

'Are you always this confident?' Tansy unlocked her phone and gave it to him solely to be polite.

Brilliant dark golden eyes raked her troubled face as he punched in the number. 'Always.'

As Tansy vanished into the lift, Jude was perplexed, striving to understand her behaviour, because it didn't make the smallest sense that a woman willing to marry him for money would baulk at the inclusion of a little sex. A venal nature was rarely accompanied by much in the way of finer feelings. As a rule, Jude had discovered, gold-diggers were very single-minded, willing to do and say anything and deceive anyone to enrich themselves. Could she really be a virgin or was that some kind of ruse? His suspicious nature was honed by having been for years a prime target of female manipulative wiles.

Tansy travelled home on the train in a daze. She couldn't possibly have agreed to sleep with him, could she? That would have been indecent, she assured herself, and yet the closer she got to home, the more apprehensive she became about the decision she had made. She would lie to Calvin when he asked, she decided. She would say Jude had said she wasn't suitable. It was perfectly understandable that she wasn't willing to go to bed with Jude Alexandris just to secure her baby sister's future… wasn't it? It wasn't as though he were unattractive, however, wasn't as though she were hanging on to her inexperience for any particular reason. It would be more truthful and accurate to say that confronted with the unexpected—the sex—she had panicked and fled.

In the event, what to tell Calvin Hetherington no longer mattered when he jerked open the front door at her approach and glowered at her. 'You told Alexandris *no*? You turned him down?' he roared at her in disbelief.

Tansy paled. 'Don't shout…you'll upset Posy.'

'Susie's taken her out to the park.'

'How did you find out I said no?' Tansy asked flatly.

'I rang him to ask how it went...and you blew it, for some crazy reason, *you blew it*!' Calvin snapped at her furiously. 'He was willing to proceed, you *weren't*. What happened? What are you playing at?' her stepfather demanded in a rage.

Recognising that Jude had protected his own privacy, Tansy shrugged. 'We just didn't gel.'

'Well, too bad for you!' her enraged stepfather launched back at her. 'You can go upstairs right now and pack and get out.'

'Get out?' Tansy echoed in shock.

'Why would I let you stay on here after you've wrecked the best opportunity we were ever going to get of saving this situation?' he slammed back at her, full of rancour.

'Because I look after your daughter and the house,' Tansy reminded him gently.

Calvin studied her with hard, resentful eyes. 'Susie will take care of both from now on. Go on, pack... I want you *out* before the end of the day!'

Tansy went upstairs on wooden legs and collapsed down on the edge of the bed. That was the moment that it dawned on her that she had no rights whatsoever in the situation she was in. She had no right to stay on in the house, which had originally been bought by her own father, because it now belonged wholly to Calvin and she wasn't a tenant. She had no right to interfere in Calvin's care arrangements for his daughter either because she was only a half-sister.

Susie would be free and unsupervised to do as she

liked with the little girl. She could lose her temper and shout at Posy and slap her when she cried. Tansy shuddered at that memory. She could leave Posy unchanged in her cot whenever she liked and for as long as she liked, walk away while the child was in the bath, careless of her safety, and feed her inappropriate food because there wasn't going to be anyone around to object.

Tansy's chest went hollow at the thought of the baby she loved being subjected to such treatment round the clock. Susie didn't mean to be cruel, she was just too immature to be looking after a baby that wasn't her own, but she was also too much in love with Tansy's stepfather and too keen to move in with him to admit that unwelcome truth. It would be Posy who suffered for Tansy's refusal to consider having a 'normal' marriage with Jude Alexandris.

Her bedroom door was thrust open and two suitcases were set down firmly in front of her. 'It's best you go,' Calvin told her curtly. 'I could never forgive you for this.'

As he slammed the door behind him again, Tansy pulled out her phone and agonised while she looked for Jude's number in her contacts. She couldn't find it until she read 'future husband' in the list, and almost spontaneously combusted in rage because there was ordinary confidence and then there was the kind of glaring discordant confidence that made a woman want to run over a man with a steamroller to painfully squash the attitude and bravado out of him. And that was Jude's variety.

She called the number. 'Hello? Would that be future husband I'm addressing?'

'I don't know. Am I?' Jude enquired, not one whit surprised, it seemed, by her callback.

'That would have to be a yes,' Tansy bit out between clenched teeth. 'If you still want me to marry you, I'll agree.'

'We still have more to discuss,' Jude retorted crisply.

Tansy breathed in sustaining air fast and hard and wondered what it was about him that filled her with such irritation and rage. It wasn't reasonable. She might find his marital terms offensive and unpalatable, but he had presented them calmly and politely. It was not *his* fault that Calvin had tied her up in knots over Posy's future. It was not *his* fault that she loved her half-sister as much as if she had given birth to her, which was hardly surprising when she had been looking after the child since the day of her birth. Like any new mother, Tansy had done the sleepless nights, the anxiety attacks and fears that she was doing something wrong, and then the moments of pure gold when she looked down at Posy and her heart just threatened to burst with sheer love.

'When do you want to see me again?'

'This afternoon at my office. I don't have time to waste,' Jude told her with audible impatience. 'I'll text you the address. Come as soon as you can—I'll fit you in.'

Not very gracious, Tansy mused, her face burning as she kicked off the shoes and tore off the dress. The deal was done now, so it didn't matter what she wore, did it? She pulled on a stretchy, comfy skirt and teamed it with flat ankle boots and a floral top before putting on her coat and heading downstairs to see her stepfather again.

'I've agreed to marry him… OK?' she proclaimed as she stood in the living room doorway. 'So you'll need to make legal arrangements for Posy coming to live with me… I should tell Jude Alexandris about her now.'

Calvin vaulted upright, taken aback by her change of heart but visibly energised by the news. '*No!* You can't risk it. Why would he want a baby in the picture and all the noise and inconvenience that go with her?' he demanded. 'Use your brain, Tansy. Don't be a fool! The kid could make him back out. You can't afford to tell him about Posy until that wedding ring is safely on your finger.'

Tansy swallowed hard at that advice because honesty came more naturally to her than lying by omission, but if that was what it would take to safely and legally remove her sister from her father's mediocre care, she would do it. That penthouse apartment was huge and could probably absorb a couple of hidden babies without causing anyone any annoyance, she thought ruefully. There was no reason why Posy's existence should impact that much on Jude, she told herself firmly, squashing that memory of him saying that they would scarcely be apart the first few months of their marriage and reminding herself that she was marrying him for Posy's sake, which meant that Posy's interests had to come first and ahead of everything else. Even ahead of honesty and fair-mindedness? a little voice nagged in the back of her brain, but she silenced it because she couldn't afford to make a mistake when it came to Posy's future well-being.

* * *

Alexandris Industries occupied a landmark skyscraper in the City of London. By the time Tansy made it to the top floor, she was wishing she owned more formal clothes because her casual, youthful outfit seemed out of place. Her wardrobe, however, was depressingly slender because she hadn't had the money to add anything to it since her mother's demise and had never had cause to own dressier outfits.

The receptionist signalled Tansy with a discreet lift of her hand while she sat in the waiting area. Tansy stood up. 'Mr Alexandris will see you now...he has squeezed you in. Are you one of his godchildren?' the young woman asked, curiosity brimming in her keen gaze.

'No,' Tansy replied, reckoning that absolutely nobody would pick her unimpressive, rather ordinary self out as his future wife.

She was shown into a very large and empty office and ushered over to a sofa in the corner where coffee already awaited her. After a couple of minutes alone, she helped herself and tried to relax. When Jude blew through another door like a tornado ten minutes later, she almost dropped her cup as he strode towards her, unnervingly different and formal this time in a dark designer suit that fitted his lean, muscular physique to perfection. Yet that restive, powerful energy of his still fizzed in the air like a storm warning.

'Tansy...your name is rather unusual,' he remarked, disconcerting her with that opening greeting.

'For a couple of generations all the children on my

mother's side of the family were named after plants or trees,' Tansy told him with a reluctant smile. 'All the obvious names for girls like Violet and Rosie and Daisy had already been used by the time I arrived.'

'A charming tradition,' Jude commented, his attention lingering on her, taking in the delicate curves beneath the close-fitting top, the long slender legs crossed, the feet in shabby boots. 'You look like a teenager in that outfit. I'll be accused of cradle robbing by the press—'

'Hardly. I'm almost twenty-three,' Tansy cut in defensively.

'I'm twenty-nine. It's still a big gap,' Jude told her stubbornly.

'If you say so.' *Yes-woman, yes-woman,* Tansy chanted soothingly inside her head. He didn't want an argumentative woman with opinions of her own and if she worked at it she could keep a still tongue for her sister's sake, of course she could. Posy was worth the sacrifice of a little pride.

'I have something important I want to discuss with you before we get down to the nitty-gritty of wedding arrangements,' Jude revealed. 'But I need you to agree to listen to me first without interrupting. I don't require an answer from you right now. I simply prefer to be upfront. Our relationship will be easier if we are honest with each other…'

Tansy went pink and dropped her head, that reference to honesty cutting into her. After all, she was not being truthful with him about the reality that she would come with the extra responsibility of a young child in tow. 'I can listen,' she muttered tightly.

'My original plan when I believed that I was marrying Althea was to use this marriage to father a child. Althea had agreed to that option,' Jude told her. 'And I would be delighted if you were willing to consider that possibility as well.'

Tansy was so astonished by that statement that her head swept up, stunned green eyes locking to his lean, darkly handsome features. He need not have worried about her interrupting him. She was so taken aback by that utterly unexpected confession that she could only stare in wide-eyed shock at him. A *baby*? He was actually asking her to have a *baby* with him? Was he out of his mind?

CHAPTER THREE

'EVIDENTLY I NEED to explain my point of view,' Jude breathed tautly as he recognised her incredulity while marvelling at how little control she had over her facial expressions. He wasn't accustomed to a woman who wore her thoughts on her face like a banner. It was educational and oddly satisfying.

'I have good reason for my aversion to marriage,' Jude contended with studious cool. 'Historically the men in my family have either made extremely poor husbands or they have married troubled women. I have no wish to follow in their footsteps and make several marriages or go through the disputes and the messy divorces that follow.' He shifted a fluid brown hand in repudiation of that depressing prospect. 'I've already lived through that pattern when I was a kid with my father and it's not for me, nor is it an ideal background against which to raise a child.'

Tansy nodded understanding of that outlook because she had checked out the Alexandris family online. Stormy separations, flagrant infidelities, divorces, custody battles and bitter feuds documented his family's shockingly volatile history in the relationship field. With those statistics behind him, it was hardly surprising that he would be especially wary of matrimony.

'But in a marriage like this, where there is no shared history or baggage, having a child could be a practical option and I am, at heart, a very practical individual. Although I have no desire to make a real marriage, I still very much need a legal heir,' Jude admitted calmly. 'It would be easiest to have one with you. I can also assure you that any child we had would be loved and cared for and that you would be richly rewarded for providing me with one.'

Tansy stared woodenly down into her coffee cup, her natural colour evaporating at his assumption that she was mercenary enough to conceive a child for a profit. It hurt to remain silent, to compress her lips on the angry defensive words ready to leap off her tongue. Calvin had forced her into a tight corner where she *had* to play a certain role. Naturally, Jude Alexandris had assumed that she was marrying him for his money, and she could not afford to tell him anything different until *after* the ceremony when Posy's future would be secure. Calvin would get his money and then he would be out of their lives, she reminded herself bracingly, thinking that at least her stepfather would never get the opportunity to use Posy the way he was using her to enrich himself.

'We would also share custody of any child. I would be amenable to most reasonable arrangements. I can give you those reassurances but naturally there is no guarantee that we could even conceive a child together,' Jude pronounced with an ironic curl to his sensual mouth. 'I don't think the male line in my family is particularly fertile, because I am an only child and so was my father.'

'Do you want my opinion on this potential plan of yours?' Tansy asked very stiffly.

'Not at this moment, no,' Jude admitted bluntly. 'For now, I only want you to mull the idea over and see if it could be a fit for you but, obviously, it's *not* a required condition for this marriage to happen.'

Some of the tension in her slight shoulders eased at that assertion and she looked back down at her coffee, forcing herself to sip it again in an effort to behave normally.

'Possibly you feel that you're too young to be tied down with the responsibility of a child,' Jude continued. 'But with my wealth, you could have nannies round the clock and becoming a mother would not deprive you of your freedom.'

Tansy almost choked on her coffee and her face burned with guilty heat because she already knew what it was like to be a young mother and there had been neither nannies nor babysitters to take the weight of responsibility off her shoulders. But, of course, she wasn't able to share that truth with him yet.

'You're keen on this idea,' Tansy said stiffly instead. 'Why? I mean, you don't even know me—'

'I don't need to,' Jude intoned confidently. 'In fact, I think it would be an advantage that we are strangers. Having a child would be a project rather than a burning mission. Emotions wouldn't be involved, and we have no past history or romantic expectations to complicate our relationship. Both of us already know that the marriage will end in divorce. I see innumerable benefits to such a detached arrangement and such arrangements are not uncommon in today's world. Friends sometimes have children together.'

Tansy's head nodded with obedient marionette stiffness. He was insane, she reflected ruefully, and as emotionally aware as a big dumb rock. He honestly believed it was possible for them to marry, have a sexual relationship and conceive a child together without anyone's emotions getting involved! What planet had he grown up on? What sort of women was he accustomed to dealing with? Had no woman ever told him that there were good reasons why human beings weren't supposed to carelessly mate like animals to reproduce? She drew in a slow, deep, self-soothing breath and remained studiously silent.

Seemingly released from tension after having broached the topic of having a child, Jude poured himself a black coffee and strode away from the table again, a tall, lithe silhouette suddenly revealed and gilded as he stepped into a shard of sunshine. 'Now, we'll get down to the basic stuff we have to organise.'

'I'm sure *I* will not be organising anything,' Tansy volunteered deadpan. 'I believe that's your department.'

Suspicious dark eyes struck hers at unnerving speed and Tansy flushed and went back to surveying her coffee again, censuring herself for having let that sarcastic comment escape, particularly when she had been doing so well at keeping quiet. Jude sank down casually on the arm of the sofa opposite her, innately graceful in his every movement. He was too close now for her to relax because her attention continually wandered back to his stunningly handsome face, tracing the sharp high cheekbones, the strong black brows framing his deep-set eyes and the lush, sensual lips that softened those arrogantly masculine features and somehow made her own tingle. When he looked directly at her, her breath caught in her throat, her heart hammered and her mouth ran dry. She shifted uneasily in her seat, alarmed by the sheer strength of his sexual attraction.

'You're quite correct. I do have everything in hand,' Jude confessed. 'Althea has even given us our cover story but I'm afraid it has put a price on your head with the paparazzi.'

'Cover story?' Tansy repeated blankly, still struggling to pull free of the dreamy sensual spell he could plunge her into with a mere lingering glance.

'Althea and I were supposed to be getting married next week. Now I'll be marrying you instead,' Jude extended a dry explanation. 'The press and the general public will assume that I ditched her for you, which will make us look more realistic to my family since that is exactly what my father did in order to marry my mother thirty odd years ago. He was engaged to a very respectable Greek girl when he ran off with my mother.'

'Charming...so I'll be posing as the sort of woman who has no objection to carrying on with another woman's man,' Tansy commented curtly.

Jude shrugged a wide shoulder in an infuriatingly careless motion. 'Does it matter? Once Althea backed out, it was never likely to be plain sailing for us as a couple because Althea was the perfect bride as far as my relatives were concerned. *Any* other bride would be a controversial choice, so don't take that angle personally. I don't give a damn what anybody thinks, nor do you need to. All you have to do is get through the wedding reception and then we're pretty much done with family ties and socialising.'

Tansy nodded with a sinking heart, resisting the urge to say that that sounded very cold to her. But family wasn't always perfect. Didn't she know that herself? With a mother with whom, sadly, she had barely had a thought in common and a stepfather she had actively disliked? She had no excuse to feel superior, but she wasn't looking forward either to being a target of dislike and disapproval with his relations when she hadn't actually committed the sin for which she would be judged.

'The wedding will take place next week in Greece.'

'Greece?' Tansy gasped in shock, prompted into jerking forward in her seat and setting down her coffee to gape at him. 'We have to get married abroad?'

'I was born there. It's not "abroad" to me,' Jude fielded very drily.

In a frantic state of mind, Tansy wondered how on earth she would get Posy a passport in time and, indeed, whether her stepfather would be willing to travel out to Greece with his daughter. Complications she hadn't expected were suddenly piling up around her, throwing her naive plans and expectations into crisis.

'Couldn't we just get married here?' she prompted hopefully. 'In a register office or something?'

'But that would mean that you could miss out on all

the bridal pomp and ceremony—a choice which would make you a very unusual woman,' Jude remarked, subjecting her to a considering appraisal as if her suggestion were distinctly unusual and unfeminine. 'It would also greatly disappoint my grandfather who is, I'm certain, looking forward immensely to his leading role as host and master of ceremonies...'

'I'm not much for pomp and ceremony,' Tansy confided unevenly, still anxiously concerned about how she could possibly fit a ten-month-old baby into such elaborate arrangements.

Jude lifted his chin, a sudden, breathtakingly charismatic smile flashing his shapely, wilful mouth as he sprang upright without warning, that buzzing energy of his pronounced again. His smile turned the beauty of his eyes to pure glittering gold enticement. 'Yes, I'll do it!' he proclaimed, utterly disconcerting her. 'Disappointing my grandfather, Isidore, would come very naturally to me at the moment and us arriving already married will annoy the hell out of the old man. I'll arrange a register office wedding here before we fly out, but courtesy demands that we'll still have to go through the motions in Greece and suffer through a church ceremony and a party.'

Tansy nodded slowly, barely able to credit that she had succeeded in changing his mind about something, but relief was already overpowering her in a wave. At least, if he married her in London, she would be able to immediately gain custody of her little sister and she would not need to ask Calvin to put himself or his girlfriend to any extraordinary inconvenience.

'Where will we be living?' she pressed, belatedly forced to consider such facts on the back of the sudden realisation that her whole life was about to undergo a radical change.

Jude's brow pleated. 'I move between properties, as and when suits. Nothing's set in stone, but much of the time we'll be "abroad", as you call it.'

Tansy lost colour, knowing she would have to get a passport for her sister as quickly as possible, realising that out of ignorance she had totally underestimated the practicalities of life with an Alexandris. A guy as rich as Jude owned more than one home and travelled whenever and wherever he wanted, probably in a private jet. The routine restrictions that limited the choices and movements of ordinary people were unknown to him.

'You'll need a wedding gown and a new wardrobe. I have a stylist waiting next door to take your measurements,' Jude volunteered, startling her once again with that announcement. 'You will be provided with appropriate clothing to wear.'

'Provided? But—'

'Don't quibble about the unimportant details, Tansy,' Jude urged silkily. 'It's all part of the same deal and you're being paid to take on this role.'

No, *Calvin* was being paid, Tansy reflected angrily, compressing her lips on an outburst, keeping Posy's welfare first and foremost in her mind every time Jude said something that set her teeth on edge. Future husband might be an absolute dream of a fantasy man to look at, but actually living with him struck her as likely to provide a much tougher challenge. It didn't matter where or how she married him or what she wore in that temporary fake life, she reminded herself firmly. In that field Jude was undeniably right: those were insignificant details.

'I'm also hoping to keep a lid on your identity until after the wedding,' Jude informed her. 'I don't like the paparazzi. Don't talk to anyone about this marriage… and I mean, *anyone*. From you I will expect total discretion with regard to every aspect of my private life and family.'

Gripped by the warning onslaught of those piercing dark eyes set hard as granite, Tansy swallowed with difficulty. 'Yes, of course. You've got it.'

Jude wore doubt on his lean, darkly handsome features. 'I'm well aware that a lot of women like to see themselves in print but, unless it's a fashion shoot, you won't be seeing yourself in print and you won't be giving any interviews, either before or after our marriage. Is that clear?' Jude intoned.

'Crystal clear,' Tansy parried stiffly. 'Any other rules?'

'Don't tell me any lies. If you make a mistake, *own* it and tell me about it. I despise liars,' he admitted with a ringing authority that chilled her to the bone. 'The stylist is waiting for you through that door…'

Tansy rose unsteadily and moved forward, involuntarily intrigued by a man capable of arranging so much without input from anyone else. He had a strong eye for detail, she acknowledged, a knack for grasping potential problems in advance, even the little ones like what his fake wife might wear. *And he hated liars.* Her conscience twanged as she acknowledged guiltily that even he could not be expected to have guessed about the existence of a baby girl whom nobody had dared to mention. 'How did you know what time I'd be arriving to arrange a stylist?'

'I didn't.' Jude shot her an amused look. 'For the kind of money I'm prepared to spend the woman was willing to practise patience and wait until you showed up.'

As Tansy drew level with him to head towards the door he had indicated, he caught her hand in one of his to bring her to a halt. 'Let the stylist be your guide. I don't want a bride who dresses like a teenager.'

Shaken to find herself that close to him and in actual physical contact with the warmth of his big hand engulfing hers, Tansy gazed up uneasily into tawny gold eyes that were as primal to her in that moment as a lion's tracking prey. 'I only look like a teenager because I'm so skinny,' she muttered awkwardly. 'I just never rounded out like my friends. I kept on waiting for it to happen but…it *didn't…*'

As Tansy heard those unnecessarily frank words fall from her lips scarlet heat rushed into her cheeks and she wanted to bite her tongue off. But there it was: she was indisputably tiny in the places women were supposed to be curvy and feminine, more boyish than lush in shape. On the plus side she could eat whatever she liked and burn it off again without much effort, but she had always longed for the curves she lacked.

'You're not skinny, you're…slender,' Jude contradicted soft and low, something in that dark purring drawl sending a tide of awareness currenting through her from head to toe. 'Some men prefer that. Personally, I put a higher value on a more natural appearance.'

'So you say,' Tansy breathed, unimpressed by that claim, which she had heard before and found not to be true. 'But it's my bet that you wouldn't be too impressed if you got treated to natural *all* the time. Men always think they don't like make-up on a woman but I'm not sure that's the case.'

'You do have opinions,' Jude noted.

'Didn't think you wanted to hear them.'

'I do and I don't,' Jude confided. 'I prefer to keep this relationship impersonal.'

Tickled by that unlikely possibility and the sheer ignorance of human interaction with which he made that admission, Tansy shot him an amused glance. 'Well, you *will* have to work very, very hard at making sure that you don't fall madly in love with me because, I'm telling you now, you're not my type,' she heard herself tease.

Jude gazed down in visible surprise at those clear almond-shaped green eyes sparkling with laughter and the pulse at his groin kicked up a storm of interest, disconcerting him. He rested a hand down on her slight shoulder, wondering what sort of sexual chemistry it was that felled him where he stood with a totally ordinary young woman. Gold-digger, he reminded himself darkly, but inexplicably it didn't quell the desire and, with a sudden fierce impatience new to his experience, he stopped holding back and he bent his arrogant dark head and kissed her.

Tansy hadn't been prepared for that move. Later

she thought that she should have been, when they were standing so close and alone and supposedly on the brink of what he *in his insanity* saw as a normal marriage. But the sensual, seeking brush of his mouth over hers made her stop breathing and freeze in astonishment. For a split second, he owned her with that kiss, *owned* her as no other man ever had because it was so exciting. Sensation burst low in her tummy and stabbed an arrow of heat down into her throbbing core. She pressed her thighs tightly together, struggling to kill that surge of awareness. And that fast, she was drinking in the unfamiliar but ridiculously arousing scent of him, discovering that that was an added aphrodisiac. He smelled good enough to eat, she found herself thinking as his arms came around her and her knees wobbled, and that all-pervasive heat spread like a traitor up through her entire body. Her hands closed on to his sleeves to steady herself.

She felt alive and blazing with energy in a way she never had before and his lips were parting hers and hers were still clinging to his, her slight frame jerking in a shocking spasm of electrified pleasure as his tongue pierced the sensitive interior of her mouth. It was like a burning torch bursting into flame inside her and every skin cell was urging her to get closer to him. Her head swam with the dizzy intensity of it, every thought overpowered by physical reaction.

Fully aroused and tense, Jude set Tansy back from him and dealt her a sizzling smile of appreciation. 'Getting to know you better promises to be especially entertaining,' he quipped as he tugged open the door that led into the room beyond.

Not if I can help it, Tansy thought, gritting her teeth, torn between wanting to slap him and slap herself for succumbing to him like a dizzy, never-been-kissed adolescent. For goodness's sake, she had literally been clinging to him! Her colour was high as the stylist approached her with a tape measure and the door behind her closed again. There was no time then for her to agonise.

The other woman was hugely efficient, questioning her about colours and styles, likes and dislikes, while bringing up outfits on her laptop for Tansy to scrutinise. Tansy, who hadn't had new clothes in longer than she remembered, found it a startling experience and when her companion moved on to asking her to preview wedding gowns on screen, it felt even more unreal to her. She was measured for every possible garment from the skin out and assured, when she tried to argue, that Mr Alexandris had specified that she was to have 'everything'. And everything in Jude's parlance seemed to encompass more clothing options than Tansy could ever have dreamt of owning and hinted at a lifestyle she had only glimpsed in her mother's favourite glossy fashion magazines.

She was on the way home again when Jude texted her the date and time for the register office wedding. It was only three days away and her eyes widened because even though Calvin had warned her that Jude was on a tight timeline, she had still underestimated the speed at which events would unfold and her life would change.

But so would Posy's, she reminded herself more cheerfully. She would be able to buy new clothes and toys for her sister. There would be no more scrabbling round charity shops for garments and playthings that some other child had outgrown. With hindsight she could see that her stepfather's financial problems should have been obvious to her sooner, but then Calvin had always been very stingy about spending money on anything that did not directly benefit him.

The next day, Calvin informed her that his boss was coming out personally to the house with the prenuptial contract for her to sign. 'He's going to be very curious about how Alexandris got to know you. Just act mysterious,' he advised her.

Tansy was not required to act anything because Calvin's boss was scrupulously businesslike and polite, and he asked her no awkward questions. He even advised her to take the document to her own legal representative for a consultation. Tansy demurred and, after glancing through several pages, her brain staggered by the huge sums of money being offered to her as a mere 'allowance', insisted on signing then and there. After all, she didn't have time to waste either, not if her stepfather were to feel secure enough to sign over custody of his daughter to her.

She was not, however, that surprised when Calvin came through the front door in a rage that evening, slamming into his home study and, when he saw her in the doorway, throwing her a furious look. 'I've been made redundant by the firm…overstaffed, according to the big boss. Load of rubbish! They've worked out that I must have lined you up with Alexandris and they see it as a breach of client confidentiality!' he framed bitterly.

Tansy said nothing. Indeed, she found herself thinking that, for once, smooth, smug Calvin had got his fingers deservedly burned for his manipulative ways, but ultimately he would be richly rewarded for the marriage he had made in her name, so the punishment of losing his job wasn't that great. And *that* stung, that he could use Posy as a bargaining tool to satisfy his own greed and still have the nerve to pretend that he cared about his daughter.

The following afternoon Jude phoned Tansy.

'I've received a warning that the paparazzi may be on the brink of identifying you,' Jude offered flatly. 'To protect you, I need to remove you from that address. No newspaper will publish your name without a photograph at the very least. A car will pick you up in thirty minutes.'

'A car? In thirty *minutes*?' Tansy repeated, nervous perspiration beading her upper lip at the prospect of her situation and potentially the reference to her baby sister being published in a newspaper. 'To pick me up and take me where?'

'A hotel, where you will remain undetected and safe until we meet at the register office tomorrow—'

'I *can't* move into a hotel!' Tansy exclaimed, worrying about Posy.

'You will accompany my security team to the hotel. I don't want you exposed by the press before my family even meet you. You don't have a choice about this,' Jude informed her grittily, and that was the end of the call.

'Jude thinks the press may be on to me,' Tansy told Calvin as she hurried downstairs and her stepfather appeared in the lounge doorway. 'He wants to have me picked up and moved to a hotel until the ceremony but I can't just walk out on Posy.'

'Of course, you can. Susie's on her way over,' Calvin told her in impatient disagreement. 'I've already warned you, Tansy. What Alexandris wants, he has to get because he could still walk away. You're not dealing with Mr Average or Mr Obliging here.'

'You could hire a nanny for Posy until tomorrow. You're about to come into money. You can afford to hire someone,' his stepdaughter reminded him doggedly. 'Then I wouldn't have to worry about her.'

'You make such a fuss about her. The kid will be *fine* with Susie. Good grief, I can't wait until you move out of here!' the blond man admitted in a burst of unhidden irritation. 'You're one of those women who always thinks they know best about everything. Alexandris is welcome to you!'

Tansy concentrated on packing an overnight bag. That she was getting married to Jude the next day felt surreal. None of the new clothing she had been promised had arrived as yet and she still only had her green dress to wear. Of course, he wasn't expecting her to appear in a wedding gown at the register office. The bridal finery would be reserved for Greece and the first day of her official wife role. She bustled next door into Posy's room where the baby was napping, and she crept about filling a bag with the baby necessities she would require for her sister's benefit the following day and set the bag aside.

Downstairs she tackled her stepfather about a topic that had begun to worry her. 'You haven't asked me to sign anything yet to take charge of Posy,' she reminded him nervously.

'It's not that simple…' Calvin frowned at her. 'Social services would insist on being involved in any change of child guardianship. The only way you can legally *have* Posy is to adopt her, but you're getting married and because of that Alexandris would have to be part of the adoption application. I suggest you take it up with him after the ceremony.'

'Adoption?' she questioned in complete bewilderment. 'But you *told* me you could *sign* Posy over to me.'

'Alterations in child custody arrangements are more formal than that and hedged around by legal safeguards,' Calvin informed her loftily. 'I can give you permission to take her abroad and I've pulled every string in the Alexandris armoury to get the kid her passport in time without Alexandris realising that it's the kid and not you who needs the passport. But I'm afraid that's the best I can do for now.'

'That's not fair, Calvin. That's not what we agreed,' Tansy protested in consternation.

At that point, her mobile rang again, and a man called Spiros, as mentioned and named by Jude, informed her that he was waiting for her at the back entrance to the house. Regretfully appreciating that she couldn't just tuck Posy into a case and pack her as well, Tansy grabbed her overnight bag and warned Calvin that Posy would need to be accompanied by her baby bag and her stroller when Tansy took charge of her the next day.

'I'll drop her off with you after the ceremony. I'll be outside the register office,' he promised cheerfully.

Tansy gritted her teeth because she didn't trust him. He had already grossly deceived her by promising to sign over custody of Posy when, as a lawyer, he must have known from the outset that that wasn't legally possible without the involvement of the local authorities. How could she have been so stupid as to trust Calvin's word about anything? On the other hand, as long as Posy seemed to be only a burden in her father's eyes, it was unlikely that he would want to reclaim his daughter in the future, Tansy reasoned, striving to silence the anxious insecurities pulling at her.

She compressed her lips as she emerged from the house. Her bag was immediately claimed by an older man in a suit, who directed her towards the narrow rear gate beyond which a car was parked in readiness.

The city hotel was famous and exclusive. Tansy felt like a fish out of water from the moment she walked through the lofty-ceilinged foyer with its marble floor and magnificent glittering crystal chandeliers. The opulent formality of her surroundings was overwhelming. She was wafted up in a lift and shown into a superb suite that included a spacious living area as well. In the bedroom she found a small selection of the garments she had chosen with the stylist awaiting her, and relief filled her because a smart outfit had been included and she thought the dress and toning jacket would be perfect for the civil ceremony. After carefully trying the clothing on, she sat in the silky robe that had been included with the gorgeous lingerie and wondered how to fill what remained of the day.

It had been so long since she had had time to herself because, for months, every day had revolved round her baby sister's feeding and sleeping schedule. She walked through her ridiculously luxurious accommodation and smiled with rueful appreciation, curling up on a sumptuous sofa to watch TV before calling room service to order an evening meal. Replete from those treats, she ran herself a bubble bath and lay in it, fretting about whether or not Susie had remembered to put Posy to bed with her favourite toy. Recalling her stepfather's accusation that she was too fussy, she wondered if that was true. Not long afterwards she climbed into the extremely comfortable bed, set her phone as an alarm and lay back, thinking in disbelief, *I'm getting married tomorrow...*

CHAPTER FOUR

TANSY ROSE INCREDIBLY early the next day and then had to fill the empty hours that stretched before the late-afternoon ceremony.

Only after lunch did she begin getting ready. She slid into the diaphanous lingerie, relishing the smooth, unfamiliar slide of silk against her skin and the pretty adornments of lace and ribbon. The dress zipped, she slipped on the high-heeled courts and donned the jacket. The unruly tumble of her hair round her shoulders made her wince because it looked untidy. Her hair needed to go up to set off the stylish rose-coloured suit. With deft fingers she braided her hair and anchored it to her head. A text arrived to tell her when she would be picked up and she was down in the foyer ahead of time, nervous as a cat on hot coals.

It isn't every day you get married, she soothed herself, but it wasn't as if it were a real marriage. Love didn't come into their agreement and she had to admit that that made her sad, because she had always assumed that when she got married she would genuinely care about her partner. This marriage is for Posy though, she reminded herself, don't make it personal. But the recollection of her little sister frightened her as well at that moment because she was imagining how Jude Alexandris might react to the revelation that she had been less than honest with him. He would be angry. She hadn't told him an actual lie, but she certainly hadn't matched his forthrightness either.

Pale and taut, Tansy entered the waiting room in the register office feeling slightly nauseous with nerves. Jude was already there, tall, dark and devastatingly spectacular in a dark grey designer suit that accentuated his sleek, athletic build. Just looking at him stole the breath from her lungs. From the bronzed glow of his skin to his glossy black curls and wide, sensual mouth, he emanated compelling masculine allure. Her tummy flipped and her heart thumped in her ears as she collided with glittering dark golden eyes enhanced by inky black lashes. All of a sudden her legs felt disconnected from the rest of her. A hint of a smile curved his beautifully shaped mouth, lighting up his lean, shockingly handsome features, and she blinked, utterly dazzled by that sudden flash of powerful charisma.

'Who will be acting as the witnesses?' she whispered as she drew level with him.

'My security guards. These past weeks I've seen enough of lawyers to last me a lifetime,' Jude confided with grim amusement, a big hand curving to her spine to urge her forward as the registrar's assistant signalled them.

He didn't like her hair up, Jude mused, but she did look very stylish and rather more mature, although when her eyes danced with amusement, her inner teenager shone out like a neon light. He suspected she was the sort of woman given to giggling at inappropriate moments. But that sassy smile, accompanied by the downward-cast eyes and the soft flutter of her lashes as she nibbled at her fuller lower lip, ensnared his attention every time. That hint of uncertainty and shyness was incredibly enticing. He invariably went for bolder women, who laid out sex like an all-you-can-eat buffet, no questions asked, nothing on the forbidden list. He liked straightforward, he liked simple, he didn't like room left for misunderstandings or women who played games, available one day, strategically unavailable the next.

Tense at the awareness that matrimony was a solemn event and shaken by the knowledge that she was, in many ways, making a mockery of it, Tansy bolted her knees together and stood as straight and still as she could. Without fanfare the ceremony began. Jude lifted her hand and slid a fine-plaited platinum wedding band onto her finger. Her hand trembled damply in his, her responses breathless as her apprehension climbed. No matter how hard she tried to stay in the moment, her brain kept jumping ahead to Jude's likely reaction when she collected Posy from her stepfather, and she was soon right on the edge of panic. My goodness, Calvin had better be outside waiting on time, she reflected anxiously!

'So, now I'm a married man,' Jude mused reflectively as Tansy roamed ahead of him, impatient to leave the building. 'We're not in a hurry. We've plenty of time to get to the airport.'

'We're going straight to the airport?' Tansy checked in apparent surprise.

'Didn't I tell you that?'

'No,' she said flatly, because she had already noticed that he didn't bother telling her anything that he didn't think she needed to know.

'Our Greek wedding is tomorrow.'

'Oh, joy,' she muttered tautly as she stepped out onto the street, several other men joining the pair that accompanied them and fanning out across the pavement while a limousine nudged in at the kerb ahead of them.

But Tansy shifted sideways, her attention locked not to the car but to the pretty young blonde holding a baby several feet away. 'Susie…' she framed in relief, reaching for her sister and anchoring the smiling baby on her slim hip. 'Where's her stuff?'

'What stuff?' Susie asked blankly, already backing away. 'Look, I have to go. Calvin will go spare if he gets a ticket—'

'I packed a bag for her… I need her pushchair!' Tansy gasped.

Susie shrugged. 'Sorry… I didn't see it. We only brought her.'

Tansy watched incredulously as her stepfather's girlfriend hurried off without a care in the world, indeed, probably glad to see the back of both of them. Tansy out of the house and Susie freed of the expectation that she would ever have to look after Calvin's daughter again could only be a win-win on Susie's terms.

'What's going on?' Jude demanded with a frown of bewilderment, watching the baby cling to Tansy like a little limpet and dab playful little kisses across Tansy's face in what was obviously a regular game between them. Mother and child? Jude froze, shattered by the suspicion.

'Sir...?' Spiros prompted, standing at the open passenger door of the limo in readiness for their departure.

Jude unfroze with difficulty and pressed a hand to Tansy's spine to move her towards the car. With a presence of mind that astonished Jude, Spiros leant into the car and popped out a built-in child's car seat in readiness for the unexpected passenger. Jude hadn't even realised the limo offered such an option.

The woman who had told him that she was a virgin was a *mother*? And she had deliberately concealed the fact? Jude was in shock. But he *had* married a woman who was a stranger. All he knew about her was that she liked money enough to sell herself into marriage for it. He had taken a huge risk, hadn't he? He should have had Tansy fully investigated in advance instead of simply taking her at face value. What madness had possessed him? The simple fact that the minute he had laid eyes on her he had wanted to lay her down on the nearest bed and lose himself in her? Yet when he knew so little about her, she could never have been the safe option her stepfather had sworn she was.

It was his own fault: he hadn't been willing to spare the time it would have taken to run the usual checks on Tansy. He had been in too much of a hurry, too eager to press ahead with the marriage after Althea had let him down. And his impatience had brought its own punishment.

In the ghastly silence that stretched inside the limousine, Tansy, having secured Posy in the car seat, broke out in nervous perspiration. 'I'm really, *really* sorry that I didn't tell you about her beforehand,' she whispered guiltily. 'I was scared you would change your mind about marrying me.'

Jude shot glittering dark golden eyes to her corner of the limousine and flung her a sardonic appraisal. 'You think?'

'I'll grovel if you want me to but please don't shout in front of Posy. I don't want her to get upset,' Tansy confided. 'If you're *still* taking me to Greece with you—'

'You're my wife now. I don't see that I have much choice.' Jude ground out that admission.

'I'll have to buy a load of baby things at the airport because Calvin didn't send any of her stuff with her,' Tansy muttered apologetically.

Jude knew nothing whatsoever about babies. A few of his friends had reproduced. He might be a godfather several times over but his dealings with babies were very much of the hands-off, admire-the-kid-from-a-distance nature. And then, just like that, his agile brain snapped back into gear and he dug out his phone to start handling the situation. He called his PA and told him to hire a rota of three nannies to provide the child with round-the-clock care and to ensure that the first one joined them in time for the flight out to Greece. He called his head housekeeper to order a nursery to be set up in all his homes. Those practicalities dealt with, he lounged fluidly back and simmered with pure burning rage.

The baby kept on stretching out little starfish fingers

in his direction and he ignored it. It was an absurdly friendly little creature, quite impervious to the chilly atmosphere and the silence surrounding it.

He had married a single parent, a young woman with a child by an unknown man. And it would be a waste of time to set a private investigation agency on to Tansy now because within the week the international press would have exposed every single secret she had, including the identity of her child's father. Jude was rigid with anger, enraged by her brazen dishonesty from the outset of their acquaintance.

Had he known the truth about her, he wouldn't even have considered her, he reasoned angrily. He did not need nor want the hassle and inconvenience of a very young child in his life! He had nothing against children. *Thee mou*...did he not want one of his own to silence for ever Isidore's lectures about family bloodlines, duty and loyalty? But having his own child, and curbing his freedom to meet the needs of that child, was a far different prospect from the situation that Tansy had landed him into without his agreement! Unaccustomed to anything but his own will restricting him, Jude fiercely guarded his ability to do as he pleased when and where he pleased.

They arrived at the airport. Tansy bundled the kid into her arms like an unwieldy parcel and struggled to keep up with Jude as he headed for the peace of the VIP departure lounge.

By the time they arrived there, Tansy was a hot perspiring mess because Posy was a solid little girl and Tansy wasn't accustomed to carrying her for so long.

After a moment of hesitation, she settled her down on the carpet at Jude's feet. 'Look, I have to go and buy essentials for Posy and she's too heavy to carry. Can you just keep an eye on her for ten minutes?' she almost whispered, her face flaming at her nerve in even asking. 'I'm sorry, I don't even have a pushchair to put her in.'

'What do I do if she starts crying?' Jude asked drily, ignoring the sudden grin that spread across Spiros's usually expressionless face.

'Lift her?' Tansy gave him a pleading look. 'She's very friendly.'

Raising her rump, the very friendly baby crawled under a chair and got stuck there. She set up a hullabaloo of complaint until Jude lifted the chair away and freed her from her self-imposed cage. By then Tansy and two of his security team had departed. Not a fast learner, Posy crawled beneath another chair and ducked her head away before whipping it back and looking expectantly at Jude with huge blue eyes. She was trying to play peekaboo without anything to hide behind, Jude registered, blanking her while a woman nearby obliged and the baby shook and wriggled with delighted laughter at the response, tousled blonde curls bouncing.

It was probably the cutest baby that Jude had ever seen, but then he didn't look at many babies and he could well be mistaken. That cuteness factor did not diminish his rage and disbelief one jot. He was appalled by the extent of Tansy's deception.

Tansy was disconcerted by the amount she had to buy merely to get Posy through a couple of days. Nappies, wipes, powdered milk, bottles, cereal, bibs, dummies, changes of clothes, a toddler cup, a couple of basic toys. A bigger embarrassment was reaching the till and realising she did not have enough in her bank account to cover such a spending spree and then Spiros startled her by stepping in with a black credit card and taking care of the payment for her. She went weak with relief. They arrived back in the VIP lounge festooned with bags of supplies. Tansy was hot and bothered and her feet were in agony from the tightness of her new shoes. She was taken aback to see a strange young brunette down on her knees on the floor entertaining Posy.

'Who's that?' she asked.

'Our new nanny. Her name's Kerry, pleasant girl, enjoys travel,' Jude advanced coolly.

'How on earth did you acquire a nanny before we've even left the airport?' Tansy whispered in disbelief.

'She's emergency cover from an agency. I have very efficient staff.'

'Posy doesn't need a nanny, and this is *not* an emergency.'

'How are you planning to get through the wedding tomorrow without a nanny?' Jude asked drily.

Tansy stiffened because she hadn't thought ahead to that challenge and her shoulders slumped as she recognised her oversight. 'I'm really sorry about all this.'

'Not one half as sorry as I am to discover that I've married a liar and a fraud,' Jude imparted with a soft chilling bite that cut into her tender skin like the slash of a knife blade.

Momentarily tears stung the backs of her eyes and she twisted her head away to hide that weakness. She wanted to defend herself, but it was neither the time nor the place. Instead she moved forward to introduce herself to the nanny and scooped up her sister to give her a cuddle. A liar and a fraud, she thought, wincing from the description until she reminded herself impatiently that, having secured Posy's future with their marriage, she was now paying the price for her deceit.

The private jet was a great deal larger than she had naively expected. The stewardess led the way to one of a set of sleeping compartments at the rear of the plane, which was already set up with a crib for Posy.

'She's such a happy baby!' Kerry remarked cheerfully of her new charge. 'Is she always like this?'

'Pretty much and she sleeps like a log too,' Tansy confirmed with pride as she finished changing her sister and slotted her into fresh clothing, a tight knot of tension forming in her stomach as she contemplated having to face the showdown with Jude. Time to pay the piper, she told herself ruefully, because she had neither an escape hatch nor an adequate excuse for what she had done.

She walked back to the spacious living area with its groups of opulent cream leather seats and tables. A stewardess was already serving Jude with a drink and Tansy asked for a white wine, feeling she needed something to stiffen her backbone. Her anxious gaze settled on Jude's hard classic profile. From the slash of his black brows, the angle of his strong nose and the corner of his lush shapely mouth, he was compellingly male and absolutely gorgeous, especially with the shadow of darkening stubble emphasising the sculpted hardness of his jawline.

'I know you must think very badly of me for not telling you about Posy,' Tansy said as soon as they were alone.

Jude averted his attention from the shapely length of her legs, cursing his male susceptibility for distracting him. He dealt her a lacerating glance in punishment. 'Don't fake regret with me. Why didn't you tell me that you had a baby?'

'I couldn't risk it. You might have changed your mind about marrying me,' she admitted honestly.

'*Thee mou…* I don't need any explanation for your motives!' Jude derided.

Tansy lifted her chin, a hint of challenge in her bright gaze. 'Well, actually you *do*. I didn't agree to marry you for the reasons you probably think I did.'

'I'm pretty certain that your reasons are no more complex than the size of my bank balance and the money I was willing to offer,' Jude pronounced with sardonic bite.

A wave of angry pink ran up Tansy's throat over her cheeks and up to her brow. Deeply insulted that he had dared to call her a gold-digger to her face, she gritted her teeth and settled herself down in a comfortable seat to have her drink. In an effort to fake a relaxation she was far from feeling, she kicked off the shoes that were pinching her poor toes black and blue and slid off her jacket because she was too warm. 'Well, since you already know everything there is to know about me, there's no reason for me to keep talking, is there?'

Jude surveyed her with a daunting air of incredulous hauteur, his spectacular dark golden eyes gleaming with irate warning. Tansy hitched her chin even higher in challenge, green eyes gleaming with furious defiance and determination. 'I've said sorry but I'm *not* going to grovel any more. I did something wrong and I've acknowledged it. I will do everything I can to ensure that Posy does not interfere too much with your life but there's not much more I can offer to do.'

'Of course, she'll interfere with my life!' Jude ground out, incensed by that unexpected rebelliousness of hers and her anger. She was angry with him? How *dare* she be angry with him? What right did *she* have to be angry?

'Not if you can help it…you hired a nanny fast enough!' Tansy could not resist sniping back at him. 'And you called me a liar and I'm not!'

'How do you make that out?'

'I didn't actually tell you any lies. You didn't *ask* me if I had any dependants.'

'That was for you to tell me upfront,' Jude incised crushingly.

'You're not being fair. If you were going to be so blasted picky, you should have known what questions you needed to ask,' Tansy argued defensively. 'And if you *had* asked, I would have had to answer truthfully because, whatever you think, I'm *not* a liar.'

'I wasn't prepared for someone as inventive with the truth as you appear to be,' Jude fired back at her. 'Althea has her faults, but she didn't tell me any lies.'

Tansy flushed. 'Althea said she would marry you and then changed her mind last minute!' she reminded him shortly, needled by his reference to the other woman. 'She let you down—I haven't and don't intend to! I keep my word.'

'How do you expect me to believe that now? There's nothing straight or honest about your dealings with me,' Jude condemned with icy scorn as he set his empty tumbler down with a jarring snap. 'Bringing a young child into this changes everything!'

'Maybe so,' Tansy conceded reluctantly. 'But Posy's the only secret I have.'

'Yet you even chose to pretend that you were still a virgin...*why*? Did you somehow imagine that virginity made you more appealing?' Jude demanded with lacerating contempt. 'Most men prefer an experienced woman.'

And it was only then that the extent of Jude's genuine incomprehension engulfed Tansy. He now thought she had been lying when she had admitted her lack of experience. Why was she surprised that he had no idea that Posy was her sister and *not* her daughter? Understandably, he had assumed that she was Posy's mother. Why had she not immediately realised that that was what he would think? Not that the identity of Posy's mother could have much bearing on the current situation, she conceded ruefully. After all, the key issue was that Tansy had chosen to conceal Posy's existence and her intention of bringing the child with her into their fake marriage.

Pale and taut, Tansy stood up. 'I *wasn't* lying about that. Posy's my sister, not my child.'

His strong black brows drew together and he shot her a disbelieving look. 'Your...*sister*?' he scorned. 'There's twenty-odd years between you!'

'My mother was forty-seven when Posy was born

and died soon after giving birth to her,' Tansy told him tightly, her eyes shadowing at that unhappy memory. 'I've been looking after her ever since she was born. I left my course at university while Mum was pregnant because she needed help with her business and after she died, I stayed on because...' She made an awkward gesture with her hands, her lips compressing. 'Well, Posy still needed me.'

'She's your stepfather's child?' Jude prompted with a grimace. 'So, why are you looking after her?'

Tansy tensed. 'I'd prefer not to get into that. Calvin's never been my favourite person but he wasn't cruel to Posy,' Tansy stressed uncomfortably, reluctant to tell him about her stepfather's financial stake in their marriage, for she suspected that that might cause more trouble than she was equipped to handle just at that moment. 'He just wasn't interested and his girlfriend, whom he wanted to replace me with, was only willing to look after Posy to please him and didn't have any affection for her. My sister deserves better than that.'

Jude breathed in slow and deep, slightly mollified that the baby was not *her* child and that she had not lied to him on that score, but he was equally quick to recall the conversation he had had with her when he had broached the topic of her having a child with him. He tilted his arrogant dark head back, furious condemnation in his piercing gaze. 'Even when I asked you to consider having a child with me and suggested that you might not be keen on taking on the responsibility of becoming a mother at so young an age, you didn't admit the truth,' he reminded her lethally. 'Let's be frank—not even a direct question from me would have persuaded you to reveal that child's existence!'

Guilt lacerated Tansy because she remembered that same moment and that conversation very well and knew she could not excuse her silence. 'As I said earlier, I was keen for the marriage to take place. I didn't want to give you a reason to write me off as a possibility.'

'And, of course, it's too late now,' Jude completed flatly and then his eyes fired pure scorching gold with rage as he narrowed his fierce gaze on her. '*Thee mou…* no wonder you were so eager for us to marry *before* we went to Greece! That's what made it possible for you to continue concealing the child's existence from me. You were determined to have that ring safely on your finger first.'

There was no way of arguing that point and Tansy bit her lower lip and nodded grudging agreement. Jude, it seemed, had a forensic brain. He would unpick and expose every evasion and half-truth she had given him until there was nothing left for her to hide behind. She glanced up, encountering liquid golden eyes that sent a buzzing energy pulse through the most sensitive areas of her body and the sensation shook her inside out because no man had *ever* made her feel like that before. Her nipples tight buds pushing against her bra, her slender thighs trembling, the heart of her hot and damp, she hastily averted her attention from him.

The same heat pulsed through Jude like a drumbeat and he was furious with himself. The throbbing swelling at his groin was an unwelcome reminder of his lack of control around her. Although shouldn't that persistent sexual attraction be something to celebrate rather than something to regret when they were already married? He wanted the full truth of what was going on with her stepfather and then he wanted her in his bed to ease the hard edge of frustration she induced. Whether he liked it or not, evidently they were stuck with the baby and condemned to be a family of three rather than a carefree couple. Dark fury rippled through his big, powerful frame.

'There's an imbalance here,' Jude mused. 'You've landed me with a child in my life for the next couple of years. I'm not the forgiving kind, but if you were willing to consider compensating me for your lies and omissions I may be persuaded to overlook your flaws.'

Tansy lifted clear green eyes full of incomprehension and her smooth brow pleated. 'I don't understand.'

Jude studied her with angry, calculating intensity. 'Try to give me that baby I asked you to consider having and I will not only forgive you but I will also treat your sister as though she were my own child.'

Silence fell. Tansy's eyes rounded and widened. 'Oh, my word, you're trying to use this to put pressure on me! That is so…*so* unscrupulous.'

'And you're *surprised*?' Jude sliced in very drily. 'You're dealing with an Alexandris, not an angel. I was taught to wheel and deal from childhood.'

Shock set in hard on Tansy. She could barely credit that he would use her plight and her current guilt to bargain with her and do so with such a shameless lack of remorse. But what was even worse, she discovered just then, was that softly given promise to treat Posy the same as his own child. That was *huge*, particularly when it related to a little girl who had never known a father in her short life. Tansy knew how much she had missed having a daddy and some day her sister would go through the same experience, only not if she agreed to Jude's suggestion that she try to have a child with him.

'One question,' Tansy muttered unevenly. 'If I were to agree to this, would you be willing to apply to adopt Posy with me?'

'Of course.'

Tansy felt dizzy with relief because her stepfather continued to lurk at the back of her mind as a lingering threat to his daughter's security. Removing Posy from Calvin's care without Tansy having any legal right to keep the child had worried her. Calvin had deliberately misled her by not delivering on the promise he had originally made and why was that? Only if Tansy adopted her sister could she feel that the child was safe from her father's intrigues, and with Jude by her side, Posy would then be fully protected.

'If you're willing to adopt Posy with me, I'll agree to try to have a child with you,' Tansy conceded tautly, wondering if she was crazy to lay so much of herself on the line, but then thinking about Posy and knowing she would do anything to keep that little girl safe and secure. And providing her sister with that security and possibly the joy of another sibling as well would be a good result, she told herself squarely.

A slanting smile slashed Jude's beautiful mouth and her heart skipped a beat and her mouth went dry. 'Let's have dinner, *hara mou*,' he suggested smoothly.

CHAPTER FIVE

'I'LL TAKE POSY,' Jude offered as he lifted Tansy down out of the helicopter and turned to Kerry to extend his arms.

Cross at having her night's sleep disturbed, the baby pouted and then succumbed to the invitation, a man being a new source of attraction in her mainly female world. Ensconced in Jude's arms, Posy smiled sleepily.

'That's the first time you've used her name,' Tansy remarked as she accompanied him into the waiting SUV.

'She will be family now.'

His statement felt reassuring because Tansy had yet to have anyone stand by her side when it came to guarding Posy's welfare and her fear of Calvin's potential interference receded a little. It was getting dark rapidly and Tansy peered at the formal gardens stretching ahead of them and then off into the distance at the walls she could dimly see in one direction. 'Where's your grandfather's house?' she asked.

'Over the hill. The estate is gigantic. Other people downsize at his age but Isidore *upsized*,' Jude told her wryly. 'This place used to belong to one of his biggest business rivals and he bought it the minute it came on the market. He's very vain and he likes to live like a king.'

'He sounds quite a character,' Tansy commented as the car mounted the hill and turned down a central drive to begin an approach to a huge building that, with its twin wings, resembled a French chateau and was lit up like a firework display both inside and outside. 'Wow…'

'Isidore may be terse with you,' Jude warned her. 'He expected me to marry Althea and he doesn't like surprises. He won't like you having a child in tow either and probably won't believe that she's your sister.'

'I can cope with rudeness,' Tansy said ruefully.

'You have my permission to be equally rude back. He thinks women should be seen and not heard and all three of his late wives fell into the quiet-little-mouse category.'

'Oh, dear.' Tansy grimaced, nervous perspiration dampening her upper lip as the vast dwelling ahead drew closer and the SUV pulled up at the foot of the steps.

Jude strode up the steps, Posy still safely held in his arms. The opulence of the big foyer was overpowering. Mirrors, gilded furniture and giant crystal chandeliers obscured Tansy's vision and made her blink in disorientation. Jude addressed an older woman who approached him with pronounced subservience and he handed Posy back to the nanny.

'Cora will show them to their rooms.'

'I should go up with them,' Tansy contended, the food she had eaten earlier sitting like a lead weight in her tense stomach.

Jude closed a hand over hers before she could accompany the nanny. 'No, we don't run scared in this family,' he told her firmly, urging her on with him into a room where a small portly man stood by a huge marble hearth.

'Jude!' Isidore Alexandris exclaimed in welcome, his heavily lined face smiling even while his deep dark eyes remained steady, and that was the only word Tansy understood because a flood of Greek followed.

'And this is my wife, Tansy.' Jude switched smoothly back to English as he moved her forward.

'Tansy…' The smile on the older man's face melted away and he dealt Tansy a brusque nod of acknowledgement before continuing his conversation with his grandson in Greek. He was virtually blanking her, Tansy registered, but she rather suspected that being ignored by Isidore could be more comfortable than attracting his attention. The exchange between the two men was sharp-edged and Isidore pursed his thin lips, his displeasure at Jude's replies patent but the affection in his gaze when he looked at his grandson remained, despite his irritation. While Jude might seemingly be either unaware of or indifferent to his grandfather's attachment to him, that warmth was blatantly obvious to Tansy.

Feeling like a third wheel, Tansy hovered until Jude wrapped an arm round her stiff spine and guided her back out of the room. 'Doesn't he speak English?' she whispered as they crossed the echoing foyer towards the sweeping staircase.

'Like me, he was educated at Eton,' Jude offered. 'He was being cutting.'

'Did you have an argument about me?'

'No. He will accept that you're my wife for the foreseeable future. He's not happy about it but he'll settle because he's finally got me married off,' Jude breathed sardonically.

'Have you been that hard to get to the altar?' Tansy teased in an excess of relief at having so swiftly escaped his intimidating grandfather.

Long powerful legs ascending the stairs, leaving her breathless in her efforts to keep up, Jude vented a humourless laugh. 'You have no idea. Marriages don't work out very well in my family. Of course, I was avoiding it.'

'Then why now?' Tansy asked curiously. 'What's changed?'

Dark golden eyes swept her face assessingly on the landing. 'We'd have to be a lot closer for me to explain my reasons.'

Tansy flushed and jerked a slight shoulder in receipt of that snub, falling silent as Jude strode through a door at the foot of a corridor, strolling confidently through a beautiful sitting room adorned with fresh flowers into an equally large bedroom.

Jude approached a pile of boxes sitting on a low table. 'Isidore is loaning you some family jewellery to wear tomorrow. Festoon yourself in diamonds. Don't worry about being vulgar or excessive. He loves to show off our wealth.'

'OK,' Tansy muttered.

'I have business to discuss with Isidore,' Jude told her, striding towards the sitting room. 'I'll see you later.'

Tansy fell still. 'We're both sleeping in here?'

Jude hitched a mocking black brow. 'We're married, and did you really expect separate rooms when the old man is desperate for me to provide the next generation of the family?'

Tansy shifted uneasily where she stood. 'You said you'd give me time.'

'And so I will,' Jude murmured lazily. 'I'm not sex-starved. I can share a bed with you and resist temptation.'

On the way out of the room, he came to a sudden halt and glanced back at her from lushly lashed narrowed eyes. 'I should warn you. Althea Lekkas will be one of the guests tomorrow. Isidore invited her and I suppose, on the face of things, it will look better from the guests' point of view that there's no apparent bad blood between us,' Jude declared with a curled lip because he was already weary of Althea's numerous texts begging for details about his replacement bride. He just wanted her to back off and leave him in peace.

'No skin off my nose,' Tansy countered brightly. 'I know nothing about her or your relationship.'

'We've known each other since we were kids. She was my first love. It didn't work out but we've remained friends,' Jude advanced with a shrug.

His *first* love. She wondered why that description only increased her curiosity. It wasn't as though she were attached to Jude in any way or possessive of him. Tansy stiffened, irritated by her desire to know more about Jude's past than she had any good reason to know. Keep it impersonal, she urged herself, keep that distance. They could be polite and civilised *and* sexual, she assured herself, without bringing any real feelings into it. It *had* to be that way; she couldn't afford to get involved on any deeper level because that way she would get hurt. Jude needed a wife and he would be happy if she gave him a child, but he had said that at most they would be together for only a couple of years. Nothing lasting or permanent was on offer and it would be a disaster if she allowed herself to become fond of him on any level.

Jude departed and Tansy investigated the other doors that led out of the bedroom, discovering a packed dressing room. Her wedding dress was there in a protective wrap and she uttered a quiet prayer that it would fit. All the other clothes that had been ordered that first day in Jude's office sat in neat piles on shelves, hung from rails and tumbled in a rainbow of opulence in drawer after drawer. Shoes and bags filled an entire cabinet. She had only ever seen such an array of clothing inside a big store.

In a haze of growing exhaustion, she left the suite to check that Posy had settled for the nanny. Unsure where her sister had been put to sleep, she had only reached the top of the stairs when the housekeeper, Cora, appeared and showed her where to go. Posy was soundly asleep in a fancy cot with Kerry in the room next door. On the way back to bed, Cora asked Tansy if she had any special requests for breakfast the following morning while informing her that Jude's grandfather had instructed that the usual technicians attend Tansy to prepare her for her wedding day.

* * *

Tansy twirled in front of the cheval mirror, pleased with the perfect fit of the gown. An off-the-shoulder neckline and tight half sleeves completed the sophisticated look. Delicate beads and fabulous diamonds shimmered as she moved. Romantic lace motifs overlaid the tulle that snugly encased her from the shoulder, with the skirt falling in soft layers to her feet, hemmed by the same lace that swept back into a small cathedral train. Her mass of hair was up to anchor the magnificent diamond tiara that sat like a crown on her head, while the collar of diamonds encircling her throat and the matching bracelets cast rainbow reflections on the rug below her feet.

From the moment Tansy had wakened she had been waited on hand and foot. Her breakfast had been served in bed with the indent on the pillow next to hers the only evidence that at some stage of the night Jude must have joined her and slept beside her. Tansy remembered nothing after climbing into the blissfully comfortable bed. A hair stylist had arrived after breakfast, soon followed by a nail technician and a beautician. Tansy had insisted on doing her own make-up because she didn't like it too heavy. A maid arrived to tell her that Jude's grandfather, Isidore, was waiting downstairs to accompany her to the church.

Tansy descended the stairs with great care because her heels were extremely high. She was disconcerted when the older man extended an arm to her and murmured almost pleasantly, 'You look very well indeed, my dear, and the diamonds are the ultimate embellishment. Do you like them?'

'Yes… I've never worn diamonds before. Have these pieces been in the family long?'

It was a lucky question. Isidore Alexandris smiled and rested back in the limousine to tell her the history of the jewellery she wore, careful to tell her the worth of each item as well as what was paid for it at auction. She was suitably impressed. That conversation lasted them through the heavy Athens traffic all the way to the doors of the grand church chosen for the traditional ceremony. There she was surprised to see Jude in the entrance hall waiting for her, surrounded by his bodyguards.

Tansy walked through the double doors and Jude fell silent. An impossibly slender figure in delicate white draperies, she looked dazzlingly beautiful. The superb collar of diamonds encircling her elegant white throat and the tiara shining in her luxuriant dark blond hair were the perfect additions. He was stunned by the smile on his grandfather's face because it looked genuine.

'You look superb,' Jude breathed, handing her a beautiful bouquet of tumbling white roses and gypsophila.

Pleased colour brightened Tansy's cheeks as she looked up at him. Even in her high heels, he still towered over her and he looked hotter than hot in a splendidly tailored dark grey tailcoat, waistcoat and narrow trousers, his glossy black curls glinting in the sunshine illuminating the glorious stained-glass window behind him. Shimmering dark golden eyes of appreciation were welded to her and slow, pervasive heat filtered through her, making it a challenge to breathe.

'You may not have done as badly as I thought with her,' Isidore whispered, startling his grandson before he could walk down the aisle with his bride. 'She's bright and she may be penniless but so, essentially, is Althea, and Althea's flighty into the bargain, which is worse.'

Jude almost laughed, astonished that Tansy had won even that amount of grudging approval from the older man, who only the night before had sworn that no Alexandris had ever chosen a less worthy bride.

Tansy hadn't realised that the Greek Orthodox ceremony would be as long or as elaborate. The exchange of rings, the carrying of a candle followed by the symbolic crowns and the circling of bride and groom were driven by Jude's nudging guidance and she blushed and stumbled and hesitated more than once, just praying that her uncertainty went unnoticed. The church was packed. At the end of the service, her slim shoulders relaxed from rigidity and she was able to accompany Jude back outside with a little more assurance.

'I could have done with a rehearsal for that,' Tansy quipped, ready to reach for Posy when she saw her in the nanny's arms but prevented by Jude.

'You can see her at the reception,' he pointed out smoothly as a wall of cameras and shouted questions greeted them outside the church.

'When did your mother pass away?' Tansy asked curiously as they climbed into the waiting limo.

'Clio's still alive. Where did you get the idea that she was dead?' Jude demanded.

'I just assumed. I mean, I read online about the divorce and your father's car crash but that was years ago.

I thought that a mother would always attend her son's wedding and there's been no sign of her—'

'Clio would sooner drink poison than come to an Alexandris social event and run into my grandfather. They hate each other.'

'That's sad,' Tansy opined. 'When you don't have much in the way of close family you'd prefer them to get on.'

'That's life,' Jude pronounced cynically but his lean, strong face had clenched hard, hinting that he was less comfortable with those divisions than he was prepared to acknowledge. 'I may not have close family but I do have numerous cousins. I saw little of my mother growing up. We're not close. She's Italian and she returned to Italy following the divorce.'

It all sounded very detached to Tansy and she wondered if that was why Jude was so hard and unemotional or if, indeed, that facade of his was simply a pretence, because she could sense that his reaction to any reference to his mother was sensitive and guarded. What was that reserve of his hiding? 'Were you close to your father?' she asked curiously.

Jude turned exasperated dark eyes on her. 'What is this? Psychology for beginners?'

'Never mind. I like knowing what makes people tick. I didn't mean to pry,' she responded lightly, stealing a glance at his unimpressed expression and then laughing out loud. 'Well, yes, I *was* being nosy but you weren't supposed to pick me up on it!'

A reluctant grin slashed his sculpted lips. 'I spend my life in business meetings interpreting body language and expressions.'

Tansy had the tact not to remind him that he hadn't contrived to read her very well and guess that she was hiding things when they first met. The wedding breakfast was being held in a pillared ballroom in the mansion. Reunited with Posy, Tansy ignored the questioning appraisals coming their way and settled in for a stint of polite socialising, eating and smiling dutifully at the many toasts. She noticed Althea Lekkas long before she realised who the other woman was and that was only after someone hailed her from across the room. The glowing glamorous blonde, her gold metallic dress melded to her shapely curves, was fizzing with energy, flirting like mad and attracting a lot of male attention.

When Jude was taking Tansy round to meet people, the same woman walked right up to them. 'Hi, I'm Althea,' she said brightly. 'May I steal the bridegroom for a little private chat?'

Keen not to seem territorial while marvelling at Althea's nerves of steel, Tansy stepped away and headed for the cloakroom to freshen up, wondering if it was too soon to get changed because they were leaving in an hour. Jude had told her so without telling her where they were going. But then, explaining himself was not Jude's strongest talent. He behaved as though he had never been a part of a couple before and was unable to make that mental shift to sharing details in advance or even discussing his plans. Or possibly that arrogance was simply part and parcel of his attitude to her, the woman he had *paid* to marry him. And maybe it was rather naive of her to believe that he should consult her about what happened in their lives.

Walking back to the ballroom, Tansy heard raised voices and recognised Jude's. Her smooth brow furrowing because he sounded both angry and frustrated, she crossed the hall to a light-filled room full of exotic plants where Althea and Jude appeared to be involved in an argument. Of course, they were conversing in Greek, so she had no idea what they were saying. The blonde appeared to be trying to soothe Jude, tugging down and clinging to his arms when he lifted them high in a gesture of seething impatience and then leaning forward to plant her full pink mouth on his in a fervent kiss. That display of intimacy, that assumption that her kisses would be welcome, was blatant as a police siren in its boldness. In response, Jude pressed the blonde back against the wall, pinning her hands to her sides, speaking to her in a low intense voice. What she was witnessing struck Tansy as the very essence of passion playing out before her appalled gaze.

Although it was the hardest thing she had ever done, Tansy snapped her spine straight, turned her head away and went upstairs to remove her wedding dress and change. Jude's relationship with his old friend and former first love was none of her business, she told herself briskly even while another, more primal voice in the back of her mind was shouting something far more aggressive. Jude was her husband and he was already cheating on her and that hurt her like a knife thudding into her chest, igniting a host of reactions she had not expected to feel. Instead of cool, critical detachment she found angry, bitter resentment and revulsion roaring through her and she shuddered with the force of her feelings. So much for all that talk of his about respecting fidelity within marriage! Possibly, though, she was a little oversensitive to the pain of being cheated on because it wasn't the first time it had happened to her. And watching the speed at which Calvin had moved on after her mother's death had only reinforced her trust issues.

At nineteen she had lost faith in her own judgement when a spiteful girl and a lying, manipulative boyfriend had conspired to hurt and humiliate her. Egged on by her flatmate and supposed friend, Emma, Ben had tried to get her into bed with him to win a bet. In effect a price tag had been put on Tansy's virginity and that had destroyed her pride and hurt her heart because she had fancied herself in love with Ben. Emma's cruelty had inflicted another wound, particularly once Tansy had realised that Emma had been sleeping with Ben the whole time he had been dating Tansy.

Shaking free of that sordid recollection, Tansy studied Posy, snug in her cot and blissfully, innocently asleep, leaving her big sister longing to experience that same sense of peace and security. Kerry hovered in the doorway. 'We'll be joining you again tomorrow, Mrs Alexandris. Don't worry about her.'

Tansy flushed as she registered that even the nanny seemed to know their schedule and destination while Jude had chosen to leave his bride in the dark. She found two maids packing her clothes in the bedroom and scooped up cropped linen trousers and a comfortable ivory top to wear with flat sandals. She got changed in the bathroom, but she still couldn't think straight.

Every time she tried to focus on something else, she would see Althea's mouth plastered to Jude's.

Why on earth had Althea cancelled the wedding if she still wanted Jude? It could have been Althea in the church today marrying Jude, Tansy reasoned painfully, and she felt like an idiot for believing him when he had said he and Althea were only friends. What sort of weird relationship did the two of them have? Perhaps they had one of those passionate on-and-off relationships that people sometimes got caught up in, a relationship full of drama and confrontation and feverish reconciliations. Yet he had married *her*, Tansy reminded herself, compressing her lips, bewilderment lacing the other fiery emotions she was experiencing.

Tansy was pacing and lost in troubling thoughts when Jude strode into the bedroom, dismissing the maids at almost the same time as he began stripping off his formal wedding attire. His lean, strong face was set in grim angles and hollows, his tension palpable.

'I saw you kissing Althea,' Tansy told him, not having planned to admit that but finding those incendiary words flying straight off her tongue.

Jude grimaced. 'That's all I need!' he bit out in a raw undertone, stripping off his boxers to stride naked into the bathroom.

Her face hot from being exposed to all that bronzed masculine nudity, Tansy was nonplussed by that lack of response. What? No apology? No explanation? Not even a thin tissue of lies aimed at staging a cover-up? She could hear the shower running full force, a cascade of water splashing down on the tiles. Only minutes later, Jude emerged again, his wet curls wildly tousled, a towel loosely wrapped round his lean hips as he stalked into the dressing room. Sheathed in what she suspected to be his favourite ripped faded jeans and a loose black shirt that was still unbuttoned, parted edges showing off a slice of broad brown muscular chest, Jude joined her again. A dark shadow of stubble framed his strong jaw line, a jaw that was set granite hard.

'We'll discuss Althea later. I've just spent thirty minutes clearing that car crash up without causing a public scene. I refuse to deal with another scene from you in my grandfather's home, where nothing is truly private,' Jude intoned with chilling cool. 'This is *not* your moment.'

Utterly taken aback by his brazen lack of discomfiture, Tansy raised her head high. 'Obviously not, since even though you married me yesterday I seem to be the only person round here who doesn't know where we're heading next!' she proclaimed heatedly.

Dark golden eyes rested on her. 'My bolthole in Rhodes. It's private and on the beach. It's also a short flight.'

'You should have answered me about Althea,' Tansy condemned, thoroughly enraged by his self-control and his unrepentant attitude.

'We haven't got the time to get into something that complex right now,' Jude countered drily, planting a directional big hand to her spine. 'Come on. I can't wait to get out of here.'

He escorted her down the stairs, where he exchanged a few fleeting words with his grandfather in the hall before urging her out of the mansion and into an SUV that ran them back down to the helipad, where the helicopter awaited their arrival.

As she boarded, sidestepping Jude's attempt to lift her, Tansy's hair blew back from her delicate features, highlighting the almost aggressive angle of her chin. Just his luck, Jude thought, he had married a gold-digger with moral principles and a surprising amount of backbone, because she had done the unexpected: she had challenged him openly.

As the helicopter took off, however, Jude compressed his wide, sensual mouth hard. He would have to tell her about his history with Althea and he was outraged by the prospect of having to explain himself to *any* woman. Sadly, circumstances were about to force him to share private stuff that he did not usually share with anyone, but it was necessary to keep Tansy on side. He *needed* a child with Tansy, and he could not afford to alienate her. Hadn't he thrown his life open to a stranger? Hadn't he married her in the hope of having a child and to protect his mentally fragile mother from a loss that might break her again? It was unthinkable to him now that he would not ultimately win his complete freedom with the sacrifices he had already made.

And yet Tansy had already *deceived* him, *lied* to him, *cheated* him of his expectations, he reminded himself fiercely. His lean brown hands clenched into fists because he was so bitterly weary of women trying to use him, trying to profit from him. Yet if she did give him a child it would be a commercial transaction like their marriage, so how was he any better than she was? He himself might have been conceived in love but even by the time he was born his mother had hated his father as much as she'd loved him.

He was an Alexandris and that was how it was for an Alexandris, he reasoned grimly. He got the money, the worldly acclaim and success, he got nothing else deeper or more meaningful from anyone…even Althea. Her love had been whisper-thin and warped. As for his troubled mother, she could barely tell the difference between her adulterous late husband and her living son, who had learned very young never, *ever* to cheat on any woman because that pain could *break* someone vulnerable…

His brilliant eyes shadowed with his most tragic memory of his mother, Clio, and he paled. Of course, he had naively believed that there might be more to Tansy before he'd married her, *before* she'd chosen to show him her true colours of lies and deceit. But she was a gold-digger, there was no denying that now, and, ironically, he was much safer with Tansy, a tough, greedy little woman who likely wouldn't care if he bled to death in front of her…

CHAPTER SIX

THE HELICOPTER LANDED in what looked like a forest glade.

Tansy jumped out, full of curiosity. 'You have a cabin in the woods?' she remarked in surprise, briefly forgetting that she wasn't actually speaking to Jude as yet. Ironically, though, the fact that he hadn't even tried to communicate with her during the flight had left her feeling ridiculously excluded.

'No, not a cabin,' Jude asserted, leading the way down a path through the pine trees, dense vegetation on all sides preventing her from catching much of a view of anything.

But the smell of the sea flared her nostrils and she saw a glint of water through the forest of tall straight trunks surrounding her. They emerged out of the shade into the evening sunshine and her eyes went wide as she saw the ancient stone walls intersected by ornamental turrets rising in front of her. 'A castle?' she whispered in disbelief.

'I saw it from the water one afternoon a few years ago. It was a medieval ruin until it was illegally developed by a rich eccentric in the nineteen twenties. It was almost derelict again by the time I bought it and fixed it up. It's the smallest property I own. I had to renovate a terrace of farmworker cottages nearby to accommodate staff.'

'I suppose it's unthinkable that you could manage for yourself,' Tansy sniped.

'I will never be able to live safely without security, nor will you. The family name does come with a downside of high risk,' Jude told her drily.

'Oh, believe me,' Tansy said tartly, 'I've already seen that for myself!'

Jude gritted his even white teeth and shot her a shimmering dark golden glance of condemnation. 'You're wrong about me, *very* wrong!'

Tansy said nothing more, accompanying him into an unexpectedly cosy hall and up a stone staircase into a spacious bedroom, made airy by contemporary furniture in spite of the natural stone walls and narrow window embrasures through which sunshine glimmered in long shards across the floor. 'A drink?' Jude prompted.

'Wine,' Tansy said flatly. 'Please...'

'Althea and I...a tangled tragic tale,' Jude murmured grittily as he opened a cupboard kitted out with a comprehensive bar and refrigerator. 'We were childhood sweethearts with the approval of both families. Isidore very much approved of the Lekkas pedigree, if not their lack of fortune. At sixteen, she was my first lover and I was hers and I adored her. My best friend, Santos, was in love with her as well but I trusted him, I trusted them both...' Jude glanced up from the beer he was pouring and saluted her with it, a cynical curve to his expressive mouth. 'You're only that young and innocent once.'

As Tansy guessed with a sinking heart where the tale seemed to be going, she tensed, suddenly feeling that she was being made aware of stuff she wasn't entitled to know, and then reddening on the memory that she had seen him in Althea's arms and that, as his wife, she *did* have a right to know their back story if it was relevant.

'I did a business degree at Harvard and one summer I worked as an intern in New York.' Jude poured wine and extended a glass to her. 'Althea slept with Santos while I was away. It only happened once but there was no reasonable excuse for it and, even though I believed her when she said it wouldn't ever happen again, I couldn't forgive her for it.'

Her back stiff with the tension in the atmosphere, Tansy sat down in an armchair and clutched her glass with both hands as if it were a lifesaver. 'I can understand that.'

'But Althea has never understood or accepted it,' Jude declared flatly. 'Initially I refused to have anything to do with her. I was very bitter. It was only after her father approached me on her behalf that I appreciated that our friends had made her a social pariah. That was more punishment than I felt she should suffer, and I made an effort to tolerate her again.'

'What about…er…your friend Santos?'

Jude gave her a wry glance. 'I found it easier to forgive him because he genuinely loved her. He asked her to marry him afterwards and she said no. He was devastated. He got drunk one night and crashed his motorbike. I've always secretly blamed Althea for his death as well.'

Tansy sipped wine into her dry mouth in fascination because she couldn't take her eyes off his darkly handsome face while one emotion after another flickered there, teaching her that he felt much more than either he or she had been prepared to acknowledge. Just like her, he knew exactly what hurt and betrayal felt like and what it felt like when the object of your love revealed clay feet and came crashing down off a pedestal. 'What Althea did was a disaster for all three of you,' she remarked ruefully. 'So why, bearing that problematic past in mind, were you, only a few weeks ago, considering marrying her and having a child with her?'

'She offered when she found out that I was in a tight corner. Initially I said no, but I was desperate and I did think better the devil you know,' Jude admitted, startling her once again with his frankness. 'After all, it's been almost nine years since we were together and I thought it was safe. She was married to someone else for four of those years and was recently divorced. I assumed she'd moved on long ago.'

'Only she hadn't,' Tansy guessed.

'When she said she couldn't go through with the marriage she insisted she still had feelings for me, so I backed off immediately,' Jude clarified. 'That was a major turnoff for me. But today when she came to the wedding, she told me that I wasn't supposed to run off and find someone else to marry after she dropped out.'

'Why? What were you supposed to do?' Tansy pressed with bemused curiosity.

His stunning dark golden eyes shadowed, and his beautiful shapely mouth twisted with exasperation. 'Apparently, Althea had her moves all planned out. The cancellation was a power play. She thought that when she dropped out at the last minute I would panic and come back and offer her *more*.'

'More?' Tansy queried, smooth brow pleating.

'A more lasting marriage, maybe even love.' Jude winced in disquiet at the concept and sprawled fluidly down on a love seat, one denim-clad knee gracefully raised. 'But I couldn't do it. I didn't want to be with her long-term and I couldn't ever love her again because fidelity for me is an unbreakable rule.'

'Then what was that I saw between you this afternoon?' Tansy asked him baldly, wondering if any man had ever looked so spectacularly beautiful in ripped jeans and a shirt, the sheer breathtaking perfection of his sculpted face and lean, powerful physique compelling.

'Althea losing the plot at our wedding. She had taken something…she was as high as a kite and furious with me. That's when she told me she'd deliberately cancelled the wedding, expecting me to offer her a more permanent deal, and I was disgusted with her because she should have moved on from me long before now… Wouldn't any normal woman have moved on?' he prompted in a raw undertone of appeal.

Tansy nodded weakly, marvelling that Althea had betrayed him in the first place, while thinking that most women would be challenged to fully get over a guy as rich, beautiful and sexy as Jude Alexandris. It had been a fatal mistake for Jude to offer that convenient marriage, so near and yet so far from what Althea still so desperately wanted to reclaim.

'She's just had bad luck with other men, that's why she keeps on coming back to the idea that—'

'You're the one and only who got away,' Tansy slotted in wryly. 'So, what about that kiss?'

'*She* kissed me! By then, I'd regained my temper and I was trying to get her to pull herself together and calm down. Her brother took her home. He was very apologetic. I think her family are considering putting her in rehab.' Jude grimaced and raked long brown fingers through his glossy curls in a gesture of frustration. 'I feel guilty about her. I even feel guilty for being grateful that she *did* cancel the wedding because if I had married her, it would have turned into a nightmare.'

Tansy wanted to hug him for being so honest with her and she could only be impressed by the sheer depth of feeling he had hidden so well from her. He wasn't a bad guy. He wasn't a cheat and he still had sufficient generosity and compassion to be concerned for the woman who had once cruelly betrayed his trust. 'I misunderstood. I thought I was seeing a lover's quarrel… That argument and her behaviour seemed so intimate,' she confided uncomfortably. 'And there's no way I would be sleeping with you if you were carrying on with other women at the same time! I couldn't live like that, so if you're planning on playing away, please leave me out of it.'

Jude lifted and dropped a broad shoulder. 'It's really not a big deal for me to promise you that I will not be with anybody else while we're together. Cheating is against my principles,' he confided in a driven undertone, his strong facial bones standing out stark beneath his bronzed skin. 'I grew up with a father who screwed around on my mother and I watched his affairs drive her into a nervous breakdown because she couldn't cope with his behaviour.'

'Oh...' Tansy was shocked because, while she had read about his father's womanising reputation online, she had not factored in the damage that his parents' broken relationship must also have inflicted on Jude. His compassion for his mother's suffering during her time with his father impressed her. He might not be close to the woman, might not see much of her, but he clearly still cared deeply about her.

'I'm probably the last man alive who would cheat on you,' Jude quipped with grim amusement, setting down his glass and opening his arms. 'Now come here... I want to...*finally*...kiss my bride.'

Tansy stood up, uncertainty stamped in every line of her bearing. Jude dropped his legs down and eased her closer to stand between his spread thighs.

He plucked at the waistband of her cropped trousers. 'Is it possible to lose the trousers? I prefer skirts.'

'Trousers are more practical for travelling.'

'You've got me now, and first-class travel. You don't ever need to be practical again,' Jude intoned, flipping loose the button at her waist slowly enough to allow her time to back away if she wanted to.

Only, Tansy discovered, she *didn't* want to because she was much more invested in wondering what Jude would do next. His action released a heady mix of terror and longing inside her. The relief of his explanation about Althea, the sudden loss of her every excuse to stay distant from him, had left her dizzy, unsure and confused. And then there was the warmth he had evoked while he spoke, the emotion he so rarely showed but so definitely felt, the pain he had exposed. All of a sudden, gorgeous, sexy, intimidating Jude was a human being, who had been wounded just as she had been by betrayal, and he no longer felt like a potentially threatening stranger she had to be on her guard with.

He ran down the zip and the trousers fell round her ankles. He lifted her out of them and held her stationary, smoothing appreciative hands down over slender hips covered by the thin band of the lace thong she wore, trailing long, lazy fingers over the long length of her shapely legs, sweeping them up again to briefly encircle her tiny waist before stroking up over her narrow ribcage. *'Like,'* he stressed without embarrassment. 'Beautiful, utterly perfect...'

Tansy could barely believe what he was saying. Colour lanced her cheeks as he lifted her and tipped her forward so that she straddled his lap, the denim of his jeans rubbing against her knees as she splayed her legs, so self-conscious now that she felt as though a burning torch were flaring up inside her. He framed her face with his big hands and captured her parted lips with his and it was as if an adrenalin rush engulfed her, his tongue darting into her mouth as subtle as a sword and then plunging deep, and her head spun while the edge of his teeth plucked at her full lower lip. And that fast she was on fire, rocking back from him, feeling her shirt drift down her arms as his palms grazed over her bra-clad breasts until the bra too was gone and he was toying with her achingly sensitive nipples, making her gasp into his mouth and struggle for breath. Liquid flame ran to the heart of her and pooled there even as his hands slid down to her hips and ground her down on the hard thrust of his erection below the denim.

And the most ridiculous thrill ran through Tansy that it was she who had aroused him, not beautiful Althea in her daring golden dress in all her extrovert attention-seeking glory. She blushed for her own petty and pathetic sense of achievement but there it was, an inescapable fact that she was as competitive when it came to Jude as any other woman. It was *her* he wanted, not his childhood sweetheart, his once-adored first love.

Bending her back over his arm to support her, he closed his lips round a swollen rosy nipple and suckled strongly. Her breathing grew choppy in her throat as he attended to the other straining peak, that heat at the heart of her spreading into a torturous ache as he ground her down on him. Long fingers laced into the fall of her hair.

'I love the different colours in your hair and I love it when you wear it loose,' Jude confided, watching the dying sun glimmer across the lighter strands where the tips touched the floor as he bent her back. 'You're also remarkably flexible—'

'Gymnastics.' Tansy laughed. 'It was much more fun than ballet classes.'

And she thought abstractedly that that had to be the

true definition of a womaniser, a man capable of making her laugh in a sexual situation where she was less than confident of her body or of what happened next. His mouth brushed against hers again while his fingertips glanced expertly over the absurdly responsive tips of her breasts, tugging, gently twisting and rolling, making her squirm and moan while arrows of craving stabbed deep in her pelvis, starting up a tingling, throbbing burn between her thighs.

Without warning, Jude stood up, carrying her with him, her legs anchored round his waist. 'Let's get more comfortable,' he urged, tumbling her down on the bed, her hair fanning out wildly around her head, her green eyes huge at that sudden change of pace. 'Relax,' he urged. 'We take this as far as you want and no further.'

Tansy went pink and winced. 'Am I that easily read?'

'Pretty much, *koukla mou*.' His slanting grin of affirmation was pure charismatic gold as he stood beside the bed, hauling his shirt off over his head to reveal the defined sheet of lean muscle that corrugated his broad chest. He cast it off to embark more languidly on his jeans.

As the jeans began to fall and she realised that he was wearing nothing beneath, she stilled. A dark happy trail arrowed down to a very substantial erection. He was long and wide and she wished she had the nerve to tell him that, with every skin cell in her body jangling with a terrifying overload of sexual response, he could go as far as he liked because she was done with waiting to find out what all the fuss was about.

He came down on the bed beside her, gloriously, unashamedly masculine, and she shimmied over to him and kissed him with lingering pleasure. He smelled so good she wanted to bury her nose in him, and he tasted even better. Her hand speared into his black curls to hold him fast. A long finger scored across the taut triangle of cloth stretched between her legs and she almost spontaneously combusted from the jolt of excitement that shot through her.

Jude rolled her over and flat against the pillows, dark golden, glittering eyes hot as a predator's as he lay over her, supporting his weight on his arms. 'If we continue, do you mind if I don't use protection? Or is it too soon for you to want to try conceiving?'

Her brain was in flux and she had to struggle to grasp what he was asking, blinking up at him without immediate comprehension.

'You look like a baby bird when you look up at me like that,' Jude husked.

The concept of immediately trying for the pregnancy she had agreed to stunned her, but that there might be a fast result struck her as so off-the-charts unlikely, she couldn't even picture it. From what she had read and heard, however, it could take months to conceive, which meant that waiting too long to try could be unwise. 'It's all right with me,' she muttered.

He tugged off the thong, cast it aside, smoothed a carnal fingertip gently over the tiny bundle of nerves below her mound. The hunger awakened with extreme force and flooded her like an addictive drug, tiny nerve endings firing up for the first time, her whole body tensing and trembling as he explored her maddeningly sensitive flesh. She pressed her hot face into a satin-smooth brown shoulder, startled by the sheer pleasure thrumming through her. And then the tightening at the heart of her gave way and the world went white as she climaxed in his arms, gasping and shuddering in the aftermath.

'No matter what I do, this is probably going to hurt,' Jude murmured intently.

'I *know* that… I'm not that naive!' Tansy protested breathlessly.

'And you're very, very sexy,' Jude growled. 'Because I did intend to keep my hands off you for at least a few weeks!'

'Well, the best-laid plans…' Tansy chided with a face-splitting grin of pride, relieved that she wasn't the only one tempted in their relationship, the only one surrendering to that hunger she had never really felt until that moment.

Jude laughed, brilliant, dark, golden, heavily lashed eyes spectacular in his lean, sun-darkened face. He wondered how long it had been since he had last relaxed to that extent with a woman in bed. He couldn't remember because all his more recent dealings with women had been of the most basic variety, consisting of nothing more than casual encounters.

He kissed her again with more passion and less restraint as he shifted against her, allowing her to feel the hard thrust of him against her tender core. Her heart hammered as he crushed her lips under his and she strained against him, seeking that pressure, that friction, every fibre of her demanding more sensation.

Jude pushed into her narrow channel very slowly, lifting her slight body up to him. His stunning eyes stayed welded to hers even as a low groan of sensual pleasure escaped him. '*Thee mou*…you're so tight, *moraki mou*.'

Melting within at the erotic enjoyment he couldn't hide, Tansy tipped up more to him and he slid in deeper and faster than he might have intended and she jerked as a sharp sting of pain shot through her lower body. Betrayed into a muffled moan, Tansy briefly froze. 'It's all right. Don't stop now,' she mumbled, red-faced.

Jude shifted his lithe hips and sent sweet, seductive sensations shimmying through her pelvis to replace the discomfort. Her heart thumped faster, her body quivering from that shock invasion that came with a stark jolt of pleasure and left her wanting more.

'Still hurting?' Jude pressed.

'Not any more,' she proclaimed breathlessly, rocking up into him in helpless invitation.

His fluid movements controlled her with mounting pleasure, tiny little tremors coursing through her as her tension and the ache of need built ever higher. The pace increased and her heart raced, her nails digging into the smooth skin of his back as the excitement took over, urging her hips up to his, her body jolting in satisfaction from his every powerful thrust. And then the tension splintered, and fireworks burst inside her and she was overwhelmed by the blissful convulsions of pleasure that flooded her.

Jude released her from his weight and lay back.

Tansy breathed in deep and slow, all the tension that

had wound her up tight for days drained away. For the first time she felt truly close to Jude and even more regretful of the fact that she had concealed her sister's existence, starting off their marriage on a wrong note. In an effort to diminish that sin, she murmured, 'You know…er… I would have told you about Posy upfront if Calvin hadn't warned me not to.'

'At what stage did he decide to dump his daughter as well as his stepdaughter on me?' Jude enquired smooth as glass.

Tansy stiffened and compressed her lips, taken aback by his tone. She turned her head to study his taut, perfect profile. 'Nobody has been dumped on you! You needed a wife. Posy needed me. It's kind of ironic too that you're lukewarm about her, because she's truly the *only* reason I'm here with you now.'

Ebony brows drawing together, Jude locked narrowed dark golden eyes to her. 'How so?'

Tansy sighed, deciding to tell him the truth because she saw no point in concealing it any longer, and if she could improve his view of her, it could surely only make their relationship run a little more smoothly. 'It was never your money I was after. I'm not a gold-digger,' she murmured tightly. 'It was Calvin's idea. I had to agree to marry you and give my stepfather that initial financial settlement for marrying you before *he* would agree to sign over my sister into my care…'

Jude absorbed that bombshell in total silence because it plunged him deep into shock and into thoughts he did not want to have. 'Are you seriously telling me that you're planning to give *him* that money?' he demanded rawly, his lean, dark features taut with anger and incredulity. 'And that that little baby was the price of your compliance?'

Unable to grasp why that seemed to annoy him when she had naively believed that information would improve his opinion of her, Tansy sat up, hugging the sheet to her. 'Yes, and it's already done. I wouldn't have married you for any other reason… I mean, *why* else would I agree to marry a stranger? Particularly one who wanted sex included in the deal?' she countered ruefully. 'Calvin had no idea at all about that aspect. He believed you only wanted a paper marriage. But let's face it, he didn't care about the details. All he saw was an opportunity to profit.'

Jude sprang off the bed, dark colour overlaying his sharp cheekbones, rage and consternation leaping through him. 'You had sex with me because of that baby?' He stared down at her in irate disbelief.

Tansy went even more red in the face, annoyed that he didn't appear to be listening to anything she said or reacting as she had expected. 'No, I wouldn't put it that way. I wouldn't say that,' she mumbled uneasily, shying away from that too personal and private subject. 'I mean, how is that worse anyway than me being a golddigger willing to do anything for money?'

Contrary to that protest, outrage was filling Jude to overflowing. He could see, however, that her green eyes were clear and steady on his. She didn't get it, she really *didn't* get how offensive what she had just told him was. 'You let that creepy bastard pimp you out to me like a hooker!' he accused rawly.

'How dare you?' Tansy snapped back at him in disbelief. 'How *dare* you say that to me?'

'You think I feel any warmer towards you knowing that you only let me bed you because a child's welfare was at stake?' Jude roared. 'It didn't occur to you that that is more than a little sleazy?'

Tansy stared back at him in a fury, green eyes bright as gemstones while she struggled to conceal her hurt from him. 'Well, maybe it didn't occur to me that someone like you would be that sensitive, since you believe that you can buy *anything* you want...and you proved it with me,' she completed less boldly, still shamed by that awareness. 'But I'm not one bit sorry either!'

'I can see that,' Jude seethed, thrown off balance by her unapologetic defiance.

'Good. Then we understand each other perfectly,' Tansy told him, ripping at the sheet to wind it clumsily round herself and slide off the bed to head for the door she reckoned led to a bathroom. 'I didn't care what it cost me to get Posy out of that house and away from Calvin and his girlfriend. And unless you plan on going back on your word like *he* did, we'll adopt her now and she'll be safe, and he'll never be able to use her the way he's used me!'

And with that ringing assurance and tears blinding her, Tansy plunged through the door only to find herself in a large dark cupboard, fitted out as a closet.

'Bathroom's next door,' Jude informed her gently as he lounged back against the tumbled bed, clad only in his unbuttoned, ripped jeans, the dark dangerous rage still smouldering in him but restrained by the innate caution of a man who had seen, growing up, what a man's unfettered ire could do to a woman. 'Couldn't get permission to knock a door through in a protected building.'

Feeling even more foolish, Tansy stalked down the corridor, trailing the sheet and stifling a sob. Her first sexual experience had come complete with a distressing aftermath. There had been no reassuring physical closeness, no show of affection. That was stuff a woman could only hope to receive from a guy who cared about her. Jude had treated her like a one-night stand because he didn't see her as being any different, indeed might even see her as being less after what she had revealed about Calvin and Posy. Her heart squeezed inside her as she worried about what the future might hold with Jude when he was that furious with her…

CHAPTER SEVEN

JUDE BREATHED IN slow and deep to calm himself.

Calvin Hetherington had to be dealt with first. No way should he profit from the morally unforgivable arrangement he had set up! That poor baby, Jude reflected with deep repugnance that a father could place such little value on his own flesh and blood. As for Tansy, she suffered from tunnel vision where her sister was concerned. She had not even paused to consider that Jude might not be as corrupt as her stepfather, had not even contemplated telling Jude the truth until the die had been cast. And now he had to sort the mess out and he needed the details to accomplish that feat. Digging out his phone, he contacted his top-notch Greek lawyer, Dmitri, and made him aware of the situation, gritting his teeth when the older man came close to questioning his judgement in entering such a marriage without having taken due consideration and care.

Jude already knew that he had been reckless. It was an Alexandris trait, but it was the first time ever that *he* had committed that sin. Maddeningly, he had only become reckless after he had first laid eyes on Tansy and she'd turned him down, he acknowledged grimly. He had wanted her the instant he'd seen her, the light glimmering over her long streaky hair, those luminous green eyes wary and anxious, the pulse beating out her nerves at the base of her elegant white throat. And Tansy had spoken the truth when she had accused him of being accustomed to buying anything he wanted, and he had bought himself a wife with no more forethought than a man buying a product off a shelf. That was a sobering truth. What right did he have now to complain about the complications Tansy had brought with her? Dmitri had warned him that it was even possible that, after he contacted the British legal team to check the facts, he would have to start paperwork to safeguard the baby by applying to have Posy made a ward of the court.

While Jude ruminated about what complications might lie ahead and sank entirely naturally into problem-solving mode, Tansy was being a lot less productive. In the spacious shower she let the pent-up tears stream down her face under the cover of the water. Posy was safe now, wasn't she? That was the all-important bottom line, wasn't it? Only she hadn't been quite truthful with Jude when she had acted as though her sister had been her only motivation. She hadn't intended to play the martyr, but she had been even less keen to admit that she found him incredibly attractive and had been intrigued and fascinated by him from the outset. Ought she to admit that? Why should she expose herself to that extent?

A knock sounded on the bathroom door while she was splashing cold water on her face in an effort to chase the puffiness of tears from her eyes. 'Yes?' she called loudly.

'Dinner in ten minutes,' Jude told her.

Tansy swallowed hard and waited a few moments before dashing back to the bedroom in a towel. A single case sat there, and she dug into it, rustling through the neatly packed garments to extract a long cotton skirt and a light strappy top. She dressed in haste, combing out her wet hair, scrutinising her wan face with critical eyes, rubbing her cheeks for some colour and then scolding herself for even caring about her appearance around Jude. After all, he was on another level of gorgeous and always would be and she was never going to catch up. Had Jude not needed a wife he could sign up on a temporary basis, he would never have considered someone as ordinary as she was for the role.

As she reached the foot of the stairs, a small, older Greek woman stepped into view and greeted her and moved forward to open a door and show her the way. Smiling politely, striving to conceal her nervous tension, Tansy stepped out onto a terrace and looked in wonder at all the fairy lights strung up above the table and the tea lights burning everywhere, illuminating the walled courtyard and the box-edged beds of herbs planted within its boundaries that sweetly scented the air. Jude leapt up from his seat, his visible discomfiture at the celebratory bridal setting almost making Tansy laugh.

'Oh, how pretty the table looks!' she exclaimed for her companion's benefit, because someone had gone to a lot of trouble stringing up those lights and setting out all those little candles.

Jude spoke in rapid Greek to her companion and the woman beamed happily at Tansy. As she vanished back indoors, Jude lounged back against the low wall edging the terrace, his long powerful legs splayed in tailored chinos. Tansy blinked, freshly assaulted by his vibrant sexuality, mortifying heat blossoming low in her body at the recollection of just how intimate their connection had been only an hour earlier.

'We have to discuss your arrangement with your stepfather,' Jude informed her, sending her thoughts crashing back to practical issues again. 'Did he somehow grant you legal custody of Posy?'

Tansy's face dropped in dismay at that direct and precise question and she shook her head. 'He assured me beforehand that he would, but that turned out to be a lie and we got married so fast I didn't pick up on it until it was too late. He told me that the only way I could have legal custody of my sister was by adopting her and, of course, that would mean that you had to be part of the application as well.'

Jude looked unsurprised by her explanation. 'His deception was calculated. He won't want to surrender custody of his daughter while he thinks he could still use her as a blackmail tool.'

Her smooth brow indented. 'How?'

Jude sprang upright and reached for the bottle of champagne awaiting their attention, unsealing it with a pop and filling the glasses. 'Hetherington could demand that you return his daughter to him…or that you compensate him accordingly. As my wife, you have access to a great deal of money.'

'I wouldn't let him *do* that!' Tansy protested heatedly.

'You've already demonstrated that there isn't much you wouldn't sacrifice in order to keep your sister with you,' Jude reminded her sardonically. 'Including your virginity.'

In the act of tossing back the bubbling champagne, Tansy almost choked on it while the heat of embarrassment enveloped her entire body. 'I've already told you... it wasn't like that. But I assure you that I have no plans to hand over any more of your money to Calvin. That would be like *stealing* from you.'

'Then it will be good news for you to hear that Calvin has yet to receive a penny of what you describe as *my* money,' Jude retorted crisply. 'But that sum was yours to do with as you wish. It became yours the day you married me.'

'As I told you, I've already transferred that money to Calvin,' Tansy muttered uncomfortably.

'You tried to but, ultimately, the transaction was blocked.'

'Blocked?' she echoed in dismay.

'Our bank accounts are heavily protected from fraud. Such a large transfer as emptying your new bank account was flagged and would have been run by me before it was allowed to proceed. Now it's permanently blocked. Hetherington is not going to get that money.'

'But then I bet he'll demand Posy back!' Tansy gasped. 'I *agreed* to give him that money.'

'Just as he agreed to give you legal custody of your

sister, which he didn't,' Jude reminded her drily. 'He's *not* getting that money, Tansy. Fathers aren't allowed to sell their children in today's world. Furthermore, any money changing hands between you and your stepfather would invalidate any adoption proceedings in the future as it would be illegal. No, we will deal with your stepfather together and only through the proper legal channels.'

'But that'll put Posy staying with us at risk and I couldn't *b-bear* to lose her!' Tansy framed with a stifled sob of sudden fear half under her breath.

'We won't lose her,' Jude swore. 'I won't allow that to happen. That's the least of what I owe you.'

'You don't owe me anything, Jude. I brought Posy into this marriage without your knowledge. You're not responsible for what happens to her—'

'You're my wife. She's your blood relative. She's entitled to my protection. I also have an engrained loathing for greedy, dishonest operators like your stepfather and no child deserves a parent that heartless.' Jude yanked out a chair and gently nudged her towards it. 'Sit down. Our housekeeper, Olympia, is about to serve our meal, *moli mou*.'

'I'm not sure I could eat.' A shaky smile formed on Tansy's lips. 'You probably don't understand but I love Posy as much as though she was born to me. I was the first person to hold her after her birth and she's been mine to care for ever since.'

'What sort of stepfather was Calvin before your mother died?' Jude asked her, surprising her with that question.

Tansy compressed her lips. 'Absent, uninterested. Mum and him just led their lives and I got on with mine at school and when they went on holiday I moved in with my aunt Violet.'

'And your mother. What was she like?'

Her sense of wonder lingered, along with a growing pleasure that he was keen to know such facts about her. She wasn't used to talking about herself but there was a heady feeling of satisfaction inside her at being the sole focus of his interest.

'She was wrapped up in Calvin and very conscious that she was ten years older than he was,' Tansy confided wryly. 'That's why she was overjoyed when she fell pregnant. Neither of them had expected that but I could see he didn't share her enthusiasm. He never wanted a child. I think he married Mum because she struck him as a good financial bet. She owned her own home and business. But if you can believe what he told me, they were living well above their means and he's currently facing bankruptcy.'

'What did you inherit?'

'Nothing. Mum left everything to Calvin. If he hadn't needed someone to look after Posy, he would never have allowed me to stay on in the house for so long,' she pointed out ruefully. 'I mean, it's not like he or I were ever close or that there was any family tie.'

'And your own father?' Jude prompted.

Tansy ate the last delicious bite of the starter and set down her cutlery, surprised by how hungry she had been. She lifted her champagne glass. 'He was an accountant and he died in a car accident when I was a baby. He was a lot older than Mum. I have no memory of him at all, but he left Mum quite well off. She opened up a beauty salon and lived well on the income…well, at least until she and Calvin got together.'

'A beauty salon?' Jude was disconcerted because there was nothing remotely artificial about Tansy and, to his way of thinking, artifice flourished in beauty salons.

'And it made no impression on me… I *know*.' Tansy laughed, her small straight nose wrinkling. 'But if you'd met my mother you'd soon have guessed what the family business was. She had every beauty enhancement on the market and wouldn't have opened the front door without her false eyelashes on. I was a *huge* disappointment! She wanted a daughter who was just like her and, although I did all the training courses to please her and worked at the salon whenever I was needed, it never interested me the way it did her.'

The main course arrived, and Tansy realised she had been chattering nonstop about herself and she flushed and fell silent.

'I was saving the main question until last,' Jude murmured softly as he watched her, entranced by her pale porcelain skin and delicate features, the strap of the top she wore sliding off one slender shoulder. 'Why was such a beautiful girl still sexually innocent?'

Tansy dragged in a long, quivering breath, unable to accept that he saw her as beautiful, suddenly plunged into horrible awkwardness by such a query. 'I'm not going to talk about that on the grounds that it makes me feel like a fool and as days go, this has already been a very long and trying one.'

As her voice fell away Jude simply spread long fingers in an accepting gesture, although he knew that he would be revisiting that topic. 'You'll be reunited with your sister tomorrow. My yacht is travelling here overnight.'

'Your…yacht?' Tansy repeated.

'*The Alexandris*—my twenty-fifth birthday present from Isidore,' Jude told her flatly.

'Pretty over the top as gifts go, but then, as you said, he is that way inclined. But even so, he's enormously attached to you. I could see that.'

Jude glanced across the table with startled dark golden eyes. 'You *could*?'

Tansy marvelled at his inky black lashes and the length of them and stiffened at that abstracted thought, shifting in her seat and feeling the soreness at her still-tender core, the legacy of that new experience he had mentioned. Her face burned as she fought to concentrate on the conversation. 'Yes, it's obvious. He's proud of you. It shines out of him every time he looks at you,' she muttered ruefully.

Jude had never thought of Isidore, his grandfather, as being personally fond of him. For most of his life, albeit secretly, he had viewed his family history from his mother's side of the fence and had seen both his father and his grandfather as ruthless, often cruel predators with few saving graces, who saw in him only that all-important necessity: the heir to the Alexandris wealth to be groomed to follow in their footsteps. Had he been blind or was Tansy naive and mistaken?

He shook off that wandering thought, acknowledging the armour he had put on from childhood once he'd understood that his father, Dion, didn't expect him to get emotional about anything because an Alexandris male only expressed violent anger. Dion had been unable to control that anger as Isidore did, and Jude could remember his father raging at staff, at office workers, at his cowering mother, in truth at anyone who ignited his hair-trigger temper. Dion Alexandris had had all the self-control of a spoilt and indulged toddler and, having witnessed that, Jude had learned young to control his anger. In a real rage, Jude turned to ice.

As they ate the main course, Jude talked about the yacht and Tansy giggled at some of the revealing extras that his grandfather had thought to include, like a stripper pole, a giant hot tub and mirrored ceilings. 'Not really my style,' Jude insisted. 'But Isidore and my father were the ultimate playboys back in the days of their youth.'

Unimpressed by the claim, Tansy rolled her bright eyes. 'I'm pretty sure you're not that innocent.'

'I'm not, but I was only a man-whore for a couple of years after Althea when I was wrapped up in being bitter as hell,' Jude admitted. 'I'm an adult. I got over it eventually.'

'But by the sounds of it, your father never did,' Tansy slotted in before she could think better about getting that personal.

'That's how he was raised. Any woman he wanted he should have, regardless of whether or not he was married or with anyone else. He bedded my mother's sister, her maid, my nanny,' Jude enumerated drily.

Tansy was truly shocked but fought to hide the fact. 'I don't think much of a sister that would do that.'

'You'd be surprised how easily tempted people can be to do unforgivable things,' Jude murmured very seriously. 'I should've been less honest…you're shocked.'

'I thought Calvin was bad when he brought a woman home for the night less than a month after my mother passed,' Tansy muttered uncomfortably. 'I just ignored it, acted like it wasn't happening because I didn't have any alternative.'

'Hetherington didn't ever come on to you?' Jude prompted tautly.

'Oh, my goodness, no!' Tansy laughed outright at the idea. 'That's one sin he didn't commit. I'm not his type, though. His type is big blond mane of hair, large boobs, very decorative. Didn't you see his girlfriend outside the register office? Susie is like a much younger version of my mother.'

Olympia brought coffee. Jude stepped away from the table and sank back down with careless grace on the wall to survey Tansy with an intensity that made her uneasy. He had beautiful eyes, but they could also be very piercing and distinctly intimidating.

'What?' she said defensively, as though he had spoken.

'Now we have to talk about the elephant in the room… the topic you don't want to touch,' Jude extended softly. 'I want to know *why* you had sex with me this evening. And I need an *honest* answer. I think I deserve that from you.'

Caught unprepared by that demand, Tansy was aghast at his candour; her lips rounded and her eyes were huge and green with stricken dismay. 'I… I—'

'You need to think about it?' Jude elevated a sardonic ebony brow. 'Really? Nobody should need to think *that* hard about telling the truth.'

And that genuinely put Tansy in the hot seat and she sat as stiff and expressionless as a statue in her chair. 'I can't even understand why you would be asking me that question,' she argued.

'From what I understand, Hetherington virtually blackmailed you into agreeing to marry me. You wanted to protect your sister and that's why you agreed…correct?'

Tansy nodded as jerkily as a marionette hanging taut on uneven strings.

'How do you think *I* feel knowing that you were pressured into sharing my bed?'

'But you didn't pressure me…*not at all*!' Tansy stressed in fierce disagreement.

'That doesn't add up. Before we married you asked me to give you time to get to know me,' Jude reminded her, causing hot colour to sweep into her cheeks. 'Then we marry, you produce Posy like a rabbit out of a hat and then all of a sudden you decide you don't need getting-to-know-me time and we have sex. Was that because you felt you had to please or soothe me in some way to persuade me to accept your sister?' Jude demanded with all the cool, critical fire of a hanging judge.

'No!' Tansy slashed back at him in a temper at being mortified to such an extent. 'I had sex with you because, *stupidly*, after you confided in me about Althea, I felt closer to you because someone I cared about was once unfaithful to me as well. Why the hell should you even need an explanation for why I chose to be with you?'

'Because I will not accept an unwilling partner.'

'I wasn't unwilling, you stupid, *stupid* man!' Tansy launched back at him in a towering rage such as she had never, ever felt before. 'I just like you...*why else* would I have broken my own rule?'

Jude froze as though she had struck him and he was, she reckoned, lucky that in her anger she hadn't lashed out physically, because she felt absolutely humiliated at being forced to go into the reasons why she had succumbed to his irrefutable attraction. In all her life she had never felt sexual chemistry as powerful as what she felt around him, had never even dreamt that a guy could affect her with one look or one touch the way Jude did. And it truly was scarcely a mystery that, married off at speed to an absolutely beautiful, sexy man, she had succumbed to that irresistible attraction. Only a complete idiot would have required such a fact spelt out to him!

'I'm not stupid.' Jude caught her hands in his as she attempted to move past him and walk indoors. 'I simply had to know whether or not you were with me because you wanted to be and not because you felt you *had* to be.'

Face burning, Tansy flung back her head and slung him an angry, mutinous glance. 'Well, *now* you know! I hope it was a moment worth embarrassing me for to this extent!'

Scorching golden eyes smouldered down at her. 'I'm sorry—'

'No, you're not!' Tansy argued helplessly because she could see a positively platinum glow of satisfaction shining from him. 'You heard exactly what you wanted to hear, only you can't have *needed* to hear it.'

'It never mattered so much before,' Jude framed, gripping her small hands tight when she tried to break free of him.

'In a few seconds I am going to kick you very hard,' Tansy warned him between clenched teeth.

In a sleight of hand and at a speed that took her utterly by surprise, Jude released her hands and bent down to scoop her up into his arms instead. A disconcerted squeak escaped Tansy before his warm, sensual lips engulfed hers and he tasted so good her head spun, her toes curled. The pulse of hunger renewed, disconcerting her because she had thought that crazy, clawing need was sated. After all, her body still ached, and yet when Jude tumbled her down on the wide bed and kissed her breathless, she wanted him again with a wildness that shocked her. The heat in her pelvis induced a craving that she couldn't fight.

Her fingers raked through his hair, her body lifting in delight to the weight and hardness of his, hands sliding down over his back, that insane excitement building and building to an incredible height and making her feel shameless and greedy.

'I can't get enough of you!' Jude growled, burying his mouth in the soft, sensitive skin between her nape and her shoulder, letting her feel his teeth and sending shock waves of arousal coursing through her.

'Is it always like this?' she mumbled dizzily, angling

back her head to allow him easier access to the tender slopes of her unbound breasts.

'Are you kidding?' Jude laughed, unholy amusement illuminating the dark golden eyes locked to her face, colour lying along his high cheekbones. 'If it was always like this for me, I'd be a sex fiend!'

CHAPTER EIGHT

POSY'S CHUCKLES SHOOK her squirming little body as she rolled away from being tickled and crawled under the desk, peering up at Jude with bright blue eyes brimming with merriment as he flung himself back into his office chair with a grin of amusement at his own behaviour.

Never having had anything to do with children before, Jude had not even considered that he could be fascinated by a baby, but he had discovered that the very simplicity and lack of guile in so young a child appealed to him. Posy liked or disliked stuff or people. There were no shades of grey with her, nothing fake. She didn't care who he was or what he could give her as long as he played with her and made her feel safe and appreciated.

He had been married to Tansy for six weeks and, very much to his surprise and in defiance of his ingrained cynicism, Jude was extremely satisfied with the wife he had picked and the life they were sharing. Tansy was a breath of fresh air in his world. Watching her with Posy, he was impressed by her warmth and affection for the child and the sacrifices she had been willing to make to keep Posy in her care. She didn't have a gold-digging gene in her entire body. When he had presented her with a phone she had been shocked to realise that the blue and white diamonds on the case were real and had tried to return it to him. She had even lectured him about how appalling it was to *waste* that amount of money on a phone, because she had yet to grasp that, on his terms, what he had spent was *not* a huge amount of money.

On a practical basis, Tansy was perfect. As for the 'having a child' part of his marriage, Jude had, for the present, pretty much buried that ambition at the back of his mind. Of course, he reflected, it *would* be helpful to his future plans if a conception took place, but it could also change things in his relationship with Tansy and, right at that moment, Jude wanted nothing to change because he liked it just as it was. Indeed, he liked it a whole hell of a lot. Their sex life was off-the-charts fantastic. He couldn't keep his hands off Tansy and she was pretty much the same with him. He had never enjoyed that level of sexual chemistry with a woman before and that told him that it had to be incredibly hard to find that enhanced buzz and thrill, because he was no innocent. His liberal upbringing and his opportunities had made his sexual experience a fact of life.

'Are you tormenting my sister again?' Tansy teased as she walked into his office and discovered that there wasn't a lot of work getting done just at that moment. A colourful cascade of toddler toys lay scattered across the rug. Safe playing spaces suitable for a baby had appeared all over the magnificent yacht after Posy had slid and banged her head on a hard wooden floor. *The Alex-*

andris had not been designed with a baby in mind and Jude had had to ensure that, where possible, the vessel was child-friendly for her sister's benefit.

'She's much more fun than a coffee break,' Jude informed her with gravity, his lean, strong face full of contrasting amusement. From his flaring black brows, bronzed skin, lion-gold eyes and taut jaw line, he remained as spectacular as a living, breathing vision to Tansy's admiring gaze.

Turning pink, Tansy reflected on how very far their relationship had progressed over the past six weeks. All three of them had travelled an impossible distance from that difficult start, not least her baby sister, currently engaged in trying to climb onto Jude's chair with him to regain his attention. Posy adored Jude. The little girl squirmed and slid back down again and started to cry and Jude reached down a long arm and automatically hauled the baby up. Posy clambered across his lap with a beaming smile, sat down, rested her curly head calmly back against his chest and stuck her thumb in her rosebud mouth, her satisfaction unconcealed.

'Although she's not quite as much fun as you are, *moli mou*,' Jude intoned thickly, lushly lashed dark golden eyes narrowing to wander over her slight body. His intense gaze lingered on the soft pink fullness of her mouth, the sun-streaked fall of her hair and the pouting profile of her breasts in a halter-neck top before literally devouring the long, smooth, golden length of her legs in casual denim shorts.

And below that scorching appraisal, which was now so awesomely familiar to her, Tansy's whole body lit up like a torch with heat and awareness. Her nipples tightened, something clenched low in her pelvis and her insides turned liquid and melting.

A knock sounded on the door and Posy's nanny appeared. Jude sprang upright and passed over the sleepy child, crossing the floor as the door closed again to tug Tansy up against his tall, powerful frame. One hand wound into the thick, silky length of her hair to tip her head back and the other flirted with the fashionably frayed edges of her shorts so that she quivered against him, as on edge as a cat on hot coals.

He crushed her mouth under his, his tongue delving deep, and a low whimper of helpless response escaped low in her throat. 'We only got out of bed a few hours ago,' Jude grated above her head, bumping his brow against hers in apology while she struggled to breathe again. 'This is crazy.'

'Yes, it is,' Tansy muttered, trying to call a halt on her own runaway hormones. 'We shouldn't give in to it.'

Jude ground the thrust of his arousal into her stomach. 'To hell with self-denial,' he groaned raggedly.

'You're not into that,' she conceded shakily.

He tipped up her chin to gaze down at her. 'Are you too sore? Oh, don't go all shy about it. I *know* I'm demanding.'

'You're not too demanding,' Tansy framed, biting at her full lower lip, her face rosy. 'I would tell you if—'

'The same way you would tell me why you were still a virgin when I married you?' Jude scorned, unimpressed. 'If you're embarrassed, you won't tell me anything.'

'Right… OK. I'll tell you why I was inexperienced… *later*,' she promised reluctantly.

'It's a deal.' Jude treated her to one of his wide, charismatic smiles that dazzled her. 'It annoys me when you won't tell me things.'

'I know, but I'm getting better,' she pointed out. 'I just never had anyone to confide in before.'

And the very thought of what she had just admitted hit her like a resounding crash of doom. What did it say about her that she was confiding in a fake husband as if he were the real thing? A loving, affectionate guy, who was intending to stay with her? That awful truth was so clear to her but, even so, somehow all her boundaries with Jude had blurred and every time she tried to take a sensible step back from him he inexplicably contrived to yank her closer.

That they had spent the past six weeks behaving like a *real* couple on a honeymoon certainly didn't help her to retain rational barriers. Initially she had been overwhelmed by the giant yacht and the sheer luxury of its appointments, but somewhere along the line, she conceded guiltily, she had become accustomed to living with meals served whenever hunger struck, a maid, a team of nannies and an onboard beauty salon where she could have her hair done any time she liked. And with all the practicalities of life taken care of for her, so much time had been freed up, time she had spent with Posy and Jude while *The Alexandris* sailed round the Greek islands, stopping off wherever took their fancy.

As he yanked the door open again, Jude closed a hand over hers and they headed down the passageway and up the stairs to their gorgeous cabin. For a split second Tansy tried to break free of that sensual haze that entrapped her, but, one step into complete privacy, Jude scooped her off her feet and tumbled her down on the bed and the allure of the sheer excitement he sent cascading through her overwhelmed her again. Heart hammering inside her chest, she exchanged kiss for kiss as they rolled across the bed, engaged in a frantic effort to rid themselves of their clothing and connect at the fastest rate possible.

There was nothing cool about that urge, nothing controlled or disciplined. In fact, the insanity that often seemed to grip her in Jude's radius bewildered Tansy as much as it dominated her, because she had no previous experience of the woman she became with Jude. She ripped at his shirt, pressed her lips hungrily to a satin-smooth brown shoulder and trembled at the aphrodisiac of his scent. She couldn't get enough of him, couldn't deny the needs of her own body. The instant he touched her she went up in flames. He was *her* source of irresistible temptation and she wanted to savour every moment with him just as feverishly as she told herself that she needed to learn to control her susceptibility.

Skilled fingers traced the sensitive skin at her core and she jerked, frantically opening her mouth to the delve of his tongue. All of her was on fire, the tips of her breasts straining and stiff, the heart of her damp and pulsing. He flipped her over as easily as though she were a doll and ground into her hard and fast and the pleasure was almost more than she could bear. She arched her back and moaned, the delight of pure unvarnished sensation screaming through every fibre of her being. Her climax still quivering through her limp body, Tansy finally flopped back against the sheets, absolutely wiped out by the experience.

With a glimmering smile, Jude reached for her and drew her under a strong arm, disconcerting her so much for a moment that she froze.

'What's up?' Jude prompted.

'Nothing, absolutely nothing,' she hastened to tell him, as though that small affectionate gesture were an everyday occurrence.

It wasn't. Jude didn't cuddle or snuggle or hug after sex. He was very much an island, a loner in intimacy. From the sidelines she had watched him slowly, almost clumsily learning to respond to Posy's unrestrained baby affection. She had seen him freeze in shock the first time her sister dabbed playful baby kisses all over his face in the same game she often played with Tansy. But Posy had forged her own path with Jude and he was returning her hugs without restraint now, and it seemed as though that had changed something in him, Tansy acknowledged with quiet pleasure, ridiculously pleased by that arm anchoring her to him in the aftermath. Why? It gave her a sense of achievement and the conviction that she was humanising Jude, who could often seem remote from the concerns that troubled others.

'So,' Jude murmured softly. 'You agreed to tell me why...'

'Is that why you're hugging me for the first time ever?' Tansy demanded with sudden anger. 'You want me to bare my soul, so you come over all manipulative and finally hug me?'

A frown line drawing his ebony brows together, Jude studied her in apparent wonderment. 'You will be *"baring your soul"*?' he queried.

Tansy went red. 'Well, that was a bit of an exaggeration,' she conceded, marvelling and mortified that that angry outburst had emerged from her without her volition.

'But the use of that word, "finally", suggests that I'm a major fail in the hug department?' Jude pressed. 'Well, that's not surprising. I didn't get hugged as a child very often—'

'But surely your mother—'

'No, when she visited me after losing custody of me to my father, she wasn't allowed to touch me. Isidore and my father hated her and considered her a malign influence and restricted her access to me as much as they could,' he took her aback by revealing. 'A nanny with strict instructions always acted as a chaperone.'

'But why on earth did they hate her so much?' Tansy exclaimed, wide-eyed.

'I think because she fought back and wouldn't lie down to be walked over. All their lives Isidore and my father were all-powerful in almost every sphere and virtually everyone set out to please them. To be fair to them, though, Clio can be very difficult to deal with. In the end they dealt with her by almost destroying her,' he breathed tautly. 'But we're not going to get distracted by my background just when you were about to spill the beans about why you were still a virgin when we met.'

Tansy gritted her teeth at the reminder and lay as still as a statue beside him. Her mind was still clinging to what he had told her about his background though. Growing up in such a difficult family situation had damaged Jude too. She was trying to imagine his childhood without hugs and winced in sympathy. The adults around him had been at daggers drawn and he had suffered accordingly. Distrust and intolerance had deprived Jude of the loving care he should have enjoyed.

Certainly, Tansy had had a better experience as a young child, but her face shadowed when she recalled her teenaged years when her peers had been dating and getting sexual experience. By that stage, the lack of understanding and shared interests between Tansy and her mother had become more obvious. She admitted to Jude that she had never had time at that age to get out and about. Either she had been swotting for exams, off on a beauty training course or working in her mother's salon.

'There wasn't room for anything else in my life.' She sighed. 'And in any case, nobody was interested in me that way.'

'I don't believe that.'

Tansy rolled her eyes, unimpressed, thinking back to her almost prepubescent lack of curves in her teens. 'When I started university I was sharing a flat with five girls. For the first time I was having a social life. The others were much more comfortable with boys than I was, and they all had active sex lives. I didn't realise it at the time but afterwards, after what happened, I think a few of those girls disliked me just for being different. Early on I admitted I was a virgin but that I was hoping to meet someone special. I was teased a lot, but I didn't let it bother me.'

'Why should you have?' Jude breathed above her head.

'One of my flatmates became my best friend, a girl called Emma. I fell madly in love with Ben, who was on Emma's course, and we started dating. I was quite frank with him about not being willing to jump into bed with him straight away. I wanted to see if we could go anywhere first,' Tansy admitted ruefully. 'I suppose that was pretty naive…me expecting him to wait.'

'No. It was his choice, whether he did or not,' Jude chipped in, being more supportive than she had expected.

'We were dating a few months and I was so *happy*,' Tansy recited with a groan of embarrassment. 'He was my first boyfriend and we were holding hands! And then one weekend, when I was supposed to be going home, I accidentally found out the *real* truth of what was going on behind my back. Mum cancelled my visit at the last minute because she and Calvin had been invited away by friends. I returned to the flat unexpectedly and found Emma and Ben in bed together and heard them laughing about me.'

Jude turned her face towards him as she fell silent. 'What did you do?'

'I confronted them. Emma admitted they'd been together from the start and that she and her friends and his had bet Ben that he couldn't collect my V-card,' Tansy confessed stiltedly. 'They'd all set me up for a joke. I was horrified, humiliated, awfully hurt because, not only did I love Ben, I believed Emma was my best friend.'

'I bet Ben tried to get you back afterwards,' Jude surprised her by remarking.

Tansy frowned. 'He acted like a freaking stalker… I couldn't believe that after what he'd done he could even think I'd have anything more to do with him! How did you know that he did that?'

'Because I'm a man and I would assume he was simply using Emma for sex until he got you. He wouldn't have wasted all that time on you if he hadn't been keen. I would also suggest that she was in love with Ben too and jealous of his attraction to you,' Jude summed up with confidence.

'And what made you the teenage love guru?' Tansy whispered, turning over to look at him, her heart tightening. 'A very misspent youth?'

'I was with Althea. There was nothing misspent about my youth,' Jude reminded her wryly. 'That's why I went off the rails after her. I felt like an idiot for looking for *"for ever"* when everyone around me the same age was settling for a "just for now" option.'

Tansy smoothed a possessive hand down over his well-defined abs, honed to perfection as she knew by daily early morning gym sessions, which she often shared although her passion was running. 'I think that's admirable, that you rejected the life your father and grandfather had led and set your heart on something more lasting.'

'No, it was naive, stupid,' Jude argued. 'I was too young to know what I was doing—'

'No,' Tansy continued to disagree. 'You just picked the wrong girl.'

An involuntary laugh escaped Jude. 'You make it sound so simple.'

'Sometimes it is. Someone like me would have appreciated your values,' Tansy muttered, engaged in kissing a haphazard line down over his rippling stomach, one small hand tracing a long muscular thigh.

'Yes, but we're not in this long-term, are we?' Jude muttered thickly, one hand sliding into her hair, keen to urge her in the right direction, unashamed lust gripping him with need all over again. 'So that angle doesn't come into it.'

Momentarily, Tansy froze and tried to make herself continue what she was doing, but it was impossible when she felt as though Jude had dropped a giant rock on her from a height, squashing breath and hope from her as he forced her back into the world of reality, rather than the world of fantasy where she had been getting rather too comfortable.

'My goodness, I'm starving!' she exclaimed, sitting up suddenly, rescuing herself.

Jude frowned, not an easy man to deflect, and he caught her hand before she could move off the bed. 'What did I say?'

Her fine-featured face froze. 'You didn't say anything.'

'About us not being long-term?' Jude pressed. 'But that's a *fact*.'

'Yes, of course, it is,' Tansy agreed, still trying to work out how best to evade that awkward subject.

Jude scrutinised her with shrewd dark golden eyes. 'Don't get attached to me, *moli mou*. I'm a bad bet.'

Tansy flipped her rippling hair off the side of her face with a steady hand. 'I wouldn't get attached to you. You're not my type,' she replied flatly.

'How can you say that?' Jude demanded, thoroughly disconcerted by that reply, and spreading lean brown hands to indicate the tumbled bed she had just slid off as if it were evidence to the contrary.

Tansy steeled herself to stand where she was, naked and vulnerable and seemingly unconcerned. 'That's simple chemistry and basically meaningless,' she downplayed, reaching for a robe with studious calm.

'We'll be flying back to Athens for my birthday party tomorrow. Isidore insisted. He always insists on throwing me a party,' Jude imparted ruefully. 'One would think that a thirtieth celebration could be left for me to enjoy in my own way.'

'But listening to you, one would also think how very spoilt and entitled you are,' Tansy incised thinly. 'Nobody ever threw a party for *me* in my entire life! Your grandfather loves and cares about you. For goodness' sake, the man's on the phone to you every day, interested in every breath that you take! What does it take for you to appreciate what you have?'

Colour scored Jude's high cheekbones. He clenched his teeth together on an acerbic response. Tansy viewed his family through a different scope, possibly because she had been pretty much neglected by her own mother, he reasoned inwardly. Tansy had never been put first or spoiled or indulged by a proud or loving parent. But he *had* been, Jude registered for possibly the first time, thinking of how every household he had lived in from childhood had revolved around him and of how Isidore had scrupulously made time for him whenever his father was unavailable. It was strange how Tansy's opinions were changing his outlook on some areas of his life, he acknowledged uneasily.

Isidore had instilled his grandson with the belief that women were innately untrustworthy, probably in the hope of driving another wedge between Jude and his mother. After Althea had proved Isidore's theory, Jude had strongly resisted the concept of being influenced by any woman. As for love, he was never doing that again, that went without saying. He got by fine without love, had done so for years. But the suggestion that he might have been blind to the reality that his grandfather loved him pierced him on a deep level, cutting through the barriers that his mother had set up inside his head when he was much younger. He wasn't enjoying Tansy's insight into his family as an onlooker, but it was certainly making him think for the first time in a long time about how his dysfunctional background could have moved certain facts weirdly out of focus.

'I appreciate what I have,' Jude countered ruefully. 'Enough serious talk though…let's concentrate on what you're wearing for the party. It will be a very glitzy event.'

Tansy nodded with a jerk and vanished into the palatial en suite bathroom, her eyes burning with moisture. He had warned her not to get attached to him. He had missed the boat, Tansy reflected wretchedly. She had done what she had believed she would not do, had let feelings take hold, because it would *never* be just chemistry for her with Jude. There was just so much she liked and appreciated about him that he made her head spin.

Foremost in that line was his uncompromising honesty and his compassion for his troubled mother, whom he rarely saw. Then there was his quick and intelligent brain, because there was no denying that a clever man was the most entertaining and the best company. His kindness towards Posy, his lack of snobbishness when Tansy sometimes got things wrong because she had grown up at another social level, his generosity with other people because, for someone she had called spoilt, he was remarkably tolerant. She could have kept listing admirable attributes for longer, she conceded while she stood in the shower, letting the tears finally fall, but what was the point?

She had fallen in love with a guy who would never love her back and that broke her heart. She had nothing to hope for either, when their arrangement excluded love in favour of practicality. Jude had ringed their entire relationship with boundaries. In addition, she felt guilty about loving him, about having failed to keep emotion out of their agreement while at the same time Jude was fully meeting his end of the deal to be a father to Posy. How could she complain when she had caught feelings for him? He had specifically warned her against getting attached to him. He had, in short, given her exactly what he had promised, and it would be ridiculously naive of her to hope for anything more permanent when he had been so candid from the outset...

CHAPTER NINE

'IT'S GORGEOUS,' TANSY whispered as Jude clasped the fragile emerald and diamond necklace at her nape.

'And this set isn't an Alexandris heirloom which you can only borrow. It's yours,' Jude stressed, sending a shard of pain winging through her that he felt as though he had to make that fine distinction because she *wasn't* a genuine Alexandris wife, with him for the long haul.

A fixed smile in place, Tansy shifted her head so that the matching earrings shimmered in the light. 'It's a really beautiful gift. Thank you very much,' she murmured quietly. 'But I don't know when I would ever wear it again after we're divorced. I can't see me living the high life.'

Jude's lean, strong face clenched hard. He might have warned Tansy not to get too attached to being his wife, but he didn't like it when she referred to their eventual divorce...particularly as though it were just a heartbeat away when it *wasn't*! Strangely, that outlook of hers should have been welcome but instead it set his teeth on edge. They had been together less than a couple of months, yet, all of a sudden, Tansy seemed to be racing for the finishing line as though she couldn't wait to get away from him.

Yes, virtually overnight something had definitely *changed* in Tansy because she was on edge and curiously quiet. All day he had been struggling to get her to talk and relax the way she usually did. Her new reserve made him tense and made him question his own behaviour and it was already driving him absolutely crazy.

Tansy cast a last glance at her reflection in the cheval mirror. Jude's birthday party was a very formal event. The green ballgown with its beautiful stylish embroidery glittered with crystals in the dusk light. It hugged her slender figure like a glove, fanning out below her knees in a profusion of fabric above high-heeled sandals the exact same colour.

'You look like a Venus…it's outrageously sexy,' Jude intoned huskily, long fingers stroking down her slender spine.

Her breath caught in her throat and she quivered, but still she stepped away, practising the self-denial he had once mocked. 'I'm not curvy enough for that comparison.'

'Curvy enough from what I can see, *moraki mou*,' Jude remarked with amusement, narrowed eyes resting pointedly on the delicate but full pout of her bosom below the fitted dress.

My goodness, had he noticed that she had got a little bigger there? Tansy frowned, suspecting that she needed new bras because her opulent lingerie was becoming too tight. Had she been overeating? But she so rarely put on weight, she mused in bewilderment.

When had she last had a period? Tansy froze at that sudden thought and then opened her phone, where she had always kept a note of her cycle, only to discover that she hadn't even set up a record for the simple reason that she had not had a period since her marriage. *Not one single one!* Could it be that she was pregnant? The shock of that possibility thrilled through her and she thought of the pregnancy tests she had purchased some weeks earlier for just such an occasion, resolving to utilise one as soon as possible.

'Althea's been invited,' Jude informed her grimly, interrupting the frantic surge of her thoughts. 'Unfortunately, Isidore regards her as an old friend of mine. I should've told him what's been happening with her.'

'Just smile pleasantly at her and keep your distance,' Tansy advised.

'She's too brash to take the hint whereas you are probably the least pushy woman I've ever met,' Jude mused. 'I'm not sure that's always an advantage with me.'

'Well, I've never aspired to being perfect,' Tansy countered a shade tartly.

'And you're so prickly all of a sudden!' Jude complained, closing a hand over hers to walk her out of the bedroom, a tall, devastatingly handsome figure in an exquisitely tailored dinner jacket and narrow-cut trousers. 'You didn't used to be.'

Tansy reddened because she knew that she wasn't in the best of moods after the sleepless night she had endured, agonising over her feelings for him. 'There's a first time for everything.'

'I still like you, prickly or not, *moli mou*,' Jude teased, closing a powerful arm round her narrow spine as they came to a halt in the door of the nursery.

Shaking off her bedding, Posy clawed her way upright in the cot, little eyes bright as she gripped the top rail and bounced in mad excitement. 'Da... Da!' she yelled, round little face wreathed in welcome.

'I still can't get over the fact that, although you say he didn't receive that money, Calvin hasn't been in touch to *demand* it,' Tansy admitted half under her breath as Jude cheerfully broke her rules to lift her sister out of the cot and cuddle her.

'She's supposed to be in bed to sleep for the night, Jude,' she scolded. 'That's unsettling for her. Routine is important—'

Jude dealt her an amused glance. 'It's equally important to be spontaneous sometimes as well,' he retorted in direct disagreement. 'As for Calvin, his number's blocked on your phone, which is why you haven't heard from him.'

'Blocked?' Tansy exclaimed in disbelief. 'How did that happen?'

'It was set up on your new phone before I gave it to you,' Jude admitted without apology. 'I didn't want him harassing you.'

'You don't have the right to make that kind of decision on my behalf!' Tansy whispered in fierce dismay. 'Because he hasn't heard from me, he'll be even more furious and that's *not* a good idea with Calvin.'

'Allow me to deal with Hetherington,' Jude countered smoothly. 'He's my headache now. No way will I allow him to get his paws on this little girl again.'

Colour had burnished Tansy's face into animation and anger. 'That's not the point.'

'It's exactly the point,' Jude incised with cool, crushing finality as he settled the baby back in her cot and gently covered her up again. 'I am better equipped to deal with the Calvins of this world than you are.'

Having had access to the angry texts that Calvin Hetherington had already sent his stepdaughter, Jude was relieved that he had protected Tansy from them. So far, her stepfather had threatened to sell his story to the media and set the police on them for abducting his daughter without his permission. Tansy didn't need the stress of those threats. Jude was using every expert in the field to keep Posy's father at bay until another investigation by Calvin's former employers was complete. Regaining custody of the daughter he had never wanted was likely to be the last thing on Calvin's mind once he had more worrying developments to consider, Jude mused.

Jude's arm enclosed Tansy again on their passage down the sweeping staircase. Her colour was high, her mood on edge. Jude had a tendency to just take over, convinced that he knew better than her. But he should have told her about blocking her stepfather's calls, shouldn't have he? She would have panicked, she acknowledged, because she was horribly conscious that the law would be on Calvin's side as a birth parent and not on theirs.

As for Jude's words earlier… *I still like you.* It was

better than nothing, she supposed unhappily. Not a lot to write home about though, when she was insanely in love with him! Perhaps she was a glutton for punishment, she conceded as they descended the stairs into a crush of the most unbelievably beautiful and glamorous women, who were all keen to personally congratulate the gorgeous heir to the Alexandris fortune on his birthday. In short, Jude was being mobbed.

As Tansy stood off to one side, a waiter served her with a glass of champagne, and she asked him to bring her a sparkling water in a champagne glass instead.

Isidore Alexandris appeared in front of her. 'I believe Jude is taking you to meet his mother tomorrow—'

'Yes.' But Jude had mentioned that fact only in passing, and not for the first time she had received the impression that questions about his surviving parent were not a welcome source of conversation. Jude, she had sensed, was very protective of his mother.

Isidore compressed his lips. 'Stick by his side. Clio was difficult and Dion and I were hard on her because she did a lot of damage to Jude when he was a boy,' he breathed in a driven undertone. 'Her bitterness was like poison. Jude had been indoctrinated and traumatised by the time his father won custody of him. I still can't abide the woman but, to be fair, there were faults on both sides. None of us deserve a trophy for our behaviour back then.'

'Jude did refer to the…family bad feeling,' Tansy selected with tact. 'But he doesn't discuss her with me.'

'He wouldn't,' Isidore commented wryly. 'He's very

loyal to anyone he cares about, but I have never believed that she deserved that loyalty.'

As Tansy accompanied Isidore into the crowded ballroom, she saw Althea, glowing and gorgeous in a tight black dress that showcased her bountiful curves, and quickly looked away again. She was disconcerted when Althea approached her, dropping down fluidly into the vacant seat beside her. 'We didn't get to talk at the wedding,' the blonde declared. 'How are you finding married life?'

'It's wonderful,' Tansy responded with a smile to equal the brilliance of her companion's.

'Jude and I are incredibly close. I hope you don't intend to interfere with our friendship. Jude would be furious with you,' Althea informed her smoothly.

'I think that since you confronted him on our wedding day some things may have changed,' Tansy countered with quiet dignity. 'Jude wouldn't enjoy another scene—'

Althea's eyes flared with resentment. 'Who the hell do you think you are to tell me that?'

'His wife.' Tansy breathed in deep, studying the blonde, seeing what Jude probably did not see in his first love: a pampered and arrogant beauty unaccustomed to meeting with rejection. 'You had Jude once and you blew it. That's not on him, that's on *you*.'

As Althea spluttered in fury at that blunt rejoinder, Tansy eased upright in her high heels and walked away. A hand closed over hers and steered her behind an ornate pillar. She glanced up in consternation to see Jude gazing down at her with a dazzling smile of appreciation.

'I can't believe that I've reached the age of thirty before meeting a woman who wants to *rescue* me, *protect* me...'

'What on earth are you talking about?' Tansy asked, still flushed from her encounter with his ex-girlfriend.

'I overheard your conversation with Althea. You were warning her off for my benefit. That was very sweet,' Jude labelled softly. 'And very sexy.'

Relief that he wasn't offended, allied with that comment, made Tansy laugh. 'According to you, everything I do is sexy.'

Glittering dark golden eyes full of heat swept her animated face. 'It is,' he confirmed.

Tansy mock-punched his shoulder. 'You're full of it! Do some women actually believe that nonsense?'

'Unluckily for me, *not* my wife.'

Tansy stretched up on tiptoes and pressed her lips briefly, helplessly, against his. 'Give it up now,' she told him, wide green eyes locked to his compellingly beautiful face. 'You couldn't fake dejected, no matter how hard you tried!'

Jude pressed her back against the pillar and covered her parted lips hungrily, deeply with his and she trembled in response, every sense engaged in that intensely erotic connection. She could feel the fast beat of his heart, his arousal, the raw sexual tension in his lean, powerful frame and as always it thrilled her and only an awareness of their surroundings made her push jerkily against his shoulders to separate their bodies again.

Jude stared down at her. 'This is the first time you've been yourself with me today,' he told her, filling her with dismay with that unexpected insight.

'There's nothing wrong with me,' she protested weakly. 'You're imagining things.'

'I'm neither stupid nor blind, *moli mou*.'

Tansy set her teeth together. How on earth could Jude read her so well? How did he know that she was desperately trying to pull back from him to protect herself? Having realised that she was in love with him, Tansy had backed off. She would do the pregnancy test tomorrow, get that out of the way. If she *was* pregnant, it would take Jude's keen focus off her, wouldn't it? He would be delighted, and he would relax then and might well assume that any change in her was due to hormones.

All she had left now was her pride, she reasoned ruefully. The last thing she needed was to be humiliated by Jude starting to handle her with kid gloves in the same careful way that she saw him trying to handle Althea. Women who made the mistake of getting too keen on Jude might annoy and exasperate him but they also seemed to awaken his compassion. Perhaps that was a result of his recollection of his father's cruel treatment of his mother. But the very last thing Tansy wanted to be when they divorced, and remained in contact for him to see Posy and the child she hoped she was carrying, was an object of pity.

The giant tiered birthday cake was cut on the terrace beyond the ballroom where a firework display was staged simultaneously. After supper had been served, they were on the dance floor where Tansy was apologising because all she knew how to do during a slow dance was shuffle while Jude, of course, was as skilled on the floor as a formally trained dancer. In the midst of that, Isidore stood up and the music stopped abruptly as the older man called for attention.

Jude's hand, splayed to her spine, flexed and froze as Isidore addressed his guests with a beaming smile and called for Jude to join him at his table. As they moved forward, Isidore continued speaking in Greek and there was a loud round of clapping and many shouts of approval. Unaware of what was happening, Tansy stuck by Jude's side as he was slapped on the back and his hand was shaken by the many people approaching him. All she registered was that Jude appeared to be stunned but struggling to conceal that reality.

'Sorry, what's happening?' she whispered apologetically to Isidore.

'I've announced my retirement. Jude will now be taking over control of the Alexandris empire. It's time for me to step down,' his grandfather told her with satisfaction.

That announcement had made Jude even more the centre of attention. Tansy listened to him talk in Greek with apparent calm, but she remained conscious of the dazed light in his dark eyes that suggested that his grandfather's retirement had come as a complete surprise to him. She wanted to ask him why that was so, but Jude had been plunged into talking business with various guests and it was some time before they were finally free to head upstairs to bed and talk. It was two in the morning and Tansy was smothering a yawn, wondering if her bone deep exhaustion could be another sign of pregnancy, because usually she could take one late night without it being a problem.

'You're very tired,' Jude noted.

'Yes. Are you going to tell me why Isidore's announcement shocked you so much?'

'I had no idea that that was his plan. In fact, I thought he wouldn't even consider it until I was married with a child,' Jude admitted tautly.

Tansy stopped in the doorway of their bedroom and stared back at him. 'That's why you needed a wife and wanted a child,' she guessed.

'That possibility only added an inducement, but it's not why I needed a wife or chose to marry. Ever have the feeling that you've been played?' Jude breathed in a raw undertone as he doffed his tuxedo and poured himself a whiskey from the bar in the sitting room, kicking off his shoes, unbuttoning his shirt, the seething tension in his big, powerful frame blatant 'That's how I feel right now. Isidore *played* me—'

Tansy gave him a bemused look. 'I don't understand.'

'My mother, Clio, lives in an Alexandris property in Italy. She's lived there ever since the divorce. She got virtually no money when she left my father and Isidore allowed her to move into the Villa Bardani because initially she still had custody of me. He did offer to buy her a house in Greece, but she refused to come back here. A couple of centuries ago the gardens at the villa were a showpiece but over the years they were allowed to fall into ruin. After she lost custody of me, Clio became obsessed with restoring the villa's gardens. She had nothing else in her life to focus on.'

'Why did she lose custody of you?'

'She had a nervous breakdown and slashed her wrists when she was alone in the house with me,' Jude offered flatly. 'For that reason, she was deemed mentally unfit by the courts to look after a young child.'

Shock engulfed Tansy, for she had never dreamt that something so distressing lay behind Clio's loss of custody of Jude. His parents had had a dreadful marriage and it made Tansy wonder how much that truth had influenced Jude in his desire for a more practical union, shorn of emotion. After all, powerful emotions had proved destructive in his parents' marriage and must have damaged Jude's faith in them as well. How could he ever approve of love or even want it when some kind of love had originally brought his parents together? And Althea had claimed to love Jude as well, even after betraying his trust.

'Oh, my word…that's a horrible story,' she whispered in a pained tone of sympathy. 'Divorce, then a breakdown, followed by the loss of her son into the bargain. Your mother suffered.'

'Exactly,' Jude incised, his lean, strong face grim and taut. 'This family *destroyed* Clio. I have a difficult relationship with her as well. She can't seem to separate me from my father inside her head. But I still care about her and believe that she deserves happiness. The gardens she restored over the past twenty years are now world-renowned and she's out there labouring in them from dawn to dusk with the gardeners. Those gardens mean everything to her…and Isidore threatened to send her an eviction notice.'

Tansy blinked rapidly. 'He…*what*?'

'She has never had a legal right to live there or even be on the property because it belongs to my family. My grandfather said he would throw her out and refuse her access to the gardens which belong to the villa unless I was married by my thirtieth birthday. I believed he would do it too, because he loathes her,' Jude admitted curtly.

'And that's why you needed a wife,' Tansy whispered, sinking down into the nearest seat before her wobbly legs could betray how much shock *she* was in. She had simply assumed that he had some business or inheritance reason for requiring a wife and it had not seemed worth her while to dig any deeper. She had never dreamt that his motive might be so personal or so family-oriented. And that he had gone to such extremes to protect a woman whom he rarely even saw impressed her even more.

'Isidore was playing me,' Jude bit out harshly. 'He wanted to see me married and settled before he retired, but I suspect that he never had any serious intention of evicting Clio from her home.'

'Perhaps not.'

'Because it would have alienated me for ever,' Jude delivered with a bitter edge to his intonation. 'I assumed the worst of him, and he encouraged me to do so.'

Isidore had fooled him, Jude acknowledged, but, even worse, Isidore had *known* that his grandson would believe the very worst of him and that fact bothered Jude. Had he shown his distrust to his grandfather so clearly? Evidently he had and Jude's lack of faith would only have increased Isidore's resentment of his daughter-in-law. A tangled mixture of shame and guilt and resentment infiltrated Jude. Somewhere during the years of his childhood, he had discarded the ability to stand back and clearly read those closest to him. He had believed blindly in everything Clio told him, had judged his grandfather to be a cruel, hard man. Yet that same cruel, hard man had proved to be a loving grandparent, indeed a much more caring and supportive parental figure than Jude's distinctly distant father.

'Well, you may be married but I wouldn't say you're *settled* with a divorce already organised as a happy ending,' Tansy pointed out in consolation.

'I'm so comforted,' Jude bit out with a razor-edged smile, jolted more than he liked by that unwelcome reminder.

'I'm off to bed,' Tansy said, surrendering to the tense atmosphere, reminding herself that the perplexing rights and wrongs of Jude's family were not really any of her business because she wasn't a true wife. Not that Isidore appeared to appreciate that fact, she conceded ruefully. She saw that just as Jude had not realised his grandfather was wielding an empty threat as a weapon, Isidore had not realised that Jude might choose to make a *fake* marriage rather than a real one. Two tricky, too clever, too stubborn personalities from the same family, she acknowledged, well, fancy that. Jude and his grandfather were chips off the very same block.

Freshened up and sheathed in a silk nightie, she climbed into bed. Jude paced the sitting room, initially outraged that Isidore had duped him and unable to get past that fact. He had raced off like a knight in shining armour to come to his mother's rescue, but it hadn't been necessary. That was a galling footnote to the sacrifices he had made and yet hadn't Isidore created a better outcome for all of them? Clio was safe, Jude was, to all intents and purposes, happily married and newly conscious that he had a grandfather who appeared to love him.

Not a grandfather who viewed him solely as a necessary heir, but a man who had seen and possibly understood Jude's reluctance to risk his emotions in *any* close relationship. After all, emotions were messy and made you vulnerable, and Jude had perfectly grasped that fact after his mother, distraught over Dion's many infidelities, had tried to take her own life. Jude had been prepared to marry only if emotion could be removed from the equation.

And his marriage of convenience with Tansy had scarcely proved a punishment, he reflected with a sudden grin at his own melodramatic frame of mind. Tansy was wonderfully straightforward, and hadn't he ultimately received everything that he had once craved? His freedom in business from Isidore's interference? The right to steer the Alexandris empire in a more innovative direction? It had taken the wife he had never thought to have to persuade him that his grandfather was not the callous monster Clio had once depicted. Jude had finally seen his grandfather's love for him as clear as day and it had shaken him almost as much as Isidore's retirement plans.

Naturally, his mother had had a confrontational relationship with his grandfather, who had remained loyal to his only son. There was more than one side to his parents' broken marriage and the divisions in his family were not as black and white as Jude had once believed. In a much better mood at having faced that truth, Jude went for a shower.

Gentle fingertips smoothed down Tansy's thigh, trailing against silk, piercing through her drowsiness. 'Jude,' she muttered.

'I'm sorry I was angry. It was nothing to do with you,' Jude husked, tugging her back against him.

'It's OK…' she mumbled, wriggling her bottom back into the heat of his arousal, registering the sizzle of awareness travelling through her whole body.

He kissed the nape of her neck, dallied there, found the slope of her shoulder and let his teeth graze the tender skin and a tiny moan was wrenched from her parted lips, eyes opening in the moonlight as she stretched back into the heat of him. His hands found the achingly sensitive peaks of her breasts and she flipped over and arched into him like a shameless hussy, finding his carnal mouth for herself. And all the inner tensions and insecurities she had been crushing down blew her wide open with hunger for him.

In one powerful stroke he drove into her and the excitement took over, pushing her into an electrifying climax that almost wiped her out into unconsciousness.

'That was absolutely incredible,' Jude husked, and that was the last thing she remembered until she shifted awake soon after dawn, dug out one of the pregnancy tests she had bought and crept off to the bathroom to use it.

Tansy stared in near disbelief at the positive result on the wand. She had had her suspicions, but she had not really believed until that moment that she *could* be pregnant. Her brain hadn't quite been prepared yet for that development and for a long time she sat on the edge of a glitzy bathtub, set in marble, contemplating the test. Her hand splayed across her stomach as she pictured a tiny version of her and Jude and her heart raced with happiness and a hundred expectations of the future.

Jude strolled into the bathroom naked as she emerged. 'You're up early—'

Tansy spun round to face him. 'I've got news!' she heard herself exclaim, excitement and a sense of achievement bubbling through her.

Jude switched on the shower and sent her a level glance. *'Yes?'* he pressed with subdued amusement, wondering what the heck she was so pleased about.

'I'm pregnant!' she told him.

And halfway into the shower, Jude froze, and he unmistakably paled as though she had given him bad news. 'Right… OK,' he breathed, vanishing into the shower, turning to face the wall, the tension in the muscles of his smooth golden back unhidden.

Tansy's excitement drained away like sand through an egg timer. She blinked, utterly at a loss as to why her announcement had proved to be a damp squib instead of a source of satisfaction and pleasure.

Jude wanted to punch the wall. The terms of the pre-nup they had both signed were etched in letters of fire inside his head. He had had every clause written according to how *he* wanted the marriage to play out. He had wanted his freedom back as soon as possible, had wanted a separation the minute he estimated it could reasonably be demanded. Back then everything had seemed so simple to him because he had assumed he would want his life back as it had been. But now, all of a sudden and without the smallest warning, he was discovering that what he had thought he had wanted wasn't actually what he wanted at all…in fact it was the very last thing he wanted.

CHAPTER TEN

WHAT WERE THE odds of a pregnancy occurring in so short a time? Jude asked himself, thinking of his grandfather, who had fathered only one child even though he had had three wives, and his own father, who had cast his sperm even more liberally and had *still* only managed to produce one child. And *he* got a conception in the space of a couple of months. Isidore would be jubilant, any kid, boy or girl, figuring as a virtual miracle in his eyes. In other circumstances, Jude might have been jubilant as well, especially if he could picture a baby like Posy, except with Tansy's hair and maybe Tansy's smile. Or a little boy. It wasn't as though he had any preference…

But for now he had to make the best of things, particularly because he had got what he had asked for, what he had bargained so hard to have. Where had his wits been? Why had he not foreseen what might happen? What might go wrong?

Later that morning, Tansy toyed with the idea of saying several tart things to Jude once they were ensconced in the private jet and flying to Italy. But in the end she said nothing about the baby she was carrying, noting instead the frequency with which Jude's gaze rested on her stomach while realising that, in spite of his silence, he was hugely conscious of her pregnancy. And since that was the case, why did he have so little to say about it? In fact, it seemed as though her little announcement had utterly silenced him. Or was it that Jude was not looking forward to introducing her to his mother, who was, by all accounts, a challenging personality?

Tansy could only suppose that Jude was brooding because he now appreciated that everything he had done had been for nothing. He had gained a wife, a child in Posy and conceived another, radically altering his lifestyle for no good reason. In the end, after all, Isidore had handed his grandson everything he wanted on a golden plate. Yet, angry and hurt as Tansy was with Jude, she could not judge him harshly for striving to protect his mother. Conceding how hard she had worked to protect her little sister from harm, she had no right to judge anyone.

'How did your mother meet your father?' Tansy asked Jude abruptly.

'She was the gardener at a house he visited in Florence. He said it was love at first sight.'

'But from what you've said it was a love at first sight that only lasted about five minutes,' Tansy qualified ruefully.

'According to him, he told her before he married her that even though he loved her he could never be faithful.'

'When did he tell you that?'

'Shortly before he died when I was eighteen. I don't think Clio ever got over him. She still keeps a portrait of him in her cottage, which is a little strange if you consider the level of animosity there was between them.'

Tansy frowned. 'She lives in a cottage? I thought she lived in some big villa.'

'She *did* up until she lost custody of me. After that she moved into a house on the Bardani estate because she said she didn't want to owe the Alexandris family anything.'

'But presumably the cottage belongs to your family as well.'

Jude shrugged in dismissal of that point.

'I imagine developing a world-famous garden doesn't come cheap in execution or maintenance either,' Tansy murmured curiously. 'Who finances all that?'

'I cover her expenses, but the gardens are now open to the public and more or less pay for themselves.' Jude grimaced. 'The prenup she signed was so tight that she was left flat broke after the divorce. My father was needlessly punitive because she demanded a divorce that *he* didn't want and she had no family of her own to fall back on for support.'

'I can imagine that she didn't want to fall back on the sister who had slept with her husband,' Tansy said with distaste.

'Clio's still very much a loner.'

'What age were you when she had her breakdown?' Tansy pressed curiously.

'Six.'

'Did you find her after her…attempt?' Tansy asked tautly.

Jude nodded. 'The memory of it still haunts me. She was lying in a pool of blood, unconscious, and it was the staff's night off.'

'I'm so sorry,' Tansy breathed heavily as she attempted with an inner shudder to picture how such a scene would have affected a six-year-old. 'What did you do?'

'I phoned Isidore.'

'Not your father?'

'No, I knew he was partying in his yacht on the other side of the world because Clio had shown me the photos that day in a newspaper. I think even at that age I suspected that he wouldn't be much good in an emergency. Isidore sent help to the villa and then flew straight to Italy. He took care of everything and brought me back to Greece with him. It was two years before I saw Clio again because she was in a rehab unit for a long time and when I finally did, she and my father had a massive row, which just made everything worse. He had remarried by then and she couldn't cope with that. Their relationship was toxic long after the divorce.'

'I hope that when we part we can, at least, stay friends,' Tansy muttered tautly.

His brilliant dark golden eyes hardened and took on a glittering intensity that seared her. His lush black lashes swiftly screened his expression. 'I'm the last person likely to make the relationship difficult after the way I grew up,' he parried stonily. 'The children's security must come first.'

'I think you'll miss Posy when we split up,' Tansy forecast, feeling very brave in making that comment and admiring the steadiness of her own voice, but she felt the need to continually remind herself that their marriage was only temporary. 'I miss her now.'

Jude tensed and stared down at the laptop in front of him. 'It would have been selfish to make her do this journey with us when we'll only be at the villa one night—'

Tansy nodded agreement because she liked to try and keep her sister to a stable routine, which was difficult, she allowed ruefully, when Jude seemed to live flitting from property to property, country to country, and then there was the yacht to throw into his options as well. It was something they would have to discuss because there had to be one place he would surely be willing to call home where they could settle like a normal family. Only they weren't a *normal* family, she acknowledged with a sinking sensation in her tummy.

As they were driven from the airport it was a beautiful sunny day with the sky a clear cerulean blue and the landscape lush and green with the promise of spring moving into summer. Orange and olive groves and serrated lines of vines marched over the rolling hills and a colourful selection of wild flowers flourished on the verges of the lane they drove down.

'We'll head up to the villa later. Clio is expecting us,' Jude told her.

The limousine drew up at a picturesque old stone building embellished with glorious roses and greenery. 'It looks like a painting,' Tansy whispered admiringly.

'Wait until you see the gardens,' Jude advised. 'The whole place is like this—'

A tall, beautiful blonde appeared in the doorway and smiled widely at Jude. 'Come in…lunch is ready.'

'This is Tansy,' Jude murmured. 'Clio…'

Clio looked twenty years younger than Tansy knew her to be and she was still gorgeous, from her long blond hair and bright blue eyes to her leggy grace in workmanlike jeans.

'Tansy.' Clio extended a cool hand. 'Rather a common, ordinary herb, I'm afraid.'

Tansy went pink and smiled, ignoring the comment.

'There's nothing ordinary about Tansy.' Jude laughed, resting a hand against her taut spine.

A light lunch was served in the dining room. The room was dominated by a large portrait of a young, handsome man with black curls, his likeness to Jude so strong that it could only have been his father.

'The resemblance between father and son *is* striking,' Clio commented when she saw what had stolen Tansy's attention.

'It certainly is,' Tansy agreed, disconcerted by the older woman's brittle manner and tart tongue while marvelling that Jude was so tolerant of her idiosyncrasies. His kindness, his fondness for his only surviving parent were palpable, but it also helped her to understand why he would be so keen to steer clear of emotional entanglements in his own life after his experiences at his mother's and Althea's hands.

'Why aren't you drinking your wine?' the blonde

woman asked abruptly. 'Don't you like it? Perhaps you'd prefer red or rosé? Or perhaps you don't drink?'

'Tansy's pregnant,' Jude said quietly.

The announcement dropped into a sudden sharp silence. His mother stared at him in dismay. 'You *can't* make me a granny! I'm far too young for that,' she objected vehemently.

'Fortunately, we don't need anyone's permission,' Jude countered quietly.

Clio settled indignant blue eyes on Tansy. 'Jude will ruin your life. He'll cheat on you like his father cheated on me. The last thing you should be doing is bringing a child into the chaos ahead of you!'

Tansy breathed in slow and deep to restrain her temper. 'You can't know your son very well if you think he would cheat on me. He has an aversion to infidelity that makes me feel safe on that score. He is *very* loyal,' she stressed defensively.

Jude closed a soothing hand over hers where it sat knotted into a fist of tension on her thigh. It infuriated Tansy that a mother could think so little of her own child that she denigrated him in front of an audience.

Clio snorted. 'You'll learn otherwise…eventually.'

Jude, evidently accustomed to his mother's attacks, made light conversation for what remained of the meal. Clio didn't even ask Tansy when her baby was due, indeed appeared to have no interest whatsoever in the topic. By the time coffee was served their hostess was becoming restless and she mentioned a media interview she had mid-afternoon before suggesting that they tour the gardens.

'Your mother's rather thorny,' Tansy said ruefully as they walked down an informal path from the cottage. The path gave way into a wide grassed area enclosed by a tunnel of low-hanging trees. An imposing stone temple sat as a focal point at the far end. It was spectacular.

'Always was. Essentially, if you had roots you would get much more attention from Clio,' Jude remarked wryly.

'No, I wouldn't, not with the connotations of a name as humble as mine. I think I'm the equivalent of a weed in her eyes!' Tansy opined with a helpless giggle.

'Thank you for not taking offence.' Jude sighed. 'She was rude but that's not unusual for her. She's not very fond of her own sex and she doesn't like to share my attention with anyone else.'

'Or the thought of being made a grandmother.'

Jude flung back his curly dark head and laughed with appreciation. 'You weren't one bit bothered by her, were you?'

'No. You did warn me.'

'Years ago, she deeply offended Althea.'

'Althea has more of an opinion of herself than I do.' As they wandered below the trees, Tansy was relieved that she was wearing comfortable sandals and a light linen dress because, even in the shade, it was very warm. She was enjoying the fresh air and a sense of relaxation after spending half the day trapped in a seat.

'We have to talk,' Jude intoned tautly.

ESP fingered down Tansy's spine like spectral fingers of warning and her delicate features tensed. As her pace slowed Jude closed a hand over hers to urge her on. 'About what?' she said stiffly.

'I would suggest…a potential renegotiation of terms,' Jude murmured sibilantly.

'What terms?' Tansy almost whispered, so drawn tight were her nerves at that proposal.

'The legal terms of our marriage,' Jude specified.

Tansy tugged her fingers free at the edge of a mossy stone fountain ringed by wild pink orchids. Sunlight glinted on the clear water and the brightness made her blink several times. 'Why would we need to renegotiate anything?' she asked uneasily, her heart beating very, very fast in the heat, perspiration breaking out on her upper lip.

'You're pregnant. That changes everything,' Jude pointed out, lowering his lean, powerful body in a graceful sprawl of long limbs down onto the stone steps leading up to the temple. The fluid, careless elegance of the movement implied he had not a care in the world, Tansy thought painfully.

To Jude, Tansy looked very pale. But then that flawless porcelain skin of hers was very pale and translucent in comparison to his own, he conceded, studying her while willing her to respond as he wanted her to respond. In full sunlight, her dress was gossamer-sheer, outlining long shapely legs and the shadows of her areolae, accentuating the reality that she was not wearing a bra on her small pouting breasts. The tightening at his groin, the pulse of arousal made him grit his teeth, but she looked utterly incredible with her long streaky hair tousled in waves and catching the light across her shoulders, her clear green eyes fixed to him.

'I don't understand what you're getting at,' Tansy admitted shakily.

'In our marital agreement it states that the instant a conception occurs we can separate,' Jude recounted curtly. 'Of course, you're free to make your own decision and if that's what you *want*—'

'Separate...like *now*? Immediately?' Tansy prompted half under her breath, her lungs feeling deprived of sufficient oxygen in the hot, still air. 'Where did it say that? I don't remember reading that.'

'It was one of the clauses in the marriage contract.' She was looking at him as though he were talking in a foreign language, eyes wide, complexion white as milk below the sun.

Tansy was feeling impossibly dizzy and slightly sick and much too hot for comfort. She made a belated move back towards the shade beneath the trees, but it was too late. Darkness stole her vision, her body swaying, and she folded down on the grass in a heap as she fainted.

For a split second, Jude almost panicked. He raced down the steps to lift her up and she looked so white and delicate in his arms. He dug out his phone and rang the villa for a staff member to collect them in one of the buggies that were used by his mother's gardening team. Tansy stirred in his arms and moaned. 'I'm so hot.'

'You're going to be fine,' Jude said unevenly, trying to inject confidence into that optimistic assertion but very aware of his ignorance and digging out his phone again to organise a doctor's visit to check her out.

She was pregnant, rather fragile in his estimation and he had sprung a huge choice about the future on her without the smallest preamble. It wasn't only the heat that had got to her but probably the stress he had heaped on her as well and he felt appallingly guilty.

'You're holding me too tight,' Tansy whispered shakily, her head still woozy as she peered up at him, noticing that his stunning dark golden eyes were awash with emotions she couldn't interpret.

'Sorry,' Jude breathed tautly, his grip on her loosening a little.

'I'm still so dizzy.' She sighed apologetically as the world tilted and she was laid into some sort of compact vehicle.

'Close your eyes, relax,' Jude instructed.

But Tansy was incapable of relaxation with Jude's words still weighing heavily on her mind and shadowing everything: separation after conception. A clause in their premarital agreement? Why hadn't she read it properly? There had been pages and pages and she had given up ten pages in while the document went on to cover every possible and unlikely development under the sun. Even so, separating as soon as she fell pregnant? That was *so* cold-blooded, she reflected wretchedly. Had she been aware of that fact from the start, she wasn't sure she would have agreed to consider having a child with him.

Jude carried her up steps and she heard the low mutter of voices talking in fast, liquid Italian. Her head was still swimming but her lashes fluttered up and she saw a very grand landscape painting and she closed her eyes again, just relieved that they were indoors again and out of the heat.

He laid her down carefully on a mattress and she looked up into a crown from which elaborate brocade drapes were festooned. Eyes widening, she sat up, ignoring Jude's advice to stay flat. 'Good heavens, this place is like a museum—'

'Isidore loves the villa's antique grandeur but he won't come here in case he runs into Clio,' Jude explained with a wry smile. 'It's not my style though.'

'You surprise me,' Tansy told him sharply, angry green eyes locking to his devastatingly handsome features. 'I would've thought the medieval vibe of magnificence would have appealed to you since your ideas seem to be equally barbaric.'

Jude stiffened, his dark eyes narrowing. 'I won't argue with you when you're in this condition and the doctor's about to arrive.'

'What condition? *Raging?* How dare you think for even one moment that it was appropriate to persuade me into a pregnancy when you planned to cut and run as soon as it happened? You think that's acceptable? I don't!' she snapped furiously. 'I don't need a doctor. I need a big stick or something to thump you with!'

Jude spread lean brown hands wide in an eloquent soothing gesture that had no effect at all on his irate wife. 'You're right.'

Tansy just glared at him, eyes as bright and luminous as jewels. 'You… *You!*' Words simply failed her and with difficulty she got a grip on herself again and twisted her head away sooner than look at him. 'I really don't want to talk to you right now. To have such a clause in the agreement you had drawn up…' she condemned. 'It was callous, selfish and unfeeling to ask me to have a child with you when you planned to walk out and leave me before it was even born.'

'I assumed that you would want your life and your freedom back as I believed I would want mine…but everything's changed since then,' Jude intoned, striding back towards the bed. 'Why aren't you listening to me?'

'Go away,' Tansy mumbled wearily, not in the mood to be placated when she was faced with the knowledge that she had been behaving once again as though their marriage were normal when it was not. How could she expect a level of support she was not entitled to receive? He had not told her a single lie about what their marriage would entail.

Of course, he hadn't planned to stay with her until the baby arrived! Why would he put himself through that boring duty of care when he didn't love her or plan to remain married to her? Jude was accustomed to doing what he liked when he liked. Great wealth had given him a freedom that less fortunate people could only dream about. She had been an idiot to make any kind of assumption about their convenient marriage, and what underlined that fact more than anything was a husband who talked blithely about *renegotiating* terms with her as if they were involved in a business deal.

'Tansy?'

'You can come back when the doctor arrives to translate,' Tansy told him grudgingly. 'Otherwise I don't think we have anything more to say to each other.'

As the door closed behind Jude, Tansy patted her flat stomach guiltily, tears burning her eyes as she thought of how much she would love her baby. She questioned if she would ever tell her child the truth of how she had ended up married to Jude Alexandris. Would she lie to conserve her pride? Pretend they had fallen in love? Jude being Jude would probably insist on telling only the truth. Her lower lip wobbled at the prospect of her son or daughter looking at her with less respect and more judgement. A business deal based on money. It sounded so sleazy and yet nothing with Jude felt sleazy. Why was that? Was she simply a pushover for his compelling appeal?

A doctor arrived, middle-aged and pleasant and with sufficient English to enable her to pretty much ignore Jude, which suited her mood perfectly. He told her that fainting was not that uncommon in early pregnancy, particularly when she had been tired and struggling to deal with the heat. She stole a glance at Jude, who looked as guilty as if he had pushed her down a flight of stairs and, instead of reassuring him that it had not been his fault, she hardened her heart and watched him leave with the doctor.

The salad she had requested arrived on a tray and she clambered off the bed and went for a shower before eating. She tugged on a light robe afterwards, reluctant to get dressed again.

When she emerged again, Jude was lounging up against the foot of the tall bed, looking ridiculously beautiful in his favourite ripped jeans and a T-shirt. 'You haven't eaten anything,' he pointed out.

'I wanted a shower first,' Tansy said stiffly, averting her gaze from his riveting sensual allure. 'I shouldn't have shouted at you earlier. I shouldn't let my emotions go around you. After all, we made a business deal, not a marriage.'

Jude set his even white teeth together and flashed her a pained glance of reproach. 'That is not how I think of us being together. Our marriage is not a deal and it's got nothing to do with business.'

Tansy sat down at the table by the window and lifted her knife and fork. 'It is what it is,' she responded stonily. 'No point wrapping it up in euphemisms at this late stage. You *paid* me to marry you.'

'You married me to save Posy from an unhappy childhood. You didn't want the money for yourself. Obviously, that makes a difference.'

Tansy lifted a cool, doubting brow. 'Does it? You referred to renegotiating *terms*. That's business talk.'

'I was trying to be cool, clever. I shot myself in the foot,' Jude breathed in a driven undertone. 'I got it wrong. I get a lot of things wrong with you, but I don't really know how to tell you what I'm feeling right now...'

'Honest and simple works best for me,' Tansy told him, stabbing a fork into a piece of avocado, savouring its flavour while he studied her in growing frustration. She marvelled at the perfection of his lean bronzed features, the piercing intensity of his extraordinary eyes, and forgave herself for getting too attached to him. After all, she was only human.

Jude straightened his broad shoulders and rose to

his full height. '*Thee mou*... I fell in love with you! I wasn't expecting it and I didn't immediately recognise it, so I messed up everything. I didn't even realise how I had changed until you began referring to us getting a divorce and it bothered me. I didn't want the clock to start ticking on a separation either.'

Her fork fell out of her nerveless hand with a clatter. 'You f-fell in *love* with me?' she stammered in disbelief.

'Understandably, I don't *want* a separation or a divorce now but there is no allowance for a change of heart in the terms of our marriage agreement. Nobody, least of all me, foresaw this development and, of course, it alters everything between us. I need you to give me the chance to prove that this can be a real marriage.'

Tansy had stopped breathing as well as eating. 'A real marriage,' she echoed weakly.

'I can see this has been a shock to you as well,' Jude commented, hunkering down beside her to settle dark golden eyes on her transfixed face. 'You'll need time to think about this.'

'Don't try and wriggle out of it again,' Tansy whispered with dancing eyes. 'You said you loved me… I want to hear the proof.'

'How do you prove something like that?' Jude groaned. 'The practical marriage I originally intended would exclude almost everything we have done together. I tell you everything. I've told you stuff I've never told another living soul. I feel very comfortable with you in every situation. You're very grounded, very calm and thoughtful. I appreciate that because I'm more volatile and impulsive. I think we are a very good match but whether we are or not doesn't matter because, at the end of the day, I don't want to go on living if I haven't got you beside me...'

Tansy dug her hands into his T-shirt and dragged him closer, almost knocking him off balance. 'Be warned. I won't *let* you live without me. I'm hopelessly in love with you but I'm terrified this is all some insane misunderstanding and any minute now I'm going to wake up and realise it was all just a dream!'

Jude's dark golden eyes blazed like molten metal as he vaulted upright and lifted her up out of her chair. 'It's not a dream. I was just a little too slow to recognise how I felt about you. There's been no special woman in my life since Althea and what I feel for you is much deeper than anything I *ever* felt for her.'

'Honestly?' she pressed as he brought her down on the bed and kissed her breathless.

'That was all first love, hurt pride and ego.'

'I still don't understand why Althea let you down in the first place,' Tansy admitted ruefully.

'We were each other's *first*,' Jude murmured. 'Even though we had no problems in that department, she was determined to try sex with someone else as a comparison.'

'Oh...' Tansy's green eyes had rounded in surprise at that information.

'So...' Jude purred, staring down at her with a new tenderness glowing in his beautiful eyes and a dazzling smile tilting his lips. 'You will have to content yourself to never ever having a comparison.'

'I'm very attached to what I got first time around,'

Tansy confided as she struggled to extract him from his T-shirt. 'In fact, so keen am I that I just enjoy try, try, trying you again.'

Wicked amusement lit his amazing eyes. 'I love you so much,' he husked, claiming her parted lips again in a passionate kiss.

The robe fell open, exposing pale silky skin, and Jude took full advantage. Both salad and conversation were forgotten as the fever of desire took over and drew added fire from the depth of their new attachment. Passion and excitement combined until Tansy finally flopped back against the pillows and gazed at Jude with loving tenderness in her eyes.

'Why on earth did you talk about renegotiating terms when you *loved* me?' she demanded without comprehension.

'When you told me you were pregnant I panicked because I assumed that you would also be thinking of that clause in our prenup and you had already mentioned the prospect of us getting a divorce,' Jude reminded her. 'I honestly believed that you might already be planning to walk out on our marriage.'

'Idiot!' Tansy scolded, running gentle fingers along his strong stubbled jawline. 'You were the guy who warned me not to get too attached—'

'When I was already insanely attached to you…only I hadn't put a label on those feelings.' Jude flung his head back with a sigh, skimming narrowed dark golden eyes to her. 'It wasn't until you said this morning that you were pregnant that I realised why I was so happy with you.'

'And then you decided you needed to renegotiate.' Tansy grimaced.

'Not my most shining moment. But after getting to know Posy, I am incredibly excited about our baby,' he confided, warming that cold spot that his silence had inflicted earlier that day. 'I love her too…you know that, don't you?'

'There's a lot of love in the air right now.'

'But it was you who taught me to love again. Until I met you, I was so closed off from my emotions that I couldn't even see Isidore's affection for me,' he confided guiltily. 'I misinterpreted everything he did. I saw my mother's pain and blamed Isidore for it, but it wasn't his fault that my father was continually unfaithful to Clio, and I can understand that at the end of the day he chose to support his son, only he shouldn't have been so cruel about it.'

'She's your mother and she did suffer at their hands. Your father treated her badly and her experiences with him are still influencing her now. There's not much you can do about that.' Tansy sighed. 'But, thankfully, Isidore looks spry enough to be around for many years more and you still have the chance to show him that you care.'

'He really likes you. When he hears about the baby, you'll be the eighth wonder of the world!' Jude teased.

'I'm more worried about keeping Posy with us,' she admitted anxiously.

Cradling her tenderly in his arms, Jude gazed down at her with an air of satisfaction. 'I have good news on that front…although it's not good for your stepfather.

I received a call about him late last night and another confirming his situation only an hour ago.'

Tansy stared at him. 'Calls from whom?'

'His former employers, my UK legal team. Apparently, Hetherington was helping himself to money from clients' accounts at the legal firm. That's why they laid him off—they needed time to bring in a forensic accountant to investigate. They have concrete proof now and he's been charged with theft. He'll go to prison,' he forecast grimly.

Shaken by those facts, Tansy swallowed hard. 'Prison? My goodness, Calvin is not going to like that.'

'He was in a position of trust. That kind of crime is severely punished.'

Tansy nodded, shaken to think of Calvin in a prison cell and so grateful that her little sister had been safely removed from the fallout of such a crisis.

'If he agrees to surrender his parental rights to Posy, I will offer him the services of the best criminal defence lawyer in the UK,' Jude told her. 'I think he'll go for it. After all, he's not interested in his daughter and doesn't want the responsibility for her. The lawyer won't be able to get him off the charges, but he may well be able to win him a shorter sentence.'

'Let's hope he accepts your offer,' Tansy murmured heavily. 'You know I never liked him, but I'm shocked that he was actually stealing.'

'I bet you made all sorts of allowances for him because your mother loved him. You have too much heart, but I'm not about to complain when you managed to fall in love with me even though I was behaving like a four-letter word of a guy.'

'I want to record that admission and use it against you in the future,' Tansy confided with eyes brimming with laughter as she laced her fingers in his ruffled black curls and drew him down to her again.

'You do realise that I'm never ever letting you go?'

'Cuts both ways,' Tansy warned cheerfully.

'How could I not love a woman who makes me this happy?' Jude purred, stretching against her, lithe and lazy, and pulling her close. 'You're my personal gift of sunshine and I love you.'

The same happiness swelled inside Tansy, assuaging all fear and insecurity. He loved her. He loved Posy and hadn't she seen that love in action? And he would love their baby as well. Contentment settled over her as she closed her arms round him, full of joy and love and possessiveness and no longer afraid of what tomorrow would bring.

EPILOGUE

FOUR YEARS LATER, Tansy sat on the beach on Rhodes, enjoying the sunshine while Posy and her little brother, Bay, built a sandcastle. Posy chattered incessantly, telling Bay what to do, groaning when his foot knocked a carefully built wall flying. Bay's mouth compressed and he loosed a shout of frustration, kneeling down and striving to rebuild what he had ruined.

'Let him have a go,' Tansy urged Posy before she could take over and do it for him.

'He can't do it,' Posy muttered in a long-suffering tone.

Tansy watched without surprise as her son carefully, clumsily patted the wall back into place. It was neither so neat nor so tall a wall as it had been, but it was a good effort for so young a child. He had phenomenal concentration for a toddler, and he preferred to build rather than destroy. Satisfied, he stepped back, watching Posy stick the plastic flag on top, and he beamed.

'Daddy see,' he said with decision.

Hearing voices, Tansy got up from the lounger she was on. She was slow because she was five months into her second pregnancy. Pulling on a beach dress, she heard the children yell, 'Pappi!' in excitement and race off to greet Isidore, who could always be depended on to visit with toys and treats.

Kerry, who had stayed in their employ, began shepherding the children back to the castle, but Bay was clinging like a leech to his father's leg, determined that Jude should first admire his castle.

The little boy looked very like his father, but he had Tansy's streaky light hair, though it was curly rather than wavy. Jude grinned at Tansy and performed the official sandcastle inspection for the kids, making acceptable noises of admiration. Isidore swept up Posy, who was chattering away to him.

Since Tansy and Jude had settled into a more permanent home in the UK, Isidore had become a frequent visitor. He loved to see his great-grandson and he did not make a difference between Bay and Posy, which had won over Tansy to his side. Jude had, however, had some difficult conversations with his grandfather about his mother and Isidore had acknowledged the part he had played in Clio's breakdown, admitting that his punitive approach and his unhesitating support of his son had gone too far.

He had made a magnificent cash gift to the Villa Bardani gardens in an act of contrition but Clio had had to be persuaded to accept it. Jude and Tansy visited Clio in Italy, but she had yet to visit them because she refused to leave her garden. While fences were gradually being mended and a new spirit of openness was growing in the family, they had yet to persuade Clio and

Isidore to occupy the same room at a family gathering. Even so, Clio had made tentative moves towards being friendlier with Tansy, and the older woman was unreservedly fond of her grandson, Bay. These days Jude was a little more relaxed in his mother's company and she uttered fewer dire warnings about the likelihood of his continuing fidelity. Tansy was hoping that, for Clio, the past was finally staying in the past.

Her stepfather was still in prison. He had received a heavy sentence for his crimes in spite of the excellent defence that his lawyer had made for him in court. That he had embezzled the funds of a disabled client had counted heavily against him. He had, however, surrendered his paternal rights over his daughter and, eighteen months after his court case, Jude and Tansy had become Posy's adoptive parents.

'We're dining on the yacht tonight, birthday girl,' Jude reminded Tansy. 'And you're all sunburned and covered in sand.'

It was her twenty-seventh birthday. Tansy lowered her lashes and then looked up at the husband she adored with gleaming green eyes of innocence. 'I suppose you'll have to harass me into the shower. Maybe you should have married a more decorative woman, who makes more effort.'

'But would she be as hot and willing in the shower with me?' Jude husked in her ear.

Tansy went red. 'Who can tell?'

'I can,' Jude purred, running a possessive hand down her slender spine as Isidore, the nanny and the children disappeared into the castle. 'I choose the sex bomb every time.'

'I don't look like one of those right now,' Tansy lamented. 'I'm all tummy—'

'That's my baby in there…that's wonderfully sexy,' Jude insisted, pausing on the path to crush her ripe pink mouth under his, tugging her up against his lean, powerful body and sending her temperature rocketing sky-high.

In the bedroom he presented her with an eternity ring. 'Eternity won't be long enough for me with you,' he swore.

Giggling helplessly at that high-flown assurance, Tansy headed for the bathroom, only to be scooped off her feet and taken there even quicker than her own feet could have carried her. Off came the beach wrap and the bikini beneath. Jude knelt at her feet, nuzzling against her swollen stomach while his deft and clever fingers made her writhe and gasp.

'We're heading out on a moonlight cruise, special dinner, all that jazz,' he told her thickly as she moaned at the zenith of her climax and went limp against him. 'I'm making you pay in advance in case you fall asleep early on me.'

'Took a nap this afternoon. I love you,' she whispered contentedly against his shoulder.

'And I adore you, Mrs Alexandris. You're the sun at the centre of my world,' Jude swore with passionate certainty.

* * * * *

THE MAN SHE SHOULD HAVE MARRIED

LOUISE FULLER

To Lori. I miss you. x

CHAPTER ONE

SMOOTHING HER LONG, dark blond hair away from her face, Nia Elgin took a deep breath and followed Stephen, the butler, through the wood-panelled hallway of her family home, Lamington Hall.

Except the beautiful Georgian manor house wasn't her home right now.

For the next year at least, she would be living in the gardener's cottage along the drive.

And Lamington was being rented out to Tom and Diane Drummond, an American couple who were taking a sabbatical in Scotland to research Tom's ancestral roots.

This evening was her first visit to the house since the Drummonds had moved in a week ago, and it felt strange walking past the family portraits and suits of armour as a visitor.

But that wasn't the reason her heart was in her mouth.

As Stephen's fingers rested on the door handle, she took another breath, forcing herself to stay calm, trying to prepare for what lay on the other side of the door.

Not what, but who.

Her heart lurched.

Farlan Wilder.

Even now, she could still picture the first time they'd met.

He had been twenty-two, three years older than her, with eyes the exact same green as summer bracken and a smile that had made Morse code messages of excitement beat through her body.

It had been love at first sight, at first touch, at first everything—swift and as certain as a swallow returning home from its wintering grounds in spring.

And he had loved her right back, just like the heroes in her favourite books.

That year, the summer of their love, time had slowed, days had lengthened and the warm, lazy heat had spilled through September, nudging into the first few days of October.

Six months and two days after they'd met Farlan had proposed. She'd accepted, but they'd decided to go travelling first.

Her breath burned her chest.

And then, just as swiftly, it had been over.

Ended by her.

And, just like the swallows, he had upped and left the cool, inhospitable shores of Scotland for a new life in another country.

She shivered.

The fact that he was back in Scotland at all made her want to reach past Stephen and clutch the door handle for balance.

But the fact that he was here, at Lamington, was the cruellest cut of all.

Her stomach dipped with a desperate, panicky plunge, just as it had been doing ever since Tom and Diane had invited her to join them for Burns Night supper and she had stupidly agreed to join them.

Would she mind awfully if there was one extra for dinner? Tom had asked, and of course she had said no without thinking.

'It's a big deal for us, him coming. He wasn't even supposed to be getting here until next week,' Tom said slowly. 'You see, he hates Burns Night.'

She hadn't known who 'he' was then, and—incredibly—she hadn't cared.

Tom had shaken his head, as though not able to believe what he was saying. 'Something to do with a woman, I think. But I told him, you can't hate Burns Night, my boy, not if you're a Scotsman.'

The look of outrage on his face had made her burst out laughing. 'So why did he change his mind?' she'd asked.

He'd grinned. 'I played my trump card.'

'And what was that?'

'*You.*' Tom had grinned again. 'Changed his mind real quick when I told him Lady Antonia Elgin was going to be here. Apparently, you and he crossed paths once a few years ago. Must have made quite an impression on him.' He'd winked. 'I've gotta say I was surprised. I've never known anything or anyone change Farlan's mind before, and that's a fact.'

He had carried on talking, but she hadn't been able to hear what he was saying. Her heartbeat had swallowed up his words.

Inside her head, her thoughts had started to unravel.

It must be a coincidence.

It couldn't be Farlan—not *her* Farlan.

But apparently it was.

She glanced at Stephen's back.

Her stomach knotted. If only she could just turn and run away, hide in the bothy on the estate, where she had always gone as a child to escape her parents' incessant demands.

Or, better still, if she could just rewind, smile apologetically to the Drummonds and say, *How kind, but unfortunately I have other plans.*

But she could neither change her character nor turn back time, so she was just going to have to get through it.

Stephen opened the door, and as she followed him through her heart stopped and for a few agonising half-seconds she scanned the room.

But it was only Tom and Diane, turning to her and smiling.

She forced herself to walk forward as Tom held out his arms in welcome.

'Good evening, Lady Antonia—or should I say *fáilte*?'

She smiled. Whatever her feelings about seeing Farlan again, Tom and Diane must not be made aware of them. Not when they clearly knew nothing about their past relationship.

But what about Farlan?

How was he going to react?

It was a question that had been playing on a loop inside her head. And she was still no closer to answering it.

'Farlan will be down in a minute,' Diane said, her face softening. 'He only arrived in Scotland at lunchtime.'

'Got his own private jet.' Tom grinned. 'And then he flew himself down in a helicopter. Landed right out back.'

She kept smiling somehow. 'Really? That's amazing.'

Tom handed her a glass of champagne. 'To a Burns Night to remember. *Slàinte mhath*.'

She raised her glass mechanically, then took a deep drink.

Part of her couldn't believe this was happening. She'd have sworn this house was the last place on earth Farlan would ever want to visit again. And she knew that because he'd told her.

Her heart felt like a crushing weight in her chest as she remembered that last terrible stilted telephone conversation.

Except the term 'conversation' implied an exchange of ideas and views, and she had been the only one doing the talking, trying to apologise, to explain, pleading with him to understand.

He hadn't spoken until right at the end, when he'd told her that she was a fraud, a coward and a snob, and that she was less than nothing to him now.

His silent anger had hurt; the ice in his voice had hurt more.

But not as much as the one-note, accusatory disconnection tone when he'd hung up on her.

With an effort, she dragged her mind back into the present. *'Slàinte mhath,'* she repeated.

Tom grinned. 'I can't tell you how happy it makes me, Lady Antonia, to finally say those words in the land of my forefathers and in your beautiful home.'

'It's *your* beautiful home tonight,' Nia protested. 'And please call me Nia. Being called Lady Antonia makes me feel like I'm about to open a fête.'

He roared with laughter. 'Nia it is, then.' He glanced at her glass. 'Now, let me top you up—we've got some celebrating to do.'

Panic was prickling beneath her ribs.

She didn't feel like celebrating.

But she was a guest, and she could almost hear her mother's smooth, polished voice telling her that a guest should always be 'pleasant and accommodating.' Tilting her glass, she let Tom refill it with champagne, his undisguised happiness making her smile properly.

'Tom, you look magnificent. You know, being an Elgin, I shouldn't really admit this, but the Drummond tartan has always been one of my favourites.'

It was true. The red and green weave was so gutsy and vibrant, so defiantly and unapologetically proud of its clan roots.

In contrast, the Elgin tartan of brown and cream seemed inhibited—timid, almost.

But perhaps, like dogs and their owners, a tartan reflected the character of the person wearing it. Farlan would certainly think so, she thought dully.

Obviously pleased, Tom gave a mock bow. 'It is a fine tartan, and it looks particularly attractive on my beautiful wife.'

Tom pulled Diane closer, planting a kiss on her lips as he did so.

Such easy, open displays of affection were rare in this house. In fact, Nia couldn't remember the last time anyone had held her close or kissed her.

She felt her face start to tingle.

That was a lie.

She could remember exactly when she had been held, and how she had been kissed. More importantly, she could remember who had been doing the holding and the kissing.

Only she couldn't think about that now.

It would hurt too much to have the past and the present in the same headspace, and so, pushing the memory back into the darkest, most remote corner of her brain; she said quickly, 'I agree. You look amazing, Diane.'

Diane laughed. 'I do feel rather regal.' Her face softened. 'But you, my dear, are quite, quite lovely.'

Glancing down at her sleek one-shouldered black dress, Nia felt a blush creep up over her skin.

Compliments were also in scarce supply in her daily life.

She knew that she was a good boss, and her staff liked her, but it was her job to offer praise and encouragement, not theirs.

And although her parents loved her, they both had that tendency common in the spoiled and wealthy to expect perfection and focus on the tiniest of flaws.

Without any siblings to divert their focus, being Lady Antonia Elgin was both a privilege and a burden. It had been lovely growing up surrounded by Old Masters, and being able to ride across the estate on her pony, but there were so many expectations and responsibilities to shoulder.

She felt her throat tighten. It was only after she'd met Farlan that it had involved making sacrifices too. He was the one person who had made her feel she was special, and she had let him go. Actually, she had pushed him away.

The glass felt suddenly slippery in her hand, and she tightened her grip. 'Thank you, I haven't got dressed up in a while so it's a real treat.'

Basically, her social life consisted of an occasional lunch with girlfriends and those events in the social calendar that were absolutely unavoidable.

'Well, it was worth the wait,' Diane said gently. 'And what a beautiful brooch.' She stared admiringly at the striking thistle-shaped diamond and amethyst brooch that was holding Nia's sash in place. 'Is it a family heirloom?'

Nia nodded. It was one of the few pieces she hadn't been forced to sell.

'It was my great-grandmother's. My mother gave it to me on my eighteenth birthday.'

Once upon a time her beauty had pleased her mother. Now, though, her delicate features and soft brown eyes seemed mostly to remind the Countess of Brechin of her daughter's failure to find a suitable husband.

Diane sighed. 'It's perfect. You're perfect—' She glanced over Nia's shoulder, her eyes lighting up. 'Don't you think so, Farlan?'

Nia felt her whole body turn to stone. The familiar details of the drawing room spun around her as if she were on a fairground ride.

Earlier she had wanted the evening to be over as quickly as possible. Now she wanted the floor to open and swallow her whole.

Frozen to the spot, she watched Farlan Wilder walk across the room, her pulse slamming in her throat.

It was seven years since he had left Scotland. Seven years of doubt and loneliness. And regret.

She had never expected to see him again.

But now he was back, and how things had changed.

When they'd met, outside a pub at the Edinburgh Festival, she had been out with friends, enjoying a gap year before taking up a place at Oxford to study history.

Seeing him that first time had made her shake inside. He'd been cool, cocky, outrageously flirty and heart-stoppingly beautiful. An art school dropout and wannabe film-maker with nothing to his name. No money, no family and no belongings. Just raw, untried talent, an unshakable self-belief and plans and promises aplenty.

Her throat tightened. Plans that had worked out just as he had promised.

Not only was he a *bona fide* film director now, he had already won multiple awards, and his latest movie had been *the* blockbuster of last summer.

And it showed, she thought, in the casual confidence of his walk.

The cockiness of youth had shifted into an unmistakable authority that came along with crossing an ocean in economy class and returning on a private jet.

She watched, her smile pasted to her face, as he grabbed a tulip-shaped glass of champagne and kissed Diane on the cheek.

'She certainly is quite something,' he said coolly.

He shifted his weight and, expecting him to lean forward and kiss her too, she braced herself. But instead he held out his hand, the dull metal of his expensive Swiss watch glinting in the firelight.

At the touch of his fingers his eyes met hers and a burst of quicksilver darted through her veins.

She had thought about this moment so many times—

dreamed about it, conjured up almost this exact same scenario.

She would turn to face him, and he would be angry, but not with the ice-cold fury of that last conversation.

In her imagination, his anger was hot and spilling over with the passion of so many wasted years apart so that within seconds they were both crying and he was pulling her close and she was kissing him—

As she stared at him, for a few half-seconds she actually thought she might still be asleep and it was all just a dream.

But then he lifted his chin and, gazing into his narrowed green eyes, she knew with breath-crushing certainty both that she was awake and that nothing had changed.

Farlan hated her.

Nia couldn't move. Her body, her limbs, seemed to have stopped working, and her ribs seemed suddenly to have shrunk.

She had thought herself prepared for this.

But too late she realised that nothing could have prepared her for this tumultuous rush of feelings, none of which she could reveal as her eyes met his.

He might have become a big shot in Hollywood, but he hadn't changed much physically—or if he had it was for the better.

Seven years ago he had been a beautiful boy, with a scruffy mohawk and a heart-splitting smile. Now he was a wildly attractive man.

Yes, he was, she thought, her stomach clenching in a sharp, unbidden response.

He wasn't wearing a kilt, or even a hint of tartan. Instead he had chosen to wear a snow-white shirt and dark grey trousers, and yet his conventional clothing only seemed to emphasise his extraordinary bewitching beauty.

The leanness of youth had matured into broad shoulders, and the dark mohawk had been replaced by a buzzcut and a shadow of stubble that showed off the perfectly contoured planes of his cheekbones and jaw.

But he was no longer smiling.

Or at least not for her, she thought, her heart contracting as he withdrew his hand and switched his gaze to Diane, his mouth curving upwards.

'Sorry I'm late, Dee. My head's still back in LA. With my razor.'

He ran his hand over his stubbled jawline, smiling crookedly, and for a moment Nia couldn't breathe, couldn't think. All she wanted to do was reach out and touch his face, stroke it like she'd used to.

He had been like a cat that way, lying on the sofa with his head in her lap, hitching his chin to push up against her hand.

Her head was spinning, her heart crumbling, but if Diane sensed the flickering undercurrent of hostility in the room she gave no sign of it.

'Thank you for coming, darling boy.' She smiled up at him. 'I know this isn't your favourite night of the year so I really appreciate it, and Tom does too.'

'It's the least I can do.' Farlan smiled back at her. 'You were there for me when I needed you. I was pretty hard work back then, but you never pushed me away.'

Nia felt her whole body tense as his eyes locked with hers.

'Most people don't have your heart, Dee. They don't have the courage to trust their own judgement.'

His face was blank of expression, his voice too, but his eyes were the same dark forbidding green as the pine forests that edged the estate.

'Well, you've been there for us too.' She glanced at Nia. 'It's thanks to Farlan we're standing here right now—isn't it, Tom?'

Clapping his hand on Farlan's shoulder, Tom nodded.

'We've been talking about it for years, but something always got in the way. Would have been the same this time only he got mad. Told us we needed to make a decision and stick to it. That's how he got himself all those awards. It's not just about having a vision. My boy doesn't falter.' He winked at Nia. 'I bet you knew he was going to go all the way to the top.'

Farlan's gaze scraped against her skin like sandpaper.

'Yes, I mean… I didn't—' she began, but Farlan interrupted her.

'I'm not sure I made that big an impact on Lady Antonia. I was just a farm boy—a stupid, naive kid. Of course I've grown up a lot since then.'

His pointed use of her title made swallowing difficult. 'I remember you perfectly,' she said quietly.

It was like drowning. She could see every single moment of her life with him playing out on fast forward in front of her eyes.

'When we met. How we met. You were making a film about the Fringe,' she said.

He smiled at her now, but it was a smile that stopped at his mouth. There was no corresponding warmth in his eyes. It was just a consequence of muscles moving beneath the skin.

'Not about the shows. It was the performers that interested me.'

His eyes met hers, the green irises steady and implacable.

'All the sacrifices they made. I wanted to document that commitment. Show people what they could achieve if they believed in themselves and others.'

I did believe in you, she wanted to say.

But before she had a chance to open her mouth, Diane tapped Tom on the arm.

'We need to call Isla and Jack.' She turned to Nia. 'We

usually have a Burns Night supper with our Scottish friends back home, and we said we'd call them and show them how it's done in the old country.'

Still flustered from her showdown with Farlan, Nia stared at her blankly. 'Show them…?'

Pulling herself together, she realised what Diane was asking.

'You might have to go to the kitchen to make a video call. The internet never really works in this part of the house—'

'The kitchen?' Diane hesitated. 'Oh, we don't want to leave you two—'

'Just go, Dee.'

Farlan was smiling, but there could be no mistaking the authority in his voice. Nia could almost picture him behind the camera on set, his all-seeing gaze directing every line, every glance.

'You don't need to worry.'

She tensed as his gaze flicked towards her face, his green eyes hardening.

'I'll take care of Lady Antonia.'

As the door closed behind them there was a beat of silence. Glancing at Nia's face, Farlan thought she'd flinched. Then again, it might just have been the flicker of the candlelight, but a part of him would have liked to know that she was feeling even just a fraction of his pain. A pain that seeing her had resurrected with a speed and sharpness that alarmed him.

He tried to calm his mind. Only that was hard to do when she was so close. Close enough to see the flecks of gold in her light brown eyes and the pulse pushing frantically against the smooth, pale skin of her throat.

Maybe he'd be doing better with it if it hadn't been so sudden. Not the ancestry stuff—Tom and Diane had been talking about that for ever—but coming here, to this particular house.

When Tom had first told him that they had rented Lamington Hall he had actually thought he'd misheard. That there was another Lamington Hall, a different one, that had nothing to do with the Elgin family.

Or more specifically with Nia.

Of course when finally he'd accepted that it was *that* Lamington, it had felt like a bad and not especially funny joke, and he had cursed himself for having not paid more attention to the Drummonds' whole house-hunting business.

His breathing stalled in his throat, and suddenly he had that too-big feeling in his chest—the one that made him sometimes wake up with his nails biting into the palms of his hands.

Only what difference would knowing have made really?

Even without the memory of what had happened with Nia, Scotland was still such a raw wound.

Tom and Diane had helped open doors for him in the States, even as they'd opened their hearts to him, but he had held back so much from them about his life, his past.

Even now, after all these years, the thought of telling them everything made his stomach tense.

They had met by chance. Their car had broken down and he'd stopped to help. Of course Tom had noticed his Scottish accent right away and instantly invited him over for a drink.

Drinks had turned into dinner, and soon he had been dropping round all the time.

And then Diane had offered him a room.

Even though he'd turned her down, then spent months avoiding them, they had never faltered in their friendship. It was only after spending yet another night on their sofa he'd realised that he'd already crossed the line.

But there were still so many locked rooms inside his head. So many doors that needed to remain closed.

Including the one at Lamington.

His shoulders tensed. It had simply never occurred to him that Nia would leave her home, much less rent it out to strangers. Clearly her father's need for a warmer climate had forced her hand, made some unwanted but necessary changes.

He glanced over at her set, pale face. Nia hadn't changed, though. She was still the most beautiful woman he had ever seen.

Nothing—no amount of time—could change the delicate bone structure beneath the smooth, flawless skin or thin that full, soft pink mouth.

His eyes snagged on the curve of her lower lip, his body tightening without warning as he remembered the feel of her mouth on his, the way she had moved against him—

Blanking his mind to the Nia of seven years ago, he forced himself to look at the woman standing in front of him.

He was wrong. She had changed; she'd lost weight. A little too much, in fact, he thought critically, wanting, needing, to have that small victory. And it wasn't just her weight. Her light brown eyes had lost their sparkle.

Aged nineteen, with her long dark blond hair falling in front of her face and that pale peach-soft skin, she had looked like a goddess or a princess in a fairy tale.

Sounded like one too.

It had been one of their shared jokes that he had been born in London but had a broad Aberdonian accent, whereas Nia—thanks to her expensive boarding school in Berkshire—spoke with a kind of smooth drawl that held no trace of her Scottish upbringing.

The chill in his stomach began seeping through his body. Her voice wasn't the only misleading thing about her.

He had thought she loved him without reservation. She had told him that she did.

And yet when it had come down to choosing between him and a bunch of bricks and beams she had left him sitting at the train station like an unwanted suitcase.

'So what happened?'

She glanced up at him. A flush of colour crept over her cheeks and her eyes widened with shock, or maybe confusion. 'What do you mean?'

'This…' he gazed slowly round the room '…was once so very important to you.'

It was why she had broken up with him. And the other side of that statement, the unspoken truth, was that he hadn't been important enough for her to walk away, to leave Lamington behind.

'So what changed?' he asked. 'Why are you playing house down the drive?'

This time there was no mistaking the swift, startled flinch in her eyes, and a part of him hated it that he had caused that flicker of pain. But another part—the part that had never fully forgotten or forgiven the pain she'd caused him—felt nothing.

She shook her head. 'I'm not playing at anything.'

His chest felt suddenly too tight. She sounded as shaken as he felt. And he knew it wasn't just his accusation. He knew she was feeling the shock of this encounter just as much as he was.

'You played me.' His voice cut through the air like a blade. 'You made me think it was real.' She had made him care and hope and believe. 'So what was I? A gap year adventure? A way to shake up your family a little?'

'No, that's not true.'

'Really?' He rolled his eyes. 'You know, I might have believed that. *Once upon a time.*' The tension in his voice was making his accent more pronounced. He could hear the influx of glottal stops, the rolled 'R's. 'But guess what, Lady Antonia? I don't believe in fairy tales any more.'

'It's not a fairy tale.' Her voice was fraying. 'It's the truth.'

'Is that what you tell yourself?' He shook his head.

She had gone to talk to her parents. Left him standing in the kitchen like some delivery boy.

His heart twisted. He should have known then how it was going to go.

But he had loved her, trusted her—

Even at that distance it had stung, hearing her father say that she would lose her inheritance if she went ahead and married him. But not as much as when she had broken up with him the following day over the phone.

The unrelenting misery of those hours swept over him, the shock of her betrayal as raw and intense as it had been on the day.

'You used me, Lady Antonia, and then you dumped me.'

Lead was filling his lungs. That first year away from her had nearly broken him. And the worst of it was, he had been there before. A different time, a different kitchen, but the same old story. And yet even though he had heard the thin, shrill whistle of the missile and known what it meant, he still hadn't seen it coming.

He'd thought Nia was different—special. And he'd been so smitten with her that he'd ignored both the obvious and the lessons of the past.

Idiot that he was, he had actually believed that he was special to her.

'Your parents thought you might follow your heart. They needn't have worried. You don't have a heart, do you, Lady Antonia? Plenty of pride, but no heart.'

'Just saying things doesn't make them true.'

Her voice was still shaking, but maybe with anger now, and that was good. Anger was easier to fight. It made it easier for him not to care about the way she was bracing her shoulders.

'Oh, I know that—thanks to you. How about "I love you, Farlan. I want to be with you." Or maybe, "Wait for me at the station." Yeah, you're good at saying things that aren't true.'

'I was nineteen.'

Her cheeks were flushed, but the rest of her face was paler than the marble statues in the garden outside.

His breath caught.

It had been close to freezing that night at the station. He had sat there for three hours. He had called her maybe thirty times.

When, finally, she had called back, he had known even before she'd started talking that it was over.

The Scottish were supposed to have over a hundred words for different kinds of rain. He knew from experience that there were almost as many kinds of silence.

There was the silence of wonder.

The silence of fear.

And the silence just before that moment when the woman you love tells you she doesn't want to be with you any more.

He could still hear it now, inside his head, whenever he was with a beautiful woman—that flutter of hesitation. It would start small, but it always ended up swallowing him whole, and he was sick and tired of it.

Life was good—most of his life anyway. He had friends, more money than he could spend, a career he loved. And Tom and Diane.

Even now their generosity and faith both astonished and scared him. He had been so angry, so wary when they'd first met, but they had persisted.

And that, in part, was why he was here. To try and repay them for giving him what his own flesh and blood had failed to.

A home.

Not grudgingly, or reluctantly, or as some kind of temporary fix, but a real home.

They had done so much for him, and he had told them what he could bear to share. But nothing about Nia. Not even her name. It hurt too much—and, besides, they couldn't fix everything.

He couldn't either, apparently, judging by his complete lack of any love life.

Sex, yes. But love…

Tom and Diane were right.

He was ready. He wanted what they had. Only the memory of that last conversation with Nia still haunted him.

It was certainly the reason he avoided Burns Night. But then Tom had told him on the phone that Lady Antonia Elgin was joining them for supper and he'd felt that fate was giving him a chance to put the past to rest.

It was why he'd flown five thousand miles.

Only he wasn't going to share that fact with Nia.

He shrugged. 'And now you're twenty-six.' His eyes locked with hers. 'How are you finding living in the gardener's cottage?'

She opened her mouth to reply, but as she started to speak, the door opened.

'I am so sorry.' Diane hurried in. 'I didn't mean for that to take so long but they were so excited to see everything. Anyway—' She broke off, her eyes shining with excitement, as from somewhere in the house a distant melancholy wailing swelled up. 'I think we're ready to eat.'

CHAPTER TWO

As the piper marched slowly into the room, his fingers moving deftly over the chanter of the bagpipes, Nia managed to keep smiling. But inside, she was reeling at Farlan's words.

Given how it had ended between them, she had expected him to be distant with her. But the fact that he had been willing to see her at all had given her hope that time might have diminished his hostility.

She'd been wrong.

His attack had been so swift, so bitter, so unfair, it had left her breathless.

Tom held out his arm. 'Would you do me the honour, Nia?'

She nodded mechanically. 'Of course.'

Diane and Farlan followed them, and she was so conscious that he was there, behind her, that she forgot where they were going.

They stood behind their chairs and she felt a buzzing in her ears as she saw that she was seated opposite him. Feeling slightly sick, she waited as the piper finished playing, and then joined in the applause round the table.

'Great job.' Tom was grinning like a small boy. Turning round, he shook hands with the piper. 'You think maybe you could give me a couple of lessons?'

Nia barely heard the reply. She was too busy trying to make sure that her face was giving away none of the feelings that were turning her inside out.

It should be easy—she had lived most of her life hiding her thoughts from her parents—but Farlan had been the first person to bother looking beneath the surface. He had made it easy for her to talk, for her to be herself. And that was why having to close herself off to him had been so hard, and hurt so much.

Tom solemnly read the Selkirk Grace, and then it was time to eat.

The meal started with a traditional cock-a-leekie soup.

'That is the best darn soup I've ever eaten,' Tom said, laying down his spoon.

Nia nodded. 'I don't know anyone else who can turn a chicken and some vegetables into something so sublime. Molly calls herself a cook, but I actually think she's an alchemist.'

Farlan leaned back in his chair, his green eyes glittering in the candlelight.

'That probably says more about you than her,' he said softly.

'What do you mean?' Her face felt warm and she knew that her cheeks were flushed.

'Look at all of this.' He gestured towards the gleaming cutlery. 'Everything you own is gilded, Lady Antonia. Why should the food you eat be any different?'

His eyes locked onto hers and she felt ice tiptoe down her spine.

'You more than anyone should know that there's no place for base metals at Lamington,' he added.

He was smiling, so that it looked and sounded as if he was teasing her, but she could hear the edge in the voice.

Her mouth was bone-dry. 'I just meant that in my opinion Molly is modest about her talents.'

'In your opinion?' He held her gaze. 'It's good to know you have one.'

She swallowed past the lump in her throat as he turned towards Diane and began asking about the house.

After that he avoided speaking to her directly. Not that he made it obvious. In fact, he was so subtle about it she was pretty sure Tom and Diane hadn't actually noticed.

Somehow when he spoke he made it seem as though he was including all of them in his stories and jokes, expertly directing the flow of conversation so that she was simply required to nod and smile.

It might feel organic to everyone else, but she knew he was pulling the strings, that he had already planned this scene in his mind, and now it was just playing out under his critical green gaze.

Probably that was why he was such a successful director.

As if on cue, the piper returned to a roar of approval from Tom, and this time he was followed by Molly, carrying the haggis on a silver-gilt platter.

As the host, it was Tom's duty to address the haggis, and his chest was swelling with such obvious pride and emotion that Nia felt tears well in her eyes.

Soon it would be over.

And afterwards there would be no risk of them ever having to meet again, she told herself. Farlan would make sure of that.

The meal was excellent. Crisp pan haggerty, creamy *neeps* and *skirlie.*

The nutty, toasty stuffing wasn't traditionally served on Burns Night, but Molly knew it was Nia's favourite. Only tonight it might as well have been sawdust.

'I'm guessing this is a big night for your family, Nia,' Diane said, pouring some whisky cream sauce over the haggis. 'You must have a whole bunch of traditions.'

Did having your heart broken count as a tradition?

Nia couldn't look at Farlan. Instead, she smiled across

the table at Diane, hoping the misery in her heart wasn't visible on her face.

'Before I went to boarding school it was like having a second Christmas. It was so exciting. All the staff used to come to Lamington in the afternoon, and then my parents had a big party in the evening for their friends.'

But for the last seven years there had been nothing exciting about Burns Night. Instead, everything from the first champagne cork popping to the final chord on the bagpipes was just a tortuous reminder of all the what-might-have-beens in her life.

It was the one day in the year she wanted to be anywhere but Lamington. Only not being there was impossible, for it would mean having to explain to her parents, and she couldn't face having that conversation.

To her mother and father the whole affair with Farlan had been an unfortunate, imprudent aberration to be quickly forgotten.

And she *had* forgotten.

Months, days, goodness knows how many hours of her life had passed since, and she couldn't remember how she had spent any of them. And yet she could still remember Farlan's exact words, and the intensity in his green eyes as he'd pulled her against him on that snowy afternoon.

They'd been sledging in Holyrood Park in Edinburgh. It had been a cold day, but with Farlan's body pressed close to hers she hadn't noticed. As they'd tumbled into the snow he had held her tight and kissed her fiercely.

'I want this to last for ever, Nia.'

The heat of his mouth had burned her lips and stolen the air from her lungs, so that she had thought she might faint. And then he'd slid the ring onto her finger and she had known a happiness like no other.

'Let's go away—just the two of us. Let's not get caught. Let's keep going.'

She had wanted to go with him so badly it had made her whole body ache, and in those sweet, shimmering moments of unrestrained happiness she'd even thought she might go through with it—

But of course people like her, the sensible, reliable ones who never broke the rules, always got caught.

Glancing up, her eyes rested on his flawless profile.

And she was still being punished for it now.

Raising the glass of Laphroaig to his mouth, Farlan tried to remember why he had decided this was a good idea.

They were sitting in the drawing room now, drinking coffee and whisky. He had purposely taken an armchair—there was no way he was going to end up sitting on some sofa with Nia—only that meant uninterrupted views of the room.

Success in Hollywood had given him an entrée into some of the most beautiful homes in the world. But the grandeur and scale of Lamington still jolted him more than he was willing to acknowledge.

The first time he had come here he'd barely noticed anything other than the shift in air temperature as they had sneaked into the house through the back door.

The memory snatched at his breath.

The warm, peppery smell of gingerbread cooking, the gleam of copper pans and Nia's fingers tightly wrapped around his like mistletoe around the branches of an oak tree.

He had stayed in the kitchen, but he doubted he would have noticed anything that day even if she had given him a guided tour. He had been too cocooned by the immense certainty of what he was feeling, what she was feeling—

Or rather what he'd thought she was feeling…

His gaze snagged on the Turner watercolour on the wall opposite and he felt suddenly blazingly angry.

Somehow it made it worse, finally seeing it again in person, knowing that Nia had quietly and calmly weighed him up against all of this.

Back in LA he'd been stunned, and then almost blinded with fury to learn that Tom and Diane would be staying here. But after he'd cooled off coming back to Lamington had seemed to make perfect sense. There would be a certain satisfaction in knowing that he was staying there, in *her* house.

His spine stiffened.

Much as he didn't like to admit it, his reaction had confirmed what he already knew but had ignored.

Nia was still in his head.

In his head, in his dreams, and sometimes he would even see her in the street or a restaurant or climbing into a cab.

Of course, it was never her, and he knew that.

But it always stopped him in his tracks just the same—left his whole body trembling with a longing and a loneliness that made it hard to stand up, to sleep, to eat, to think.

He'd hoped that seeing Nia again would flip some kind of switch inside him, and at first, in the drawing room, it had felt as if it had.

Now, though, he wasn't so sure.

Confronting her had felt good, satisfying. He hadn't wanted or needed to hear her excuses or explanations. But throughout the meal he'd kept feeling his gaze drawn to her beautiful pale face at too frequent intervals. Not so he could feel some kind of triumph, but because he hadn't been able to look away.

Not liking the implication of that particular thought, he lowered his glass and tugged at Diane's hand. 'So, Mrs Drummond, when are you and the big man here meeting the genealogist?'

'On Friday. And then next week we're going to take a

field trip up to Braemar. That's where Tom's family originally came from,' she said to Nia.

Keeping his gaze fixed on Diane's face, he felt rather than saw Nia nod.

'It's very beautiful round there,' she said, 'and the castle is quite significant historically.'

'Is it?' he asked softly. 'I thought it was just a hunting lodge for the Earls of Mar. But I suppose I've been spoiled. I mean, Craithie is a piece of Scottish history.'

So much for not talking to her.

Her eyes jerked up to meet his. 'What's Craithie Castle got to do with anything?'

'Oh, didn't Diane and Tom tell you?' He let his gaze drift lazily over her face. 'I'm thinking of buying it. Partly as an investment, partly as a retreat. These last few years have been hoachin', and I want somewhere I can kick back and relax. Do some creative thinking.'

A flush of colour was spreading over her cheeks. She looked stunned—probably because she knew the asking price.

Tom grunted. 'Make sure some of that creative thinking is about more than just work. I'm not saying it doesn't matter,' he said, picking up his wife's hand and pressing it against his mouth, 'but other things matter more. Like finding Mrs Wilder.'

Mrs Wilder.

The words spun in front of his eyes, glittering like the snowflakes that had fallen on Nia's face that day in Holyrood Park when he'd proposed.

Did she even remember it? Or know what it had taken for him to say those words? Even now it made his heartbeat slide sideways like a car on black ice.

He held up his hands in surrender. 'Then I know you'll both be pleased to hear that I'm ready to make a fool of myself over a woman again. Any number of women, in fact.'

That wasn't quite true.

He knew he would never let any woman get close enough to do that and, glancing over at Diane, he felt a spasm of guilt. She cared about him. Tom did too. They were the parents he'd never had. Kind, loving, warm. And, like any child lucky enough to have that kind of parent, he knew they only wanted the best for him.

Always had, even when he'd been at his worst.

His jaw tightened.

And his worst had been pretty appalling.

But they had stayed calm and firm, somehow sensing—although he'd never done more than hint at his past—that he needed proof they would stay the course. And they had given him that proof.

They had shown him love—shown him how to love, and why love mattered. Passion mattered too, but mostly they wanted him to have the kind of love they shared.

And theoretically he wanted that too.

Only that kind of love required a trust that wasn't in him to give.

Thanks to the woman sitting opposite him.

He let his eyes rest on her face until finally she looked up at him.

'You know the type,' he went on. 'Beautiful, beguiling and believable. But then a poor farm boy like me shouldn't expect anything else. Wouldn't you agree, Lady Antonia?'

'Oh, take no notice of him, Nia,' Diane said, shaking her head. 'He's not poor, and he wouldn't know a tractor if one ran him over. And you—' She turned to Farlan. 'If you really are serious about finding the love of a good woman, my boy, you need to think seriously about what you want.'

For a moment his reply stalled in his throat. That was the point. He had been very serious—once. His feelings for Nia had been sacred almost. For him, she was the mythical 'one.'

There had been others over the years, but in truth he'd only ever wanted one woman. Nobody else had come even close to matching Nia.

'You're right, Dee. I have thought about it, and the one thing I really want in a woman is that she has to know her own mind.'

He glanced over at Nia. The edges of her face seemed blurred, almost like the brushstrokes of the watercolour behind her head.

'That's what matters to me,' he reiterated.

'Well, we'll have to see what we can do. I'm sure they'll be no shortage of takers.' Tom grinned at him. 'Now, how about another drop of whisky? And then I might see if I can have a little try of those pipes. Nia, another glass?'

'Oh, no, thank you, I really should be going. I have such a lot on tomorrow. But thank you so much for a wonderful evening—'

Something in her voice pinched him inside.

He knew he had been cruel, and purposely so, but then he remembered how she had made him feel.

Getting to his feet, he watched as Diane and then Tom hugged her, steeling himself for the inevitable moment when he would have to embrace her.

'Now, Farlan will see you home. Farlan—?'

His pulse jerked as Diane turned to him expectantly.

'Yes, of course,' he said finally, filling the small, awkward pause. 'Let me get your coat.'

It seemed to take for ever to get out of the house, and for Nia, every second was agonising.

Now her pulse beat in time to the crunch of Farlan's footsteps as he strode down the drive.

She could easily have walked home alone, so why hadn't she said so? Why did she always choose the path of least resistance?

Her gaze lifted irresistibly to Farlan's face.

She might have lost his love, but she still had her pride.

As soon as she was certain they were out of sight of the house, she stopped and turned to him.

'I'll be fine from here. It's not even a half a mile.'

She made to step past him, but he blocked her path.

'I know where it is.'

His eyes found hers. In the darkness they seemed more black than green, but the hostility in them was still unmistakable.

'Good. Then you'll understand.' Her voice sounded odd, as if someone was squeezing her ribs, but she didn't care. She just wanted to get away. Not just from Farlan, but from the whole damned mess of her life.

'It's pitch-black.'

'I know the way.' Before he could respond, she moved past him, darting forward into the darkness.

It was starting to rain, and a brisk breeze was blowing thick dark clouds across the sky, playing peek-a-boo with the moon. But even if it had been a dry, clear night she knew he wouldn't have followed her.

Why would he when she had given him a ready-made excuse not to bother?

It's finished, she told herself. *You did it. You saw him; you talked to him. The worst is over.*

Why, then, did she feel not relieved but miserable?

She had barely started to answer that question when she heard him moving swiftly through the darkness, his long strides easily catching up with her.

'Hey, slow down—'

Catching her sleeve, he spun her round, staring down at her as if she was a disobedient dog who had slipped its collar.

'Look, I get it, okay? You'd rather break your own neck

than let me walk you home. Well, guess what, Lady Antonia? I don't want to walk you home either.'

She stared at him, mute with emotions she didn't want to feel.

Back at Lamington, with his expensive watch reflecting the flames from the fire, he had seemed both familiar and yet unnervingly different. Like the large Flemish tapestry in the drawing room after it had been taken away for refurbishing and returned with its previous faded tones restored to lush colour.

But out here, with his coat hunched around his shoulders and his rain-splashed face tipped up accusingly, he looked exactly like the beautiful wild boy she had fallen in love with at first sight.

Only he no longer loved her. Instead, she was just a woman he had agreed to walk home for a friend.

It was too much to bear.

The misery inside her twisted sharply, flared into an unfamiliar anger. 'So don't do it, then. Just turn around and go back the way you came.'

His face hardened. 'If it was up to me I would. But unfortunately Diane asked me to walk you home and I said I would.'

Even through the thick wool of her coat, the disdain on his face made her skin sting.

'And, unlike some people, I keep my word.'

She tugged herself free. 'Fine—but let go of me.'

'With pleasure.'

They stepped apart, squaring up to one another like two squalling cats, and then he handed her the umbrella Diane had insisted he take.

'Here, have this.'

She was about to refuse, but he had already turned and was walking away.

The moon peeped out from behind the shadow of a cloud

and then instantly retreated. *Lucky moon*, she thought, feeling bubbles of anger and misery bobbing inside her chest as he silently kept pace with her.

The worst is over.

The words replayed inside her head and she breathed out shakily. How arrogant, how naive, how frankly ridiculous that sounded.

The worst wasn't over—it was just beginning.

She might have finally seen Farlan again, but they hadn't so much met as *un*met.

Her heart beat unsteadily in the darkness.

Seven years ago they would have found it impossible to be so close and yet not touch or talk. Despite coming from such different backgrounds, they'd had more in common than any two people she had ever known. Their tastes so similar, their feelings so in tune.

Now, though, they were walking at arm's length in silence, and it felt as if they were strangers.

Except that strangers at least had the chance to get to know one another better.

She and Farlan wouldn't even be able to do that.

Up ahead, she could see the porchlight of the gardener's cottage. Relief flooded her body, and she sped up so that two minutes later she was standing on the doorstep.

She closed the umbrella and half turning, not wanting to see his face, said stiffly, 'Okay—I'm home now, so you've kept your word. Thank you and goodnight.'

She pushed down on the handle and opened the door.

'Are you kidding me?'

The snap in his voice made her hand jerk backwards. She turned towards him, her eyes wide. He was staring at her as if she had grown horns.

'Please tell me you didn't leave the house unlocked.'

He was outside the circle of the porchlight, his face in

shadow, but she could see the tilt of his jaw, hear the tension in his voice.

'I never lock it. Well, I would if I was going away. But I was only down the road—'

Farlan was already moving past her into the cottage.

Heart pounding, Nia stumbled through the door after him, smoothing her damp hair away from her face. 'You don't need to—'

She blinked. He had found the light switch and she watched dazedly as he stalked from one room to the other, then up the stairs.

She heard his footsteps reach her bedroom and suddenly she was undoing her coat, making her way to the kitchen. Finding a glass, she filled it from the tap and gulped greedily, the chill of the water burning her throat.

'You need to be more careful.'

She turned to where he stood, his shoulders grazing either side of the doorway.

'The back door doesn't even lock.'

His voice was rough, raw-sounding, and she stared up at him, wanting to believe that there was concern beneath the anger, but also not wanting to add to the tangle of feelings at being alone with Farlan.

'It does. You just have to jerk it a little—'

He was staring at her in disbelief.

'Just get a new lock.' His lip curled. 'Oh, sorry, I forgot. You need to run everything past a third party before you make up your mind.'

Her anger flared again at this sudden, unexpected, unasked-for confrontation.

'That's not fair, Farlan.'

'Fair? *Fair!*' He stared at her disbelievingly. 'That's rich, coming from you.'

She took a breath, the bitterness in his voice making her head swim. Stepping back, she gripped the kitchen counter.

'Look, I get that you want to punish me for what happened between us, but my door locks have got nothing to do with you. In fact I don't even know why you're here.'

He took a step closer, so close that she could feel the tension radiating from his skin.

'I'm here because I wasn't going to make it awkward for Diane and Tom.'

'If you didn't want them to feel awkward then maybe you shouldn't have come in the first place.' She knew he was angry with her, but it was unjust of him to blame her for this. 'You knew I was going to be there. If you didn't like it you could have just stayed away.'

His jaw tightened.

'Why should I stay away? They're my friends and, in case you hadn't noticed, you don't live there any more, Lady Antonia.'

Her eyes were suddenly blurry with tears. She hadn't wanted to leave Lamington, or to rent out her home. But she'd had no choice. The alternative would have been to sell it, and that had just not been an option.

It shouldn't have come to this. For years now she had tried talking to her parents, explaining their finances over and over, showing them how their outgoings always outstripped their income.

But the Earl and Countess of Brechin had both been raised to pursue their every whim, and it had been impossible to make them understand the severity of the situation.

Her mother had reacted with outrage; her father had simply refused to discuss it. It was not possible for him to spend less, and that was that.

Persuading them that it was a matter of urgency had been an exhausting and thankless task, but she hadn't cared.

What mattered was keeping Lamington safe.

Now more than ever.

Her fingers pinched the kitchen counter.

She'd always loved her home, but for the last seven years it had been the focus of her energies—her whole life, really.

It wasn't the first time she had acknowledged that fact. But it was the first time she'd done so standing next to Farlan, and it hurt in the same way as seeing him walk into the drawing room, with a sting of regret travelling a beat behind her pulse.

Feeling his gaze on her face, she looked up into his eyes, saw the pride smouldering there.

'But I suppose the Elgins have been kicking people off their property for four hundred years. I guess old habits die hard.'

Her head was spinning, his accusation jamming up against the memory of telling her parents about Farlan.

She closed her eyes briefly. 'My father shouldn't have said what he did.'

'Actually, it was what you *didn't* say that mattered more to me,' he said coldly.

She stared at him in silence, wanting to say it now. Only it was too late. Too much time had passed…too many things had happened.

'So staying at Lamington is your way of getting back at me,' she said hoarsely. 'For what I didn't say.'

His eyes glittered, the green vivid against his dark brows. 'I hadn't thought about you in years, but when Diane invited me I guess I was curious.'

He was so close she could see the muscles clenched in his jaw.

'I wanted to see whether Lamington was worth it.'

She felt his eyes rest on her bare shoulder, and then his gaze tracked slowly round the small living room, seeing what she could see and had tried to ignore—that it wasn't just her home that had shrunk, but her hopes, her dreams, her life itself.

'And was it, Nia? Do you still think keeping your title

and your ancestral home and your wealth was more important than me? Than us? Than our love?'

It was the first time he had called her Nia and her heart clenched as she wondered if it would be the last time too.

'I didn't think that,' she whispered.

'I know.' His smile made her heart twist. 'You let yourself be persuaded into thinking it.'

It was true—her parents *had* persuaded her that marrying Farlan would be a mistake. Telling them that he was brilliant and talented and special had done nothing to dent their opposition. And yet if it had been just her parents' objection she would have resisted them.

She could feel the words building, backing up in her throat. *Let me explain.* She almost said it out loud but what was the point? Farlan didn't want explanations. That wasn't why he had come back to Scotland or why he had wanted to see her again.

Like he said, he was just curious.

'I should probably go—'

'Yes.' She managed to nod.

Good manners dictated that she should show him out, but her body wouldn't respond. And he didn't move either. Instead, he stood staring down at her, and then her breath stalled in her throat as he reached out and touched her thistle-shaped brooch.

'Do you remember that day?'

She nodded slowly, her pulse skipping like a stone across her skin.

They had gone to the seaside. It had been the hottest day of the year—so hot that the sun had looked like a scoop of melting ice cream.

'*Taps aff*,' he'd yelled, dragging her across the dunes.

They had walked and talked, picking up the shells and wave-tumbled pieces of smooth glass that were scattered at the shoreline. After weeks cooped up in Farlan's tiny, airless flat, the air had been so fresh and clean they'd been almost high on ozone.

But it had been more than that.

Walking along the seafront, they had understood that this was it for both of them. There would be no one else. It didn't matter what anyone said or did, they had known.

It wasn't young love. It was a love that would span a lifetime, cross oceans, scale peaks.

And so they'd decided to get tattoos.

Her breath echoed in her ears, short and uneven.

It had been a dare at first, and then a test of how much they trusted one another.

Farlan would choose hers, and she'd choose his.

The catch: they wouldn't get to see them until after they were finished.

But of course they had chosen the exact same tattoo of a thistle.

'Every moment,' she said quietly.

His eyes found hers and she felt her pulse start to hammer, softly at first, and then more heavily, so that it felt like an undertow, pulling her down and back through time to those frantic, endless moments in his small flat.

Mesmerised, she watched his fingers trace the outline of the brooch—and just like that she remembered the warm caress of his hand, the way she had burned so feverishly at his touch.

A current of heat rippled through her body, wrapping itself around her heart. It had been there right from the moment she had seen him walk into the room, simmering beneath the surface, only now he was too close for her to pretend it wasn't happening. So close she could see the colour streaking his cheekbones, feel his warm breath mingling with hers.

'Farlan…' she whispered.

Their lips were barely an inch apart.

His eyes widened, and every part of her tightened in anticipation. She wanted to kiss him so badly she didn't even realise she was leaning into him until the sharp, ragged screech of a vixen punctured the quivering silence.

Abruptly his face was shuttered and he withdrew his hand. 'Get some sleep. You look tired.'

Completely unable to speak, and sure that her face was showing everything, she watched as he walked swiftly to the door.

As it closed, she moved across the room on autopilot, locking it this time.

It's over, she told herself.

Only this time she wasn't talking about the ordeal of seeing him—she was talking about the tiny, involuntary hope that maybe, possibly, there might be a second chance for the two of them. That somehow she might manage to persuade him to try again.

Whatever had just passed between them had made it clear that it was too late. There was no hope. There would be no reprieve.

And she was going to have to live with that for the rest of her life.

CHAPTER THREE

PUTTING HIS FOOT down on the accelerator, Farlan eased the big car forward, his eyes tracking the low pale sun in the blue sky above the Cairngorms.

Having got used to the warm, sun-filled days of life in Los Angeles, he'd almost forgotten the fickle Scottish weather.

Four seasons in a day, his grandmother used to say.

And it was true. Right now the white clouds scudding above the heather-covered hills looked positively jaunty, but when he'd set off this morning it had been drizzly and dreary and grey—*dreich*, in other words.

Dreich.

Now, that was a word he hadn't used in a long time.

No need for it, living in Los Angeles. Not that anyone would have known what he was saying anyway.

His mouth twisted up at the corner. When he'd first arrived in California it had been so difficult to get people to understand what he was saying. It hadn't just been his accent, although that hadn't helped. It had been all the words he'd used without thinking—like *dreich* and *scunnered* and *clarty*.

They had mostly slipped from his speech through lack of use, and his accent had softened over time. But other things had stayed as solid and immutable as the granite tors that reared up across the moorlands.

He felt his lungs tighten, so that he had to force himself to breathe.

Eyes narrowing, he slowed down and scooted past a racing cyclist in a glaringly luminous green jersey, then accelerated. He felt a childish but undeniable rush of satisfaction: the seven hundred and ten horsepower, four-litre twin turbo engine was explosively fast.

He wasn't really fussed about the money he was making now. It was nice not to have to worry about it any more, and he liked being able to look after people. Mostly, though, he just liked the 'convenience' of being rich.

Doors really did open if you had a lot of money. Everything was faster, slicker, less stressful. There was never any waiting around for a table in a restaurant. When you wanted to leave a limo was always on hand to whisk you away. And you didn't have to bother with shopping. People just sent you stuff. Clothes. Sunglasses. Smartphones.

He glanced at his wrist.

Watches.

Maybe that was why he hadn't been tempted to go on a spending spree.

That could be about to change, though.

He glanced admiringly at the smooth leather and carbon fibre interior of the supercar that had been delivered to him this morning. Another perk of being Farlan Wilder, film director.

He had met the racing team last year, when he'd flown to Austin for the United States Grand Prix. As a VIP, he'd been invited into the paddock and told to get in touch if he ever wanted to test drive anything.

He'd just been waiting for the right moment.

And where better to put this incredible machine through its paces than these endless empty roads with their backdrop of stunningly beautiful scenery?

Thankfully, LA's bumper-to-bumper gridlock didn't seem to have impaired his driving skills.

He shifted in his seat. For him, being in a car had always

been a means to escape reality, to suspend real life. His mother used to put on some music, and for however long it had taken to get where they were going all of them—he and his parents and his older brother, Cam—would act like a normal family.

Briefly, the rows had stopped.

He stared at the horizon.

They'd stopped permanently when his mother had left. It had been all right for a while, and then his dad had basically moved in with his new girlfriend, Cathy, and he and Cam had been left to raise themselves.

In those years before his brother had left too, he and Cam had gone on 'road trips.' Of course, that had been just something Cam had called them, to make it sound cool.

They hadn't gone anywhere special—just far enough away to make it feel as though they had left themselves behind.

But he knew better now. He knew that it didn't matter how fast you drove, how many miles you put between yourself and the person you blamed for the dark cloud spreading inside your chest, you never left yourself behind.

As what had happened in the cottage with Nia had so gut-wrenchingly proved.

He thought back to that moment when he had stepped towards her.

Or had she leaned into him? He couldn't remember. Memory required a functioning brain, and his had melted into his heartbeats the moment he had looked into her eyes and seen—

Seen what?

He swore softly.

Seen what he'd wanted to see. Or, more precisely, seen what his body had wanted to see. Nia's eyes…those beautiful soft brown eyes…misty with desire.

But it had been a mirage. An illusion. A teasing, flickering slideshow made up of memories and wish fulfilment.

Gritting his teeth, he pushed up the revs.

He understood wish fulfilment better than most of the population. As a film director he produced movies that were designed to satisfy people's conscious and unconscious desires.

His mouth twisted.

Clearly, though, he should have been concentrating on satisfying his own—then maybe he wouldn't have found himself standing inches apart from his ex with what could only be described as a hard-on.

He still couldn't quite believe it. Walking back to Lamington afterwards he had felt as if his body had betrayed him. Nia had broken his heart. It made no sense for him to feel anything for her but hostility and resentment.

Okay, she was still a beautiful woman, and they'd been alone, and they had a history, but surely her crime should have stifled his desire. Why, then, had his body reacted in that way?

But he knew why.

It had been an instinctive response. Like reaching for something when you saw it fall. Automatic, unthinking. *Foolish.*

He had come so close to kissing her…so close to pulling her body against his and giving in to the sharp pull of desire.

The fact that he hadn't done so was less to do with will power and more to do with a chance encounter between a fox and a vixen.

A soft, expensively restrained ringtone filled the car's cabin and gratefully he pulled his mind away from Nia's soft lips.

'Answer phone,' he said curtly.

'Farlan.'

It was Steve, his producer. He had noticed a missed call from him yesterday, and had been meaning to get back to him.

'Steve—sorry, man. I was going to call you—'

He glanced at the clock on the dash. It was barely six a.m. in Los Angeles, but it didn't surprise him that Steve was already up and making business calls. Most people he'd met in the movie industry seemed to work all hours of the day and night, and he was no exception, only today it had slipped his mind.

His hands tightened around the steering wheel.

Or perhaps it might be more accurate to say that it had been squeezed out by thoughts of Nia.

'No worries. I just wanted to let you know the good news.' Even from five thousand miles away the elation in his voice was unmistakable. 'Travis Kemp loved the pitch. So it's on, baby.'

The road dipped but that wasn't what made Farlan's stomach plummet.

The pitch.

How had he forgotten? That should have been first on his agenda, and normally it would have been, but thanks to Nia his mind had lost its usual razor-sharp focus.

With an effort, he kept the confusion and irritation out of his voice.

'That's great news, Steve. Really great news. Thanks for letting me know and thank you for making it happen. I know you put in a whole lot of effort on this one.'

'It was an easy sell. They loved it, and they love you. In fact, Travis is having a gathering this weekend and you're on the guest list. Check your in-box. You'll need the zip code to find it. It's in the middle of nowhere.'

Farlan gazed blindly at the view through the windscreen.

The weather had changed again. Dark swollen clouds were rolling low over the hills, swallowing up the light, turning the landscape bruise-coloured and carelessly flinging raindrops at the car like a commuter chucking coins in a busker's hat.

Travis Kemp was a 'name.' He didn't just greenlight films—he made legends. Even to be invited to one of his 'gatherings' was a coup.

He felt a hum in his chest…could feel it spreading out, fluttering down his arms.

Tom and Diane would understand. Particularly Tom. He was close enough to the movie industry to know what a connection to Travis Kemp could mean.

There was every reason to go back to California, and only one to stay here in Scotland—and it had nothing to do with Nia.

The reopening of the Gight Street Picture Palace was his project, and he'd always planned on visiting it while he was over here. But in the run-up to his leaving LA the trust that managed it had invited him to the reopening ceremony, and he'd agreed.

He could cancel. Only he could still remember his own disappointment when he was at the beginning of his career and people had blown him out.

And then there was Nia.

Her face, her soft brown eyes wide and drowsy with desire, slid into his head.

The memory of her rejection had haunted him for seven years. Seeing her was supposed to have changed things. Put the past back in its box. And yet it wasn't her rejection that was playing on a loop, but those few, febrile unfulfilled seconds when he had unleashed a different part of their past.

A part that was nothing to do with rejection and everything to do with attraction.

In the distance, the sun was pushing back at the clouds. Suddenly everything was brilliantly illuminated in colour, the hillsides a jigsaw of sapphire and rust and gold like a stained-glass window.

If he went back now she would always be there in his head.

This was his one chance to erase her for ever and have a chance at finding the happiness that Tom and Diane so wanted for him.

That he wanted for himself.

'I can't make it, Steve. You know I was heading back to Scotland for a couple of weeks? Well, I decided to go a little earlier.'

'You did? Are you there for the shooting? Or just catching up with "auld acquaintances"?' Steve made a poor attempt at a Scottish accent.

'Nice try, mate, but I'm from Scotland—not Ireland.'

Just as he'd intended, Steve laughed.

But Farlan didn't join in with the laughter. Instead, staring coolly at his own narrowed green gaze in the rear-view mirror, he slowed the car and, using the passing place, turned it around.

Just one 'auld acquaintance'—and he was going to do whatever it took to make sure that this time he would forget her.

'Oh, my dear, you made it. I am so pleased.'

Nia smiled as Diane hurried towards her and kissed her on both cheeks. She held up a pile of books. 'I thought I'd pop these back in the library. I borrowed them before I moved out.'

'Well, we're all in the library right now, just this moment stopping for tea. It's going very well.' Diane's eyes were shining with excitement. 'How was your trip to London?'

'It was fine,' Nia lied. 'But I'm always happy to come back to the Highlands.'

Sometimes she met a friend for lunch or shopping, but

after her meeting with the family accountant she hadn't been in the mood for either small-talk or tapas.

Douglas McKenzie had known her grandfather. He was nearing retirement now, but he was still sharp and straight-talking.

'Your parents' personal expenses are not just ridiculous—frankly, they're jeopardising everything you are trying so hard to prevent,' he'd said, with typical bluntness. 'If this carries on, you're going to have to seriously consider letting out Lamington for longer. Two, maybe three years.'

It had been like a sharp slap. 'Surely that can't be the only option, Douglas?' *Two, maybe three years* was too long to live in limbo.

Catching sight of her face, his expression had softened. 'I'm sorry, Nia. I don't want or need to scare you. You know what's at stake. It's your parents who simply refuse to deal with the reality of their finances.' He'd hesitated. Then, 'I know it's none of my business, and I'm sure you had your reasons for turning down Lord Airlie, but he's a good man and I think if he had the slightest encouragement from you...'

Breathing out slowly, Nia blinked as the library came back into focus. Through the long windows at the end of the room, she could see the distant heather-covered hills.

The Most Honourable the Marquess of Airlie—or Andrew, as she called him—lived just over those hills, in a castle that made Lamington look like a dolls' house. He was one of the wealthiest men in Scotland, a handsome blue-eyed Highlander, and a kind and generous man.

When he'd proposed to her a year ago she had known that he would be a kind and generous husband. But she could no more marry him than she could marry Douglas McKenzie.

She felt a shiver run over her skin.

Her parents had been apoplectic with fury when she had

turned him down. They had raged, threatened, pleaded with her, but she had been firm.

This time she had been firm.

Her mouth compressed.

After what had so nearly happened at the cottage with Farlan she had sworn to stay away from Lamington. He was only staying for a fortnight. She could easily avoid having to see him again.

Then, just as she'd been boarding the plane back, Diane had called and invited her to tea, and to meet Finn McGarry, the genealogist who was researching Tom's Scottish roots.

The hope and warmth in her voice would normally have made Nia accept immediately. But even the thought of seeing Farlan again had made panic swamp her and, stammering slightly, she had started to make her excuses.

It was very kind of her, but they already had a guest staying, and Farlan was only over for such a short time—

Diane had laughed. Not so short, she'd said, that he couldn't take himself off on a round trip to Inverness.

Nia had felt relief wash over her.

Apparently Farlan had arranged for some amazing supercar to be delivered to the house and would be heading off after lunch.

But just to make sure… 'So did Farlan get off all right?' she asked now, casually.

Or at least she had been aiming for casual.

Even just saying his name out loud made her skin heat, just as it had in the cottage when he'd reached out to her. She could still feel it now—the way the air had changed around them, how it had seemed to turn liquid.

Or maybe that was just her…

Her cheeks felt as though they were burning. It had been instant and un-tempered, and for a few glorious half-seconds she had forgotten the past as a dizzying rush of hunger had risen up, drowning out logic and the unchangeable fact that it didn't matter how badly she wanted to reach out and stroke his face, or press her lips against his beautiful mouth, she had forfeited her right ever to do so again.

'He did.' Diane turned to her and shook her head. 'But then he changed his mind. He got back about a quarter of an hour ago.' She lowered her voice. 'I don't know what's up with that boy. He's been like a cat on a hot tin roof since he got here. Can't seem to sit still for more than five minutes. Tom… Farlan,' she called out as they walked into the library, 'look who's here!'

It was only good manners and some kind of residual momentum that kept Nia walking forward.

Farlan was sprawled across a sofa, the sleeves of his dark jumper rolled up.

She tried so hard not to look at him that she almost tripped over the edge of one of the rugs, and her cheeks flared anew as she imagined him remarking on her clumsiness.

But when she stole a quick glance in his direction, he wasn't even looking at her. He was looking at Finn McGarry.

She took a breath, forcing air in and out of her lungs. Had she given it any thought, she would probably have expected the genealogist to be an elderly man in a shabby, tweed suit.

But Finn was apparently short for Finola—and Finola McGarry was young and slim, with huge blue eyes and a dark pixie haircut.

She was also very pretty.

Farlan certainly seemed to think so, she thought, a slippery unease balling in her stomach as Diane handed her a cup of tea.

She watched as he gave Finn one of his slow, teasing smiles.

'All these questions, Ms McGarry…you're making me feel nervous.'

'Please call me Finn—and I doubt much makes you nervous, Mr Wilder.'

'It's Farlan. And a beautiful woman cross-examining me makes me very nervous.' His green eyes glittered. 'Unless, of course, you're a fan.'

'I am. I did an internet quiz on you the other day. Got every answer right except one.'

'Which was…?'

'Your middle name.'

Nia froze, her fingers tightening around the handle of her teacup, chanting the answer inside her head.

I know his middle name, she wanted to shout. *Jude. It's Jude. And I know that he always falls asleep with his arm under the pillow, and I know that* Plein Soleil *is his favourite film. I know him as well as I know myself, maybe more.*

Farlan's chin jerked up, his eyes locking with hers, and for a horrible moment she thought she had spoken out loud.

But then he looked away, almost as if he hadn't seen her. 'It's Jude.'

'Like the song?' asked Finn.

Farlan shook his head. 'The saint, actually,' he explained.

Nia was starting to feel sick. It had been painful enough accepting that Farlan could not forgive her, and that there would be no second chance for the two of them. But imagining him in a relationship with another woman was a whole new level of agony.

She leant forward to put her cup down, letting her hair fall in front of her face so that she could no longer see Farlan and Finn.

Farlan and Finola Wilder. Even their names sounded good together.

'Could I have some milk?'

The cup in her hand jerked as she realised Farlan was standing beside her. 'I didn't think you liked it in tea—'

'My taste has changed,' he said flatly.

His gaze rested on her face and she felt her heart contract with shock at how much it hurt to look up at him and no longer find love in his eyes.

As she drank her tea, she managed to keep up a flow of polite conversation with Diane, but her ears kept tuning in to the couple talking on the other sofa.

'Unusual job for someone your age,' Farlan was saying, leaning back against the sofa cushions and stretching out his long legs. 'Was it always the plan?'

'Yes.' Finn nodded, then frowned. 'Actually, that's not strictly true. It was *my* plan. My parents wanted me to be a lawyer, and I did do a term at Edinburgh, but it wasn't what I wanted.'

Nia felt rather than saw Farlan lean forward.

'So…what? You dropped out?'

'Yeah, my parents went ballistic. They're all lawyers in my family, and they tried every which way to talk me out of it, but…' She shrugged. 'I wasn't going to change my mind.'

Farlan's eyes were fixed on her face. *'"I have dared to do strange things—bold things, and have asked no advice from any."'*

The sudden intensity in his voice made Nia spill a little tea in her saucer.

Diane looked up and sighed. 'That is so beautiful. Is it Robert Frost?'

'Emily Dickinson.'

Nia and Farlan both spoke at the same time.

His eyes locked onto hers, and for a few pulsing seconds it was as though they were alone in the vast book-lined room.

'Oh, I almost forgot.' Diane put her cup down with a clatter. 'Finn, we have a book of photographs we want to show you. The packers put it in the wrong crate, but you must see it. Farlan, could you help Tom get it down for me?'

Nia watched as everyone left the library.

She took a shivery breath, feeling the gap in the room where Farlan had been.

Nobody had asked her to go too. And nobody would notice that she hadn't followed them.

Picking up the pile of books she'd brought back, she made her way to the spiral staircase that led up to the galleried second floor of the library.

She felt adrift.

Her body felt as though it had short-circuited.

She couldn't do this—couldn't just sit by silently and watch Farlan fall in love with someone else.

Her heart twisted.

How could he not fall for Finola McGarry?

She was beautiful, and passionate, and she knew her own mind. Finn had followed her heart, and Nia knew that to Farlan that made her irresistible.

Slowly, she made her way along the shelves, sliding the books carefully back where they belonged. Typically, the last one, the biggest and heaviest of all of them, came from a higher shelf.

Glancing down at her high-heeled court shoes, she frowned.

She could just squeeze it in anywhere—only then finding it again would just be down to luck. Picturing her mother's face, she sighed and, gripping the ladder with one hand and clutching the book in the other, she began climbing.

Annoyingly, it was still a little out of reach, but if she just leaned over—

'Nia!'

She jerked round, her foot slipping sideways, and suddenly the book was sliding from her fingers and she was grabbing for the ladder.

Strong hands grasped her waist and she felt her body connect with a hard chest.

'What are you doing?'

Those same hands spun her round and lowered her to the floor. Looking up, she almost forgot to breathe. Farlan was standing next to her, his green eyes narrowed in disbelief.

'I was just trying to put a book back.'

'In *those*?'

Farlan looked down at her shoes and then immediately wished he hadn't as he felt a stealthy stirring of lust at the sight of her long, slender legs in what were quite conceivably stockings.

Watching her eyes widen at the harshness of his voice, he felt like a jerk. But Nia wasn't the only one who had been caught off balance.

Imagining what would have happened if he hadn't been there to catch her made him feel sick.

But it was his body's swift, treacherous reaction to how good it felt to have her pressed against him that had shaken him more.

In the car, everything had seemed so clear. Deep down he'd known he was avoiding her, and that was why he had turned around and driven back to Lamington. To prove to himself that what had happened in the cottage had been either a fluke or just a final twitch of muscle memory—that there would be no next time.

And he'd been doing just fine.

Until Nia had sashayed into the library with her hair falling in front of her face, looking like a cross between Jessica Rabbit and a Hitchcock heroine in a pencil skirt and shiny high heels.

Who the hell wore heels like that when they were popping over for tea?

Realising he'd lost his train of thought while he'd been

staring at her legs, he gritted his teeth. 'Why are you even up a ladder anyway? Don't you have staff to put your books back for you?'

Her hair had fallen back from her face and, gazing down at her, he felt his heartbeat accelerate. She looked stunned, and furious, and for a moment he thought she might slap him or stalk off, but instead she just shook her head.

'No, I don't. Now, do you mind?'

He felt a tic of anger and something else pulse through his chest as she pushed his hands away from her body and edged backwards, as if he'd been trying to mug her rather than save her from breaking her neck.

Her neck...

His eyes were a beat behind the words, but as they dropped to the smooth, creamy skin of her throat he felt the hum in his head slither down his veins.

Had those pearls she was wearing been a gift? And, if so, who had given them to her?

The most likely answer to the question sharpened his anger to a point. 'Yeah, I do mind, actually,' he said curtly. 'I mean, do you have any idea what would have happened if I hadn't been here?'

A flush of colour spread over her cheeks. 'Nothing would have happened.'

'So no need to thank me, then?' he said sarcastically.

She frowned. 'Thank you? For what? Haranguing me?'

Containing his temper with an effort, he shook his head. 'If I hadn't come along when I did it would have been like a game of Cluedo in here. Lady Antonia, in the library, with a ladder.'

'Why are you making this such a big deal? My foot slipped—that's all.'

He stared at her in frustration, maddened by both her lack of gratitude and the smooth Englishness of her voice.

'I was fine. In fact, if you hadn't scared me I probably wouldn't have lost my balance.'

So what was she saying? That this was his fault?

He stared at her in silence, her words and her light floral scent tangling with the emotions in his chest.

Reaching down, she picked up the book she'd dropped.

He plucked it from her fingers. 'I'll do it.'

She snatched it away again. 'I don't need your help. I don't need anything from you.'

'I know. You made that perfectly clear seven years ago when you chose this house over me.'

The memory of it echoed inside him like a bomb blast.

She took a step closer, close enough that he could almost see her heart beating beneath the fabric of her top.

'That's not how it was,' she said.

'That's exactly how it was.'

Bitterness was rolling through him like a juggernaut. She had never needed him. Wanted him, yes, but not for ever—not like she'd promised.

'I was there, remember? We were both there. Only at some point you started reading from a different script.'

The script her parents had written.

She blinked. 'We weren't in a movie, Farlan. You can't just write the ending you want.'

'You did.'

There was a beat of silence and then she shook her head slowly. 'No. I didn't. I did what I thought was right for both of us. But it wasn't what I wanted.'

'What *did* you want?' He'd meant to sound scornful, but instead his voice was shaky, urgent.

Her eyes found his. 'I wanted you. I've only ever wanted you.'

He stood, frozen. For a few seconds they just stared at one another, and then she took a step closer, and his heart jerked as she brushed her lips against his.

It was a light, tentative, tantalising not-quite kiss. She had kissed him like that once before, that very first time. Before all of this had happened, when there had been nothing but hope and hunger and heat between them.

Heat was filling his lungs. He had come back to Lamington to put the past behind him. Only not this piece of the past.

Pulse stuttering, his hands moved automatically to her waist and he kissed her back.

He heard the book fall to the floor, and then her fingers began moving down his body, roaming clumsily over his shoulders and chest, pushing up his sweater, pulling his T-shirt aside.

He breathed in sharply as her hands slid over his bare skin, feeling his body harden. Pressing her closer, he tugged at the buttons on her cardigan until she was open to him. His fingers splayed over her stomach…his heartbeat melted into her skin.

She moaned softly as he cupped her breasts and then, lowering his face, he sucked a swollen nipple into his mouth. His blood pumped faster as she arched against him, and then his hand was pushing under the hem of her skirt, finding more warm, irresistible skin and the tops of her stockings.

Breathing raggedly, he found her mouth again and, walking her backwards, slid his hand through her hair, cradling her head so that he could deepen the kiss.

There was a muffled thump as they collided with the shelves, and then more thumps as books began falling to the floor, but he didn't care. All he cared about was the fierce, hot pressure in his groin.

'Farlan—'

His eyes fluttered open. She was staring at him, her hair mussed, her lips swollen. From somewhere inside the house he heard Tom's booming laugh.

What the hell were they doing? What the hell was he doing?

Drawing back, he watched her grab the front of her cardigan. Clearly Nia was thinking the same thing.

'I'm sorry,' she said shakily.

Her eyes dropped to the books on the floor and, crouching down, she started to pick them up.

'Leave it.' He pulled her to her feet. 'I'll sort it out.'

'You can't just put them back anywhere.'

Her eyes were too bright, but her words gave him an excuse to vent his panic and confusion.

'It's just a few books, Nia.' He shook his head. 'What is it with you and this damn house? Always wanting everything to be perfect.' And obviously that excluded some nameless nobody like him.

Her face stilled. 'It's not just a house. It's my home.'

Something in her answer, in her voice, made his chest tighten. 'Nia, I—'

But she stepped past him, moving so swiftly that she was already halfway down the spiral staircase by the time his brain had caught up with his breathing.

He stood for a moment, heard her words echoing around the still, silent room, and then, bending down, he picked up the books and began slowly and carefully putting them back exactly where they belonged.

CHAPTER FOUR

GAZING OUT OF her bedroom room, Nia felt her heart swell. No matter how many times it happened, it was still magical.

It had snowed overnight, transforming the drab, muddy fields and spiky hedges of the Scottish countryside into an endless white wonderland.

There must be six inches, at least. Enough to cover the lawn in a thick blanket and make the *philadelphus* and camellia bushes buckle.

Not enough to make the world stop turning.

Her throat tightened.

No, only Farlan Wilder had the power to do that.

She glanced across the fields to where Lamington rose, pale and splendid, beneath a pewter-coloured sky. It felt strange, knowing he was there, that he was sleeping in the guest room just yards from where they would have shared a bed *together* if she hadn't broken up with him.

Although, judging by yesterday's performance in the library, they didn't actually need a bed.

She felt her face heat.

Even now the memory of that kiss stunned her.

It had been such a stupid thing to do, and it should have felt wrong on so many levels.

They had parted on such bad terms, and he didn't even like her. Yesterday, after the way he had acted, the way he had spoken to her, she hadn't liked him very much either.

But when her lips had touched his she had more than liked him. She had wanted him with every fibre of her being.

And he had wanted her too. She had felt it in the urgency of his mouth, the press of his fingers against her skin.

She stared blindly through the glass at the glittering white landscape.

Time was like snow. It covered everything so that after a few weeks—days, even—you forgot what lay beneath.

But all it took was a few moments of intense heat and things started to reveal themselves.

Or, in this case, feelings. Feelings she had buried… feelings she'd thought had faded to manageable proportions.

But here, in this small, neat bedroom, with its chintz curtains and low beams, she could admit that even after all this time a part of her still wanted Farlan.

Was that really so surprising?

It was hardly unusual for ex-lovers to feel desire long after affection had faded.

Farlan being back had obviously stirred up all kinds of feelings.

Add in to that already potent mix the fact that he was staying at Lamington, and it would have been incredible if there hadn't been any repercussions—

But was that enough to explain how she had acted?

Could desire really overrule everything? Not just the past, but all the anger and confusion that still simmered between them?

Her heart began banging against her ribs.

It wasn't just desire.

Remembering Finola McGarry's wide-eyed beauty, she clenched her hands, her nails digging in deep.

The years had softened the ache of Farlan's absence. But seeing him with Finn had been a new, fresh pain, even though it shouldn't have been that much of a shock.

After all, he'd made it clear just a couple of days ago

that he was looking to 'make a fool of himself with any number of women.'

Yet she hadn't been prepared for exactly how much it would hurt. How every time his eyes had skimmed past her to settle on Finn's face it had felt as though the air was being ripped out of her lungs.

But he wanted me as much as I wanted him.

It was so tempting to listen to that tiny, treacherous voice in the back of her head…to think about the tantalising possibility that they might get back together.

Only what would be the point?

There could be any number of reasons why he had kissed her like that. Habit…curiosity. Or perhaps, like her, he had just lost control and given in, momentarily, to the pull of the past.

It didn't much matter either way, and it certainly wasn't going to happen again.

She and Farlan had split up for multiple reasons.

Maybe those reasons had been misguided, and maybe she had spent the last seven years regretting her actions and resigning herself to never meeting a man like him again. But no matter how passionate the kiss, it didn't change the facts.

Whatever it was she and Farlan had shared, it hadn't been solid or strong enough to survive real life.

The thought of deliberately drawing a line under their relationship made her shiver on the inside. But she knew what it had taken for her to get over him the first time. She couldn't relive that. The time for what-might-have-beens was over.

And if she needed further proof of that she should remember how he'd looked at her when she had tried to pick up the books. There had been nothing lover-like about him then. He'd been just as angry and resentful as he had been all those years ago.

On the table beside her bed, her phone pinged.

Glancing down at the screen, she frowned. It was a text from Johnny, the head ghillie at Lamington, asking if she still wanted to meet and would she like a lift.

Of course—how could she have forgotten?

Tom and Diane might be living at the big house, but she was still overseeing the running of the estate, and she had earmarked today for catching up with the outdoor staff. The ghillies, stalkers and gamekeepers who knew the hills and the winds and the waters of Lamington best.

It would be a long, tiring morning, spent trundling round the estate in a car without a fully functioning heater. But on the plus side she would be too busy to give any more thought to the enigma that was Farlan Wilder.

Having texted back yes to the first question and no to the second, she showered and dressed and ten minutes later was bumping over the snow-covered road in her battered Land Rover.

When she arrived at Johnny's house, a trio of khaki-green ATVs were already waiting for her. Leaning against them, a cluster of men all dressed identically, in boots, thick trousers, quilted jackets and beanies, were talking and drinking what she knew would be hot, sweet tea from Thermoses.

As she slid out of the car, the men all turned to face her. 'Good morning, Lady Antonia.'

'Good morning, everyone. I know you're all dying to have some fun with all this lovely snow, and hopefully there'll be some time later for that, but first—'

'Sounds great.'

Looking up, she felt her stomach jolt even before she recognised his voice.

Shifting against the bonnet of the nearest ATV, Farlan downed his tea and screwed the top back on his Thermos as though this was all completely normal to him.

'Are we talking snowballs or sledging?'

She stared at him in silence. 'I didn't know you were joining us, Mr Wilder?' she managed finally.

'I wasn't.' He gazed at her, his green eyes clear and steady. 'But Johnny dropped round to the house to pick up the key for this.' He patted the bonnet. 'So we got talking, and he told me you were all meeting up, and—'

And what? she wanted to scream.

His smile could have melted a polar ice-cap. 'I don't have much on today, except a call to my producer. So I thought I'd tag along. Have a tour of the estate.'

Tag along?

She felt blindsided, just as if he'd scooped up a ball of snow and thrown it at her head. Surely he wasn't planning on spending the whole morning with them?

As if he could read her thoughts, his eyes met hers. 'But only if that's okay with you, Lady Antonia?'

No, it's not. It's actually extremely inconvenient, she thought, biting back a strong desire to tell him so. *And unfair.*

It felt as if the whole world was weighted against her, tipping her ever more into his orbit just when she had come to terms with their last encounter.

'It's really not very exciting,' she said.

'Good,' he said softly. 'I've had quite enough excitement in the last twenty-four hours.'

His eyes rested on her face, and for a second she couldn't breathe as his words wound around her skin.

'Well, I don't have any objections,' she lied. 'So, shall we get on? Or does anyone have anything they want to discuss before we leave? Any questions?'

There was a general shuffling of feet and then Johnny raised his hand. 'Just the one. Is Mr Wilder going to be using Lamington as a location for one of his films? Only Allan, here, got his drama badge in Scouts…'

Everyone roared with laughter.

Farlan grinned. 'That's my leading man sorted, then.'

Watching him, Nia felt dizzy. Most of the men who worked on the estate were reserved with strangers, and yet here they were, chatting to Farlan as if they'd known him their whole lives. As if he was one of them.

But Farlan had a knack of engaging with people…making them see the world differently, act differently. It was what made him such a successful film director, she thought. With him, everything seemed possible.

Unlike her family, he made everything feel as simple and certain as the heather-covered hills.

She had felt more sure of herself when she was with him. He had seen qualities in her that others had ignored…seen beneath the poise and reserve and made it clear how much he liked what he saw.

For those six months they'd been together she had never been happier. It had been an actual tingling feeling, like sherbet exploding on her tongue. And in that state of unending, incomparable happiness she had thought that she could have it all. Farlan and Lamington.

Only life didn't work like that. You could never have it all. Sacrifices had to be made.

But she hadn't wanted him to have to make them.

He'd had so much passion and talent and determination. He'd wanted to travel, to see the world and seize his place in it, and she hadn't been able to bear the idea of tethering him to her.

But without him her world had shrunk…grown small and domestic. The days had slipped by unmarked. Outside of Lamington's thick walls the seasons had changed, but she had stayed in hibernation, neither asleep nor awake.

Until yesterday.

'I'll drive.'

Her chin jerked up. He was beside her, and somehow the air no longer felt cold, but warm.

'Or do you not mind driving in the snow these days?'

It was a deliberate hook to their past, but if the last few days had taught her anything it was that returning to the past was a bad idea.

She glanced pointedly over his shoulder. 'I'm sure you'll have a lot more fun in one of the ATVs.'

'You didn't answer my question.'

'That's because the answer is irrelevant. I'm not spending all morning sitting in a car with you, Farlan.'

'Why not?'

'You know why,' she whispered, glancing over his shoulder again. Johnny and Allan were looking over at them curiously.

'You mean because you're worried you won't be able to keep your hands off me?' he murmured.

'I am *not*.'

'So what's the problem?'

You—you are the problem.

Biting her tongue, she stared at him in mute frustration. She didn't do confrontation very well. As an only child she'd never had to fight her corner, and by nature she was shy and moderate.

Now, though, she wished she could just get into her car and drive off, like a character in a film. But if she did that it would be all over the estate by noon, and then Tom and Diane might hear something, and—

'There is no problem,' she said crisply. 'But if you change your mind you'll have to walk back. This is a working estate, and some of us are still working.'

With twin bright spots of colour burning her cheeks, she got into the driver's seat and slammed the door.

As they slithered along the road he leaned back, stretching out his legs. 'It's pulling a little to the left—you might want to check the brakes.'

Staring stonily ahead, she followed the ATVs up over the snow-covered hills. Her heart had begun to thump loudly.

Last time they'd parted he had been tense and sparring for a fight, the heat from their kiss still flooding his veins. But his mood seemed lighter this morning. Probably because he was back in the director's seat. Or rather the passenger seat of her car.

'So where are we going?' he asked.

'Up to Inverside. It's at the far edge of the estate. We'll go there first and work our way back. The radio doesn't work so well around here, but if you want to listen to music there's a couple of CDs knocking around.'

At least that way she could just concentrate on driving and try and forget he was even there…

'Actually, I thought we could talk.'

Her spine tightened so swiftly she thought it might snap. 'Talk?'

'About what happened.'

She jerked round, her eyes widening with shock. When the car followed the direction of her gaze he reached across and gently straightened the steering wheel.

'You know… In the library.'

Her breath was trapped in her throat, the memory of that moment echoing through her like the bells of the local church.

This was one of the many differences between them. His directness.

Most of the people she knew—herself included—fudged things, and in the past she'd always admired Farlan's ability to go straight to the point.

Not right now, though.

'There's nothing to talk about,' she said.

She felt his gaze on her face.

'Really? So that's an everyday occurrence for you, is it?'

An everyday occurrence? Hardly.

Even now the memory of his lips on hers made her feel as if her skin was on fire. The last time she had kissed a man had been over a year ago, and it had borne no resemblance to what had happened with Farlan in the library.

She felt a prickle of guilt.

Andrew was quiet, and a little old-fashioned, but he was also sweet and generous. And sensitive. They could have had sex. She was on the pill to help manage her hormone-related migraines, and part of her had wanted to sleep with him—the same part that had wished she could fall in love with him.

But it hadn't felt right.

So she had told Andrew she wasn't ready and he had said he was happy to wait. Not once had he put pressure on her or badgered her for an explanation.

She frowned. What would she have said if he had?

Seven years was a long time *not* to get over someone.

Most people—her parents, for example—would think it was melodramatic and self-indulgent to hold on to pain for that long, to let the absence of something—*someone*—put a grey filter over the rest of your life. But that was what it felt like to have loved and lost Farlan.

Not that she was about to tell *him* that.

Ignoring his question, she bumped over a snow-covered cattle grid.

'It shouldn't have happened.'

'And yet it did,' he pressed. 'You kissed me, and I kissed you back. In the library at Lamington Hall. What would the Earl and Countess of Brechin say?'

On the surface his tone was mild, as if he were just enjoying a pleasant conversation. But she heard the taunt in his voice, and the hurt pride.

'Where are they, by the way?' he asked.

'They're staying with my aunt and uncle in Dubai. My father needs a warmer climate for his chest.'

She parroted the 'official' explanation for her parents'

decision to leave their home. The one that would allow them to hold their heads up high.

'Why didn't you go with them?'

'Lamington isn't just where I live,' she said quickly. 'I run the estate.'

That wasn't the only reason. Seeing her aunt and uncle would have been just too painful. But she couldn't explain why to Farlan—*especially* not to Farlan.

'Couldn't you get in a temporary manager?'

'That would just mean even more disruption for everyone.' She stared through the windscreen, over-concentrating on the road. 'Besides, I don't like the heat.'

'I wouldn't say that was true…'

Her mouth was suddenly dry, and she felt her belly clench. She wanted him, but she was fighting the attraction.

'We're not doing this, Farlan,' she said slowly. 'I get that you're still angry with me for what I did. And I'm sorry I hurt you. If it makes you feel any better, I hurt myself too.'

In front of her, the ATVs were slowing. She watched distractedly as they stopped and parked in a line. Breathing out unsteadily, she stopped the car behind them, her fingers curling around the door handle.

'But we don't need to discuss what happened in the library. It was meaningless for both of us, I'm sure.' His eyes flickered but she ploughed on. 'It was a mistake. I wasn't thinking. But it won't happen again.'

She was already halfway out of the car. 'Now, if you don't mind, I need to get back to work.'

She was wrong, Farlan thought as he followed her across the snow. That kiss hadn't been meaningless for either of them. It had been too raw, too desperate, too spontaneous to be anything other than sheer compulsion.

Something she had confirmed in her next breath.

'It was a mistake. I wasn't thinking...'

His pulse dipped.

He was pretty sure that, like most people, Nia had chosen those particular words to distance herself from her actions, to make it sound as though there was some cosmic force in play over which she had no control.

Ironically, in claiming that, she'd made their kiss more, not less, meaningful.

Nia hadn't been thinking because lust didn't require thought.

Kissing her back hadn't required any input from *his* brain either.

Lust was an inarticulate craving, a wordless hunger that overrode logic and self-preservation.

The difference was he could admit that—privately anyway.

His chest tightened. For him, too, it had been involuntary. He hadn't wanted his body to respond to hers, and he was angry with her and himself.

She had lied to him seven years ago, deemed him unworthy, and he couldn't understand how he was still so drawn to her.

After what had so nearly happened in the cottage, he'd been sure he would call a halt. That he hadn't—or rather *couldn't*—had been the reason he'd been so brusque with her afterwards.

But, like hers, his mind and body had been playing push-me-pull-me with the past.

It was inevitable—and entirely predictable. Of *course* he wanted to taste her again.

Only now he wanted more than just a taste…

The rest of the morning was spent crossing the vast estate, checking the herds of deer and cattle and inspecting gates and fences.

Nia was a good boss, he thought, watching her with Johnny and the other men. Maybe that shouldn't have surprised him, but when he'd found out from Tom and Diane that she 'oversaw' the running of the estate, he'd been more than a little sceptical.

At nineteen, she'd been the smartest, most cultured person he'd ever met. And the sweetest. Picturing the shy, quiet girl of seven years ago, he'd found the idea of her running anything improbable, and had assumed that it was a vanity job for the daughter of the house.

But Nia clearly knew what she was doing. And it was clear that her staff liked and respected her. Probably because she listened and valued their opinions.

'How big is the estate?' he asked.

She turned. It would be natural to think that her cheeks were flushed from the cool air, but the slight tension around her jawline told a different story.

'It's just under twenty-eight thousand acres.'

He stared at her. Her hair had come loose and was framing her face, and he wondered why he'd thought she had lost her sparkle. There was a luminosity to her skin that rivalled the glittering snow, and the delicate curve of her jaw and high cheekbones made the faces of those around her look smudged and unfinished.

'And you manage it all?' Gazing across the white hills with their craggy outcrops, he couldn't help but be impressed.

'With help,' she said quickly. 'I couldn't possibly do it on my own. I don't have the expertise or the experience.'

'So what? I couldn't make a film on my own, but I'm still the director.'

She frowned, her forehead furrowing as a patch of sunlight bowled across her face. 'Exactly—you make it all happen,' she said.

'With help,' he echoed. He saw her eyes drop to his

mouth and he smiled. 'I mean, I know how to work most of the equipment, but I'm no expert—and I certainly can't act. Although I have tried.'

He felt his heart start punching against his ribcage as her mouth fluttered at the corners.

'I thought that memory might be seared on your brain.' He screwed up his face. 'Probably trying a cockney accent was a little ambitious…'

She bit her lip. 'The high heels were a nice touch, though.'

His eyes held hers. 'Fortunately for me, you're my only witness.'

'True. But, unfortunately for you, I didn't sign an NDA.'

He knew he was staring at her again, but it was impossible to look away from her soft brown eyes and even softer pink lips.

'Oh, I can think of more enjoyable ways to stop you talking,' he said slowly, his eyes holding hers, letting her know what he wanted.

The silence shivered between them.

Watching her irises darken, he felt his body harden, and then her eyes jerked away from his as they heard someone shout.

It was lunchtime.

'Let me drive.'

Farlan held out his hand and this time Nia handed him the keys with some relief.

The Land Rover was a solid workhorse, but the brake pads were a little worn and sometimes it felt as if the wheels were slipping away from her.

And Farlan liked driving. He had that combination of focus and control that made it look effortless.

Suddenly she realised he had peeled off from the line of ATVs heading down to the lake. 'Where are you going?'

'You did say there'd be time for a little fun later.'

'And you said that you had a call with your producer—'

'I'll speak to him tomorrow. Right now, you and I have a date with a hill and a sledge.'

A date.

The air thumped out of her lungs, his words spinning inside her head, glittering and fragile, like a flurry of snowflakes.

'I don't have a sledge with me,' she said quickly.

'Actually, you do.' He grinned. 'I borrowed Allan's. It's in the back.'

He slowed the car. 'Come on, Nia. It's just a bit of fun. For old times' sake.' His mouth tugged at the corners.

She felt her heart hurtle as if it was on a sledge already. He was so hard to resist, and she could feel herself responding, her body unfurling as if it was reawakening after long years of hibernation.

After what had happened in the library she knew it was too risky. Only refusing would make him more determined to persuade her. He was single-minded, driven in a way she had never understood and couldn't hope to emulate.

And his eyes were so soft and intent...

'We did have fun, didn't we? It wasn't all bad,' he murmured.

Her stomach flipped over.

It had been glorious. A daisy chain of perfect hours. He had made her laugh and dream and *live.*

'It was never bad,' she said quietly.

Not until the end.

Now, more than anything, she wished she could change that.

Maybe this would make that wish come true?

'Your choice, Nia.'

She glanced down at the disappearing ATVs and then moments later, the car crested the slope.

Beneath them, the estate stretched out towards the Cairngorms in the distance. Even after all these years it still took her breath away, and always when she came up here she felt humbled.

It was epically beautiful.

But that wasn't why her heart was knocking against her ribs. After everything she'd promised herself this morning, she'd almost lost her head again a moment ago when they were talking, but now his eyes on hers were clear and determined.

'I'll get the sledge,' he said softly.

Tiny shavings of snow fluttered past her eyes. It would be too risky, too easy to lose track of time. They should come back tomorrow, or another day.

But she couldn't say the words out loud—didn't want to risk losing the sweetness of this renewed intimacy.

And yet… 'The forecast is for more snow—'

'Come on, Nia,' he urged. 'When was the last time you had some fun?'

That was easy. She knew the day…the date. She could probably tell him the exact time too. It had been a day just like this—a day of pure white snow and happiness and wonder.

How could she resist that? *Him?*

Five minutes later she was standing at the top of the hill, gazing down the slope.

'Ready?' he asked.

She nodded.

Farlan was beside her, his green eyes glittering. Taking her hand, he pulled her onto the sledge, slotting her in between his legs. His arm curved around her waist, anchoring her close to him.

She had missed this.

She had missed *him* so much.

And it felt so right—as if their bodies recognised each other.

He brought his face close to hers and she felt his stubble graze her cheek.

'Hold tight,' he instructed.

Time rewound. She was back in Holyrood Park and Farlan was in love with her. He was seconds away from asking her to marry him.

She was trying to stay strong, detached. But his nearness suffocated her resolve…her senses reacted dizzily to the snatch of his breath and the smooth muscles of his thighs on either side of hers.

Leaning back against him, she closed her eyes, her fingers gripping his arms as the sledge skimmed over the snow.

The hard heat of his body melted the minutes away. When she glanced up at the sky next, it was bleached of colour, and had that clarity that preceded a blizzard.

As the wind began whipping up the snow, she felt a prickle of warning. 'We should probably go back now. It's getting late and it's quite a way.'

They could go off-road, but it would be risky. Drifts could make it impossible to gauge how deep the snow was, and there were hidden obstacles—ditches, rocks that could take a tyre out…

'Just one more time?'

He phrased it as a question, but she knew it was a formality. He'd already made up his mind.

As if to prove her point, he smiled at her—that smile no one could resist.

She hesitated. There was just a fingernail of sun left in the sky. 'I'm not sure that would be a good idea.'

The temperature was already dropping, and she knew from experience that in this kind of environment minutes mattered.

'I really think—' she began.

But it was too late. He was already pulling her against the heat of his body.

As they ploughed into the snow at the bottom of the hill she glanced back over her shoulder.

The sky was quivering.

Pulling out her phone, she felt a sudden panic as she saw that she had no signal.

'Farlan, we need to leave before it starts snowing.'

It already was. As she spoke, fat, shaggy flakes began to drift and spin down from the sky.

Inside the car, he began fiddling with the heater.

'It doesn't work,' she said quietly.

She should have said something earlier. Farlan hadn't been in Scotland for so long he'd probably forgotten how swiftly the weather could deteriorate.

'Which way?' he asked.

'Head towards the lake.' She glanced up at the putty-coloured clouds. Hopefully they would get back to the road before the snow got any heavier.

They didn't.

She watched, with a sense of dread building in her chest, as the windscreen wipers began to grind against the snow.

He turned to her.

'Is there somewhere we could go? A barn, maybe?' His voice was calm, but she could see the tension in his shoulders. 'Some kind of shelter?'

She shook her head. 'There's nothing close…' Her stomach clenched with a rush of hope. 'No—that's not true. There's the bothy. It shouldn't be locked, but—'

Her eyes found his and, reaching out, he gently touched her cheek. 'Only one way to find out.'

It was difficult to see now. Outside the car everything was a tumbling mass of white, as if a feather duvet had burst.

'I think that's it,' she said hoarsely.

Up ahead, there was a dark, angular shape. The Land Rover crunched over the snow towards it with agonising slowness, the wind blotting out the whine of the transmission. As it juddered to a standstill, Farlan yanked up the handbrake.

'Wait in the car.'

He was gone before she could speak. Left alone, she tried to stay calm. What if they couldn't get in?

She checked her phone: still no signal.

The door opened. He was back, snowflakes glittering at the ends of his long, dark lashes.

'It's open. And there's a place where we can put the car. I just need to clear away some snow. Do you think you could drive? I might have to push if it gets stuck.'

As she nodded, he reached past her and grabbed a shovel.

'Give me five minutes.'

She clambered into the driver's seat and then slowly began inching the car forward. Even though she was shivering with cold, she could feel perspiration trickling down her back.

The windscreen wipers were too clogged to move now, and she drove blind until suddenly the noise of the wind faded. With relief, she stopped the car.

'Are you okay?' Farlan slid in beside her.

She started to nod, but he was frowning.

'You're shivering. Here.'

He yanked off his jacket and wrapped it around her. The lining of his jacket still held the heat of his body. How was he so warm? she thought.

'I'm sorry,' she said. 'This is my fault.'

'How?' His forehead creased. 'You tried to tell me and I wouldn't listen. But it'll be okay.'

He pulled out his phone and glanced at the screen.

'The signal's pretty weak, but I'll text Tom. Hopefully it'll get through at some point.'

With an effort, she kept her voice steady. 'It's probably safer to stay here overnight. Unless you want someone to come and get us?'

There was a silence. Gazing into his eyes, she felt her brain jam. As he leaned forward and brushed a strand of hair away from her face she shivered again, but not from cold.

The car felt suddenly small. Every breath, every heartbeat, was separate and audible. She could feel the leather beneath her legs and his fingers warm against her cheek.

'I don't want that,' he said softly.

The air rushed out of her body. She could feel his gaze but she couldn't look at him—knew that if she did he would see everything: her regret, her need, her hope.

'What do you want, Farlan?' she asked finally.

He didn't answer, and as the silence stretched she wondered if her words had got lost in her heartbeat.

Then, reaching over, he gently turned her face to his.

Everything blurred. She thought she was gripping the steering wheel to stop the car sliding sideways, only to realise that it wasn't moving.

'Let me show you.'

Her pulse jolted and then he lowered his mouth to hers and kissed her.

CHAPTER FIVE

NIA FELT HERSELF catch fire. His thumbs captured her face. She felt his mouth brush over hers, gentle at first and then harder, his tongue parting her lips. His hands were sliding over her body, pulling her across the car so that she was straddling him.

The space was so small that her shoulder scraped against the window.

He was very hard. She could feel him through the layers of their clothing, feel the rawness of his desire.

Heat was flooding her limbs.

She kissed him back clumsily, her mouth seeking his, her hands winding around his neck.

He drew her closer, fumbling with the front of her jacket, tugging her arms free.

She felt his hands slide under her jumper, his fingers warm and decisive against her bare skin, gasping out loud as he caressed her stomach.

Heat rippled across her body as his hands splayed against her back to find the clasp of her bra, and then his palms were cupping her breasts, the thumbs finding her nipples.

Hunger reared up inside her.

She moaned, wanting more of his touch, more of his mouth, and as though he could follow her thoughts he tipped her head, baring her throat to his lips and then, lowering his face, taking one nipple into the heat of his mouth.

Breath shuddering, she shifted against him, pushing down against the hard press of his erection, wanting, needing, to appease the pulsing ache between her thighs. And then she was pulling at his belt, her fingers yanking at the leather, releasing him—

'Nia—Nia, I don't have any condoms.'

Condoms.

Her eyes fluttered open as the word echoed inside her head.

'I mean, I wasn't expecting to—'

His face was taut with concentration and she could tell from the tremor in his voice that he was holding himself in check, expecting, waiting for her to call a halt. All it would take was one word.

'I'm on the pill.' She hesitated. 'Are you…? I mean—'

'You don't need to worry.' He took her face in his hands. 'I don't normally do this.'

'I don't either,' she whispered.

He kissed her deeply and then, lifting her hair, let his mouth find her throat.

'So are you—? Do you still want to—?'

To answer him she reached down and took him in her hand, her fingers closing around his solid, straining length.

He pulled her closer, his breath jerking against her mouth, and then he kissed her hard, his hands pushing beneath the waistband of her trousers and panties, yanking them down.

She was lifting her hips, trying to help him. Her head bumped into the roof of the car but she didn't care. Nothing mattered except dousing this heat that was both necessary and merciless.

His eyes tangled with hers and she felt him push up and push through. And then he was inside her, hot and hard and sleek, and she was reaching for him blindly, moving with an urgency that robbed her of thought, leaving only a shapeless elemental craving.

The car was rocking from side to side. It was sex at its

most basic. A frenzied assault on their senses, their mouths and hands frantic.

'Look at me, Nia.'

His voice was hoarse, his breathing staccato.

She squeezed her thighs together, chasing the heat, feeling Farlan grow even harder, and then she tensed, muscles clenching, nails digging into his jumper, body melting around his as he stiffened and shuddered inside her.

Heart pounding, she lay limply against Farlan's chest, her face buried in his jumper, breathing in the warm scent of his body.

The damp stickiness between her thighs was already growing cold, and her leg ached where it was wedged against the door, but she was too busy struggling with the reality of what they had just done to care.

What she had just done.

The consequences of her actions exploded inside her head in the same way that Farlan had just exploded inside her body.

She knew she should regret it. It had probably made everything a hundred times more awkward between them, and giving in to temptation had been weak and selfish and wrong. And yet how could anything that had felt so good, so right, be wrong?

It had been like skating together on a frozen lake. For those few miraculous moments they had been in harmony, their bodies perfectly synchronised, every touch, every breath flowing like water.

Farlan shifted against her—and just like that she heard the ice crack beneath them, and a cool, relentless thread of reality begin winding its way up through her body.

But this wasn't just about her and her feelings…

'Nia—'

His voice was hoarse, uncertain. Fearing his regret, or worse, she kept her head lowered. Just for a moment she wanted to linger here, in his arms, cocooned in this snow-covered vehicle, in the space between hope and fantasy, where their mutual hunger had distorted time and merged the past with the present.

'Nia.'

There was no escaping his hand, and as he tilted her face up to his there was no escaping his questioning eyes either.

But he didn't speak again, and she felt her heart begin beating faster once more.

She had been foolish and reckless, but not a day passed when she didn't feel some kind of regret for the way she had acted, for the way her life had turned out.

She was tired of living with regrets, and she didn't want to add these moments to the list. Whatever he said now—whatever happened next—she had wanted Farlan and he had wanted her.

Maybe she hadn't been in control of herself or her hunger, but acting on her desire had made her feel more powerful and alive than she had in years, and she wouldn't—*she couldn't*—wish that away.

She took a breath. 'I'm not expecting you to feel the same way...' The words spilled out of her mouth. 'But I just want you to know that I don't regret it.'

There—she had said it.

She couldn't go back in time.

She couldn't unpick the mess she had made or erase the memories.

But if this was the last moment they shared she was glad that she had told him the truth. Glad that in the future she could look back and know that this time, at least, they hadn't parted with mistrust and confusion.

'I don't regret it either.'

His hands tangled in her hair, bunching it in his fists as if to prevent her escape. He kissed her again, his mouth heating hers.

'How could I regret that? Did you think I would? That I could?'

He seemed confused, almost stunned. And, meeting his gaze, she saw that he looked as blindsided as she felt.

'I don't know.' She stopped. 'Maybe. It all happened so fast.'

Except it hadn't—not really.

Ever since Farlan had walked into the drawing room five days ago she had felt as though she was standing at the shore, watching a wave build out at sea, waiting for it to come crashing over her head.

Only the details—the time, the place—had been unscripted. As had the aftermath.

'I didn't plan it—'

'I know.'

The gentleness of his voice made her still inside. Made her remember and regret. Last time she hadn't said enough and she had made a mess of everything. This time she didn't want there to be any misunderstandings.

'You don't need to worry. This was a one-off. I'm not expecting anything from you. I know this kind of thing can happen.'

She knew she was speaking too quickly—babbling, in fact. But this was a different kind of truth. One that she didn't want to tell. And just saying it out loud hurt.

She didn't want to linger on it, or have to see the relief in his eyes, and so, shifting her weight, she leaned sideways and rooted around on the floor for their jackets.

'Apparently so,' he said.

As she handed him his jacket his green eyes locked onto hers, his expression impassive, impossible to read.

'And, just so we're clear, I'm not expecting anything from you either.' Reaching up he pushed her hair away from her face. 'So, no regrets, then?'

The past swelled up between them, but there was too much to say, too many words for this cramped space.

She shook her head.

'Good.' Leaning forward, he kissed her, gently at first, then harder. 'Then maybe we should get inside, otherwise we *will* have something to regret. Like catching hypothermia.'

Slamming the door against a flurry of windborne snowflakes, Farlan felt shame heat his face.

Had he really just made a joke about hypothermia?

His jaw tightened. He was savagely, crushingly furious with himself.

He might not have been in Scotland for seven years, but he understood the dangers of a blizzard.

Having spent his teenage years on a farm, he knew that freezing temperatures and snowdrifts killed livestock. And they killed humans too.

If their phones had had any signal then they would probably have got away with nothing worse than a few scary hours sitting in a whiteout, waiting for a rescue party. But without a phone signal, in a car without a working heater, they were always going to be in trouble.

And yet, despite knowing what was at stake, he had ignored Nia—ignored her when she had first told him that there was more snow forecast, and then again when the sky had started to bleach out.

She had tried to persuade him to leave, but instead of listening, instead of letting her change his mind, he had overridden her natural and legitimate concerns about the weather and the distance they would need to travel to reach the road.

He had told himself that a couple more minutes wouldn't matter either way.

But it had mattered.

Only what had mattered more to him—what always mattered the most—was that he had stayed firm.

It was like a badge of honour never to let himself be swayed, and because of that he had put his life, Nia's life, in jeopardy.

'We should probably light a fire.'

She had turned to face him, and in the brighter light of the bothy he saw that she was pale and shivering again.

Galvanised into action, he swore softly and, grabbing her hand, towed her across the room to one of the sofas that sat on either side of a cast-iron wood burner.

'I'll do that. You sit here.'

He glanced around. Next to the sofa there was a basket stacked high with colourful plaid woollen blankets and, tugging two from the pile, he wrapped them around Nia's shoulders.

It was the easiest fire he'd ever built. The kindling was already neatly arranged in the grate, and the logs were so well-seasoned the wood burner roared into life almost as soon as he lit the match.

She started to stand up. 'I'll make some tea—'

'Sit.' He pushed her firmly back down. 'I can make tea, Nia.'

In the kitchen, he found the tea easily, and there was long-life milk next to the tea caddy. He poured out two cups and then, catching sight of a bottle of Laphroaig, he put the milk down and took the whisky instead. Unscrewing the bottle, he tipped a measure into her cup, then his own.

The liquid burned his throat twice, heat and peat, but he was glad—grateful to have something to offset the panic building in his chest.

If the snow had got heavier more quickly…

If they had been headed in a slightly different direction…

The 'ifs' piled up like snowdrifts.

He watched her take a sip of tea, his head swimming with all the possible alternative outcomes they had so narrowly avoided.

'It could have been so much worse,' he said quietly. 'If we hadn't found this place when we did.'

He could see the car in his mind's eye a tiny speck on a white landscape, drifts of snow swallowing it whole. He felt the sharp quickening of terror. The thought was unbearable.

'I'm fine, Farlan.'

Looking up, he found her watching him, her brown eyes reddish gold in the firelight. His heart twisted with guilt. She was worried about him.

Worried. About *him*.

The fact that she could feel that way, given his utter recklessness, stunned him.

'Nia…' Taking her hand, he pulled her against him, guilt swamping his anger. 'This is my fault. This is all my fault,' he muttered.

'How is it your fault?'

She sounded almost cross, and when he looked down at her he saw that she was frowning.

'I'm not a simpleton or a child, Farlan. I've lived here all my life. I know the risks. I should have made it clearer. Insisted.'

His mouth twisted. 'You tried. I didn't listen.'

She bit her lip. 'Then I should have said it louder,' she said quietly. 'Stuck to my guns. But, as you know, I've never been very good at that.'

Remembering how the snow had blotted out the windscreen, he stared at her in silence. No, she wasn't any good at sticking to her guns. And he had crucified her for that fact—at the time and then for years afterwards.

Put simply, she had been wrong and he had been wronged. Only now he was beginning to see another side to her actions—and to his response.

Back then he had been angry with Nia for listening to her parents even though she'd been a teenager and he'd been asking her to give up everything she had ever known for him—a boy. And at twenty-two he had still been more a boy than a man.

Persuading her to spend another ten, fifteen, twenty minutes sledging was different. That's what he'd told himself.

But all that was different was he was the one doing the persuading.

And that was what mattered. It was what had always mattered.

But he couldn't explain to Nia why he needed to have that power. Not here, not now, and truthfully probably not ever.

To explain would mean talking about his past, revealing the pitiful details of a life he would rather forget—a life he'd worked hard to forget.

Maybe if he and Nia had worked out he might have told her some of it. But after what had happened he didn't trust her, and he doubted he ever would.

His eyes flicked to her face.

None of that was important right now.

Reaching out, he caught her hand in his. 'It's not your fault, Nia. I should have listened, and I didn't, and I'm sorry. Sorry for putting you in danger.'

He tightened his fingers around hers, wanting, needing, to feel the warmth of her skin.

'It's just that once I make up my mind, I find it hard to change it. You might have noticed I have a bit of a thing about that…'

He'd been trying to lighten the mood, but as she looked up at him he felt his heart slow, and all at once he was conscious only of how badly he wanted to pull her closer.

And not just to comfort her.

He let the silence drift as their eyes met. Hers were soft with whisky and fatigue and something else—something that made his thoughts turn to slow flurries.

Unthinkingly, he leaned forward, his body tingling as her lips parted. Around them the air shivered, the heat from the stove pushed against them—

They both jerked apart as a familiar sound broke the silence.

A text alert.

Her phone, not his.

'I should—'

'Of course.'

He watched, his pulse jumping with a sudden and disproportionate agitation, as she checked the message.

'It's Allan,' she said, looking down at the screen. 'He just wants to know if we got back okay.'

They hadn't. And when Allan found that out, then what?

Those ATVs did exactly what their name suggested. They went anywhere, on any terrain. It would take two maybe three hours tops for a rescue party to reach them.

He felt himself tense. *If Nia wanted to be rescued.*

She was edging away from him, texting back.

'What are you saying?'

Her eyes lifted to his and his hand moved from her waist to her hair, his fingers sliding among the strands.

'Just that we're safe, and that we'll be fine until morning.'

Until morning.

In other words they would be spending the night together.

He felt his groin turn to stone with a speed that was predictable and painful.

And pointless.

What had happened had been a one-off, right?

Loosening his grip, not wanting her to feel that he was hard again already, he nodded.

'Yes, we will.'

He forced his gaze away from her face, from the swell of the breasts that she had so recently bared to his mouth, to the far less arousing pile of logs that were stacked with aesthetic symmetry on either side of the wood burner.

'So, first I'm going to get that fire going properly, and then we should see if there's anything to eat.'

Nia looked down at their knees, almost touching, and frowned. 'We should probably get out of these damp clothes.'

He knew what she meant, but it didn't stop a tug of longing, sharp like hunger, from pulling at him inside. Or keep her eyes from jerking away from his.

'Good idea,' he said, letting her off. 'We can dry them by the fire.'

He unlaced his boots and yanked them off. Straightening up, he reached for his belt, his fingers suddenly clumsy as he realised it was still undone.

Their eyes met.

'Don't worry, I trust you not to take advantage of me,' he teased.

She smiled then, as he'd hoped she would, and began pulling off her trousers.

The kitchen was well-stocked.

'Well, we won't starve anyway,' he said, holding up a tin of caviar and a jar of Fortnum and Mason porcini and truffle tomato sauce.

'I'll put some pasta on,' she replied.

As she bent down to pull out a pan, his eyes were drawn irresistibly to the length of her legs—more specifically to where the hem of her jumper rode high on her thighs.

He felt the muscles in his arms twitch. If he was on set,

he would be yelling *Action!* right now. Suddenly, the urge to reach over and pull her against him was almost overwhelming.

'There might even be some parmesan,' she said.

Dragging his gaze away, he opened the fridge.

There wasn't. But there was a bottle of Bollinger champagne.

'Nia—' he began.

Turning, she caught sight of the bottle, and then his face, and burst out laughing. 'I suppose we do have something to celebrate.'

Farlan felt his blood lighten. He liked hearing her laugh and watching her smile. It made him think about something other than making movies. It made him forget the past.

They had a picnic by the fire. Sitting cross-legged, they ate caviar with crackers, followed by pasta and then to finish, figs in port.

'That has to be one of the best meals I've ever eaten,' he said, bouncing a smile across the space between them.

He leaned back and let his gaze slowly track around the room. Bothies were supposed to be basic. Just four walls and a roof to give temporary shelter to a hiker or a hunter stranded by dangerous weather.

That had been his experience anyway, the one and only other time he'd stayed in one.

His shoulders tensed. He'd been with his brother Cam, camping. The tail-end of a hurricane had dumped a month's worth of rain in a matter of hours.

It had been the last summer before his brother had left to go on the oil rigs.

Before Farlan's life had imploded again.

Before Cam had become the latest in the ever-lengthening line of people who had made a choice that wasn't him.

Heading off the traces of fear and misery that always accompanied those memories, he glanced past Nia at the plum-coloured chenille sofas that sat on either side of the huge log burner, wondering why the sight of them made a beat of anger pulse down his spine.

'This is a nice place,' he said tightly. 'Maybe a bit spartan for my tastes—'

A flush of cochineal spread slowly over her cheeks. 'It was one of my mother's projects. She had a very specific vision.'

The fine hairs rose at the nape of his neck. He knew all about the Countess of Brechin's vision—insofar as he knew he hadn't ever been a part of it. But Nia's parents had intruded in his life anyway. They had taken away the girl he'd loved, deprived him of the future he'd planned, and he wasn't going to let them get inside his head again now.

'I'm just playing with you,' he said. Softening his expression, he reached over and picked up a faded copy of *Tatler*. 'I guess I was expecting something a little more rudimentary. The last bothy I stayed in had no electricity or running water.'

She nodded. 'They are mostly like that—the ones that anyone can use. But this part of the estate is private and—and it was just a bit of fun, really.'

He didn't like seeing that wariness in her eyes. Knowing he was the cause of it made him like it even less.

'She did a good job. It's beautiful,' he said.

Looking across into her pale, upturned face, he felt his heartbeat ricochet against his ribcage.

'But not as beautiful as you,' he added quietly.

They stared at one another in silence, and again he felt the shock of what they had just done.

What he wanted to do again.

It had felt so right, being inside her, holding her. He had known that holding her was unnecessary, and self-indulgent, that he'd needed to break the mood, only he'd been powerless to move.

Nia had done that.

He thought back to what she'd said in the car.

'I'm not expecting anything from you. I know this kind of thing can happen...'

Was that true?

For him? No. That would require some kind of pre-existing relationship, and there had been no one since Nia. Hooking up with someone you had slept with once hardly qualified.

But for her? Had there been others since him?

He felt a sting of anger. Was that why she was on the pill? Was there some ex in the mix? Someone more recent?

His hands clenched.

Even before he'd started making movies he'd always had an ability to play things out in his head scene by scene. He'd always seen it as a gift, but now, picturing Nia, her lips kissing some nameless man, their bodies entwined in a tangle of sheets, he felt jealousy burn through him.

Suddenly he wanted to ask her why she was on the pill—except that would sound completely mad.

But this whole week had been crazy…

Coming back to Scotland, to Lamington, seeing Nia. Then today, being out there in a blizzard and having sex with her in the car like a teenager. And now being in here, with the two of them half-naked…

No wonder he wasn't himself.

Watching her kneel in front of the stove, he felt his pulse stumble. The log looked huge and brutal in her hand and, remembering the moment when the snow had blotted out the light, he felt a flare of fear, worse than before.

Putting his hand on her arm, he pulled her against him, curling his arm around her body, needing to feel the slow, steady beat of her heart. She rested her head on his shoulder and together they watched the fire in silence.

'I'm sorry,' he said.

'I'm sorry too,' she said quietly.

'No.' Shifting her weight, he looked down into her face. 'I told you—you have no reason to be sorry.'

'I wasn't talking about now.'

He stilled.

'I'm talking about what happened before. With us. How it happened. What I did and what I didn't do.'

There was a long pause.

Nia felt her throat tighten. His expression didn't alter, but there was new tension in him, like the warning hum from the electric fences on the estate.

'Hey, let's not do this right now.'

He spoke easily, but again she sensed the tension, and could hear the unspoken plea. *Don't mess with the mood.*

She hesitated, but she couldn't sit there and leave other words unspoken.

Her mouth firmed. She should have said something earlier. Only with his green gaze resting on her face, and his warm body so close, she had got lost in the moment and in her memories.

It would be so easy just to lie here next to him and listen to the sound of his breathing. But soon he would get up and leave, and once again she would be left with only memories.

It had been seven years. She needed to live. To move on. To kiss again, to love again. She couldn't do that unless she put the past behind her. And to do that she had to face what she had done—admit the truth.

'I need to say this. There were so many things I got wrong b-before—' the word snagged on her tongue '—things I didn't say. I want to say them now. I want you to know all of it.'

Maybe not everything.

She couldn't betray her aunt and uncle like that.

But she could make him understand.

'When we went to Lamington that day I was nervous. I knew my parents wouldn't be happy for me, but I didn't think they would be so utterly opposed to the idea. When they were, I panicked.' Her eyes found his. 'I should have left with you, but I thought I could talk them round.'

'But they talked you round instead.'

The bitterness in his voice whipped against her skin.

'No.' She shook her head. 'No. Of course, I listened to them—'

'Why "of course"? It was *our* lives—not theirs.'

'I was nineteen, Farlan.' She only just found the words. 'And I know you don't like them, and what my father said was completely unacceptable—'

'Unacceptable?' He shifted backwards. His whole body was shaking. 'It was appalling. He said I was a nobody.'

Her body felt as if it was splitting in two. To hear her father say those words had been horrifying. Hearing Farlan repeat them now made her feel sick—actually physically sick.

'He was wrong. You were never a nobody. You were—*you are*—the most amazing man I've ever met.'

Her heart was pounding and the need for him to feel the truth of her words was overriding everything else, even the shuttered expression on his face.

'But this is my life, Farlan. I don't think you ever understood that. I don't think I really understood it either. Until that day when we came back to the estate.'

He let his hand drop down to his side. 'You were my life, Nia, and I was supposed to be yours.'

'And you were…' She faltered for a moment. 'But even if I had done what you asked of me—if I had left my family, my home, Scotland—it wouldn't have been for ever. I would have had to come back to Lamington in the end.'

He grimaced. 'Lamington. Always Lamington. It's just

a house, Nia. A really big house, but still just a bunch of bricks and mortar. And you're a snob.'

She felt a fluttering anger rise up inside her. 'And *you're* an inverted snob. You know nothing about Lamington. Or me.'

'Oh, I know everything about you, Lady Antonia.'

'No, you don't,' she snapped. 'Lamington isn't just "a really big house", it's part of the village. We employ local people, train them, support them—'

'More like exploit them,' he said coldly.

'How dare you?' She felt her face dissolving in shock. 'They're like family to me.

'Paid family.' He shook his head slowly, the green of his eyes sharp like broken glass.

'Yes—paid. Like me.' Her voice was shaking. 'I have a role here too, Farlan. And responsibilities. And a vision that's every bit as important to me as your films are to you. Only you don't understand that, or like it, or value it, and that's why I broke up with you.'

It was suddenly difficult to speak past the lump in her throat.

'Nia—'

She put up a hand. 'I know my parents. They are snobs, and they're difficult, and sometimes I don't like them very much but I knew they would come round in the end. Only then I thought about what that would really mean. I knew that you loved me, and that you would give up everything for me, just like I was going to do for you, only I knew how unhappy that would make you, and I couldn't do that to you,' she whispered.

Lowering her head, she hugged her knees to her chest.

'Why didn't you tell me?' She heard his intake of breath, and then two strong arms curved beneath her. 'No, you don't need to answer that.'

She felt Farlan's lips brush against her hair.

'I know why. I didn't give you a chance.'

His arms tightened around her.

'I'm sorry. I should have let you talk on the phone that day, but I was so furious, and hurt…'

He sounded defensive.

Looking up, she saw that his mouth was set in a grim line. 'I know,' she said. 'I should never have told you on the phone. I was going to come to the station, but then, when I heard your voice, I couldn't bear it, so I told you, and you were so angry. I couldn't think of the words I needed to say, and then you just hung up—'

There was a long silence. A muscle was working in his cheek.

'I tried to call you back,' she said. 'I tried so many times. But your phone—'

'I threw it away.' He smiled humourlessly. 'Big mistake. My whole life was on that phone.'

Her eyes slid away from his. So many misunderstandings.

'I'm sorry.' She felt sick. 'I made a mess of everything.'

She felt his fingers touch her face, tilt up her chin.

'*We* made a mess of everything. Maybe if we'd been older, or if we'd waited a bit longer or gone travelling first—'

But it was more than that. It was easy to blame their break-up on tiny individual decisions, but none of that would have mattered if they'd been meant to be together.

Lovers who were at cross-purposes didn't stay lovers for long for one obvious reason. For a relationship to work, you needed to be able to communicate with each other, and she and Farlan had only ever communicated effectively on one level.

Her heart skipped a beat and, looking up, she found him watching her, his gaze steady and unblinking. A current of heat spiralled up inside her.

For a moment neither of them moved.

'Nia…'

He spoke her name softly and she felt her mouth turn dry.

'What happened in the car—'

'Shouldn't have happened,' she said quickly.

His hand slid among the strands of her hair. 'You said that about what happened in the library.'

'I know.' She bit her lip. 'We can't—'

'You don't want to?'

She stared at him mutely. It was a rhetorical question—they both knew that.

'We didn't plan it. It just happened. It had to happen. I don't know why.'

She knew he was right. It had felt like a compulsion—a desperate need that had overridden all rational thought. Only however frantic it had been, it had still been opportunistic. Like finding fallen apples in an orchard. But this—this would be like picking them off the tree.

She met his gaze, felt panic mingling with desire, and something in his eyes steadied her.

'It's not wrong, Nia, to want what we had.' Lowering his face, he let his lips graze hers. 'To want to make it right for just a few hours.'

They couldn't change the past. They couldn't go back to being those two young lovers. But would it be so very wrong to steal back a few hours of that time?

'One night…' She breathed it out against his mouth, and then, wrapping her arms around his neck, she shifted against him, slotting herself over the hard ridge of his erection.

'Yes, one night.' His voice was hoarse. 'If that's what you want, Nia?'

'Yes…' she whispered and, clasping his face in her hands, she kissed him.

CHAPTER SIX

SHE MADE A little sound as her lips touched his, her stomach swooping upwards like a fish on a hook. There was no need for caution. No need to balance her desire with quantifiable reality.

This wasn't about the past or the future.

There would be no tomorrow.

But she wanted this. She wanted him. And that was enough.

'Let's just have one last night, Farlan. Just you and me. And in the morning it'll be like a dream.' Leaning forward, she brushed her lips against his again, breathing in his scent. 'A beautiful dream.'

He closed his eyes, and she felt a chaos of hope and hunger beneath her skin, and then he kissed her again, and the flowering intensity of his desire made her whole body tremble.

'Wait—' With a groan, he broke the kiss and, scooping her into his arms, carried her to the sofa. 'You're probably already black and blue from earlier. This time we're going to take it slow.'

She stared up at him, her blood turning to air. And then he lowered his mouth to hers.

He tasted warm and smoky from the whisky, and she felt a fluttering heat rise up inside her as he parted her lips, kissing her fiercely, opening his mouth to her, deepening the kiss.

Only she wanted more.

'Take it off,' she whispered against his mouth. And, grabbing the hem of his sweater, he tugged it up and over his head.

Heart thudding, Nia did the same.

His eyes narrowed, and with deliberate slowness she reached behind her back and unhooked her bra, peeling the delicate straps away from her shoulders and breasts.

The air between them crackled like the wood in the fire.

Glancing up at his bare chest, she felt her breath catch.

It was the first time she had seen him naked, or nearly naked, in seven years, and her beautiful boy had filled out. To be so close, to have the freedom to touch him, stripped away all and any inhibition she might have felt.

She leaned forward and touched his skin. It was warm and a pale golden colour, like lightly toasted bread. Gently, she traced the contoured lines of his obliques, and then, with fingers that shook slightly, she stroked the fine hairs that ran down the middle of his stomach to where they disappeared beneath the waistband of his trunks.

He jerked backwards, his eyes narrowing, and then his hand caught hers. Glancing down, she felt her mouth dry. He was hard already, his erection tenting against the soft cotton…

Gazing down at Nia, Farlan felt his body turn to stone. He'd had no idea that her near nakedness could bring such a ferment of desire.

He had touched her in the car, but he hadn't been looking at her—really looking at her. Now that he was, he just wanted to gaze and gaze, to drink in the soft curve of her breasts and their taut, ruched tips.

But he couldn't not touch her.

Leaning forward, he kissed her shoulder, her collarbone, chasing the pulse in the insanely smooth skin of her throat to the hollow behind her ear.

His groin was aching, the pain almost at that peak where it was pleasurable. Lifting his head, he found her mouth again, maddened by its shape, and its softness, and by the flutter of her breath against his lips. Slowly, he teased the bow of her mouth, top and then bottom, his head starting to spin as she moaned softly.

Heat flared inside him.

He was so hard already, but he could wait. He had waited, he realised a moment later. Always he had been waiting—for this moment, with this woman.

His hand slid over her face and he pulled her closer, cupping her cheek. He kissed her again, parting her lips, tasting her, breathing her in.

Reaching out, he touched her breast, covering it with the palm of his hand, feeling the tiny shivers of anticipation dance over her skin as the nipple hardened.

'Nia,' he whispered. 'My beautiful Nia.'

Her brown eyes were drowsy with desire. She stroked his face, running her finger over his jaw, scraping the stubble, teasing his mouth with her thumb.

He dragged in a breath as her other hand began to caress the thick length of his erection. It would be all over quickly if he let her carry on doing that.

Capturing her hands, he raised them above her head and licked slowly down her body, his groin throbbing as she squirmed and arched beneath him.

When he reached the triangle of soft curls he parted her with his tongue, flattening it against her swollen clitoris, feeling her unfold, tamping down the decadent ache spreading out inside him.

He let go of her hands and her fingers found his head, pressing him closer, and then closer still, and then she was moving more urgently. 'I want you inside me.'

She was pulling him up and over her body, her hands skimming his ribs. Now he let her take him in her hand, her thumb smoothing over the hard, straining head as she fed him inside the slick heat between her thighs.

His body was starting to shake.

Sliding his hand under her bottom, he raised her hips, wanting more depth, and then she was reaching up, clasping his face in her hands, kissing him as he began to move rhythmically with her, their bodies blurring as she arched upwards and he surged inside her.

Inching backwards, Farlan gently lifted Nia's arm from his chest and waited, holding his breath as she murmured in her sleep.

But she didn't wake, and after a couple more seconds he felt around on the floor for his trunks, pulled them on and then made his way silently across the room, using the red glow of the fire to find his way in the darkness.

In the kitchen, he found a glass and filled it from the tap, gulping the ice-cold water greedily, thinking that the hollowed-out feeling in his chest must be thirst.

Only the pang didn't fade. Not even when he'd drunk another glass.

Breathing out slowly, he put the glass in the sink.

His body felt great—replete and drained in a way that only happened after sex, as if all the tension had been ironed out of it.

His head, on the other hand was a knotted tangle of confusing and conflicting thoughts.

He felt his hands twitch and he pressed them against the counter, trying to steady himself.

He'd thought he had it all worked out, that he had Nia all worked out. He'd been so sure that she was in the wrong, that she had allowed herself to be persuaded into choosing her aristocratic lifestyle over him.

And she had.

Only not for the reasons he'd believed.

The ache in his chest crept outwards.

He had been so desperate for proof that he came first, that he was everything to her, and now—guttingly—it turned out that he had been. Thanks to his obsessive need to know that, he had failed to see the truth staring him in the face.

Instead—ironically—he had let himself be distracted by the very things he had accused her of preferring.

As far as he'd been concerned she had Lamington and the estate, so he'd framed her commitment to him in terms of what she was prepared to give up.

But he hadn't understood.

His mouth twisted. It hadn't even crossed his mind that, for Nia, Lamington wasn't just a big house filled with beautiful objects. That she cared about the ongoing life of the estate and the people who lived and worked on it.

Remembering Allan's text message, he felt his chest tighten. They cared about her too.

And it wasn't just a matter of duty. She had a vision for Lamington—although, unlike his film career, they had never got around to discussing that.

No wonder she had broken up with him.

Except that hadn't been the reason either.

His fingers tightened against the worktop.

Nor had she simply given in to her parents' demands.

Instead she had thought about their relationship and their dreams, and about him and his dreams. And, knowing how much he loved her, knowing him better than he knew himself, she had correctly guessed that he would do anything to make her happy—including running the estate with her, even if it made him miserable.

And she hadn't been able even to think about that happening, much less make it happen.

His shoulders tensed.

Would it have changed anything if they had talked it through properly, like adults?

Maybe.

If Nia had been more forthright, and he hadn't been always pushing people to put him above everything and everyone else. In other words, only if they had both been different people.

Shivering, he glanced around the darkened kitchen, the chill and the darkness reminding him of another kitchen.

A lifetime ago.

Almost a third of his life had passed since he had last stepped foot in his grandparents' house. In that time so many other memories had faded, but that one remained crisp and unfiltered.

He could see the kitchen as if he was standing in it now. The faded, scrubbed table. His grandmother's enamel pans. The ashtrays piled high with the brown-stained stubs of his grandfather's cigarettes.

They hadn't been bad people. They had taken him in. Given him a bed and food and clothes, a place in their home.

But it had been a grudging place. They had taken him in because there had been nowhere else for him to go.

Only Nia—briefly—and then Tom and Diane had ever made him feel wanted and accepted for himself.

And now that was gone—ruined in a day.

'Farlan?'

He jerked round. Nia was standing in the doorway. She was naked.

He felt as though he'd been kicked in the solar plexus.

The disconnect between the desperation of his thoughts and her luminous beauty was so shocking that for a moment he couldn't speak.

'Are you okay?' she asked.

The concern in her voice made the ache in his chest

spread out like an oil spill, and suddenly the need to confess was like a weight in his stomach.

But could he tell her? Could he tell Nia the truth about why he had backed her into a corner, forced her to choose between her family and an unknown, uncertain future with a man she had known for only a little over six months?

Thinking about the tangle of fresh starts and failures that had made up his childhood, he felt his spine tense.

He wouldn't even know where to begin.

And there wasn't time to unravel everything.

Not right now. Not when all he wanted to do was spin out these precious moments with her, with this beautiful woman he had loved and lost, before morning came and he had to lose her again.

'I'm fine. I was just getting a glass of water.'

Her eyes were fixed on his face, soft and questioning, and he knew she wanted to believe his words.

And yet this was not a normal night for either of them.

Should he tell her about his life? About the loneliness and the rejection? About how for most of his childhood he had felt like an unwanted birthday present that was always being regifted?

Watching her hover in the doorway, he tried out a few sentences in his head. But then his gaze dropped from her face to the pale curves of her breasts, then lower, to the tiny thistle tattoo, and a beat of pure dark need pulsed across his skin.

The time for talking was over.

Right now he wanted—*needed*—to blank out his mind to everything except the feel of her mouth on his and, walking swiftly across the room, he kissed her hungrily, nudging her backwards into the warm darkness.

Nia woke to the sound of someone humming.

No, not someone. *Farlan.*

Rolling over, she gazed blindly across the room as memories of the night before spilled into her head.

Farlan.

She felt her face grow warm. Her body felt almost weighed down with a kind of languid satisfaction and, shifting onto her side, she pressed her thighs together, feeling a pleasurable chafe of tenderness.

Last night had been like a febrile erotic dream, every movement, every touch rich and enticing.

They had kept on reaching for each other, their mouths and hands insistent, stirring, tormenting, pleasuring one another.

It had been as though they'd both understood that time was short.

Without saying so out loud they had known that this was one night of bliss they could steal back from time, suspended, separate somehow, from the onward progress of minutes and hours.

Had known that when it was morning they would wake, and the dream would fade away, and they would go back to their separate lives.

Across the room, the pale square of the window was clearly visible behind the curtains. She hugged the blanket closer. It was morning already.

Her heart contracted.

Last night it had been so simple. Reaching for one another had been all that was required. They hadn't thought further than that. Sex had been both the starting and the finishing line.

Remembering the feel of his mouth on hers, she shivered beneath the blanket.

And that would have been fine—only last night had been more than just sex: they had made love.

'You're awake.'

Glancing over at the doorway, she blinked. If she had

been imagining that this morning they would naturally follow on from last night's intimacy, then she had clearly been alone in those thoughts.

Farlan was fully dressed, and watching her without any sign of yesterday's narrow-eyed hunger.

'It's a beautiful day. The blizzard must have blown itself out overnight. Would you like tea or coffee?'

She stared at him mutely, silenced by the cool, almost brisk tone of his voice and the unspoken message it contained.

'Tea, please,' she said quickly, trying to match his manner.

He turned and disappeared back into the kitchen and she sat up, wishing that she had paid more attention to where she had dropped her clothes.

And that she could shift the strange pang of disappointment beneath her ribs.

Kicking back from that thought, she picked up her phone.

Nine-fifteen.

She had slept so late.

'Here.'

Farlan was back. Still stunned by the time, she reached up unthinkingly and the blanket fell away from her body.

His face stilled. 'I'll put it here.' He backed away, his eyes locking on hers. 'I'll let you get dressed.'

Watching him retreat, she found her clothes and dressed hurriedly. Picking up her tea, she frowned. 'This is real milk.'

'Yeah, when I went outside to check the car I noticed a farm.'

Her eyes jerked up. He was leaning against the doorframe again, rubbing the stubble on his face. Watching the flickering tendons in his hand, she felt something tug beneath her skin.

Wrenching her gaze away, she walked across the room

and drew the curtains. When she looked outside it was hard to believe that last night's storm had even happened. Everything was so still. Beneath the clear blue sky the snow was smooth and deep and even in every direction as far as she could see.

'Classlochie Farm? That's quite a hike.'

He shrugged. 'About forty minutes. But I needed to clear my head so—'

She lifted her cup to hide the flush on her cheeks. He had thrown those words out without hesitation. Clearly he had meant what he'd said last night.

It shouldn't hurt as much as it did. It was what she'd expected and what she wanted too, she told herself.

'I told them we'd got stranded and they gave me some milk. They offered some eggs and bacon too, but I said I was already running late.' He hesitated. 'I suppose we should talk about last night…'

She felt his gaze on her face. 'Yes, I suppose we should,' she said slowly.

She smothered a gasp as he put his hands on her arms and pulled her closer.

'No regrets, right?'

For a moment she didn't answer. His hands felt warm and firm against her skin—and good, unbelievably good. She felt her heart swell for a second. Then she shook her head.

'No. No regrets. I just want it to be okay between us.'

It was incredibly tempting to believe that seven years ago they had simply been knocked off course, that Tom and Diane renting Lamington was fate stepping in to bring them back together.

But his words floated back to her from that first night in the drawing room. And she didn't believe in fairy tales any more either.

She and Farlan 'worked' here, in this remote little bothy,

for the same reason they had 'worked' in his flat in Edinburgh. Because it wasn't real life.

Only aged nineteen, and hopelessly in love, it had been hard for her to see the implications of that fact.

Her heart contracted. It was still hard to accept it aged twenty-six. And she hadn't—not really, not willingly.

But last night in the cramped cabin of the Land Rover, and then again by the glow of the fire, she had been forced to admit—to herself anyway—that what they'd shared didn't, and couldn't ever, work in a real-world situation.

It was better to know that now, before it was too late.

Her chest was suddenly a muddle of pity and panic.

Like Catherine and Richard, her aunt and uncle.

When she was younger, they'd seemed like a fairy tale couple brought to life. Her aunt so beautiful and he an aspiring artist, with a sweet smile and a spaniel. And both so young.

Watching them together, she had been transfixed by the intensity of their love. And the fact that everyone else had been appalled had only seemed to make it all so much more romantic.

Against all opposition, they had married and quickly produced two children. But with bills to pay, and a family to support, Richard had stopped painting and taken a job at an art gallery in Dubai.

Nia shivered inside.

To say that he hated it would be understatement. He loathed it. And Catherine loathed her life in her air-conditioned mansion. And a lot of the time it felt as if they loathed each other too.

She so hadn't wanted that to happen to her and Farlan, and that hadn't changed.

More importantly, he hadn't changed.

He might be a wealthy, successful film director, but

he still didn't understand her connection to her home, to Lamington.

'And we are okay.'

His voice pulled her back and, looking up, she met his gaze. His eyes were clear and green.

'It hurt both of us, the way it ended, and we needed to put that right.' His thumb caressed her cheek. 'Now we can put it behind us and move on.'

Move on.

He meant find someone else.

Her pulse quickened.

Someone he could lie beside in bed and hold as she slept.

Someone who made his heart beat faster when he saw her in a crowded room.

Someone to share his dreams.

Someone to love.

Staring out of the window, she let her eyes track across the landscape to the distant hills that edged the Kilvean estate, belonging to Lord Airlie.

She wanted that too.

She wanted to be with a man and know that she was his and he was hers and nothing could ever come between them.

'Yes,' she said quietly. 'We can both move on.'

Neither of them spoke much on the drive back down to the main road.

There was nothing more to say.

Her heartbeat jumped as they bumped over the cattle grid.

The unstoppable, irresistible bare-bones hunger of last night had been intense and all-consuming, but now they were driving through the gates and past groups of sheep as if the smooth white fields had swallowed all that passion whole.

Was that what she wanted?

Back at the bothy she had thought so, only now—

'I'll drop you at the cottage and then walk back to Lamington.'

His voice cut across her thoughts and, glancing up, she realised it was too late for last-minute doubts. They were already here.

The gardener's cottage looked postcard-pretty.

'Thank you for driving.' She gave him a small, tight smile. 'I promise I'll get someone to look at the car.'

'I wouldn't worry about that,' he said softly.

'Really? But you said that there was something wrong with the brakes.'

'There probably is. But you don't need to worry about that. Not any more.'

She watched in confusion as he turned away, raising his hand in greeting as another car came round the corner and parked behind the Land Rover.

A young man in smooth leather brogues slipped across the snow towards them. 'Mr Wilder? Gordon Muir. We spoke this morning.'

'Of course.' Farlan held out his hand. 'Thanks for making this so easy.' He turned to Nia. 'This is Lady Antonia.'

Blushing, Gordon Muir held out his hand.

'Lady Antonia. Congratulations! You're about to take delivery of an incredible car.'

Take delivery? Nia frowned. 'I'm sorry, I think you must have the wrong person. I don't know—'

Farlan stepped forward casually. 'Gordon, could you just give us a moment? I need to have a quick word with Lady Antonia.'

Turning to Nia, he spread his hands.

'I wanted to surprise you, but now I can see I should probably have said something earlier.' His green eyes rested on her face. 'Look, I know you have more than enough money to buy a fleet of Land Rovers. But I also know you have zero interest in cars and that one is old and worn-out and, frankly, dangerous.'

He smiled at her then, that smile no one could resist.

'So I bought you a new one.'

Her head jerked up. 'You did what?' She felt like Gordon Muir, slip-sliding across the snow. 'When?'

'This morning. Really, it's not that big a deal.'

Glancing over his shoulder, she saw a brand-new Land Rover. She was no expert, but she had looked into replacing her old one often enough to know this sleek, black SUV came with a big price tag.

'I can't accept this.'

He was quiet for a minute, and then he took a step towards her. 'Please, Nia. Please let me do this for you.'

She wanted to be angry, but it was hard. Hard to be angry that he cared about her. And what made it harder still was that he knew her so well.

He had guessed correctly—although for the wrong reasons—that she would never get round to replacing the car and so he'd sorted it out himself.

He had done that for her, and the pleasure and pain of knowing that made her feel slightly shaky.

'I can't—' she began.

He caught her hand. 'Yes, you can.' His eyes on hers were the soft green of young beech leaves. 'If something happened to you… I just need to know you're safe.'

Her heart thudded. 'Thank you,' she said quietly.

Their eyes met and he stared down at her, and suddenly she was breathless at his closeness.

Terrified that he would guess, she tried to smile. 'I'd better go and take a look, then.'

Watching Nia pick her way delicately across the snow-covered road, Farlan could feel his body straining towards her like a Pointer reaching for a scent.

On waking, his guilt about the night before had returned, so that buying the car for her had seemed perfectly rational.

And then he'd told her that they could both move on.

But could something that felt so momentous happen and yet leave no trace?

His eyes flickered momentarily across the smooth white fields, but he knew he hadn't been thinking about last night's blizzard.

Reaching out, he touched the bonnet of the old Land Rover. Despite the chill in the air it was still warm and, staring through the mud-flecked windscreen, he could almost picture their frantic, jerky coupling.

He breathed in sharply against the headrush.

It would pass, he told himself quickly. He wouldn't forget it, or her, but he would make it all fit into his life and find a way to move forward.

'So, what do you think?'

Having enthusiastically explained every feature of the new car, Gordon had just been picked up by his colleague, and they were alone again.

'I think it's amazing.' Nia's eyes found his. 'Thank you again for sorting this out for me.'

'My pleasure. I know cars aren't your thing.' He grinned. 'However, they are mine.'

'Tom told me about your supercar.' She smiled.

'Yeah, it's a great ride. It's just on loan, but I've actually put in an order for one back in the States.'

It had been an enthralling drive. But for some reason the memory of it wasn't giving him the same rush of excitement as before.

'How long is it until you go back?' she asked quietly.

I can go back whenever I want.

The rogue thought popped into his head unasked-for.

He glanced down at her. 'Ten days.'

For a moment she looked somewhere over his shoulder, and then she met his gaze. 'And nights?' she said slowly.

Her words floated between them, pale and sparkling like snowflakes, and a beat of heat pulsed inside him.

Was she saying what he thought she was?

The desire to pull her close, to press his mouth against hers and taste her again, was irresistible, overwhelming…

He held her gaze. 'Nine, actually.'

She nodded, bit her lip, hesitated. 'I was wrong. Back at the bothy, I was wrong.' Her voice dried up for a second and she began again. 'I thought I wanted to have just one night with you, but I don't.'

His heart was jumping in his throat. The space between them seemed both hair-fine and the size of an ocean.

He knew what she was offering because it had already crossed his mind a thousand times since he'd woken that morning.

Only thinking something and saying it out loud were a world apart—especially now, when the aftershocks were still making the ground ripple beneath his feet.

They couldn't rewrite the script or change the ending. For him and Nia the credits had already rolled.

His hands clenched, and with something approaching relief he realised that he was still holding the keys to the old Land Rover.

'I think we both got what we wanted, Nia.' He took an unsteady step backwards. 'And now I should probably get back to Tom and Diane. I'll drive this over to Lamington. It can stay there until you decide what you want to do with it.'

And without waiting for her reply he swung himself into the driver's seat, gunned the engine and drove away.

CHAPTER SEVEN

AN HOUR LATER, having showered, changed his clothes and given Tom and Diane a bowdlerised version of what had happened with Nia, Farlan sat down on the window seat in his bedroom.

He felt as if he was coming down with the flu: his limbs were leaden and he was aching all over. Probably he just needed to sleep…

Glancing over at his bed, he tightened his jaw.

It didn't seem possible that he had already got used to lying with his arms wrapped around Nia's soft body, and yet apparently he couldn't face the thought of sleeping alone.

Particularly with their last conversation buzzing around his head.

Leaning his head against the glass, he felt frustration blur his fatigue—both the sexual kind and exasperation at his and Nia's complete inability to communicate.

Although, to be fair, this time she had made her wishes quite clear.

Nine nights.

He ran a hand through his hair, unsure what was more disconcerting. The fact that Nia had come right out and said what she wanted or the fact that he had turned her down.

Outside, the wind had picked up again, and he watched enviously as a bird wheeled away across the sky, riding the uplift.

When he was directing he felt just like that bird. It was so effortless, so natural, and it had been the same with the upward trajectory of his career. Not once had he doubted himself or questioned his abilities.

But as for relationships…

The nervous skinny child he'd been had blossomed, and people were eager to know him, so it wasn't that he didn't have relationships. He did. What was hard—impossible, really—was letting his friendships develop and deepen.

He knew it was a hangover from his childhood. Basically he didn't trust anyone not to change their mind about him—except maybe Tom and Diane.

He sat for several moments, his eyes tracking the bird.

It was a big deal for him when people changed their minds. In his experience it always had consequences—rarely good, often bad. Life had been unsparing in drumming that lesson into him, and for that reason he was careful never to put his needs in someone else's hands.

Nia had been the only exception to that rule.

His jaw clenched. He hated having to admit that fear played a part in so many of his relationships with people.

But it did.

It had.

Seven years ago with Nia, and then again with her this morning, when she'd thrown that curve ball at him.

Her changing her mind had been enough to make him push her away. Even though he wanted exactly what she wanted.

He shuddered as the memory of his reply pushed its way into his head and, jerking his gaze away from the window, he ran his hand over his face.

There were a thousand ways he could have responded, and he'd had to pick that one.

Across the room, his neatly made bed mocked him.

He couldn't just sit here brooding and, standing up, he walked swiftly to the door. Maybe if he moved fast enough he might be able to put some distance between himself and all thoughts of Nia.

As he walked through the house he could hear Tom and Diane, talking to Molly in the kitchen. Of all the beautiful rooms at Lamington, he knew it was their favourite. It was warm, and bright, and they found something comforting in the hum of the refrigerator and the smell of baking bread.

He lingered in the hall, drawn to the laughter and the domesticity. But he wouldn't be much company, and the effort of pretending he felt fine was beyond him right now.

Spinning round, he made his way down to the garage.

The muscular contours of the supercar had drawn him there, but instead he found himself standing in front of Nia's old Land Rover.

He scowled.

Great, he'd managed not to think about her for roughly five minutes.

His gaze rested on the Land Rover. It looked like an old seaside donkey stabled next to a thoroughbred racehorse.

Why hadn't she replaced it before?

Then everything would have been fine.

Picturing her pale, unguarded face, he swore softly.

From somewhere nearby he heard the sharp, insistent trill of a mobile phone and, peering into the Land Rover, he saw Nia's phone juddering across the seat.

As he yanked open the door it rang out.

For a moment he stared at it in silence, remembering her words.

Nine nights.

It had caught him off guard—Nia saying out loud what he had been thinking and pretending not to think.

Only why pretend? One night *wasn't* enough. They both knew it.

But only Nia had been brave enough to say it.

Admitting it now served no purpose. It was too little, too late.

His chest tightened.

That was what his grandfather had used to say to him when he had forgotten to do a chore and then tried to make amends by offering to help the next time. It was too little, too late.

Gazing blankly out of the kitchen window, Nia felt numb. It was over three hours since Farlan had driven off and she had stumbled into the cottage, her skin hot and tight with the shame of his rejection.

She had spent almost every one of those one hundred and eighty minutes replaying their conversation and trying to work out what had possessed her to act like that.

It hadn't been planned—she knew that. On the drive back down to the cottage she had actually thought it was over, that one night of hot sex had finally done what time and absence had failed to do. She'd started to think that maybe she had a chance of finding happiness.

Then everything had slipped away from her.

Her heart thudded as she thought about the huge, glossy black car parked outside in the drive.

Back in the bothy, it had been easy to tell herself that, however wild and urgent and incredible it had been, it was still just sex.

But then she'd found out what Farlan had done.

And just like that the fact that he had been thinking about her in some way that didn't involve sex, that he cared not just about giving her pleasure but keeping her safe, had made the prospect of moving on dissolve like early-morning mist.

All she'd been able to think about was that he would be leaving soon, and the thought of that night being their last had felt like a hot knife pressed against her skin.

Gazing up into his eyes, she had thought he felt the same way.

Only he hadn't.

She had misread the signs.

Too many years spent managing her parents' whims had blunted her ability to read people. *To read men.* They had made her doubt herself, and sadly there was no one to fulfil their high expectations except her; nowhere to hide from their gaze.

And, despite neither of them ever having worked for a living, they had an antipathy to idleness in others, so Nia had never had much time for fun.

Except with Farlan.

And since him she had been too busy, too distracted by the day-to-day demands of running the estate and managing her parents, to do more than take the occasional day off.

Her cheeks burned.

And she had been celibate for so long.

No wonder everything had got snarled up inside her.

Like every human, she craved intimacy and touch, and with her body so recently reawakened, still aching from their lovemaking, she had wanted more.

She jumped.

The phone was ringing—the landline, not her mobile.

As usual, it wasn't where it was supposed to be, and after searching for some moments she found it on the windowsill by the front door.

'Darling, why do you never answer your mobile phone?'

It was her mother.

'I always answer, Mummy. I was just out in the garden and I left my phone there,' she lied.

Her phone must have slipped out of her pocket when Gordon had been talking to her, but to explain that would mean explaining about Gordon, and she didn't want to risk something slipping out about Farlan.

'Then you must have been out in the garden for a very long time,' her mother said waspishly. 'I've been calling for hours.'

'How is everything?' she asked quickly, hoping to distract her mother. 'How's Daddy and Aunt Catherine?'

'Catherine's exhausted. Run off her feet as usual. But Daddy's fine. We've been playing bridge most afternoons at the club, with Fergus and Margaret Cavendish.'

Her mother paused for just a shade too long to be natural.

'David is here too. He asked after you. I think he was rather hoping you might come out and join us.'

Nia stared out of the window.

David Cavendish was three years older than her and, thanks to his athletic good looks and his father's property empire, he was a favourite of her mother's.

Her shoulders tensed. She should be used to it by now. Her mother still hadn't forgiven her for turning down Andrew's proposal, but her furious lectures and cold-eyed disapproval had now given way to these conversational depth charges.

Mostly Nia let them explode at a safe distance. But today, in the aftermath of Farlan's rejection, she felt unusually vulnerable.

'How long is he staying?' she asked.

She could almost hear the snap of her mother's spine as she sat up straighter.

'Two weeks. He got injured playing polo. I told him you probably wouldn't be able to spare the time, but…'

The unspoken hope in her mother's voice made her wince with guilt. It might be a little old-fashioned, but was it so bad for a mother to want her daughter to find a husband?

And why shouldn't she take a few days off?

It would be fun to lounge by a pool…to have a conversation with a man that didn't feel as if every third word was boobytrapped.

Outside, she could just see the Land Rover's snow-flecked tyres.

Johnny and Allan could manage the estate perfectly well for a few days, and there was nothing else to stop her from going.

For a moment she let her imagination make pretty pictures inside her head.

Teak loungers clustered round a perfect oval of blue like an oasis in the desert. Ice bumping against a slice of lemon in a tall glass and a light breeze sending ripples across the mirror-smooth surface of the pool.

From somewhere upstairs a door slammed shut. She frowned. That wasn't a breeze.

A deafening noise filled the cottage. It sounded like the time when she and Farlan had knocked all those books off the shelves in the library, only sped up and a lot louder.

Still frowning, she walked towards the window that looked out onto the garden and the fields beyond.

Her mouth fell open.

A black helicopter, its rotors spinning at an impossible speed, was juddering downwards, whipping the snow upwards like confetti in reverse.

She cleared her throat. 'Mummy, I've got to go. Something's happening in the field.'

Ignoring her mother's squawk of protest, she hung up and, grabbing a jacket from the hooks by the back door, she stepped out into the garden and through the gate.

The blur of the rotors slowed, and then finally stopped.

Silence.

The door popped open and she watched in astonishment as Farlan jumped out into the snow.

Of course—it would have to be Farlan.

But she'd been so distracted it had taken her brain a few seconds to remember he had a helicopter.

She swallowed hard as he walked towards her. He looked pale and serious and very handsome, his black clothes stark against the white of the snow surrounding him.

'What do you want?'

She was surprised at the strength in her voice, but not by the jolt of heat as his green eyes met hers.

'You left this in the car.' He reached into his pocket and pulled out her phone. 'I thought I'd drop it round.'

'Thank you.' She took the phone, the mundaneness of their exchange hurting, if possible, more than his rejection had earlier.

Was this what they had been reduced to?

With an intensity that left her reeling, she wished suddenly that she had gone with her parents to Dubai, that he had stayed a memory. And suddenly, before she even knew what she going to do, she was turning and walking away.

'Nia—'

He caught up with her as she reached the gate, grabbing the top rail firmly, using his superior strength to keep her from opening it.

Abruptly, she let go, spinning round to face him. 'Why are you still here? You dropped by to give me my phone, right? Well, now you have—so you can go.'

His breath was white in the air. 'If it was just about the phone, Nia, I would have got Diane to drop it round. I came to talk to you.'

'Don't bother,' she said flatly. 'We both got what we wanted, remember?'

His eyes locked with hers. 'I was wrong to say that.'

Reading their expression, she felt misery and anger and frustration flood through her. So that was why he was here: he felt sorry for her.

Every cell in her body was suddenly quivering, ready to

split apart. It was all so futile. All of this. It was like trying to meet him in a maze, only with every turn they just ended up further apart.

'It doesn't matter. Really, truly. Why should it matter, Farlan?' She could hardly get her words out. 'You were wrong. I was wrong—'

'How were you wrong?' Now he seemed angry.

'For being stupid enough to want more than one night with you. And then for thinking it would be a good idea to tell you that was what I wanted.' She shook her head. 'Actually, I didn't even think about it, I just thought *This is how I feel and I need to tell him.* And so I did.' She met his gaze head-on. 'And now I get to relive my stupidity, so you can tell me how "wrong" you were to say what you were thinking.'

'I was wrong to say it.' He grabbed her shoulders. 'I was wrong to say it because it wasn't true.'

She felt as if it was only his hands that were holding her upright.

'One night isn't enough for me either. I knew that the moment I woke up this morning.'

For a moment, she wavered. She wanted it to be true so badly. But with an almighty effort she pulled away from him, shaking her head. 'I don't believe you.'

His jaw tightened. 'You think I'm lying?'

Her chest was aching. Exhaustion was rolling over her in waves. 'Yes, I do. You always know your own mind. If that's what you'd been thinking then you would have said something, but you didn't.'

For a moment he seemed almost stunned, as though she had slapped his face.

'I did think it,' he said a moment later. 'But we'd said it would only be one night, so I wasn't sure.'

He exhaled heavily. There was a tension to him that hadn't been there before. Just as there had been in the car yesterday, she thought a moment later. When he had realised that there was too much snow and the threat had suddenly become real.

She stared at him, trying to read his expression.

What threat was there here?

He took a breath. 'I don't like not being sure.'

Something in his voice wrenched at her inside. A memory of that first time they'd met, of her thinking she had never met anyone so young and yet so old at the same time.

'I don't think anyone does,' she said quietly.

Her anger had faded. She didn't know why, but it just wasn't there any more.

'I messed up.'

His hand brushed against hers and she could hear the struggle to keep his voice steady.

'I know I upset you, and I'm sorry for that—so very sorry. That's why I came over…to tell you, to explain, to apologise.'

His clear green eyes were fixed on her face, as if he was scared to look away in case she vanished.

'I know it's probably too late, and I will completely understand if you never want to speak to me again—'

'You will?' she asked incredulously.

He screwed up his face. 'Not really. I'm just trying to think of anything and everything I can say that will make things go back to how they were before.'

'Do you mean before today? Or the "before" before that?' she said softly. 'I think we need to be clear. Just to be on the safe side. I mean, we do seem to make a habit of being at cross-purposes.'

'Are you?'

A pulse throbbed through her body as he took a step closer.

'Still cross with me, I mean?'

Should she be? He had hurt her, and yet it wasn't that

simple. There were old hurts and, yes, they had talked about the past, but it was naive to think that one conversation would act as a balm to those wounds.

'I was cross, and upset—'

This time his hand took hers. 'I never wanted to upset you.' His fingers curled around hers. 'And I want to make it up to you if you'll let me. If you'll give me a second chance.'

She felt the world grow hazy. Whatever happened, he was going to leave in ten days. All she would be doing was postponing the inevitable, making him more necessary to her existence.

But he was so beautiful, and she wanted him.

'What do you have in mind?' she asked.

He pulled her closer. So close that she could feel his heartbeat slamming into her body.

'That depends. How much time can you spare me?'

She pretended to think. 'I have ten days free.'

A breeze stirred between them, loosening her hair. Reaching out, he tucked the stray strands behind her ear, his thumb caressing her cheek.

'And nights?'

'Only nine, I'm afraid.'

His eyes glittered in the weak sunlight. 'Could you pencil me in?'

Her heart felt as if it might burst. She felt almost weightless with happiness. But she needed to be sure…to make sure nothing came between them this time.

'If that's what you want. To be with me.'

Tilting her face up to his, he kissed her gently. 'I've never been more certain of anything. There's nowhere else I want to be. Unless you've changed your mind?'

'I haven't,' she said simply.

His hands surrounded her face and they kissed again. The lost look in his eyes had faded and he was back in control.

'Can I take you to lunch now? It's a hotel up near Loch Ashie. It's a bit of distance by car. But we won't be going by car...'

Now she understood why there was a helicopter sitting in the field.

'You must have been pretty confident I'd say yes,' she said slowly.

His eyes followed hers, and for a moment she expected his mouth to curve up into one of those impossible to resist smiles, but instead he shrugged.

'You know what they say. Hope for the best; plan for the worst. I was hoping—' he grimaced '—praying, really, that you would say yes.'

'And if I hadn't?'

Now he grinned. 'Kept flying till I reached Moray. There's a monastery there—Benedictine monks. I was going to turn my back on the world and join their order.'

She burst out laughing. 'Then you'd better take me to lunch right now, or I might be tempted to see if that's true.'

CHAPTER EIGHT

'SO, TELL ME about your plans for Lamington.'

Stretching out his legs, Farlan looked over at Nia, satisfaction beating over his skin.

They had reached Brude House within twenty minutes, and they were lounging in the comfortable bar overlooking the battleship-grey waters of the loch.

'You want to talk about Lamington?' she said.

She looked pleased, and with a stab of guilt he wondered why he hadn't asked her that question before. But as she started speaking about her plans for a cookery school he realised that he knew why.

Lamington had always been his glittering, faceless rival. A threat even before everything else that had happened. A threat he would never be able to defeat because Nia *was* Lamington.

She didn't just live and work on the estate, she was its custodian. It was in her careful hands to preserve and pass on to her children so they could then pass it on to their children.

The idea of Nia having children with some unknown man made him want to turn the table over and roar like a stag.

Fortunately the waitress arrived, to tell them that their table was ready.

Lunch was delicious.

Brude House might not be as old or grand as Lamington,

Farlan thought, but Lachlan and Holly had done a good job of turning it into a top-flight place to stay and eat.

The decor of the dining room was glamorous, yet casual, but it was the food that impressed.

A pea and curd cheese mousse the colour of young acorns was followed by lamb with broad beans and tiny wild garlic capers that exploded on your tongue like sherbet.

Watching Nia's eyes widen, he felt a sudden, wild thumping of his heart. There were so many places he wanted to take her. Things he wanted to show her and only her. And he could now.

This was all about having fun.

In bed, and out of it.

Forcing himself to stretch carelessly, he stared across the table, his eyes tracing the curve of her breasts against the smooth fabric.

'What do you think?' he asked.

'It's amazing.'

The excitement in her smile made something crack open inside him.

'Getting here was pretty amazing too.'

'We can do it again if you like. I can take you anywhere, Nia. Wherever you want to go.'

She bit into her lip. 'I'm still trying to work out how you found this place. I mean, how do you stroll back into the country after seven years away and find somewhere so perfect?'

The flicker of curiosity in her soft brown eyes reminded him of the dancing flames at the bothy, and he felt his body stiffen at the memory.

He shrugged. 'Goes with the territory. When you're rich and, more importantly, famous people want to know you.'

His stomach clenched. *Why didn't they want to know you when you were poor and young and powerless? You were still the same person.*

'So they send you stuff, invite you to stay in their hotels, eat at their restaurants. I get a free lunch—they get publicity. Everyone gets what they want,' he said, with no trace of the bitterness he was feeling.

But he could hear the echo of the words he'd spoken earlier—knew too that she'd heard it and that he'd hurt her. He badly wanted to undo his words—to say other words that would explain why the past wouldn't let go of him and why these ten days were all he could ever give her.

Instead he pulled her closer and kissed her soft mouth, letting the slow heating of his desire blank his mind.

'In this case, though, the owners are friends of mine.'

She frowned. 'They are? Why didn't you say?'

Her expression was suddenly intent—too intent—and he glanced away, nodding at the waitress. 'Could we have more water please?' Stretching his face into a careless smile, he went on. 'What was I saying? Oh, yes. I met Lachlan and Holly in LA, doing the catering at some VIP event. We got chatting, found out we were all Scottish and just hit it off.'

'So why did they come back to Scotland?'

She seemed genuinely interested. He liked that about her. It was one of the first things that had attracted him to her. His breathing hitched. That and her eyes, and her lips, and her laugh, and the soft curves of her body, and the fact that she was the smartest person he knew...

'Lachlan was homesick.' He grinned. 'He even missed the rain. He'd always planned on coming back, and Holly was sick of LA. Anyway, I texted him and told him I was over, and he said to drop in if I was in the area.'

She smiled. 'It was lucky for him that you didn't go and join those monks, then.'

'Lucky for me,' he said softly.

He held her gaze and then, reaching out, rested his hand on top of hers. He still couldn't believe that she was here—that she had given him a second chance. Standing in the garage, he had been so sure that he had messed it up for good. And the more he'd told himself that it didn't matter even if he had, the more certain he'd become that it did.

He glanced across the table. She had changed before they'd left into a fitted navy dress. It looked expensive, and was cut modestly, and yet it made him want to strip her bare.

But it hadn't been just sex that had made him do the unthinkable, the impossible, and go after her. Nor had it been about returning her phone.

Remembering her small, stunned face after he'd rejected her had made him feel sick with self-loathing.

Her knowing her own mind was what mattered. That was what he'd told himself. But when she had made it clear what she wanted he'd thrown it back in her face.

He'd been a hypocrite and a coward and a fool.

He was also the luckiest man in the world.

The waitress came to clear the table, and as he watched Nia smile and talk to her he felt a sense of contentment. He watched people all the time as part of his job. As a film director he was paid to do it. But he would watch Nia for free all day…every day.

And now he had ten days and nine glorious nights with her, stretching out ahead of him to a distant, shimmering horizon.

He glanced over at her and found her looking at him. Hidden beneath the tablecloth, he felt his body harden. *Was she thinking the same thing?*

She smiled. 'I've had a lovely time, so thank you for bringing me.' Her smile stilled and she began fiddling with her glass. 'I was wondering if you had any plans for the weekend… For us, I mean.'

Heat rose up over his chest, coiling around his neck so that it was difficult to breathe.

He did have plans.

And all of them involved Nia wearing very few clothes.

Sometimes none at all.

For obvious reasons, he'd given a lot less thought to what he would be wearing, but he'd made up for that by imagining various different settings and positions.

Now, though, might not be the best time to admit any of that.

'Nothing specific,' he said blandly.

'It's just that the Beaters' Ball is happening tomorrow.'

He saw her hesitate.

'At Castle Kilvean. It's Lord Airlie's home—just up the road from Lamington.'

She hesitated again.

'I usually go, and I was wondering if you might like to go with me.' Straightening her back, she glanced around the dining room. 'You brought me here, and I'd really like to take you somewhere special in return.'

Farlan leaned back in his seat and let the silence grow.

This was an affair.

Affairs were supposed to be about sex and fun.

Not getting dressed up to spend an evening with a bunch of strangers. Besides, balls weren't really his cup of tea...

He frowned. *Why did it have to be all about what he wanted?* Wasn't that part of the reason everything had fallen apart last time. Him needing to come first.

'It's okay, I know it's not your thing—'

Leaning forward, he cupped her face in his hand, his thumb caressing the curve of her cheekbone. 'It is now,' he murmured. He kissed her again, his mouth parting hers, his fingers tightening in her hair. 'I would love to go to the ball with you, Lady Antonia. On one condition.'

'What's that?' She was smiling now.

'Promise you won't run away from me at midnight.'

'I promise,' she agreed.

His throat tightened. She thought they were flirting, and if life had treated him differently she would have been right.

But for him a promise was never enough. For him promises were always just waiting to be broken.

He gritted his teeth. Even now, after all this time, he still hadn't mastered his fear. Hating the feeling, he looked away, jerking his head at the waitress to break the mood.

'So, who is this Lord Airlie?' he asked.

'He's a neighbour and a friend.'

Something in her voice, or maybe the way she'd said 'friend', made his muscles tense.

'What kind of friend? Old? New? Best?'

Was he just imagining it, or did her face change minutely? Her eyes?

'A good one,' she said.

She met his gaze. 'Andrew's a good person and a good boss. It was actually his idea to ask all of his estate workers and household staff to join in with the ball—you know, to make it more inclusive. I think you'll like him,' she added.

That was unlikely, he thought, feeling a slow swell of jealousy rising as he watched her face soften. He wanted to ask her more about this other man, only he couldn't bear the thought of how it would sound.

Or of hearing what she might say.

'I'm sure I will.'

The waitress was back. 'Would you like to see the dessert menu, sir?'

Looking up, he gave her his lazy smile. 'No need. I already know what we want.'

'How did you know I wanted the pear?' asked Nia ten minutes later, scooping up the final mouthful of poached pear.

Watching her lick the spoon, he felt his groin tighten. *Who needed dessert when you were going home with a woman like Nia?*

He shrugged. 'You love pears. Apples too. But there wasn't anything with apples on the menu so…'

'I suppose everyone is too health-conscious for puddings

in LA.' She glanced at his espresso. 'Does it make you miss Scotland ever—all that wheatgrass and kale?'

It was an innocent question, but he felt his shoulders tense. 'I miss the country,' he said slowly. 'The cities and the mountains, the history and the poetry.'

'What about your family?'

What family?

He put down his coffee cup, the bitterness of his thoughts blotting out the rush of caffeine, feeling something shifting inside him. A mass of memories, pushing forward like water in a dam.

His grandparents had been the closest he'd had to a family, in that they had been related to him by blood and had let him live under their roof. But they were dead.

He had no idea where his parents were, and he had lost contact with Cam.

Not that Nia knew any of that. They had never talked about their families except in the broadest of brushstrokes. It hadn't seemed relevant. It still wasn't.

'They had a farm, didn't they?' she asked.

He let her words fall into the comfortable hum of conversation coming from the other tables. He didn't want to talk about the farm now—or ever, in fact. And especially not with Nia.

'They sold it.'

She frowned. 'Oh, I'm sorry. Farming is such hard work right now. Some of our tenants are really struggling. Are they still local?'

He shook his head. 'I don't have anyone here left to miss,' he said lightly.

The dam was holding.

She squeezed his hand and some of his tension eased, and then his heart began beating into the silence inside his chest. That had been true then, but what about now?

What about Nia?

'I thought you had family in England too?' she said.

Her voice broke into his thoughts just as from across the room there was a burst of laughter. He felt suddenly irrationally angry.

'What if I do? Why do you care?' He shifted back in his seat. 'This *arrangement*—' he tossed the word towards her carelessly '—is about sex. I'm not in it for the pillow talk. Or any kind of talk, for that matter.'

She flinched as if he'd slapped her.

There was a long pause.

'I see. Well, I'm sorry, Farlan, but I didn't agree to any "arrangement" where you get to talk to me like that,' she said stiffly. 'I'll let you finish your coffee in peace.'

Putting her napkin on the table, she reached for her bag.

'Nia—' He caught her wrist. 'Don't go. Please. I'm sorry. I don't know why I said that—'

Except he did.

It was always the same whenever he thought about his family. The same fear—the fear that wrapped itself around him and turned his words into sharp, jagged rocks in his throat so that speaking them was impossible.

Only if he didn't say something now Nia would leave, and more than anything he didn't want her to leave.

'Please. Don't go, Nia,' he repeated. 'It's just difficult talking about it…about them.'

She was looking at him warily, but she had stopped moving, and he felt a surge of relief. He hadn't pushed her too far.

'Why is it difficult?'

The dining room was awash with afternoon sun, and her face was illuminated in the soft golden light. He felt his stomach clench. She was still angry, but more than that she was worried about him.

'I haven't talked about them for a bit,' he said. *Make that ever*, he corrected silently. 'And when I do I get lost in it—I let it get out of control in my head.'

The need to talk to her, to tell the truth, was pressing down on him. But how could he explain the threadbare patchwork of his childhood?

The Elgins ticked every box. They were rich and titled and Nia could trace her ancestors back nearly four hundred years.

'My family is not like yours, Nia. It's messy and complicated—'

Her fingers tightened around his. 'All families are messy and complicated.'

He shook his head, his mouth twisting. She had no idea, and he didn't want her to know either.

Okay, her parents were difficult, snobbish people, but the only time she had experienced the random cruelty that life could throw at people had been thanks to him.

He wasn't about to make his pain part of her life.

He couldn't do that to her.

'Not yours. Your family is perfect.'

There was a longer pause.

'It's not. It's not perfect.' She took a breath. 'That's why I broke up with you. I panicked. I thought anything was better than—'

'Than what?'

For a moment she seemed to be fumbling with something inside her head, and he knew she was deciding what to say and what to conceal, balancing an equation. He knew because he did it himself, and the fact that he and Nia should have that in common wrenched at him.

'My aunt and uncle. They were exactly the ages we were when we first met when they got married. They were so in love.'

Her mouth curved up into a smile at the memory.

'I was thirteen—just at that age when you start to question things, to look at life with your own eyes, and they seemed perfect to me. Catherine was so pretty, and Richard was an artist. A really good one. But he wasn't making any money so he gave it up.'

She breathed out unsteadily.

'They used to argue all the time, but now they just lead separate lives. I think sometimes they hate each other…' Her voice stumbled. 'I didn't want that for us. Only I didn't know how to explain without betraying them.'

So it hadn't just been a generic fear about their mismatched backgrounds. She had already seen first-hand what happened when two people put their dreams on hold…when fantasy met reality head-on. She had witnessed her aunt and uncle's slow, tortuous falling out of love.

'Are they still together?' he asked.

She nodded. 'They live in Dubai.'

Something clicked inside his head. Nia had mentioned Dubai the other day. Her parents were staying out there.

He hated seeing the strain in her eyes. 'Couldn't your father help them? I know he's not well, but couldn't he maybe loan them some money?'

Something in her face shifted, and he knew that she was doing another of those mental calculations.

Finally, she shook her head. 'He can't help. He doesn't have any money.'

There was a small silence.

'I know that sounds stupid, and I know I told you they needed to go somewhere warm for his health, but I lied. He does have a weak chest, but that's not the reason we're renting out Lamington. We need the money.'

His head was spinning. *Nia's family needed money?*

'I don't understand—'

'I found out about eighteen months ago, when I met with the accountant.' She shrugged. 'I suspected something was wrong, but I didn't realise how wrong until then.'

'Did your parents know how bad things were?'

'Not really. I've tried talking to them since, but…' She

smiled weakly. 'Their interest in money is limited to spending it. They think it will just get sorted out—and it has, always. In the past.'

He could picture her, trying to explain to them, just as she had tried to explain to them about him—could sense, too, the strain she had been under and undoubtedly still was.

His hand found hers and she met his gaze.

'There's always been something to sell. But now there's nothing left except the land. And Lamington.'

There was an ache in her voice, and an exhaustion that made his fingers tighten around hers. 'You won't lose Lamington.'

Once he had hated her home—now nothing seemed to matter more than reassuring her that it would stay her home forever.

'Sometimes I wish I would,' she whispered. 'That I could just be normal like everyone else. Like I was with you… before.'

He stared at her in confusion. Not once had it occurred to him that Nia might feel that way. 'Is that why you didn't tell me?' he asked.

She shook her head. 'It's not your problem, Farlan.'

I want it to be. The words rose in the back of his throat. *I want to help.*

But how could he help anyone—particularly Nia—when he couldn't tell her even the bare bones of his life? And yet how could he not when she had shared something with him—a truth that hurt?

Feeling his body tense, he took a moment to compose himself. 'You asked about my family's farm…'

Her eyes widened fractionally and then she nodded slowly.

'My grandfather fell over and broke his hip. My grandmother couldn't cope so they sold the farm. They moved to Elrick, but they're both dead now.'

No need to tell her that there had been no room for him at their new house—that once the farm had gone he hadn't been needed. Or wanted.

But then he'd never been wanted—not by those who should have fought tooth and nail to keep him close and safe. To his family he had always been a burden and an inconvenience.

'I'm sorry,' she whispered.

Exhaling, he lifted her hand to his lips. 'No, I'm sorry for being a jerk and messing up lunch.' He held her gaze. 'Let's get out of here. We could have a look around the town,' he offered. 'I've heard it's very pretty. Romantic…'

She lifted her chin. 'And you don't have a problem with that? You know—fitting it in with our "arrangement"?'

Groaning, he screwed up his face. 'I deserve that.'

She nodded. 'Yes, you do. But I guess we could go take a look, if you're not in any rush to get back.'

'I'm not.'

Her eyes were soft and teasing now. 'Really? Maybe you should have joined those Benedictine brothers after all.'

He felt his whole body harden, like iron quenched in a forge. 'That's big talk, Lady Antonia. And later I am going to call you out on that.'

She slipped past his outstretched hand, laughing, but he caught her easily, pulling her against his body and kissing her fiercely.

Ten days. Nine nights.

It would be enough to satisfy this craving.

Then he would go back to the States and get on with his life.

CHAPTER NINE

SHIFTING AGAINST THE warmth of her pillow, Nia opened her eyes and rolled onto her side towards Farlan, her fingers feeling for his warm skin.

There was no one lying beside her.

Frowning, she shuffled up the bed. Farlan was crouching naked in front of the fire, his eyes fixed on the darting flames as he slotted a log into the glowing orange stack.

Her mouth drying, her eyes fluttered over the curve of his back.

For a moment she just stared at him.

He looked as if he was posing for a sculptor, or about to take part in some Olympian game in Ancient Greece.

His body was a perfectly weighted balance of tension and geometry, the smooth, contoured muscles gleaming in the firelight like polished marble.

She held her breath. It still felt miraculous that he was here with her…that he wanted what she wanted.

Nine days, eight nights, and counting.

No more cross-purposes. No more confusion or hurt.

They were of one mind.

She thought back to that moment in the restaurant when she had told him the truth about Lamington and her parents' finances.

And then he had confided in her.

It was their gift to one another.

An honesty neither had managed in the past.

And this was their reward.

A honeymoon, almost, like the one they would have had if they had been meant to share their lives as they'd once hoped.

The thought made her chest burn, and for a moment she wanted to tell him that he was the only man she had ever loved, that not a day had passed without her thinking about him.

Instead, she reached over and pressed her hand against the sheet that still bore the imprint of his body.

It was already cooling.

Her heart shivered. Soon he would be gone for ever. There wasn't a moment to lose.

'Come back to bed,' she murmured.

He turned, his eyes narrowing as they took in her naked body, his body instantly all muscle and tension. His gaze was blind, hungry. His erection was heavy and proud. He wanted what she wanted.

And he wanted her.

Crossing the room, he pulled her against him, his mouth seeking hers, and her hands reached for his body.

Later, they lay on the twisted bedding, watching the fire, their damp skin blurring their bodies into one, her breasts pressing against the hard wall of his chest.

The room was blissfully warm. Outside, the sky was starting to turn clay-coloured.

What time was it? she wondered.

In answer to her unspoken question she heard the church bells chime three o'clock.

There'd been so many days like this when they had first got together. Days spent in bed, in Farlan's flat.

Whenever they'd been alone time had grown thick and amorphous, so that she would step out into the street expecting daylight only to find that day was already night.

Not that she had minded. She had loved those long, languid mornings in bed. Loved, too, those afternoons when he'd pulled her into the flat and she had unzipped him, both of them frantic, panting, still fully clothed, their orgasms so quick and sharp that they never even reached the bed.

Afterwards, it had always been her who'd broken the spell. Farlan had been happy to stay there, holding her in his arms. She had been the one needing to reinstate order and normality.

Now, though, as he caressed her hip and the curve of her bottom, she wanted to stop the church bells from chiming. To stop time itself and just stay in his arms in this cosy little room for ever. Only it was stupid and dangerous to think that way…

She felt his teeth nip her collarbone lightly.

'What are you thinking?' he asked.

'Nothing, really,' she lied.

There were rules, she was sure, for this kind of affair. Someone more experienced, more practised in the art of no-strings flings, would definitely know them, but even she could guess that talking about lying in his arms for ever would not be a good idea.

'I was just thinking about the ball,' she said quickly.

It was another lie.

The Beaters' Ball was tonight, and usually she would have been thinking about it for hours beforehand, but it had hardly crossed her mind. Farlan had made everything lose shape and colour.

He slid his hand through her hair, catching strands in his fingers and lifting them up to the light. 'What about the ball?' he asked.

He spoke casually, but she could feel the muscles in his arms tightening a little, as though her answer mattered to him.

'I was just thinking it's a shame Tom and Diane can't go.'

The Drummonds had flown to Dublin for a wedding, and were both very disappointed to be missing it.

Farlan didn't answer immediately, and then he shrugged. 'There'll be others.'

'I know.'

Shifting against the solidity of Farlan's chest, Nia looked away from the fire and tilted her head back. She felt her breath catch in her throat. He was as mesmerising as any fire. He drew the eye in the same way, and it was impossible to look away.

She knew that it wouldn't matter how many days and nights they spent together—she would never get used to his beauty. Nor find another man who would make her feel so complete and so completely desired.

So why waste time at a ball that he would probably hate?

'We don't have to go,' she said. 'Like you say, there'll be other balls.'

Not while Farlan was here, though.

Something flickered across his face, like sunlight washing over the moors, and he lowered his mouth and ran his tongue over her lips. 'I know we don't.'

He was kissing her now, following her pulse down her neck to the hollow at the base of her throat. Shivering, she squeezed her thighs together against the slow, decadent ache that was starting to build there.

There would be three hundred guests at the Beaters' Ball, and they would have to talk and eat and dance with some of them. They would be surrounded by people.

'We could just stay here—'

'We could, but we're not going to,' he muttered against her skin. 'I know I don't have a title, but just for one evening I want to be your Prince Charming, Lady Antonia.'

Her fingers moved down over his stomach, hovering over the thistle tattoo below his hipbone. She heard him suck in a breath, and then he was rolling over, taking her with him so that she was straddling his hips.

'You have a one-track mind,' he said. His eyes were dark in the half-light.

'Only with you,' she said.

He didn't smile. Instead, holding her gaze, he caressed her waist, his hands moving upwards to cover her breasts. She whimpered as he licked first one and then the other nipple, making them swell and throb.

'You're making it so much harder for me.' His voice was hoarse.

'To do what?' She was moving against him now, back and forth, so that the head of his erection pushed against the relentless ache between her legs.

'To leave.'

So don't leave, then, she thought. *Stay here with me.*

But they had tried that before and they both knew it wouldn't work.

This was all they had.

This bed.

This room.

And, leaning forward, she pulled his mouth back to her breast and lifted her hips to meet his thrusts, his hard body driving out the pain of that thought.

Smoothing his hand over his face, Farlan turned off the water. For a moment he stood in the shower, his hands pressed flat against the cold tiles, steam rising off his skin, and then he grabbed two towels, wrapped one around his waist and began rubbing his head with the other.

Depending on his mood, it usually either baffled or annoyed him how no amount of hot water and huge, feather-soft towels could erase the memory of years of shivering in unheated bathrooms.

Today he had other things on his mind.

His mouth twisted.

One thing—one woman.

Nia.

He had left her back at the gardener's cottage to get changed for the ball, and he had returned to Lamington to do the same.

Glancing down at his watch, he frowned. It had only been an hour since he had dragged himself away from her soft, pliant body, and yet already he was missing her.

He had told himself that it would be enough—that coming back here had started something between them that needed to be finished properly this time. And that if they allowed themselves these few days to let it run its course then he could finally get on with his life.

Except that wasn't proving nearly as easy as it sounded.

In the beginning they had agreed to have sex.

That was how it had started in the car.

Remembering their urgent, frantic coupling that day, he felt his body harden. It had been sex in its most basic form: to satisfy a craving. But then, in the bothy, it had shifted into something more sybaritic. Pleasure for the sake of pleasure. And it had been incredible.

His heartbeat accelerated.

If she had been anyone else he would have thought she was the one—that elusive woman who would share his life with him. She had tasted sweeter than honey, and when she'd melted into him he had found himself responding to her just as he had seven years ago.

It had felt so right.

They both knew they could never have a 'normal' relationship, but after that neither of them had been willing to walk away, so they had agreed to this affair.

He stared at his reflection in the mirror. It should be like directing himself in a movie he'd written. No surprises. No disappointments or unrealistic expectations. Just him and Nia. Simple.

Except now it didn't feel simple.

Instead it felt as if he'd pulled on a loose thread and now everything was unravelling in ways he didn't understand and couldn't control.

Like this ball.

His eyes narrowed.

Where did going with Nia to a ball at a neighbour's castle fit into this arrangement?

He felt his chest tighten as it did whenever he thought about Lord Airlie.

Since that lunch at Lachlan and Holly's place Nia hadn't said any more until just now, in bed, and he hadn't asked. But when he had mentioned the Beaters' Ball to Molly, she had gone into raptures about the Marquess.

Grabbing his toothbrush, he began brushing his teeth savagely.

Not only was the Marquess of Airlie wealthy and handsome, he also ran a philanthropic foundation and was the patron of several charities that specialised in supporting local people. He was a perfect gentleman too, according to Diane, who had been completely bowled over by his handwritten invitation to lunch at Castle Kilvean.

All that was missing from his perfect life was a wife.

Farlan spat into the sink.

He got the feeling that Airlie already had someone in mind to fill that vacancy.

Stalking into the dressing room, he stopped in front of the beautifully pressed Highland evening dress that Molly had delivered to his room earlier. He stared at it in silence, his stomach tightening.

Frankly, he couldn't think of anything he wanted to do less than spend an evening hanging out with a bunch of snobby Scottish aristocrats. Especially as he could have got out of it.

Nia had said as much.

So why hadn't he just told her he didn't want to go?

Reaching out, he touched the gleaming silver buttons on the black Prince Charlie jacket.

For the same reason he had agreed to go in the first place. He knew it would make her happy. And more than anything he wanted to make her happy, make her smile and laugh.

In other words, whatever it was that was supposedly going on between him and Nia, what was happening inside his head had nothing to do with sex at all.

Nia took a step back and turned slowly on the spot, staring at the unfamiliar version of herself in the cheval mirror. It was obviously her, but she never really wore anything but black in the evening, as her mother had a horror of anything showy.

Only this wasn't showy, she thought, turning slowly again, her gaze drifting over the old gold taffeta. It was beautiful.

She had bought it in London, after that terrible meeting when the true state of the family finances had been spelled out to her by Douglas.

Leaving the accountant's office, she had been so angry and upset. With her parents for their absurd and selfish extravagances. But more so with herself.

It had all been for nothing. That had been her first thought. She had given Farlan up and it had all been for nothing. All those long, lonely years she had spent embracing the pain had been worthless.

She was going to lose Lamington anyway.

She bit her lip. Even then he had never been far from her thoughts.

Nothing had changed, and yet everything had changed.

Over these last two days she had allowed herself to be a 'normal' woman, with feelings and needs. She had confronted the past and let go of it. For the first time in a long time, maybe ever, she liked herself.

And Farlan liked her too.

She thought back to that moment in the restaurant when he had finally told her about his grandparents. He clearly still missed them. Otherwise why would someone like him—someone so gifted at communicating, at telling stories—find talking about them so hard?

It hurt, knowing that he carried that pain, those bad memories. But tonight she was going to make sure they made some good ones.

Even though she was expecting him, the knock on the door startled her. Heart bumping, she picked up the hem of her skirt and made her way downstairs to the front door.

Farlan stood outside, his broad shoulders filling the porch. She had been expecting him to wear white tie and tails, but he was wearing a traditional Prince Charlie jacket, white shirt, ghillie shoes and a Drummond tartan kilt.

He looked devastatingly handsome and romantic.

'You look beautiful, Nia,' he said softly.

'Thank you.' She swallowed. 'I've never seen you in a kilt.' *Or anything remotely tartan.*

'Tom's chuffed to bits.' He grimaced. 'We're going to have to send them a photo or my life won't be worth living.'

Her eyes gleamed. She knew he was wearing it for her, and the fact that he would do that made a lightness spread through her whole body, so that she felt as if she might float away.

Taking her hand, he pulled her against him and kissed her softly on the mouth. 'Time to go to the ball, Cinderella.'

She felt the muscles in his face move as he smiled.

'I couldn't find any mice, so no coachmen, I'm afraid.'

She glanced past his shoulder at the sleek, dark sports car. 'Looks like we won't be needing any.'

The glare from the supercar's headlights skimmed the

hedges, tunnelling swiftly through the darkness so that they reached Castle Kilvean in just under half an hour.

After a short time spent in the queue of cars moving slowly along the drive, they were walking upstairs towards the huge ballroom.

'Lady Antonia Elgin and Mr Farlan Wilder.'

As the announcer called out their names Nia felt a shiver run down her spine. How many times had she dreamed of this exact moment? Only of course in her dreams she had been Mrs Antonia Wilder.

Farlan's wife—not just his temporary lover.

It was what she still wanted to be.

Her heart felt so full she was suddenly afraid it would burst.

'Nia?'

Farlan was looking at her, his eyes narrowed on her face. 'Is everything okay?'

It wasn't. But taking his hand was easier than dealing with the emotions that were surging up inside her.

Later. She would deal with them later. But right now they could wait.

Turning to Farlan, she smiled. 'I'm fine. Shall we go down?'

Beneath a white and gold ceiling lit by a vast number of chandeliers, the huge ballroom was already half-full of guests. She felt her pulse accelerate. It was silly in some ways, but there was something about a Highland ball. The clashing tartans, the sound of the pipes, the women in their long dresses and sashes and the men looking so handsome in their kilts.

And Farlan was the most handsome of them all.

The pipers were playing a jig—'The Major Ian Stewart.'

'Do you want to dance?' she said suddenly.

Taking her hand, he smiled the smile that no one could resist. 'I thought you'd never ask.'

* * *

They danced until they were hot and breathless. And as the music started up again Farlan pulled her closer, his fingers brushing against her dress.

He had never seen her wear that colour before and he wondered why. It was perfect, the faded gold highlighting the delicacy of her features and picking out the burnished strands in her hair.

'Let's get a drink,' he said, leaning into her.

It was incredibly noisy. Apart from the music there was a swell of voices, people shouting, talking, laughing.

He grabbed some drinks from a circling waiter and nudged her towards the edge of the ballroom, where it was quieter.

'Having fun?' he asked.

She smiled. 'Yes, are you?'

The eagerness in her voice made something pinch in his chest.

'It's a great party,' he said.

She nodded. 'Dancing always makes me feel so happy.'

Her soft brown eyes were sparkling and her cheeks were flushed pink. She looked young and carefree, and with a jolt he realised that she must have been so on edge before.

'Seeing you happy makes me happy,' he said gruffly.

His words fell away into the tune of 'The Duke of Atholl's Reel.'

Too happy.

'Nia, I—'

'Antonia! I was hoping to bump into you earlier. But there's just so many people—'

'Andrew—'

Nia turned towards a tall, handsome man in a busy red and blue tartan, her eyes lighting up with delight.

'I did see you earlier, but then you disappeared into the throng.'

They kissed on both cheeks and then Nia gestured to Farlan. 'Farlan, this is our host, the Marquess of Airlie—Andrew, this is Farlan Wilder. He's—' She stumbled.

'Staying with the Drummonds.' Stepping forward to finish Nia's sentence, Farlan held out his hand.

'The famous film director,' said the Marquess.

They shook hands.

'We quite often have guests from Holyrood, Mr Wilder, but never from Hollywood. So this is a rare treat.'

He had a voice like Nia's: smooth, English-sounding, but with a tiny inflexion of Scots. And, much as Farlan wanted to hate this man, he seemed warm and genuine.

'This is a great party, Lord Airlie,' he said.

'Please, call me Andrew. And, yes, it's going rather well.' He caught Nia's eye. 'Much better than last year's effort.'

Nia laughed. She glanced at Farlan, making their private joke a shared one. 'The dance floor broke.'

Andrew nodded. 'During a particularly vigorous Eightsome Reel. We had to evacuate everyone while they replaced it.' He grinned. 'It was chaos. But I imagine compared to what you have to oversee on set our little gathering must seem like a piece of cake.'

'Not at all. Watch out—'

Catching Nia's wrist, somehow slipping his arms around her waist, Farlan pulled her out of the way as a group of giggling teenage girls stumbled off the dance floor.

'My actors would be drinking tinted water, not champagne, so on the whole I'd say you have the harder task—but maybe you should come over to LA and see for yourself.'

He could feel the heat of Nia's body, the press of her skin against his. The girls had gone now, but he was still her partner, and it was perfectly natural to let his hand rest on her hipbone, to let his fingers splay out possessively.

'I might just do that.' Andrew smiled. 'And in return perhaps I could invite you to come over for lunch. I have a date in the diary with your hosts at the end of the month. It would be wonderful if you could join us.'

For a moment, the invitation quivered in the air.

Farlan felt Nia's eyes on his profile.

It was a reason to stay. It would be just until the end of the month.

His heart beat faster.

But staying on longer would only confuse things, and he knew all too well the painful consequences of sending mixed messages.

'I would have loved to, but unfortunately I'll be back in the States by then.'

'What a shame.' Andrew glanced over at Nia, his blue eyes politely flirtatious. 'Don't worry. I'll be happy to step in and distract her. In fact, I was wondering if I might persuade you to part with her for "The Duke of Perth."'

'Oh, I don't—' Nia began.

The idea of Nia dancing with this confident, charming man, of her gazing into his eyes and laughing breathlessly during the turns, made jealousy burn through him. But Farlan forced himself to smile.

'I'm happy to sit one out. I've had quite enough Dukes for the moment.'

His jaw felt rigid with the effort of smiling as he watched Andrew steer Nia back to the dance floor, his hand resting lightly against her back. He watched as she moved among the crowd, feeling his pulse oscillating in time with her hips.

It was obvious even at a distance that she and Airlie knew the same people. Every few yards couples stopped to greet them and share a joke. And they looked like a couple too.

Nia looked relaxed and happy. Her eyes were shining. And, watching her smile, he felt his stomach clench.

Stupid, arrogant idiot that he was, he had actually

thought that he was the reason for her happiness, that he made her happy.

And he did. In bed.

But here she was at home among friends.

She was safe. *Loved.*

He turned abruptly and walked away from the dance floor through the huge doors and outside to the gardens, following the torches along a path away from the castle. The cold air stung his eyes, but that was good. It helped blur the image that had just dropped into his head of Nia lying upstairs in Andrew Airlie's arms.

He wished it would freeze his heart too.

Why shouldn't that happen? Why shouldn't Nia have that?

Airlie was offering her more than sex. He was offering her a future. A future without the fear that it would all fall apart.

Farlan knew he could never have that for himself, but he wanted that for her. He wanted Nia to be able to love without fear. And he wanted someone to love her, to take care of her. To do what he had failed to do and put her first.

'There you are.'

He turned. Nia was standing behind him.

'I've been looking for you everywhere.'

She was alone. His relief was so overwhelming that he had to take a breath to steady himself before he spoke.

'I was just getting some air.'

She was shivering and, pulling off his jacket, he slipped it over her shoulders. 'Come on, let's go back inside.'

But she didn't move. 'Actually, if you're okay with it, I thought we might go back to the cottage.'

He stared at her in silence, his heart pounding.

'Or we could go back to Lamington…'

Her words hung between them like the moths fluttering above the torchlight.

He knew what she was offering. It was the final step in resetting their past. The two of them together in the house where they had separated.

Leaning forward, he kissed her on the mouth. 'Your carriage awaits.'

The big house was quiet and still and dark. They left the lights off, and Farlan led her upstairs and into his guest bedroom.

It was so familiar—he was so familiar—and yet she could feel her heart racing as if she had fallen through a rabbit hole into a parallel world where they had never split up.

She stopped in front of the dressing table. Farlan was behind her, his unblinking gaze reflected in the mirror, watching her image. 'Could you undo me?'

She met his gaze, her mouth drying at the heat in his green eyes as he nodded.

Turning round, she felt her pulse begin to leap in her throat as his fingers brushed against her skin, and the zip slid down her back.

'Nia…'

He whispered her name, his breath warm against her cheek, and she turned towards him as the dress slipped to the floor, pooling at her feet. Now she was naked except for her stockings, her panties and her heels.

She heard his breath hitch, and her muscles clenched as his hands slid up over her waist, capturing her breasts, his fingers pulling at the already aching tips. Pulling her round, his lips found hers, and he kissed her with an urgency that made her head spin.

'Undress me…'

With fingers that felt thick and unwieldy she pulled at his shirt, her hands growing steadier as they touched the smooth, toned muscles of his chest.

They started to tremble again as she unbuckled his kilt.

He was naked underneath.

Naked and very aroused.

Reaching out, she ran her fingers over his smooth length, feeling her stomach tipping as his eyes narrowed.

'I want you,' he said hoarsely.

'So take me,' she whispered.

He lifted her up onto the dressing table and then dropped to his knees. Hooking his thumbs into her panties, he slid them down her legs and over the tops of her stockings, and she breathed out shakily as he ran his tongue between her thighs.

She gripped the dressing table, her nails scraping against the smooth wood. Her legs were trembling and his hands splayed over her skin, steadying her as she felt her body begin to lift free of its moorings.

Moaning softly, she began to move against his mouth, her pulse beating on his tongue. Soon he pulled away and flipped her round, his hand capturing her face, his mouth finding hers. And then he was pushing into her, his hand moving to her clitoris, the slow, measured sweep of his finger making her arch backwards.

His arm was around her waist and he was lifting her body against his as she let go, crying out as he thrust the blunt head of his erection up inside of her.

In the mirror, his darkened eyes locked with hers and her muscles clenched around him. And then he was crying out too, shuddering in pleasure, pressing his face against her shoulder, his heartbeat raging in time to hers.

He pulled away gently and scooped her into his arms, carried her over to the bed.

She lay there, her body quivering with the tiny aftershocks of her release. They were both breathing unsteadily, their skin warm and damp.

After a moment or two he pulled her closer and she nestled into him. She would never get tired of this. Of how it felt to have his arms around her. Of how his body felt inside her. The heat and the pressure and the rhythm.

Already she wanted him again—only at some point all this would have to stop and he would leave.

But she wasn't ready for that to happen. She wasn't sure she would ever be ready.

She thought back to what she'd told herself earlier. That tonight was about making good memories. But what if those memories weren't enough?

'What are you thinking?' he asked, and tipped her face up to his.

'I was just thinking it was lucky I didn't know you weren't wearing anything under your kilt or we'd have had to have left earlier.'

'You'd have done that for me?

Her heart was still beating fast and, looking up into his soft, green gaze, she felt it beat even faster.

She dropped a kiss on his chest. 'Of course.'

His hand slid over the curve of her hip, his fingers grazing the top of her stockings. 'Lord Airlie must be disappointed we left. I think he was hoping to dance with you again.'

She felt a pang of guilt. She hadn't thought about Andrew once. Every thought, every breath, every glance had been centred on Farlan.

'Andrew is the host—he has lots of duty dances to perform.'

'And is that what that was? A duty dance?'

Farlan had been aiming to keep his voice casual, but clearly he'd failed.

She looked up at him, her eyes searching his face. 'What do you mean?'

He let his gaze float away to the window to where the hills met the Castle Kilvean estate.

'Just something Molly said to me when I told her about the ball. She said Lord Airlie had everything he wanted…' His eyes locked onto hers. 'Except a wife.'

She shifted backwards against the pillow, her hair like honey in the soft light of the table lamp. Outside, he thought he could hear the distant sound of bagpipes.

'He wants to marry you, Nia.'

She shook her head. 'I'm not going to marry Andrew,' she said slowly.

'He hasn't asked you yet?'

There was another long silence.

'Actually, he has.'

Her words bumped into each other inside his head like fairground dodgems. He stared at her, shock muting the pain in his chest. 'This evening?'

'No.' She shook her head. 'About a year ago.'

A year ago. So after she had found out that her family estate was in financial difficulties.

As if reading his mind, she gave him a small, tight smile. 'My parents were pretty upset that I turned him down. When Andrew proposed I think they thought it would be the perfect solution to our problems.'

Farlan could all too easily imagine her father's clipped, furious disbelief.

Glancing down at her pale face, he pushed a stray curl away from her face. 'You say he's a good man?'

She nodded. 'He is.'

'And yet you turned him down.' It was a struggle to keep his voice even. 'Why did you do that?'

Her eyelashes grazed her cheekbones as she looked down at his hand on her hip. 'I've known Andrew for ever. And I love him. But only as a friend.'

'Sometimes love can change.'

His spine tensed. Why had he said that? It made no sense. He didn't want Nia to marry Andrew-bloody-Marquess-of-Airlie. He didn't want her to marry anyone. The thought made him want to rage and smash things.

But he could feel the old familiar ache filling his chest—the swell of panic, the need to push and push and push…

'Sometimes love that starts as friendship develops into passion over time,' he said.

She was shaking her head. 'That's not going to happen.'

'I saw you tonight with him,' he persisted. 'He made you happy.'

He felt as if he was stabbing himself. But it was the right thing to do.

He edged away from her. 'I want you to be happy, Nia.'

'I *am* happy. Here. With you.'

He pushed off the bed. He couldn't do this. Couldn't say what he needed to say with her so close.

'This isn't real. And you deserve better. You deserve the best and Lord Airlie is the best. He's rich and kind and he loves you.' He went for the jugular. 'And when I've gone, he will still be here. You need to think about that—about your future.'

She was looking at him as if he was a stranger. 'And you think Andrew's my future?'

Her eyes were bright.

'I can't marry a man I don't love, and—' Her voice faltered and she cleared her throat. 'And I don't want to think about the future.'

There was a silence.

Then, lifting her face, she met his gaze. 'All I can think about is you and me and how I don't want it to end just yet.'

He could hardly believe what she was saying—or that she was saying it. For a moment he couldn't speak, so great was his fear that he had misheard or misunderstood. And then he felt relief surge through his body, driving out the tension and pain of moments earlier.

He reached for her blindly, his hands curving around her

arms. 'I don't want you to marry Airlie, and I don't want this to end just yet either.' His fingers tightened, anchoring her to him. 'There's no reason we can't carry on as we are for a month or two.'

Aside from his job, his home and countless meetings with producers and actors...

Heart thumping, he pushed the thought away. He would fly back to the States as and when it was necessary.

His eyes locked with hers. 'I can make that happen. If that's what you want. And after that—'

She put her mouth against his, her soft lips breathing warmth and hope. 'That's what I want.'

He felt his heart swell. There was no doubt in her voice or her face.

And so, not wanting anything to change the certainty of the moment, he pushed her back onto the bed and lowered his body to hers.

CHAPTER TEN

'OH, NIA, THANK GOODNESS you're here.' Darting across the drawing room, Diane kissed Nia on both cheeks and, hooking her arm, practically towed her towards a sofa. 'Come and sit down with me.' She patted the cushion and then turned to her husband. 'Tom, tell Molly we'll have coffee now.'

Grinning, Tom saluted. 'Yes, ma'am.' He winked at Nia and then pulled her into a squeezing embrace. 'She's champing at the bit to hear about the ball.'

Diane nodded. 'I want you to tell me everything. And I want to see some photos.'

Nia frowned. 'I thought Farlan sent you some?'

'He did.' A deep, familiar voice cut into the conversation. 'But apparently they didn't meet requirements.'

She felt her heartbeat accelerate, and her skin felt suddenly too hot and tight. Farlan had followed Tom into the room and, glancing over at him, she felt heat crackle down her spine.

Tom and Diane had arrived back from Dublin late last night.

Even though she and Farlan had both agreed to extend their 'arrangement', neither of them had wanted to say anything to Tom and Diane, so Farlan had waited until they'd gone to bed before making his way down the drive to the gardener's cottage.

A little bubble of happiness rose up and popped inside her chest. She had been looking out for him from her bedroom, and when he'd caught sight of her he had climbed up the front wall to her open window.

His lips had been cold from the outside air, but his kiss had been hotly passionate. And what had followed had been equally passionate—both an admission of their longing and an affirmation of what they had decided in the early hours of the morning in his guest room after the ball.

He had got up early this morning, grumbling about having to leave her, and after he had gone she had rolled over in bed, pressing herself into the heat left by his body, breathing in the intimate scent of him.

And now he was dropping into the armchair beside her sofa. Real. Warm. His green eyes gleaming as they met hers.

'Good morning, Lady Antonia. Did you sleep well?'

His leg brushed against hers and she felt fingers of heat slide over her skin. She didn't think she had ever wanted anyone or anything more than she wanted Farlan in this moment.

'Yes, I did, thank you. And you?'

'On and off,' he said softly. 'I had to keep changing position.'

As Diane looked up, Nia felt her face grow warm.

Fortunately Molly chose that moment to bring in the coffee, and a delectable array of shortbread and ginger biscuits.

'So what was wrong with Farlan's photos?' asked Nia, after Molly had left.

Diane rolled her eyes. 'I'll show you.' She pulled out her phone. 'This is why you don't ask a man to take photos at a ball.'

Nia bit into her lip, trying not to smile. In one, the plaid of Farlan's kilt filled the wing mirror of the supercar, and in several others Nia could see herself and Farlan reflected in the flank of the car.

Diane was frowning at Farlan. 'I wanted photos of the

two of you, all dressed up and looking beautiful, and you took these.'

Farlan grinned. 'What can I say? I'm a creative—I went for the artistic shot.'

Leaning forward, he put his hand around Nia's and tilted the phone towards Tom. She felt her body tingle from the contact.

'This is a great one of the brake callipers.'

Catching sight of Diane's face, Nia burst out laughing. 'Oh, please don't worry, Diane. He *did* take some of us, I promise. And Andrew had a couple of photographers there, and they took absolutely masses of photos.'

Farlan was pulling out his own phone. 'Come on, Dee. You know I wouldn't let you down. Here. Take a look at these.'

Gazing down at the screen, Nia felt her heart twist. She could vaguely remember Farlan handing the phone to someone as they'd walked into the ball. But so much had happened the memory had gone adrift. Now, though, staring down at the screen, she could almost feel the weight of his arm around her waist as he pulled her against him.

It was a great photo.

A fortuitous, few seconds when everything had conspired to capture them both in a perfect moment in time.

She was almost as tall as him in her heels, so her head was only fractionally tilted back. In the background of the photo people were milling about, but even from the static one-dimensional image, anyone could tell that they were completely unaware of anyone but each other.

She heard Diane gasp.

'You both look so lovely!'

Nia felt the catch in the older woman's voice resonate through her body.

'Oh, Tom, I wish we'd stayed.' Diane was looking up at her husband, her eyes bright with tears.

Tom squeezed her shoulder. 'Now, Dee, don't you start, or you'll set me off.'

Sighing, Farlan pushed the tray of coffee out of the way and sat down on the table. He leaned forward and smoothed the tears from Diane's cheeks. 'There's going to be other balls. This is the Highlands, Dee. There's one kicking off round here practically every weekend.'

'But not while you're here.' Diane sniffed. 'You'll be back in LA next week.'

Nia felt her pulse twitch.

There was a short silence, and then Farlan smiled. 'Actually, I won't be. I've decided to stay on for a bit longer—'

He yelped as Tom yanked him to his feet.

'I knew once you got here you'd want to stay. A true Scotsman can't resist the pull of the pipes.'

Grinning, Farlan shook his head. 'The way you play them, he can.'

After Burns Night Tom had bought some bagpipes and practised enthusiastically.

'Oh, hush, you.' Diane smiled at him. 'So, are you really staying?'

'If that's all right with you, Dee?'

'I've never been happier about anything,' she said.

As Farlan pulled Diane into a hug his eyes found Nia's, and she felt her muscles tighten in a sharp involuntary spasm.

And in the confusion of tears and laughter that followed his announcement neither Tom nor Diane noticed the way their gazes locked, or the flicker of hunger that passed between them.

Later, as they lay in bed at the cottage, Nia knew that she too had never been happier about anything than Farlan staying on in Scotland.

She glanced down to where he lay sleeping, his head

resting on her stomach, his profile cutting a clean line against her pale skin.

Not even when they had met all those years ago and she had fallen hopelessly in love with him.

That had been like a thunderclap.

When their eyes had first met she had felt it crackle down her spine and along her limbs like lightning.

Even then, with no actual physical experience of men, she had known that what she was feeling was special. Unique. Miraculous.

He was everything she had ever wanted.

But she had been too young and too sheltered, too unsure of herself to let their love follow its own path. Too conscious of her role as heir to Lamington.

Her fingers trembled against the sheet.

It had been drummed into her since birth that duty always outweighed personal desires and dreams. Was it any wonder, then, that pitting her first love against four hundred years of history had torn her in two?

She had grown up surrounded by beautiful things in glass cases. Books that were never read. Paintings and tapestries that were never allowed to see daylight.

Faced with the possibility of an imperfect 'real' love she had ended everything.

But she wasn't that same fearful, uncertain girl any more.

She had grown up.

She had learned to 'manage' her parents, and she also managed the family finances and ran a twenty-eight-thousand-acre estate.

Most important of all, she had learned to trust her judgement. She knew her own mind now—and this relationship with Farlan wasn't based on some naïve ideal.

She knew her faults—and his—and she loved him anyway.

Her heartbeat stalled.

She tried the words out inside her head.

I love Farlan.

She felt dizzy with panic and shock.

But why?

Breathing out shakily, she pressed her fingers against her eyes, blocking out the sight of Farlan's naked sleeping form.

How could she not have seen it before?

It seemed so obvious to her now that she loved him and had never stopped loving him.

It had just been easier to tell everyone that she had stopped.

To tell herself that she had.

She had buried the truth deep and learned to live a quiet, colourless life.

When he wasn't there—when their relationship had been defined by impossibility—she had been able to do it. But he was here now. And what had once seemed so impossible, so out of reach, was already in her grasp.

Her hand trembled against the soft stubble on his head.

Outside there was a growl of thunder and the sudden drumming of rain like gravel against a windscreen. The sudden intrusion of reality made her flinch.

Farlan didn't want this to end. But all he had really offered was a couple of months, and then after that…

There were too many possible interpretations of 'after that' for her to contemplate, and only one she wanted to be true.

She stared down at him, her heart racing. She could wake him now, tell him that she didn't want just a couple more months, that she didn't want him to go anywhere without her.

But he might not be ready.

He might never be ready to hear that.

Remembering how his mood had shifted in the restaurant,

she felt her breath catch in her throat. He had been angry and hostile, but there had been fear not fury in his eyes.

If that was how he reacted when she tried to find out more about his family, how might he react if she told him she wanted to share her life with him?

She couldn't risk losing what she had right now for yet another impossible dream of love.

Shifting down a gear, Farlan turned the steering wheel, his mouth curving down as he threaded it through his hands.

'What is it?' Nia asked.

She was sitting beside him and, turning, he grimaced. 'Ignore me—I'm just being a spoiled brat.' Sensing her confusion, he grinned. 'It just feels a bit "agricultural."'

'You mean the car?'

He nodded. 'Don't get me wrong, it's a great car, but…'

As he let the sentence tail off, her eyes gleamed. 'Oh, I see. It's not edgy enough for Mr Hollywood Big Shot.'

They could be playful now, teasing one another without fear of everything imploding.

He burst out laughing. 'I wish! I'm just the new kid on the block right now. Compared to the Mr Big Shots in Hollywood I'm like a firecracker. Seriously.'

Outside the window, the countryside was starting to recede. In its place, houses and shops were starting to hug the road. He could feel something shifting inside him, like the pistons and the flywheel inside the car's engine.

'If you don't believe me then maybe you should come out with me to LA and see for yourself.'

There was a pause, and then he felt her hand on top of his. 'I'd love that,' she said quietly.

He felt a swooping happiness, pure and swift like a swallow curving through the sky. And, reaching over, he caught her fingers and lifted them to his lips.

'Then I'll make it happen.'

Was it really that easy? He felt his pulse accelerate. Apparently so. Only what had changed? Why was it so easy for them to communicate now when before everything had been so charged with misunderstanding?

He didn't understand it, but he couldn't deny how easy it was between them now. Or how happy it made him.

'After two hundred yards, turn right at Lennox Place.'

The glacial voice of the satnav broke into his thoughts and he smiled at Nia. 'We're nearly there.'

It was the only 'date' he had in his diary for the whole trip. Everything else he had been happy to leave to serendipity and Diane. But this was personal: it was the Gight Street Picture Palace.

The cinema had been small and shabby, but years ago it had been his hideout. His refuge. A place where he'd been able to watch heroes and heroines defeat the bad guys, fight alien hordes, go back in time and fall in love.

From that first visit when the lights had dimmed he'd been captivated, swept away not just by the dramas playing out on screen but by the thought of being behind the camera. Telling stories where he got to choose the ending.

Most times, he hadn't even cared what film was on. He'd sat through all of them. And later, every week wherever he was in the world, he would check the listings there, always thinking of the day when his film would play there.

Then it had shut down.

He had been gutted, and as soon as he'd had the money to do so he had bought the site with a view to restoring it. Now, after nearly two years and several million pounds, the restoration was complete. Today was the official opening, and he was the guest of honour.

Nia glanced over at him. 'Do you think there'll be many people there?'

He would have been happy to keep his presence private, but he understood why the trust who now managed the

Picture Palace for him had been keen to alert the media. It was good publicity and he couldn't begrudge them that.

He shrugged. 'Maybe… I guess there would be more if I was some hot-looking actor.'

'If they're turning out on account of your hotness, there should be quite a crowd,' she teased.

They parked at the Imlah, a sleek boutique hotel with a red brick Victorian facade that was owned by some friends of Lachlan and Holly. There they were picked up in a near identical car and driven to the Picture Palace.

Nia caught his eye, and he smiled at her, a moment of recognition at a shared, private joke.

There was indeed a large crowd waiting at the cinema, including camera crews and lots of photographers, and he pulled her against him as the car drew up.

'Stay close to me, okay?'

He'd been to enough premieres for the crowd not to bother him, but he could still remember how intimidating it had been to step out into a barrage of questions and flashing cameras for the first time.

There was just time to wave at the crowd and pose for a few photos, and then he was meeting and greeting the board of trustees, the architect and the design team.

Having given a speech thanking everyone involved, he cut the ribbon.

'It's not too crazy for you, is it?' He stared down at Nia, ignoring the photographers' shouts, feeling the shock of her beauty colliding with his ever-present hunger. 'We should be able to leave soon. All the formal stuff is done.'

'There's no rush.' She smiled at him. 'Let me be proud of what you've made happen here.' She nudged him towards the crowd. 'Go on.'

He signed autographs and smiled, but without Nia beside him he felt as though he had lost a limb. Glancing over his shoulder, he caught sight of her and felt his heart thump. Okay, he was done here.

'Farlan—'

He turned automatically as someone called his name—and froze.

His vision shimmered and his throat tightened, cutting off his breath.

'I heard you were coming here today. I thought I'd come down and say hello.'

The faces in the crowd thickened and blurred.

All except one.

Farlan stared at the man in front of him, his heart slamming in his chest. Panic was seeping through his body like frostbite. He tried to will it away, but he could feel himself shutting down. He was trapped in ice.

Green eyes met his own momentarily, and then he spun away and walked towards Nia.

'We're leaving,' he said hoarsely.

He had no idea how they got back to the Imlah. His conscious mind was blank. All he could think about was getting into the car and driving as fast and as far away as he could from the past.

And the pain.

He gripped the steering wheel as memories burrowed their way to the surface. Memories of driving fast to nowhere. Only he wasn't driving the car.

From some immense, impenetrable distance away he heard Nia's voice talking to him. He couldn't focus on what she was saying, but she was talking calmly, steadily, and he felt some of the tension leave his body.

Pulling off the road, he switched off the engine and gazed down the hillside at some unnamed loch. The sun was dazzlingly bright and a light wind was sending small, choppy ripples across the mercury gleam of the water. It looked so beautiful and serene. If only he could dive beneath the mirror-smooth surface and escape the turmoil in his head.

'What is it? What's the matter?' asked Nia.

The numbness had left his body, but his brain still felt frozen. Something shivered inside him, and then he felt her hand on his: warm, soft, firm…

'Please, Farlan. Please talk to me.'

'I don't know where to start,' he said after a moment.

He felt her hesitation. Then, 'Did something happen?'

'Not something. Someone. There was someone in the crowd I knew.'

He could taste metal in his mouth. The pain felt as though it would burst through his skin.

'His name's Cam. He's my brother.'

Nia stared at him. Outside the car, clouds were starting to tumble over the hills. Seconds later fat, globular raindrops began hitting the windscreen. Inside her head she was shuffling the assumptions she'd made, thumbing through them like a deck of cards.

'I didn't know you had a brother,' she said carefully.

The expression on his face made her stomach muscles tremble.

'I didn't know if I still had one. We lost touch…must be sixteen years ago. After he moved out.'

She hesitated, not wanting to press against the bruise in his voice, but even less able to just sit and watch his pain. 'From the farm?'

He stared at her blankly, then shook his head. 'No. I had to go to the farm because he left.'

Nia blinked. What did he mean by 'had to'? She took the easier question. 'So why did he leave?'

'He wasn't going to.' Farlan's mouth twisted. 'But then he met this bloke down the pub. He was a roustabout on one of the oil rigs, and he talked Cam into taking a job on one.'

Nia frowned. Usually the answers to questions left her understanding more, but with Farlan she seemed to understand less and less.

'Why did that mean you had to move to the farm?' she said slowly.

His face shuttered. 'I couldn't live on my own. I was only thirteen.'

'So you were living with Cam? It was just the two of you?'

Was that even legal?

'What about your parents?' She'd thought they were divorced and both had remarried, but if he'd been that young…

There was a long pause.

'My mum left when I was seven. I haven't seen her since.'

Nia was starting to feel sick. In the restaurant, she had wanted him to tell her about his family. Selfishly, greedily, she had wanted to share more than sex with him. Now, though, every word he spoke hurt her.

Worse, it hurt him.

'When she left it was okay for a couple of years…'

She felt his hand tense.

'And then my dad met Cathy.' He looked away, tracking the clouds that were racing across the sky. 'She didn't really like me and Cam, and she had three kids of her own, so…' His voice faltered. 'Anyway, she persuaded my dad that it would be better if we moved out, so he bought us this caravan and me and Cam moved in there. Only then Cam left.'

Her throat was so tight it hurt to swallow, to speak. 'Why didn't you move back in with your dad?'

His eyes met hers and he smiled stiffly. 'He said there wasn't room for me, so I just stayed living in the caravan. On my own.'

She couldn't look away. Her heart felt as though it would burst. How could anyone do that to their child?

'How long were you there?' she whispered.

'About four months, and then Cam called. When he found out I was on my own he got in touch with my grandparents.'

Surely that must have been the happy ending he'd deserved—except his shoulders were still tense.

'They weren't bad people,' he said, in answer to her unasked question. 'They fed me and clothed me. They did their duty right up until I was sixteen. But when they sold the farm it was clear they weren't expecting me to go with them.'

He'd been alone and homeless at sixteen.

Six years later they had met.

It had never occurred to her that his autonomy was a result of neglect and abandonment.

She had been so in awe of him. To her, he had seemed beautiful and untamed.

Now, though, she could see that he had been not wild, but lost.

A lost boy without a mother or father.

No wonder he found it so hard to talk about his family. It was a miracle he even understood the meaning of the word.

He was staring away from her, but she didn't need to see his face. She could feel everything.

Unbuckling her seatbelt, she slid over and wrapped her arms around him. Her cheeks were wet—with her tears and his.

'I don't know what I did wrong…' he said.

'You did nothing wrong.' Eyes stinging, she lifted her face to his, her love for him exploding inside her. 'You were a child.'

'Not a very easy one.' He shook his head. 'Whatever

anyone said or did, I needed proof. I was always pushing back, pushing them away to see if they meant it.' His eyes found hers. 'I did it with Tom and Diane, just like I did it with you. When I first met them I thought they'd get sick of having me around, like everyone else had. I didn't want to believe they were different, so I made it as hard as I could for them.'

The pain in his voice knocked the air out of her body. 'I know. But you don't have to push back any more. Tom and Diane aren't going anywhere, and neither am I.'

He stared at her. 'You are an incredible woman, Nia, and I'm so sorry. For everything.'

Clasping his face, she stroked his cheeks gently. 'Everything?'

His mouth curved upwards—not quite a smile, but she hadn't lost him.

Outside the sky had split in two and a rainbow was arching across the water.

'No, definitely not for everything.' He kissed her softly on the mouth. 'Let's go home.' His face creased. 'But first I better give Rosie at the Picture Palace a call…apologise for leaving without saying goodbye properly.'

They didn't talk much on the way back to Lamington. Farlan never spoke much when he was driving, and she was lost in her thoughts.

His story had shocked her. But she understood now why he had been so unforgiving, so absolute, seven years ago. She could make sense of the anger that had always been there beneath the surface.

It was an anger that stemmed from a not unreasonable fear of rejection.

So why hadn't she told him that she loved him?

'Yours or mine?' he asked.

If only there was an 'ours.'

She managed to smile. 'Mine. Then I can change out of these clothes.'

Walking into the cottage, she could feel the need to tell him the truth like a weight pressing down on her. 'Farlan—'

'What's this?'

She frowned. He was holding an envelope with her name on it. 'I don't know…'

His eyes flickered round the room. 'It wasn't here when we left.'

She opened it. 'It's from Andrew. It's the photos from the ball.'

Glancing down at them, she felt a rush of warmth for her neighbour. He was a good man, but she didn't want him.

'How did he get in?'

Farlan was standing beside her, his green eyes narrowed.

'I keep a spare key under the flowerpot.'

'So he just lets himself in?'

'Yes, he does. Because he's a friend.'

The memory of what Farlan had told her in the car merged with the suffocating intensity of her need to tell him the truth.

'And that's all he can ever be.'

Dropping the photos onto the table, she took his hands in hers.

'The other day you asked me why I turned Andrew down, and I told you it was because I didn't love him. That was true a year ago and it's still true now.' Her hands were shaking. 'But that wasn't the only reason.' She took a breath. 'The main reason I can't marry Andrew, or any other man for that matter, is because I love you, Farlan. I've never stopped loving you.'

Her fingers curled around his.

'I know we broke up a long time ago, but in my heart I've always felt married to you—and I think you feel the same way.'

* * *

Farlan stared at her in shock.

Nia loved him.

And he loved her.

He felt a rush of relief.

It was that simple. All he had to do was tell her.

But it wasn't that simple.

His eyes flickered over the photos spilling across the table. Yes, she loved him. Andrew Airlie had seen it the moment he'd looked at the pictures of the two of them. That was why he'd dropped them round.

And Farlan loved her.

But less than an hour ago he had been crumpled up in a car, swamped by a past that still defined him.

He thought back to how he'd driven away from the cinema. He had been a slithering mass of panic. It had spread through him with a speed and a savagery that had been impossible to stop, and left him blind to anything but the need to flee.

Only he couldn't outrun the past and the pain.

It was a wound that wouldn't heal. He could never be whole.

All those times he had been handed on to the next person were like fault lines inside him—invisible, but irreparable.

Being on his own had been terrifying. Whenever he felt it was going to happen again he panicked, and all the accumulated fear and powerlessness of his childhood broke through as unstoppably as lava.

Remembering how Nia had comforted him, he felt a wave of remorse. How could he inflict that on her? Not just now, but maybe for ever?

It wasn't fair. She deserved better.

A photo of Andrew Airlie and Nia snagged his gaze. She could have better. Airlie would wait for her and one day—

He slipped his hands free of hers. 'I'm sorry, Nia, but I

don't feel the same way,' he lied. 'And I'm sorry if I gave you the impression I did.'

He stepped backwards.

She looked confused, as if maybe she had misheard him, and then her hesitant smile stilled. 'Farlan, I know why you don't trust me, but—'

'I do trust you, Nia.'

He knew she would slay dragons for him, spill every last drop of her blood to keep him safe. He just couldn't trust himself to be enough for her. Not to disappoint her as he had everyone else in his life. Because she alone would stand by him whatever it cost her.

'But I don't love you.'

The expression on her face was like a blade in his heart.

'I don't believe you,' she said hoarsely. 'I think you're just scared.'

'Then you're mistaken. I'm sorry, Nia. Truly. But this isn't what I signed up for.'

He took another step backwards.

'I think it's probably best if we call time on this—on us—don't you? I've got an interview in London tomorrow, and then I'll fly back to LA.'

Misery hammered in his head so that it hurt just to stand there.

'I truly am sorry, Nia.' He turned, then stopped. 'You'll be needing this,' he said stiffly.

He held out the car key, but she didn't move. So he dropped it on top of the photos and then, ignoring her pale, frozen face, he walked across the room and out through the door.

That was what he'd decided to do, and he was a man who knew his own mind.

CHAPTER ELEVEN

SHIFTING BACK IN his seat, Farlan glanced round the cockpit of the helicopter, steadying his breathing. Methodically, he checked the instrument panel, grateful for the distraction and the comforting familiarity of the process.

There was nothing left to do. It was time to leave.

As the helicopter rose up into the pale blue sky and swung away from Lamington some of his composure began to fail. To the left he could see the gardener's cottage, and as he passed over it his whole body tensed. But he ignored it.

He ignored the ache in his chest too.

When he had come downstairs that morning, Molly had already been up, making bread, and he had stood and watched her push and knead the dough.

It was, he knew, harder than it looked. One of those complicated balancing acts between science and intuition.

But, frankly, it had to be easier than dealing with the memories of what had happened yesterday at Nia's cottage. And infinitely less painful than remembering the stunned, devastated expression on her face.

He shifted in his seat, guilt tightening his shoulders.

It was his fault. All of it.

He'd come back to Scotland believing he could press the reset button and move on.

Walking into the drawing room at Lamington on Burns Night he'd been full of anger and resentment. He'd wanted to throw his success in Nia's face, to exorcise the ghost of the woman who had cast him aside but never left his thoughts.

Or his heart.

Only of course it had never once occurred to him during the last seven years that he still loved her.

And she loved him. *Unconditionally.*

He knew that for a fact.

The tension in his shoulders was spilling down his back now.

His heart was suddenly pounding so hard it was blocking out the sound of the rotors.

For so long he had held everything in. Directing his life as though it was a movie, treating his past like something that could be edited or touched up or just left on the cutting room floor.

Yesterday he had told Nia the ugly, shocking details of his life and afterwards she hadn't pushed him away.

She had only held him closer.

Grimacing, he stretched out his neck. His back felt as if it was on a rack. He needed to stop, move around, shift this tension.

Thankfully he'd checked out a couple of helipads en-route and called ahead. The nearest was only around ten minutes away, and twelve minutes later, he brought the helicopter down onto the landing pad with textbook smoothness.

Switching off the rotors, he unbuckled and climbed out of the cockpit. A light wind was blowing, and the sun felt warm on his face.

He had stopped to stretch his body, to release his mind, but inexorably his thoughts returned to that moment when he'd told Nia about his childhood.

Seven years ago he'd pushed her to prove her love, demanding that she leave everything and everyone behind for him. And then when, quite understandably, she had panicked, he hadn't bothered to listen or stay around long enough to talk about her reasons.

He had run away.

That had been understandable too, given how many people had made him feel he only had a walk-on part in his own life.

But yesterday Nia had offered her love unprompted.

And he was still running.

Still running—only this time he was running from a rejection that hadn't happened. It had been a hypothetical rejection of their future.

That didn't just make no sense. It was crazy.

He swore softly. He was such an idiot.

There were multiple awards back at his house in LA. As an award-winning film director he was supposed to be all-seeing. And yet he had been so focused on outrunning his fears that he'd missed the obvious, glaring truth.

He didn't need to outrun them.

It was light that drove out the darkness—not more darkness.

Remembering Cam's face at the Picture Palace, he felt his eyes blur.

Love blotted out rage and resentment.

It was bigger than fear.

He loved Nia with every beat of his heart, and she loved him. But finding a way to persuade her of that was going to be a challenge after the way he'd acted and what he'd said.

He pulled out his phone.

It was time to make a few calls.

Turning onto her side, Nia stared out of her bedroom window. It had rained most of the night, and the snow of a few days earlier had all but vanished. In its place, the raw umber-coloured bare earth looked stark against the washed-out blue sky.

She had forgotten to draw the curtains last night, but it wasn't the daylight that had woken her.

It was the distant drone of a helicopter's rotor blades.

Her eyes ached from the crying bouts that had punctuated the hours since Farlan had left yesterday, and she felt her throat tighten around the lump that refused to shift.

Then he had just been leaving the cottage. There had still been hope in her heart that he would return.

But now he was leaving for good.

He hadn't said as much, but he didn't need to.

She knew he would never be coming back, and that today would just be the first of many endless days, stretching out to the horizon. An infinite, empty expanse of regrets and shattered dreams and loss. Hope followed by despair, just like the first time.

Her heart felt as if it was being squeezed by a fist.

No, she thought, *it won't be like last time. It will be worse.*

This time there were no misunderstandings—at least not on his side. Farlan couldn't have made it clearer. He had spelled it out as if he was making a public service announcement, not breaking her heart.

He hadn't been looking for a future with her or dreaming of something fixed and for ever.

What they had shared had been enough for him.

Her fingers bit into her duvet.

The sound of the rotors was growing louder.

She knew Farlan would have to fly over the cottage on his way to London, but it was agonising to hear the helicopter getting closer, to remember the time he had landed in the field and swept her off to lunch.

That had felt like a turning point in their relationship. It had been the first time he had opened up to her about himself, about his life before they'd met. She had really thought it meant something—not just to her, but to him too.

She couldn't have been more mistaken.

He hadn't wanted a second chance.

He'd just wanted sex and closure.

The helicopter was overhead now, and she gripped the duvet tighter. And then it was gone, the sound fading faster than she could have imagined.

She glanced round the room, tears weighting her eyelashes.

He was like the snow.

There was nothing to show he had ever been here.

It was as if she had dreamt all of it.

Staring through the window, her eyes followed the movement of the helicopter as it skimmed over the fields and then dissolved into the pale February sky.

With it went the last tiniest hope she had.

Rolling over, she started to cry, huge wrenching sobs that filled the little bedroom.

But nobody could cry for ever.

And an hour later, with puffy eyes and a blotchy face, she made it downstairs and curled up on the sofa beneath the duvet she'd brought down with her.

Her phone sat on the table beside her. She had texted Allan to say that she had a 'bug', and then switched it off. She'd also disconnected the landline.

Hugging the duvet tighter, she stared dully at the phone. She fumbled with the equation in her mind.

Leave it on in case Farlan called.

Or switch it off in case he didn't.

Realistically, the chances of Farlan calling were less than zero. Plus, her mother might ring and she couldn't face that.

She flinched, imagining the stream of questions. She shivered. Her mother must never know. Neither of her parents could ever know.

A fire: that was what she needed. And then a cup of tea.

Shrugging the duvet away from her shoulders, she knelt down beside the ash-filled grate of the wood burner and began clumsily making a small pyramid of kindling. Then her body stiffened, her fingers trembling against the wood.

Somebody was knocking on the door.

Suddenly she couldn't breathe. Heart thudding, she stared at it as if it was alive.

'Nia?'

Her heart dipped with disappointment. It was Diane.

'Allan dropped by earlier, honey. He said you had a bug. I tried calling, but—'

'I'm fine, Diane,' she managed. 'Really, I'm fine.'

'I just want to see you're okay, and then I'll go.'

Nia winced. There was a steely note beneath the softness. Diane was not going to leave without seeing her.

Getting to her feet, she walked across the room and opened the door.

She had thought she had no tears left to cry, but when she opened the door and saw Diane's face, she crumpled wordlessly into the older woman's arms.

'Oh, honey…'

Diane led her back into the cottage and they sat down side by side on the sofa.

'I'm sorry.' Nia drew a breath. 'It's nothing, really. I just need to get some sleep.' Swiping at her cheeks, she edged out of Diane's arms. 'Thank you for coming to check on me, but I'll be fine. And I don't want to give you whatever this is.'

'I don't think that's likely,' Diane said gently. 'You can't catch a broken heart.'

Nia lifted her head, shock replacing her misery.

'You know…?' she whispered.

'I guessed.' Diane sighed. 'When he showed me the photos from the ball.' There was no pity in her eyes, just understanding. 'I know he's hurt you, but please try not to hate him.'

'I don't.' Nia was crying again now. 'That's the problem.'

They talked some more, and in between talking Nia cried. Finally she ran out of tears again, and Diane handed her a tissue.

'Here—blow.'

She watched as Nia obediently blew, and then, reaching over, took her hand and squeezed it.

'Right. You get cleaned up, and then I'm taking you out.'

'Out?' Nia was startled. 'No, really, Diane. I can't go out.'

'Yes, you can,' Diane said firmly. 'You have to face the world at some point, and it might as well be now. Just look outside, Nia. It's a wonderful world.' She hugged her. 'Tom's coming to pick us up, and then he's going to take us over to Braemar. Now, go and get dressed.'

Upstairs, the window in the bathroom was ajar. Catching sight of the view across the fields, Nia pushed it open. The sky was calm and clear, and the yellow sun looked as if it had been drawn with a crayon.

She breathed in shakily. The air smelled of damp earth and something else. Something fresh and green.

Spring.

Her eyes snagged on a clump of primroses by the back gate. Diane was right. The world was wonderful. And she was so lucky in so many ways.

Turning on the cold tap, she splashed her face with water and dried it on a towel. She had lost Farlan once and survived. This time she was going to do more than just survive. She was going to make her life better.

In the past, she had believed that making sacrifices meant losing some part of herself; she had thought that was her duty.

Now, though, she knew it was a choice.

She couldn't be everything to everyone and still be true to herself.

Being with Farlan had given her a glimpse of the life she

wanted and the woman she could be, and she was ready now to make the changes she should have made years ago. So she was going to keep running the estate, but she would hire a manager. And stop babysitting her parents.

Diane was waiting by the door. 'Ready?'

Nia nodded. She wasn't whole or happy. Not yet. But today she would take the first step towards getting there.

'Ready,' she said quietly and, grabbing her coat, she followed Diane to where Tom sat waiting in the car.

They got back after a late lunch in a pub. There had been a few difficult moments, Nia thought as Tom reached the village. Vivid flashes of lunch with Farlan that had made her want to fold in on herself. But she was glad she had gone. Glad that Diane had knocked on her door.

She felt a rush of affection for the Drummonds. They were such good people. They had taken care of her, and they would take care of Farlan.

Her heart beat a little faster.

She could think about him now without crying—just about—and if she could get through the rest of today surely the hardest part would be over.

'Now, you're coming back to Lamington for a cup of tea. And I won't take no for an answer,' Diane said firmly. 'We'll sit in the kitchen. It's cosier there.'

Nia hesitated. But Diane had been right last time.

The kitchen was bright and warm, as usual. Unusually, the television was on, and Molly wasn't alone. Johnny and Allan were there too, and Stephen, and Carrie who helped Molly around the house.

Molly was smiling. 'Lady Antonia, come and watch. It's Mr Wilder.'

No, no, I can't.

The words formed soundlessly in her head, panic and pain sweeping over her like a riptide. Her legs felt like wooden batons, but somehow she found herself walking towards the screen.

She recognised the interviewer. Slim, dark-haired and pretty, she was the co-host of an afternoon chat show. She was describing Farlan's visit to the Picture Palace. There was footage from the opening, and then clips from some of his films and then suddenly they switched back to the studio.

Nia's heart twisted, the pain more savage than any physical wound. Farlan was sitting there on a sofa, wearing a sleek grey suit and that impossible to resist smile.

'So, Farlan—' the interviewer gave him a dazzling smile of her own '—your first film was a cult indie drama, and your last one was the action movie of the summer. What's next?'

On the television screen, Farlan tilted his face upwards in a way that made Nia swallow hard.

'Well, Chrissie, there's a couple of things in the pipeline. Probably the one I'm most excited about is a contemporary reworking of the story of Orpheus.'

Chrissie bit into her lip. 'That sounds like a challenging project…' She leaned forward in her chair. 'What was it that attracted you to that particular story?'

Nia felt her throat tighten as Farlan looked into the camera.

'It's timeless. Boy loves girl. Boy loses girl. Boy gets girl back. But there's a twist.' His smile faded. 'Boy loses girl again through his own wilful stupidity because he doesn't have faith that what he wants will actually happen. I guess it was that part that really spoke to me on a personal level. You see, I know how Orpheus felt.'

Nia's pulse accelerated. His eyes seemed to be looking directly at her—only of course he was talking to millions of unseen viewers.

'Seven years ago I fell in love with this beautiful girl. We were young, and I was pretty intense back then. I still am now. Anyway, we broke up.' He shifted in his seat. 'I never forgot her. She was always there in my head. Her face. Her voice. Then we met again a couple of weeks ago and I realised I would never be able to forget her because I still loved her.'

'And what happened?' Chrissie was leaning forward, her mascaraed eyes on stalks.

Farlan frowned. 'I messed up again. I could have led us both out of the Underworld but I messed up. And now I don't know how to live without her.'

There was a small silence, and then Chrissie turned to the camera. 'Sadly, we've run out of time, but thank you for talking with me today…'

The presenter carried on talking, but Nia couldn't focus on what she was saying. She was staring at the pattern on the sofa behind Farlan. It was the same as the sofa in the drawing room at Lamington. Her eyes searched the screen. And that painting—

He was here.

Farlan was here.

She covered her mouth with her hand, breathing raggedly.

'Nia—'

It was his voice. So familiar, and yet not familiar. He sounded like she felt. As if he was being torn apart inside.

She turned. The kitchen was empty. Everyone had left. Everyone but Farlan.

'What are you doing back here?'

He took a step towards her. 'I can't leave. I tried, but how can I leave you? You're my soul, my heart, and I love you.'

His eyes were fixed on hers, clear and green and hopeful. It was what she had wanted to hear because she loved him so much. But then she thought about his face in the car, and then again at the cottage.

'And I love you. I've never stopped loving you. But we keep hurting each other so badly.'

'I know.' His face was pale. 'And I know that's on me. I have stuff going on in my head and I've tried to deal with it, but it's too big for me to handle on my own.'

His face, the look of pain and the shame on it, made her heart turn inside out. 'It's not your fault, Farlan.' She took a step forward, her words spilling out in a rush. 'You're not to think that.'

'Maybe not what happened in my childhood, but how I've handled this, us…that's on me.'

He took another step closer—close enough that they could touch.

'But I'm going to make changes. I've got myself a therapist. And I'm going to get in touch with Cam. I'm still angry with him, but he was just a kid too, and he did his best.' His face was strained. 'Please tell me it's not too late for us. I love you so much, Nia.'

He was struggling to speak.

'I've never loved anyone else. I couldn't. You've always had my heart. And you always will.'

Nia could feel the tears filling her eyes. She loved him, he loved her and they had fought their way back to one another. But, more importantly, they were going to keep fighting to stay together.

'You and I are poetry,' he said shakily.

Her heart tumbled inside her chest. 'And everyone else is prose,' she whispered.

With a groan, Farlan pulled her into his arms. 'I'm so sorry I left—'

'It doesn't matter.'

She could feel the tears in her eyes, but her voice rang with a love that matched his own.

For a moment they stared at one another, mute with relief and gratitude that after so much, after everything that had happened, they were finally in the right place at the right time.

'How did you do this?' she said wonderingly after a moment. 'Diane said you'd left. I heard the helicopter.'

'I did leave,' he admitted. 'But I didn't get very far. I called the studio, told them if they wanted the interview they'd have to come to Scotland.'

She bit her lip. 'Very masterful.'

He grinned. 'Well, as we both know, I am a Hollywood Big Shot. Anyway, then I called Dee and she sorted everything out. Got you out of the cottage so the camera crew could get set up. Everything just fell into place.'

'I guess it was meant to be,' she murmured.

Stepping back, he cupped her face. 'I know you said you've always felt like we were married, but I was wondering what you thought about maybe making that feeling legal?'

There was a silence.

Nia gazed up at him. Her mouth was dry and her eyes felt hot. 'Are you asking me to marry you?'

'Yes,' he said simply.

She wrapped her arms around his neck. 'Then I'd like that very much,' she whispered, her eyes closing as his mouth found hers.

'In that case...' He drew away. 'We need to start planning our big day. You and I have a date at the altar, or rather the anvil at the Blacksmiths in Gretna Green in twenty-nine days.'

Catching sight of her stunned expression, he pulled her closer.

'We've waited seven years, Nia, I don't want to wait any more.'

Her brown eyes softened. 'Neither do I.'

She was smiling, and lowering his mouth he kissed her, arms tightening around the woman he loved now and for ever.

* * * * *

MILLS & BOON

Coming next month

PRIDE & THE ITALIAN'S PROPOSAL
Kate Hewitt

'I judge on what I see,' Fausto allowed as he captured her queen easily. She looked unfazed by the move, as if she'd expected it, although to Fausto's eye it had seemed a most inexpert choice. 'Doesn't everyone do the same?'

'Some people are more accepting than others.'

'Is that a criticism?'

'You seem cynical,' Liza allowed.

'I consider myself a realist,' Fausto returned, and she laughed, a crystal-clear sound that seemed to reverberate through him like the ringing of a bell.

'Isn't that what every cynic says?'

'And what are you? An optimist?' He imbued the word with the necessary scepticism.

'I'm a realist. I've learned to be.' For a second she looked bleak, and Fausto realised he was curious.

'And where did you learn that lesson?'

She gave him a pert look, although he still saw a shadow of that unsettling bleakness in her eyes. 'From people such as yourself.' She moved her knight—really, what was she thinking there? 'Your move.'

Fausto's gaze quickly swept the board and he moved a pawn. 'I don't think you know me well enough to have learned such a lesson,' he remarked.

'I've learned it before, and in any case I'm a quick study.' She looked up at him with glinting eyes, a coy smile flirting about her mouth. A mouth Fausto had a sudden, serious urge to kiss. The notion took him so forcefully and unexpectedly that he leaned forward a little over the game, and Liza's eyes widened in response, her breath hitching audibly as surprise flashed across her features.

For a second, no more, the very air between them felt tautened, vibrating with sexual tension and expectation. It would be so very easy to close the space between their mouths. So very easy to taste her sweetness, drink deep from that lovely, luscious well.

Of course he was going to do no such thing. He could never consider a serious relationship with Liza Benton; she was not at all the sort of person he was expected to marry and, in any case, he'd been burned once before, when he'd been led by something so consuming and changeable as desire.

As for a cheap affair...the idea had its tempting merits, but he knew he had neither the time nor inclination to act on it. An affair would be complicated and distracting, a reminder he needed far too much in this moment.

Fausto leaned back, thankfully breaking the tension, and Liza's smile turned cat like, surprising him. She looked so knowing, as if she'd been party to every thought in his head, which thankfully she hadn't been, and was smugly informing him of that fact.

'Checkmate,' she said softly and, jolted, Fausto stared at her blankly before glancing down at the board.

'That's impossible,' he declared as his gaze moved over the pieces and, with another jolt, he realised it wasn't. She'd put him in checkmate and he hadn't even realised his king had been under threat. He'd indifferently moved a pawn while she'd neatly spun her web. Disbelief warred with a scorching shame as well as a reluctant admiration. All the while he'd assumed she'd been playing an amateurish, inexperienced game, she'd been neatly and slyly laying a trap.

'You snookered me.'

Her eyes widened with laughing innocence. 'I did no such thing. You just assumed I wasn't a worthy opponent.' She cocked her head, her gaze turning flirtatious—unless he was imagining that? Feeling it? 'But, of course, you judge on what you see.'

The tension twanged back again, even more electric than before. Slowly, deliberately, Fausto knocked over his king to declare his defeat. The sound of the marble clattering against the board was loud in the stillness of the room, the only other sound their suddenly laboured breathing.

He had to kiss her. He would. Fausto leaned forward, his gaze turning sleepy and hooded as he fastened it on her lush mouth. Liza's eyes flared again and she drew an unsteady breath, as loud as a shout in the still, silent room. Then, slowly, deliberately, she leaned forward too, her dress pulling against her body so he could see quite perfectly the outline of her breasts.

There were only a few scant inches between their mouths, hardly any space at all. Fausto could already imagine the feel of her lips against his, the honeyed slide of them, her sweet, breathy surrender as she gave herself up to their kiss. Her eyes fluttered closed. He leaned forward another inch, and then another. Only centimetres between them now…

'Here you are!'

The door to the study flung open hard enough to bang against the wall, and Fausto and Liza sprang apart. Chaz gave them a beaming smile, his arm around a rather woebegone-looking Jenna. Fausto forced a courteous smile back, as both disappointment and a very necessary relief coursed through him.

That had been close. Far, far too close.

Continue reading
PRIDE & THE ITALIAN'S PROPOSAL
Kate Hewitt

Available next month
www.millsandboon.co.uk